THE SCROLL

A NOVEL

THE SCROLL

GRANT R. JEFFREY
ALTON L. GANSKY

WATERBROOK
PRESS

THE SCROLL
PUBLISHED BY WATERBROOK PRESS
12265 Oracle Boulevard, Suite 200
Colorado Springs, Colorado 80921

Scripture quotations are taken from the Holy Bible, New International Version®, NIV® Copyright © 1973, 1978, 1984, 2011 by Biblica, Inc.™ Used by permission of Zondervan. All rights reserved worldwide. www.zondervan.com.

The characters and events in this book are fictional, and any resemblance to actual persons or events is coincidental.

ISBN 978-0-307-72926-2
ISBN 978-0-307-72927-9 (electronic)

Copyright © 2011 by Grant R. Jeffrey and Alton L. Gansky

Cover design by Mark Ford
Cover images by Howard Kingsnorth|Stone, Imagesource, iStockphoto

All rights reserved. No part of this book may be reproduced or transmitted in any form or by any means, electronic or mechanical, including photocopying and recording, or by any information storage and retrieval system, without permission in writing from the publisher.

Published in the United States by WaterBrook Multnomah, an imprint of the Crown Publishing Group, a division of Random House Inc., New York.

WATERBROOK and its deer colophon are registered trademarks of Random House Inc.

Library of Congress Cataloging-in-Publication Data
Jeffrey, Grant R.
    The scroll : a novel / Grant Jeffrey and Alton Gansky.—1st ed.
        p. cm.
    ISBN 978-0-307-72926-2—ISBN 978-0-307-72927-9 (ebk.)
    1. Archaeologists—Fiction. 2. Excavations (Archaeology)—Jerusalem—Fiction.
3. Copper scroll—Fiction. I. Gansky, Alton. II. Title.
    PS3560.E436S37 2011
    813'.54—dc22

                                    2011013966

Printed in the United States of America
2011—First Edition

10 9 8 7 6 5 4 3 2 1

PROLOGUE

Jerusalem, June 15, 2012

David Chambers raised his video camera and pointed it at a limestone facing that had fallen from the north wall and settled at the base of the narrow tunnel. He had seen fifteen such structural failures so far and wouldn't be surprised to see more. He was viewing work done two millennia ago—work that hadn't been seen for twenty centuries. What surprised him was that there wasn't more damage. He had been in tunnels that required weeks of clearing.

The light of the camera illuminated the larger stones that provided the structural support for the tunnel. At first glance they looked like the blocks he had seen at the mouth of the passageway, ten miles back. Aboveground surveys indicated the rough tunnel ran almost eleven miles. On even terrain, a man could make three miles an hour. Here, things went much slower.

Chambers directed the camera in a slow arc, letting the lens take in every detail. It was his first pass through the tunnel, and he wanted a record that he could study for years to come.

Archaeology had a reputation for excitement and startling discovery. Most days it was just plain hard, dirty work—labor that involved equal amounts of mind-breaking scholarship and backbreaking physical work. Scholarship, perspiration, and luck were the triplets of his science.

He turned off the camera and let the blackness envelop him. A second later his heart rate doubled, and he could feel his blood pressure rise. The last sensation, he figured, was more imagination than fact, but it was real to him.

"Easy." He whispered the word to himself. He was alone in the tunnel. That was a choice made from ego and good archaeology. He wanted to be the first human to traverse the length of King Herod's ancient tunnel since it had been closed so many decades ago; he also wanted to limit the number of hands and feet in the site until he recorded everything he could.

Chambers closed his eyes, as if preventing the darkness from pressing into his brain. He wiped the sweat with his free hand, transferred the camera, and did the same with his other hand.

"Breathe. Slow. Steady. It's all in your head."

Chambers held many secrets, but none he buried so deeply as his claustrophobia.

The darkness pressed on him, as if trying to shove him to the ground. Darkness had no mass, possessed no ill will, and was incapable of harming him. That's what his rational mind told him. His *irrational* mind begged to differ.

Taking in a lungful of the dank air, Chambers forced himself to face his fear again. He had conquered many things in his life; he'd beat this too.

Two minutes later he turned on the StenLight S7 mounted to his orange helmet. The lithium-ion-powered lamp pushed back the blackness, reducing it to shadows tucked behind fallen debris. Following guidelines created by cavers, he also carried two other light sources for emergencies.

The presence of the light slowed his heart and his breathing. He took a moment to switch the batteries in the video camera. Once done, he started forward again.

Dust covered the stone floor, dust devoid of footprints. It gave him a sense of pride to know that he was the first man to lay tracks here in a couple of thousand years. That was the real reason he walked the ancient corridor alone. This was his find, and he had earned the right to be the first to walk its length.

King Herod—a vicious, paranoid Jewish king—built the tunnel

because he feared a revolt. His radically religious people didn't consider him one of their own. Strictly speaking, he wasn't Jewish. Yet Rome sanctioned the Edomite's throne.

History remembers his great success at building. His expansion of the second temple made it a worldwide wonder. It was the temple Jesus visited, the one in which He overturned the tables of the money-changers, and the place where He often taught. That, of course, was thirty-plus years after Herod the Great's death.

"Herod the Great" was more than a title to the man. He believed his own press. But with great power came greater danger. The king grew more paranoid. Friction and suspicion filled his family, and fearing a takeover by his own sons, he ordered several of them executed. When the wise men from the East came and asked, "Where is the one who has been born king of the Jews?" Herod's fear erupted like a volcano. His order led to the slaughter of children two years old and younger living in Bethlehem, the ancient City of David where the prophets foretold the rise of one to rule the House of David.

That same paranoia led to the building of this tunnel. At one end was the Fortress of Antonia; at the other, Herodian Jericho. Chambers wondered if old man Herod had ever walked the length of the corridor.

The revolt Herod feared never came, but death did. Knowing that no one would mourn his passing, Herod gave his final royal decree: the killing of the Jewish elite he had gathered at Jericho. The slaughter was to take place upon his death. If the people wouldn't grieve him, then he'd give them something they could mourn.

The command was ignored.

"You may have been one crazy king, but you knew how to get things done." The whispered words echoed off the hard surfaces.

Sadness filled David. This was his last dig in Israel. He'd had great success, but it was time to move to another concentration. Many things drove an archaeologist to commit years to study and digging in the dirt.

Biblical archaeologists loved the history and significance of biblical sites. Some even undertook the work because of their faith. Chambers had been one of those; back in the days when he believed.

Now his faith was as dead as old man Herod.

He looked into the darkness ahead.

One mile to go.

PART 1

ONE

Cambridge, Massachusetts, March 30, 2013

I t was a good wall, a wall anyone would be proud of. Situated in such a way that someone entering the condominium would see the items hanging on its pale blue surface before noticing the rest of Dr. David Chambers's large sixth-floor residence overlooking the Charles River in the south part of Cambridge. The condo was close enough to Harvard to make commuting tolerable, and just far enough away for Chambers to feel free of the world's most prestigious university.

The condo was well above his professor's pay grade, but his last two books had done well enough for him to be free of money concerns. *Beneath Hostile Sands* sat at number six on the *New York Times* nonfiction best-seller list. It had been nine months since the announced discovery of Herod's tunnel. His publishers pressed him to include it as the final chapter in the book, then rushed to print. Then came the countless interviews. The academic papers he penned caused a furor in the tight-knit community of archaeologists, a community that never felt more alive than when being critical of one of its own. Yet no one raised an accusing finger at his discovery. They couldn't. His scholarship was beyond criticism.

Chambers stood before the wall and gazed at the items hanging there. Together they summarized a twelve-year history of his spotless career. Someone in the Harvard PR department dubbed him the most interviewed scientist in the world. That was probably true. Society could only tolerate a few scientific golden boys. The astronomer Carl Sagan had taken the art of popularizing science to rare heights. Others followed: the physicist Michio

Kaku, astrophysicist Neil deGrasse Tyson, and others were frequent guests on talk shows. The public had a hunger for news from the world of science—news most couldn't understand. The contemporary faces of science were those rare individuals who knew how to talk to the camera and do so in plain language. It was something at which Chambers excelled.

Chambers set a cardboard box on a narrow art deco–style table. All the furniture in his condo centered on the 1920s style. Someone once asked why he chose art deco. He had no answer. His interior designer had suggested it, and it sounded good to him. He was a smart man, more intelligent and insightful than most, but he excelled in only a few things. In everything else, he was blissfully dense. Perhaps if his range of interests had been wider, perhaps if he had honed his other instincts to the same edge as those that guided his career, he wouldn't be doing this today.

He eyed the plaques, photos, and framed articles hanging against the smooth surface. He took the closest in hand and lifted it from its hanger. Like all its companions, the object had been professionally framed. Inside a silver frame rested the cover of his latest book. Chambers waited for a sense of pride to wash over him, but it never came. He put the frame in the cardboard box.

Next he pulled down the framed cover of *The Fingerprints of God,* his first book. That work had been far more religious in nature as he guided the reader through the greatest discoveries in biblical archaeology. To Chambers, however, it was also a scholarly nod to William Foxwell Albright, the founder of the biblical archaeology movement. It had been Dr. Albright's book *The Biblical Period from Abraham to Ezra* that had birthed his interest in archaeology—that and the work of his father.

The thought of his dad soured Chambers's stomach. Those who knew Chambers knew of his father and assumed Chambers had chosen to follow in his old man's footsteps. Chambers never corrected the impression, nor did he encourage it. The only thing his father did to kindle the archaeological spark in his son was leave Albright's book on the shelf. Chambers found it, and it set the course of his life.

Dr. Albright died in September 1971, two years before Chambers's birth. That didn't matter. Time meant less to an archaeologist than to others.

Albright, while hailed among biblical scholars, was not as orthodox as most thought. He believed the religion of the Israelites moved from polytheism to monotheism, an idea rejected by conservative Bible scholars. Chambers had wanted to honor Albright while correcting his "more liberal" interpretations.

The last thought amused him: how far he had come. Perhaps *bemused* was a better term. If Albright were alive today, he'd take Chambers to task for his newfound disbelief.

He set the framed cover in the box and followed that with plaques, awards, and articles about himself carried in *Newsweek, Time, Biblical Archaeology Review,* and a dozen other such publications. He removed photos taken of him with Larry King, John Anderson, Ted Koppel, and Jay Leno. He had other such publicity photos that never made it to the wall.

He paused before removing the last photograph. He studied it. The time: two years ago; the place: outside Tel Aviv; the woman: his fiancée. His *former fiancée.* Amber wore jeans, a dirt-caked, formerly white T-shirt, and a pair of gloves that seemed a size too large for her petite hands. The sun shone on her brown hair and sparkled in her blue eyes. The David Chambers in the photo smiled as well. In fact, he beamed. No man had better reasons to smile.

That smile would disappear a month later.

He snatched the photo from the wall and tossed it into the box. He heard glass break. He didn't bother to look at the damage.

He opened the single drawer in the table and removed a well-worn book. He pushed back the black leather cover and saw an inscription bearing his name. Gently, he touched his mother's signature, then his eyes fell to his father's scribbling.

Chambers pursed his lips and threw the Bible in the box. Moments later, he sealed the box with packing tape and buried it in his closet: a cardboard ossuary holding the bones of his past.

He closed the closet door on his history and turned to face his future.

ᴄ⌒

Dr. David Chambers leaned back in his new ergonomic office chair with his feet on the wide mahogany desk. By executive standards, the office was small, but it was still larger than the closets most professors were forced to use. Chambers was still young, so he would have to wait for older profs to retire or die before he could expect more elbow room. Unlike his home, the office was Spartan. A bookshelf lined one wall and needed dusting. Stacks of journals, scholarly white papers, and files stood precariously on the floor. One of his students, perhaps trying to impress his teacher, said, "It looks like the salt pillars along the Dead Sea." Chambers had laughed and pointed to the tallest pile. "That's Lot's wife." It was the kind of joke that only archaeologists would appreciate.

His eyes scanned a scientific journal that reported on grants given for scientific exploration. Any that mentioned Israel or Palestine he skipped. He was done with that phase of his studies but had yet to settle on a new discipline. His interest in biblical fieldwork had departed with his faith.

He had a friend who worked in pre-Columbian archaeology, specializing in the mysterious Olmecs in the lowlands of south-central Mexico. The people group flourished from 1500 BCE to roughly 400 BCE, a time period with which Chambers was familiar. Still, his academic focus had been on the other side of the world. He had deep doubts about his ability to raise money to fund a dig in an area about which he had never written; hence the need for a friend with a credible reputation in ancient pre-Columbian history.

Perhaps he could call in a few favors and sign on as dig director, share a byline or two on some academic papers, and then fund his own dig. All that might take as little as five years—if he were lucky.

He decided to make the call. After all, any civilizations that sculpted three-meter-high human heads deserved a little attention. The recent attention and media coverage of all things related to the Mayan culture and calendar were certain to raise interest in Central American archaeology.

He reached for the phone. As he touched the handset, it rang.

"Yeow." Chambers snapped his hand back, then chuckled. "What are the odds…" He answered. "David Chambers."

"*Shalom,* Dr. Chambers."

Chambers had no trouble recognizing the voice of his old friend Abram Ben-Judah.

Maintaining a running inside joke, Chambers answered Ben-Judah's Hebrew greeting with the Greek word for peace. *"Eirene."* Old Testament versus New Testament.

"It has been much too long since last we talked, my friend."

The image of Ben-Judah flashed in Chambers's mind: tall, slightly stooped, white-and-black beard, kind gray-blue eyes, and a face that looked a decade older than his seventy-plus years. "It has, Abram, it has. How is little Miriam?"

"My granddaughter is well and not so little anymore. She turns thirteen next month."

"In my country, that's the age fathers begin loading their shotguns."

"Shotguns?"

"To keep the boys away."

"Ah." Ben-Judah laughed, but Chambers recognized a courtesy chuckle when he heard one.

"So who or what do I have to thank for the pleasure of this phone call?"

"First I must ask. Please forgive my rudeness."

"You could never be rude, especially to a friend. What is your question?"

"Is it true, what I have heard?"

"That depends on what you've heard."

"You have abandoned your first calling?"

Chambers was glad a grin couldn't travel over phone lines. "I have not abandoned my calling, Abram, I've just chosen a new focus."

No response. For a moment he thought the call had been cut off.

"You still with me, Abram?"

"I'm still on the telephone, my friend, but I am not with you on this new focus."

"I'm sorry, Abram, but I've given it a great deal of thought. It is what I must do."

"Is it what you *must* do, or is it what you *want* to do?"

Chambers rested his elbows on the desk. He didn't want to have this conversation. "What's the difference?"

"I think you know." There was an edge to Abram's voice, nothing unkind, but Chambers could hear the disappointment draping his colleague's words.

"I don't think you called just to scold me. What's on your mind?"

Another long pause. "It's time to come back to the Holy Land."

"I don't think so. My last trip was just that—my *last* trip."

"God wants you to return."

This time Chambers did laugh. "That's odd. I didn't get His memo."

The laughter wasn't returned. "We need you, Dr. Chambers."

The formal "Dr. Chambers" told him Abram was serious. "There are scores of biblical archaeologists. You don't need me. I've been lucky—"

"Do not blaspheme, my friend. Luck has had nothing to do with it. *HaShem* has had His hand upon you from the beginning."

"If you say so, Abram. Look, I appreciate the offer, but I'm moving on to other fields. I can recommend a few archaeologists who will do a good job for you."

"I want you, my friend."

Chambers stood as if Abram could see him do so. "Why? Why me?"

"Because no one understands the tunnels beneath Jerusalem like you."

"There are plenty of people who know about such things."

"But not like you, my friend. You have made the discoveries. You know the topography like no other. It was you who found the ancient clay seals of King Hezekiah's officials: Ahimelekh ben Amadyahu and Yehokhil ben Shahar."

"Names unknown to almost everyone. So what? That was a lifetime ago."

"Nonetheless, that find proved once again the accuracy and truth of the *Tanakh*."

"The Old Testament Scriptures have been shown historically accurate before. Those finds are nothing new."

That topic had been the primary cause for Chambers's research. He had wanted to prove the Bible—both the Old Testament, what Abram called the *Tanakh*, and the New Testament—was accurate in every historical detail, and thereby prove its divine inspiration. He had helped achieve the first goal but lost all faith in the second.

"The Copper Scroll." That was all Abram said, and he said the words as if he were breathing a prayer. "Who knows more about the Copper Scroll than you?"

"The Copper Scroll is not Scripture, Abram. You know that."

"No, but it will lead us to…" He paused as if the word had stuck in his throat.

"Treasure?"

"Yes, but not just historical treasures like most people think. These objects *are* history."

"You have your eyes set on finding the temple artifacts?"

"Don't you?" Abram's sigh carried over the phone. "Once we sat in the cool of the evening and talked about what the scroll might lead us to."

"Good times, friend. Very good times." Chambers could almost feel the breeze that pushed through the outdoor café as they sipped strong coffee and ate dates.

"Indeed, my friend. I long for those days and those conversations again."

Chambers's irritation slipped away. "Still, I don't see how I can be of use to you. Others have sought the treasures and artifacts mentioned in the Copper Scroll. Very little has been found. I'm no magician. I can't find what's not there."

"It is there, and I think that together we can find those items. Think what it will mean to my people. Think what it will mean to history and science. Of all men, you have the greatest understanding of the ancient tunnel systems and the ancient topography."

Chambers closed his eyes. "Abram, my dear friend, I just don't believe anymore."

"I have a grant, a grant that includes your school."

"Harvard?"

"Yes. The dig will be the most challenging you've ever faced and promises to be the most rewarding."

"Abram, I don't—"

"Billions of dollars are at stake. David, this discovery may prove as great an archaeological find as Carter's discovery of the Tutankhamun tomb."

Chambers tried to object but was stunned to realize that he couldn't.

"I am authorized by my government to offer you a substantial reward.

I know you are a man of some wealth, but this will eclipse all of that. You would be financially independent, and you could fund your own future excavations."

Chambers couldn't speak.

"Please, my friend. One more trip. For me, for your university, for science, and for yourself."

Several minutes passed without conversation. Chambers appreciated the quiet Abram allowed him. Most likely, Abram believed that silence was better than rejection.

Finally, Chambers spoke. "When?"

∽

Professor Abram Ben-Judah set the hand piece back in the phone's cradle.

A voice behind him said, "Will he do it?"

Abram didn't bother turning around. He knew who spoke. He also knew who else sat at the conference table.

"He will come."

"You do not sound so sure of yourself."

Abram inhaled deeply. "I said he would come. He will come."

April 29, 2013

The Embraer Legacy 600 business jet entered its final approach with a steep bank to the left and set down at Republic Airport on Long Island.

Republic Airport serviced many business travelers commuting in private jets. Since the airport allowed no commercial airlines, it was less crowded and much easier for pilots with impatient passengers.

The moment the State of Israel's private jet came to a stop, David Chambers stood and stretched his legs. The flight from Boston was short, just over an hour, but Chambers felt antsy. It had been thirty days since Abram Ben-Judah's first call, and each day, Chambers had questioned his sanity. He had just made up his mind to leave behind biblical archaeology and the pain and fame it brought him, then an old friend called, and he folded like a card table. Well, that and the lure of a well-funded dig—and monetary reward.

The stopover was to be short. Abram explained that a team member was in New York speaking at one of the universities. He would join Chambers on the flight to Tel Aviv. Abram didn't give the man's name and Chambers didn't ask.

Chambers arched his back and stretched the muscles. The short hop from Boston had been smooth and the hour passed quickly. It was the eleven-hour flight to Tel Aviv that concerned him. At least he wouldn't be flying alone. Not that he minded being alone. Most days he preferred it.

He had plenty to occupy his mind, but a little professional conversation couldn't hurt.

The pilot and copilot emerged from the cockpit over the long nose of the Brazilian-made aircraft. Both were short, thin men, as if small stature were a requirement for private pilots.

"Can I get you anything, Dr. Chambers?" The captain, identified by the four gold stripes on his epaulets and the gray hair that stuck out from beneath his cap, motioned to the small galley at the forward end of the compartment. "Beer? Wine? A bottled water perhaps?"

"No thanks. I'm fine for now. How long will we be on the ground?"

"Just a few minutes, sir. We have one passenger to pick up and a spare crewman. Did you want to disembark for a few minutes?"

"No thanks. I'll just pace here."

"Very well, sir."

The copilot opened the door and extended the metal stairs that slowly unfolded to the tarmac. A movement outside caught Chambers's attention. A black late-model Lincoln Town Car pulled near the front of the aircraft. The small windows of the aircraft hindered his view, so Chambers moved to the open hatch. A man in a black chauffeur's uniform exited the driver's side and opened one of the rear doors. Without waiting, the driver went to the trunk and removed two large rolling suitcases and started for the stairs.

The passenger was slow to emerge. So much so, Chambers had to move aside to let the chauffeur haul the bags up the stairs, where the copilot took them and stored them in the luggage compartment at the rear of the aircraft. Once the driver descended the stairs, Chambers returned to the door. The passenger had yet to emerge.

Another vehicle—a restored '56 T-bird—pulled onto the tarmac and stopped a short distance away. A woman was driving. Seated next to her was a thickly built man. Both exited, stepped to the front of the car, and kissed. Both wore slacks and coats to fend off the cool breeze.

Chambers turned to the copilot. "Is that your other crewman?"

The copilot looked over Chambers's shoulder. "Yep."

"Wow, he has a great car."

"Yes, he does, but I think you're confused. That's Beth Clayderman. *She's* the backup pilot."

"She is? I thought—never mind what I thought."

He watched as she stepped to the Town Car and looked in. He could see that she said something but was too distant to hear. She smiled and motioned to the business jet, then started forward. When she reached the stairs, she gave the pilot a friendly punch to the shoulder and bounded up the steps. As she did, she stripped away her coat, revealing the same white crew uniform the other pilots wore.

Chambers stepped out of the way as she entered. "Hey, Chuck." She shook the copilot's hand. "Jake says we can flip a coin for second seat. You want to kick it for a while or take first shift?"

"I got the seat adjusted for my muscular frame, so I'll go first."

Beth laughed. "Muscular frame. That's a good one."

"Hey, I been hitting the gym."

"Pumping aluminum, no doubt."

"You are a cruel woman, Beth. Just plain mean."

Chambers watched the friendly exchange. Beth turned to him. "You must be Dr. Chambers."

"Call me David."

"All right. I'm Beth Clayderman."

"So I hear."

She elevated an eyebrow but didn't question the remark. "Just call me Beth. Is there anything I can get you?"

"I've already been asked, but no thanks."

"What about our other passenger?" Chuck looked at his watch.

Beth shrugged. "I think he's on the phone."

As Beth hung up her coat, she hesitated and then swore. "I'll be right back."

She raced down the stairs, then slowed when she saw her boyfriend standing by the car holding a leather overnight bag. She took it, gave him another lingering kiss, then jogged back to the aircraft.

Moments later, she had stowed her bag and taken one of the front seats. The interior of the business jet was designed for comfort. Brown leather covered each seat, and a sofa ran along the left bulkhead. A teak table with a high-gloss finish was anchored in the middle of the passenger compartment. The rest room sported brass fixtures, marble counter, and a gold-trimmed mirror. A deep-blue carpet ran the aisle. Chambers had flown in a few business jets but nothing this well appointed.

Chambers took a seat and gazed out the window. The chauffeur stood by the limo's open door, then took a step back. A man emerged from the backseat: tall, straight in the spine, broad in the shoulders, dark skin, a thick black mustache, and head full of thick, curly black hair. He shook the chauffeur's hand, then walked to where the pilot stood at the foot of the stairs.

"You have got to be kidding." Chambers closed his eyes.

"Is there a problem, Dr. Chambers?" He recognized Beth's voice.

Chambers nodded. "Not for you." He opened his eyes again. Beth was standing by his side.

"I don't understand. Did you forget something?"

"No. I didn't forget anything."

"I don't understand the problem."

"That would be me, lovely lady." Just inside the door stood the cause of Chambers's frustration. "Hello, my good Dr. Chambers."

"Nuri. Why did it have to be you?"

Nuri Aumann grinned. "Iron sharpens iron, David."

Beth frowned. "I take it you two know each other."

"Unfortunately we do." Chambers focused on keeping his mouth shut.

⌒

"It's been two hours, David." Nuri sat in front of Chambers. Like most corporate aircraft, the Embraer Legacy was designed to facilitate conversation, not keep passengers separate. Nuri's seat faced the rear of the aircraft, while David's faced forward. David had done his best not to make eye contact with his nemesis.

"I'll take your word for it, but it seems like only two weeks."

"I had heard that you had grown more somber and depressed since we last met."

"I'm not depressed; I'm just picky about my travel mates."

"See, we do have something in common. I don't like traveling with you."

"That breaks my heart."

Nuri tugged at his mustache. Like many Middle Eastern men, he wore what Chambers's father called a perpetual five o'clock shadow.

"They did not tell me you would be the American on this project."

"They didn't tell me about you. Or…"

"Or what, David? You would have refused to come?"

Chambers looked up. "That's right. I tried to get out of this from the beginning."

"Why didn't you?"

Chambers shrugged. "Abram Ben-Judah is a friend. I feel like I owe him."

"Because he helped you get permission to dig where no one else was allowed?"

The sound of Nuri's voice grated on Chambers's nerves. "I earned those rights by hard work and superior research."

"And grant money. You had access to better grant money."

"That didn't hurt."

"So you told Ben-Judah no."

"At first."

"At first. Yet here you are."

"You see, that's what makes you such a great scientist, Nuri. You have the ability to state the obvious as if you've made an important discovery."

"Scuttlebud has it that you have left biblical archaeology."

"It's scuttlebutt, Nuri, not scuttlebud. And you heard right."

Nuri stiffened. "There are a few Hebrew words I could teach you."

"No doubt. Did Ben-Judah talk about me?"

He shrugged. "Archaeology is a small and tightly connected universe. Archaeologists talk about other archaeologists all the time. You know that.

"It's nice to know people are thinking of me."

Nuri scoffed. "I repeat: you quit your science, and yet here you are."

Chambers straightened. "I didn't leave my science. I'm still an archaeologist; I still teach; I still lecture and publish. I'm just changing focus."

"To what?"

Chambers pinched the bridge of his nose. "I've been thinking about the Olmecs—"

Nuri erupted in laughter, his deep voice rolling up and down the cabin. "The Olmecs. Mexican Indians? Surely you joke."

"They predate the Spanish influence. If you were any kind of scholar, you'd know that."

"And the Olmecs, they have changed the world how?"

"There is a great deal of mystery about them and the influence they had on other Mesoamerican people groups—"

"You would trade the history of the Jews and Arabs in the heartland of the world for that? All of this because of a woman?"

"You don't know what you're talking about." Chambers turned away, his jaw tense enough to shatter teeth.

"I am not the only one saying it, my friend. It is common knowledge. Your discovery of Herod's tunnel is what other archaeologists dream of, yet you walk away shortly after you reveal it to the world."

"I left it in good hands."

"The point is, David, you left it. Period."

"What is it you want, Nuri?"

Nuri leaned forward, invading Chambers's space. "What do I want, you ask? I will tell you, David. I want to know why you are here. Why did you agree to this expedition if your heart is not in it?"

"I told you. Abram—"

"I do not believe you are that accommodating, David. Maybe in your early career you were but not now. You have another goal, don't you?"

"What if I do?"

"It is time for honesty, Dr. Chambers. We will be working together whether we like it or not. I want to know where you stand. We owe each other honesty. It's the scroll, isn't it?"

"Abram mentioned the scroll and wants my expertise."

"The scroll?"

Chambers looked up to see Beth standing nearby.

"Excuse me?" Chambers asked.

"I've tried to take a little nap, but there are a couple of men on the plane arguing. Since I can't sleep, maybe I can learn something."

Chambers couldn't tell whether she was sincere or not. "I apologize. We'll try to control our volume."

"I too apologize, my dear lady. We archaeologists are a hot-blooded people."

"I can tell."

"Are you really interested in the scroll, or are you just trying to head off any violence on your plane?"

"Both. I have an hour before I relieve the captain, and I might as well learn something."

Chambers popped his safety belt and stood. "Let's sit around the table. I'll be right back. I need to get something."

He turned and walked the aisle past the four seats situated around a low table, past the sofa, past the bathroom, and into the rear baggage area. The compartment was large enough to hold luggage for fourteen passengers. Chambers retrieved a well-worn, soft-sided leather briefcase, then returned to the others.

Nuri sat opposite Beth. Chambers chose the seat next to her.

"This should be good," Nuri said.

"You are free to leave the aircraft anytime you like."

Beth shook her head, pursed her lips, then said in a hard, don't-mess-with-me tone, "I'm telling you, gentleman, we have handcuffs on board, and I know how to use them."

Nuri bit his lip.

THREE

No matter how many times she had done this, Dr. Amber Rodgers was surprised by how much of her life she could fit in one backpack and a single duffel bag. She traveled light, preferring not to be encumbered by anything. As she wedged a field notebook into the pack next to a paperback novel she had purchased when last in Jerusalem, she had to acknowledge that she had been far more successful freeing herself of physical things than people.

"So this is it, eh?"

The words came from a short, rotund man with a hairless scalp, a forever-red face, and an exceptional gift for sweating. Dr. Les Nordoff was a respected biblical archaeologist specializing in Roman influence during New Testament times. That period was one of the sexy eras of her discipline. The number of archaeologists working New Testament digs greatly outnumbered those working on, say, the intertestamental period—400 BCE to 1 BCE.

"Yeah, I guess so." She smiled but quickly looked away. Guilt had been leeching away her enthusiasm for her new opportunity. "Listen, Dr. Nordoff—"

"Amber, I've told you a dozen times every day of the last two months to call me Les. Save the 'doctor' stuff for the university campus. Out here, we're just a couple of groundhogs pushing dirt around, hoping to find something that makes it all worthwhile."

She chuckled. "You do more than hope to find something, Dr. Nordoff...Les. You have a stellar record of discovery. It's why I jumped at the opportunity to work with you."

"And here I thought it was my funding."

Amber readjusted her ponytail of shoulder-length brown hair, something she did when nervous. Telling Nordoff of her sudden departure had been difficult enough that it took her two days to summon the courage to make the announcement. Then one evening, while seated in front of the tent used for meetings and the midday meal, she told Nordoff her decision. Unlike archaeologists in the movies, Amber didn't sleep in a tent. None of the dig crew did, except those who remained at the site to provide basic security. At night, workers who lived in the area returned home; foreigners like her stayed in nearby hotels or kibbutzim. The northwest shore of the Sea of Galilee had plenty of both to offer. That night, however, Amber had worked late, knowing Nordoff would do the same. He always worked late. He was passionate, driven, even compulsive.

After most of the crew had left for the night, Amber set out two camp chairs, fixed two glasses of iced tea, and set out a plate of *rugelach,* Nordoff's favorite regional pastry. She then called the expedition director over and showed him the spread.

"Oh no. You're leaving, aren't you?"

"I haven't said anything about leaving." Amber couldn't make eye contact.

"You don't have to. When was the last time you brought me rugelach?" He took one of the bite-sized goodies and popped it in his mouth. "You're leaving me at the altar."

"You're already married."

"You know what I mean." He took another piece of the dessert and slowly pressed it between his lips. The next words came out mumbled. "You know what I mean." He sat, slump-shouldered, with a hangdog expression.

Amber, always sensitive to the emotions of others, slumped in her chair and helped herself to the dessert, uncaring about the effect it might impose upon her narrow waist. She gazed over the serene Sea of Galilee, watching the lights of fishing boats and the glow of a crescent moon glitter on its surface. "Yeah. I'm afraid you're right. The Israel Antiquities Authority has made me an offer I can't refuse."

"You make them sound like the Mafia."

"Let me rephrase. They've asked me to join a team working out of Jerusalem."

"They'll be digging in Jerusalem?"

"They didn't say that. The team starts there." She paused. "I can't talk much about it."

"Abram Ben-Judah." Nordoff reached for another pastry, then pulled his hand away as if uttering the man's name had ruined his appetite for sweets.

"You don't have to spit his name out." She glanced at her boss and friend.

"I don't mean to. It's just that…" He frowned. "Working in Israel is hard enough as it is. The tension with the Palestinians, the scientific authorities, the government authorities, the Orthodox Jewish authorities, the local district authorities, the antiquities authorities—the only people without authority are the people doing the work."

"It's the nature of our business." Amber let her eyes drift back to the water. A cool breeze rose and caressed her cheeks as if offering solace.

"It used be the qualities that made for a good archaeologist were integrity, determination, a good education, and tenacity. Now we must also walk on eggshells. Can't offend the Jews; can't offend the Muslims; can't offend the Christians—"

"Watch it."

He raised a hand. "No offense meant, Amber. I'm just grumpy. How am I going to replace you?"

"I'm irreplaceable, you know that."

That made him laugh.

"There are plenty of good people who can fill my boots." She pulled a piece of paper from her pocket. "I've made a list of people I think would do a good job for you."

He took the paper but didn't look at it. "They won't be you."

She ignored the comment. "It was a tough decision for me. When Nuri—"

"Nuri! Ah, now I understand."

"It's not what you think."

He eyed her. "It's not? Don't lie to me. I've seen the way you looked at him when he was here two weeks ago—wait, he's the one who asked you, isn't he? Boy, I tell you what. If I knew he was here poaching, I would have run him off with a pickax."

"He wasn't poaching. Please don't make this harder than it is."

They sat in silence, watching the undulating surface of one of the most famous bodies of water in the world, the same body of water on which Peter, James, and John made their living; the inland sea where Jesus walked on the water, stilled the storm, and used boats as pulpits.

The silence was broken by Nordoff munching another snack. "These desserts just might be good enough to cause me to forgive you. Maybe."

"I shall forever cling to that hope."

He huffed. "I didn't say they were good enough to put up with your sarcasm."

"Sorry." She turned to him and found him smiling. Amber returned the pleasantry. "Did I ever tell you why I joined your work?"

"Talk around town is that you find me irresistible. Most women do." His grin widened. It was Nordoff's way. Humor was his answer to everything. That and food.

"Okay, wise guy. Riddle me this: 1986, 8.27 meters—"

"The Jesus Boat."

"I didn't get to finish my clues."

"In 1986 a pair of brothers—fishermen by trade, amateur archaeologists by avocation—discovered a portion of a buried boat. Long story short: they found a fishing boat from the first century. Hence, the Jesus Boat. For seven years, it soaked in a chemical bath to preserve it. You can see it at the Yigal Allon Museum in Kibbutz Ginosar. It's not that far from here."

"I've visited it many times. If you're so smart, can you name—"

"Moshe and Yuval Lufan." He let loose a satisfied sigh. "You were going to ask the names of the brothers, right?"

"I'm not talking to you." She crossed her arms and looked away but couldn't keep the playfulness out of her voice.

"It wasn't a very hard question. Especially for an archaeologist who works near the Sea of Galilee. So why bring it up?"

"It was that find, almost thirty years ago, that made me want to be an archaeologist. More specifically, it made me want to be a biblical archaeologist." The image of a two-thousand-year-old boat, nothing more than the substructure of beams and wood hull, floated before her eyes. It took no effort to imagine the boat floating in the water of the Galilean sea, men dressed in long robes pulled up near their waists to better free them to cast nets.

"It was a remarkable find. It's been inspiring Bible students for decades. You know..." he said.

"That it's probably not *the* Jesus boat. I know. That doesn't matter. Still, it could be one of the boats Jesus used to cross from one shore to another. Maybe it was one of the Zebedee boats."

"Ah, the Zebedee boys and their fishing family. From fishing for creatures in the sea to fishing for men. Isn't that how Jesus put it?"

"We'll never know if Jesus ever saw that boat. It might predate Him by a couple of decades." She shrugged. "Still, the idea of finding and revealing important artifacts from biblical times took hold of me. Although the find was made before I was born, it still put the flame to the kindling of my imagination."

Nordoff laughed. "Uh-oh, now you're getting poetic."

"All biblical archaeologists are poets at heart." She sipped her tea. It was strong and sweet. "Our bodies live in the present, but our minds dwell in the past." She paused, and Nordoff let her have her moments of reflection.

"And the offer you've received is better than digging up another Galilean fishing village?"

"Yes."

"Ouch. That was brutal."

"I really am sorry, Dr. Nordoff."

"No more sorry than I." He picked up another one of the pastries. "At least I had you for a while—and I got rugelach."

That conversation took place a week ago. She had already packed the few items she kept in the kibbutz where she stayed. All that remained were the things she kept at the dig site.

Nordoff, who hadn't ceased tempting her to stay, watched her like a father watching a daughter packing for college—with a sense of deep pride and deeper regret.

She waited for the last appeal, the desperate plea, but it never came. Too many details had already transpired: her replacement would arrive tomorrow; she was expected in Jerusalem; the rest of the team, so she had been told, would all be in place by the time she arrived.

"Ever onward, ever upward, eh?" Nordoff sounded depressed. Apparently his constant cheerfulness had its limits. For the last few days, he'd pretended that her leaving was of no importance, but she had no trouble seeing through the charade.

Amber cinched the duffel bag closed and slipped the backpack over one shoulder. She started for the tent opening when Nordoff stopped her.

"Les, I was hoping to avoid a long good-bye."

"Me too. I'm stopping you for another reason." He moved past her, bent, and picked up a photo. "This must have fallen out."

Nordoff turned, and Amber saw a photo in his hand. Not just any photo. *That* photo. He held it out, and her eyes fixed on the shot taken in

Tel Aviv two years prior. She saw herself in a dirty white T-shirt, gloves too big for her hands—she had lost her good pair—and an equally filthy pair of jeans. Next to her stood David Chambers, hotshot archaeologist and former fiancé. The picture, which she had been using as a bookmark in the novel she was reading, must have slipped free while she was packing.

"Keep it."

Nordoff raised an eyebrow. "That's a bit harsh. Isn't there anything in this photo you miss?"

She shrugged. "I kinda miss those jeans."

Amber walked from the tent.

FOUR

Chambers was in his element. Nothing gave him greater joy than sharing what he knew of the past. The irony that it was biblical archaeology, which he had just told Nuri he wanted to leave behind, that caused his heart to pick up a few beats didn't go unnoticed. He tried to look and sound bored, but the herculean task was too much for him. Apparently it was easy work for Nuri, who made a point of yawning every five minutes.

Before him lay a series of large wide-format photos. He pushed one in front of Beth. "This is the Copper Scroll in its current home: the Archaeological Museum in Amman, Jordan. As you can see, there are six curved segments that made up the original scroll. When it was discovered in 1952, the copper sheet was still a scroll. John Marco Allegro retained the help of Professor H. Wright Baker at the College of Technology in Manchester to cut the sheets into twenty-three strips. That began in 1955."

"So there are more strips than the six shown in this photo?" Beth leaned over the table. She looked genuinely interested.

"Yes."

"What's the copper sheet in the wood frame in the glass case?"

"It's a replica of what the scroll must have looked like in the first century before the copper sheet oxidized. Well, a portion of the scroll."

"And this is important?"

Chambers stuffed a sarcastic remark and reminded himself that he was dealing with a pilot, not an archaeology student."

"Very important—"

"Tell her why, Dr. Chambers."

"I'm trying to, Nuri, but there's an annoying buzz in the cabin."

"You could step outside." Nuri leaned over the table that separated them.

Chambers matched the position and started to speak, but Beth stopped him before a word escaped. "Gentlemen, my boyfriend proposed to me."

The whiplash change of subject ground Chambers's mental gears to a halt. "Um, congrats."

"He's a lucky man." Nuri leaned back from the table.

Beth's eyes narrowed. "I'm telling you that so you'll understand this: one, he's rich; two, I no longer need this job; three, if I lose my job because I toss you both out the hatch, it won't matter. Not to me, at least. The way I figure it, from this altitude you can argue for several minutes before you make your first bounce off the ground."

Chambers glanced at Nuri and saw him staring back. One beat later, the men laughed.

"I think she's serious, Chambers."

"I know I'm shaking."

Beth smiled and pointed at the photo. "Okay, tell me why this is so important."

"It's a treasure map, my dear." Nuri tapped the photo. "Or so some believe."

"A treasure map? Really?"

"It contains references to treasure. Scholars still have verbal fistfights over it, but many good people believe that the scroll points to buried treasure lost almost two thousand years ago," Chambers said.

Beth tilted her head. "Whose treasure?"

"I hope you don't mind a short history lesson." Chambers didn't wait for an answer. "For centuries biblical scholars, archaeologists, and historians have wondered what happened to the sacred treasure of the temple in Jerusalem. As you may know, the temple was one of the most opulent structures ever built. The first temple, built under Solomon's reign, was a marvel of construction; it was also covered inside and out in gold. Well, much of its interior was veneered with gold. Light from high windows would pour into the structure and reflect off the gold-covered walls."

"That's hard to imagine." Beth's eyes widened. "It must have been wonderful to see."

"Not many had that privilege," Nuri said. "Only priests were allowed inside the temple building, and only one of those could go into the Holy of Holies. And that was allowed only once a year."

"In the Holy of Holies of King Solomon's temple that Nuri mentions were some of Israel's greatest treasures: the ark of the covenant was a small wood box covered in gold with a pair of gold angels situated on the top. Standing over the ark were two very tall statues of angels, also covered in gold."

"But we're not talking about the first temple," Nuri said. "That temple was destroyed in 587 BCE by the Babylonians, nearly six hundred years before the Copper Scroll was made."

"Ah, but it shows the great investment people were willing to make in their temple. Besides, some of the first temple's valuables returned with the people. Around 516 years before Christ, a new temple was built, but the people had just come out of captivity to the Babylonians. In 536 BCE, the Persians overran the Babylonians, and the Persian king allowed some of the Jewish captives to return to their land to rebuild their place of worship. It was a meager thing when compared to what Solomon had built, but the sacred temple was renovated many times over the centuries. Herod the Great did the most work in expanding and upgrading the building. Beginning in 18 BCE, Herod turned the temple into one of the ancient wonders of the world."

"So that temple was filled with valuable stuff too?"

Chambers grinned. "That 'stuff' included many temple worship objects and furnishings, all extremely valuable. In 70 CE, a long revolt ended when the Romans who ruled the land destroyed the second temple. The temple and the treasures were defended by two Jewish sects: the Essenes and the Zealots."

Beth furrowed her brow. "*Zealot.* I know that term."

"Maybe you're thinking of Simon the Zealot, one of Jesus' disciples. Some believe he may have once been part of the Zealots, a group that gave Rome plenty of grief."

"Okay, Rome destroyed the temple and took all its riches, right?"

Chambers shook his head. "There are many traditions and legends that say the portable treasures—money, objects, gold and silver bullion, furnishings—were removed and hidden during the long siege, before Rome looted the temple treasury. It appears this had been in the works for some time. There are numerous tunnels under it that lead away from the Temple Mount."

"That's what Dr. Chambers is known for: tunnels." The ragged edge had returned to Nuri's voice. "He's a tunnel expert."

Chambers shrugged. "It's one of my interests."

Beth looked at her watch.

"I'm sorry," Chambers said. "I'm boring you."

"What? No. I'm a pilot, checking my watch is a professional habit. I've got plenty of time before I have to relieve one of the guys." She motioned to the cockpit. "Carry on. This is good stuff."

"Okay. As you probably already know, in 1947 a shepherd boy tossing stones into one of the many caves in the western cliffs around the Dead Sea heard something break. One of his stones had hit an ancient pot. Inside were parchment and leather scrolls. It was not uncommon to preserve important documents by sealing them in pottery. Many such pots and scrolls were found."

"Hence the term Dead Sea Scrolls."

"Exactly. In March of 1952, scholars found other scrolls in a cave near the ancient village of Qumran on the west side of the Dead Sea. They also found one scroll that was very different. Instead of being written on parchment or leather, this singular message was chiseled into three copper sheets and rolled like a scroll. That scroll became known as 3Q15—the fifteenth scroll found in the third cave at Qumran."

"I like Copper Scroll better." Beth smiled. "That name has flair."

Nuri huffed. "Science hates flair."

"That is science's loss." She returned her gaze to the photo. "Go on. Don't keep a girl waiting."

Nuri shrugged, and Chambers wound up for his next pitch. "The scroll is made up of three copper sheets riveted together. It's about a foot wide and eight feet long. Of course, time had taken its toll as it does on all things. After many weeks of restoration work, however, the scroll became readable. It was engraved with Hebrew letters, most likely by one of the Jewish Essene priests. The scroll lists sixty-four secret locations where temple treasure was hidden. That treasure, according to the scroll, includes temple vessels, manuscripts, massive amounts of gold and silver bullion, and two very important religious artifacts: the oil of anointing and the breastpiece of the high priest."

"They hid the treasure to keep it from falling into the hands of the Romans?" Beth looked from one man to the other.

"Not just that," Nuri said. "The ancient Jews also knew the day would come when Rome would destroy the temple, so they removed everything needed to set up worship in a new temple—whenever that might be built."

Beth leaned back and shook her head. "This sounds like the premise to a bad Indiana Jones movie. A secret treasure scroll. How do you know it's not just the work of an early short-story writer?"

"You're not the first to suggest that, my dear." Nuri patted her hand, then let his hand linger a moment too long. Beth placed her hands in her lap.

Chambers held back the snide comments ricocheting inside his skull, but he communicated a great deal with his stare. He moved his gaze back to Beth. "You bring up a fair point, one I've wondered about many times. The scroll polarizes scholars. Some are quick to dismiss it as the fanciful writings of some industrious scribe, but that idea can be laid to rest. The text contains no embellishment, poetry, or symbolism, just straight descriptions, almost like an accountant's list of valuable inventory."

"Maybe the guy wasn't all that imaginative." Beth defused the cut with a smile.

"He was accurate if not imaginative. For example, he describes caves and cisterns around Wadi Ha Keppah, near Qumran."

"Near the shores of the Dead Sea," Nuri added.

Chambers ignored him. "There are ancient maps that identify the area as the Valley of Qumran. Some of these places can be identified through toponyms."

"Toponyms?"

Chambers nodded. "It's a compound word taken from the Greek *topos* meaning 'place,' and *onuma* meaning 'name.'"

Beth raised an eyebrow. "Place names?"

"Most people wouldn't get that," Nuri said and winked.

Chambers wondered if the guy ever quit. He continued, "Right. A toponym is a name derived from an identifiable topological feature."

Beth looked puzzled.

"Ever been to Yosemite in California?" Chambers asked.

"Yes. I was there three years ago. Flew some execs to Fresno for a week of meetings. I stayed for a few days. Beautiful place."

"Good," Chambers said. "So you saw Half Dome?"

"Of course... *Half Dome* is a toponym?"

"Yes." Chambers saw the light go on in the woman's eyes. "It's called Half Dome because it looks like half a dome. A toponym. Archaeologist use these name descriptors as clues. Toponyms have special meanings in any local language."

Chambers repositioned himself in his chair. All of this was old hat to him, but it helped pass the time. Even so, the second best thing to doing archaeology was talking archaeology. He would talk as long as she was willing to listen.

"The scroll mentions three significant areas including Qumran by the Dead Sea to the southeast of Jerusalem, Mount Zion, and a northern region on the east side of the Jordan River."

"Modern Jordan," Nuri said.

"I figured that." Beth kept her attention on Chambers. "And these areas are important?"

"They're known to be major settlement areas for Essenes. It was where the Essenes were most active."

"So why hasn't the treasure been found?" Beth leaned toward the aisle as if putting another foot between her and Nuri. He didn't seem to notice.

"Since these artifacts are hidden in different locations, it is best to think of them as multiple treasures, not one. The answer to your question is simple: things have changed. Some places in Israel have remained the same for millennia, but two thousand years of wind, erosion, and human activity have altered the terrain. Modern Israel is very different from first century Israel. For example, the Jordan River is very different today than it was a couple thousand years ago. In 1964 a dam was constructed near the Sea of Galilee, the major source of the river's water. In that same year, Jordan constructed a channel that bleeds water for irrigation from the Yarmouk River, another water source for the Jordan River. The Jordan feeds the Dead Sea, but since the river runs much lower now, the Dead Sea is drying up. Over time, everything changes."

Beth seemed to ponder this. "So the treasures will be lost forever?"

Chambers shrugged. "Maybe, but many scholars think that there may be other scrolls found that will help us along. The Qumran community existed for more than two hundred years. The United States has been around about as long. There may be more scrolls to be discovered."

"Ah, here's where things get interesting." Nuri straightened.

"We're moving from low-tech to high-tech. Some time back, NASA developed a technology that enables researchers to take molecular frequency analysis of underground features, features that can be several hundred feet underground. Apollo crews used an earlier version of this on the moon to determine the best places to take core samples. Well, during the last few decades, the technology has improved in accuracy and detail. These surveys are noninvasive, which is a beautiful thing. It sure beats digging acres of land before finding anything worth digging for."

"Okay, I'm pretty good with tech," Beth said, "but molecular frequency analysis is a little above my pay grade."

"Understandable. You can't pick up one of these things at eBay or Best Buy. Noninvasive frequency analysis reads the electromagnetic spectrum of elements."

"Ah, well, that explains it."

Beth's sarcasm made Chambers grin. "The system reads the electromagnetic spectrum in hidden materials and tells the user the composition of the unseen objects. Using this and ground penetrating radar, we can identify underground caves, tunnels, chambers, and even some of the objects in those spaces."

"And you've had success with this?"

Nuri answered. "Surveys have found at least forty clay jars buried in the Qumran area—intact jars with parchment manuscripts. There have been other objects found, including another copper scroll."

"What do those scrolls say?"

Chambers noticed she addressed him instead of Nuri, even though he had been the one to provide the last tidbit of information. "Those finds are recent, and it takes time to get permission and funding to do the work. Some work has already been approved by the Israeli government. The largest cave is forty feet below the surface. Archaeologists move at a snail's pace. It will take several years to dig that deep and keep track of archaeological finds they make along the way."

"I could never be that patient."

"There are many who share your philosophy," Nuri said and turned his gaze out the side window. Chambers understood the feeling. An archaeologist could end a career quickly by destroying one find to reach another. The days of gonzo, devil-may-care archaeology were gone. To let one's impatience dictate the pace of a dig would only earn the disdain of the archaeological community, a society that could be brutal to members who offend its code.

"So how much treasure are you talking about here?"

"Short answer: about 2.5 to 3 billion US dollars."

There was a pause, then Beth said. "Did I hear a *B* in that sentence?"

Chambers nodded. "Billion not million. By the Copper Scroll's accounting there are 3,282 talents of gold and 1,280 talents of silver—"

"A talent?"

"It's a measurement of weight. The term was a little, shall we say, flexible. A talent weighed between 75 and 125 pounds. To keep the math simple, assume a talent equals 100 pounds. That means 4,562 talents times 100 pounds each, yielding 456,200 pounds of precious metal, mostly gold. At today's rates for silver and gold, the whole monetary treasure amounts to nearly three billion dollars, and that's not counting the archaeological value."

"How could people of that day acquire so much money?"

"The temple treasury held more than monetary gifts from worshipers and the temple treasures. It also guarded Israel's secular wealth. In a sense, you could say the temple was the national bank of first-century Israel, serving the entire nation, the government, and private citizens."

Chambers leaned forward and continued. "Flavius Josephus, the first-century Jewish historian, noted that after General Pompey conquered

Jerusalem in 63 BCE, Crassus demanded a 10,000 talent gold payment—and got it."

"I can't begin to imagine that much money."

"It accumulated over time. The people supported their temple through a half-shekel tax. A half shekel was used only for religious purposes and equaled about two days work. Every Jewish man over the age of twenty contributed a half shekel every year. There were tens of millions of Jews spread throughout the Roman Empire. The tribute probably brought in about a billion dollars every year. Imagine that multiplied over many years. It's not unreasonable to believe the temple treasury had billions of dollars. That's just the money side of things. Again, if we think about the social, historical, and religious significance of the worship items, the value of the treasure becomes incalculable. Ceremonial items have a value all their own. Not the least of which is the fact that they're made from precious metals."

"In some cases." Chambers continued, "I mentioned some of the items in the first temple. The second temple in the first century did not have the ark of the covenant, but it had its share of gold. But there are things more important than financial value."

"Really. More important than money?"

"She sounds like you, Chambers."

"Stuff it, Nuri."

Beth rolled her eyes, which Chambers took to mean she was reaching the threshold of her patience.

"During the siege of 70 CE, while Jerusalem was in the throes of the worst turmoil imaginable—the Romans killed over a million and a quarter Jews—priests secreted away the ashes of the red heifer and other sacred objects—"

"Wait. They did what? They stole the ashes of a dead animal?"

"They didn't steal the ashes. They took them to safety. It wasn't just any dead animal." He paused as he considered the best way to make a complicated topic simple. "Okay, here it is in a nutshell. The Old Testament book of Numbers prescribes that a red heifer, one that's perfect and has never been used for work, shall be killed outside the camp and burned and that its ashes be mixed with pure water, hyssop, cedar, and scarlet."

"Okay, now that's just weird." Beth scrunched her nose.

Again Chambers paused; the archaeology fascinated him, but talking about the spiritual side of things made him uncomfortable, something that hadn't always been true. The jet bounced through some clear-air turbulence, as if prompting Chambers to get on with his explanation. "I know it sounds strange, but as an archaeologist, it isn't my job to pass judgment on belief systems. It was what it was. Besides, no matter how foolish it might appear to you or me, there are still millions of Jews and Christians who believe the red heifer is important. Observant Jews have believed this since the days of Moses, almost thirty-five hundred years ago. More on target for our discussion is the fact that the ashes of the red heifer were important enough for priests to rescue them and take them for safekeeping and do so while thousands were being killed in and around Jerusalem."

"People do strange things in adverse conditions." Nuri returned his gaze to the others and tapped his forehead. "Human psychology may be the strangest study of all. Did you know that after the Americans dropped atomic bombs on Japan, several men in Hiroshima, burned and injured, retrieved a painting of the emperor from the wall of a government building and ran through the burning streets of the city shouting, 'Make way for the emperor; make way for the emperor.'" He raised his hands and shrugged. "Who can explain the minds of men?"

"Or women," Beth said.

"No one can explain that, my dear."

Beth graced him with a smile, then asked, "So they mix the ashes of this red heifer with water. Why?"

"Initially, it was used in ritual purification. For example, the ancient Jews—well some contemporary Jews as well—believed that touching a dead body made a person ceremonially unclean. Purification could be achieved by visiting the priests who used the water and ashes to perform the ceremonial cleansing. Ironically, the process made the priests themselves unclean, and they would undergo their own ritual cleansing. Many Christians believe the act symbolizes Christ and His sacrifice on the cross."

"Christians see a lot of symbolism in the Old Testament," Nuri said.

"So how does this connect to the Copper Scroll and the temple?" The plane jostled again, and Beth tightened her seat belt.

"Purification rites were not just for ritually unclean people. It is believed that the third temple—the one yet to be built—will need to be purified before it can be used for worship."

"So by saving the ashes while the second temple was being destroyed, the ancient priests were preparing for a future temple." Beth blinked, and for the first time, Chambers noticed the intelligence in her eyes.

"Exactly. The same goes for the oil of anointing." He shuffled through the papers on the table. "Let me read a few lines from the scroll: 'On the way from Jericho to Succukah, by the River ha Kippah, in the tomb of Zaok the priest, which is a cave that has two openings. On the open side by the north, the view toward the east, dig two and one-half cubits under the plaster and there will be found the Kalah and under it one scroll.'"

"What's a Kalah?"

Nuri spoke up but sounded bored. "It's pottery made from clay and red heifer dung."

"Ew, sorry I asked." A moment later she asked, "Well, was it there?"

"Like I said, a lot has changed. It hasn't been found, but something else has, something very few know about."

"Ooh, intrigue."

"You have no idea, my dear lady." Nuri looked serious. "Archaeology has more intrigue than you can imagine." He motioned to Chambers. "Carry on with your story. I enjoy a good tale."

Chambers closed his eyes for a moment, letting the jab pass, then lowered his voice as if others were around to hear him. "I have a colleague who, using information found in the Copper Scroll, undertook an expedition to find the sacred oil of anointing. The oil has been missing since the first century. He and the others searched Cave 11 near Qumran and discovered a buried clay vessel. It is about thirteen centimeters—five inches—and contained a gelatin-like substance. He said it reminded him of molasses.

"The jar had been wrapped in palm leaves and buried in a one-meter-deep pit. That protected the oil from the high heat of the Dead Sea area. Now here's the kicker: the *shemen afarsimon* goes back to the days of the Exodus—"

"The what?"

"Sorry, the term means persimmon oil. The book of Exodus describes the five special ingredients necessary to make this anointing oil. Analysis of the oil residue in the container revealed myrrh, sweet cinnamon, sweet calamus, cassia, and olive oil. The oil was used to anoint kings, priests, and certain sacred objects. Tests showed the oil in the little jug matched this unique recipe."

Chambers rubbed his fingers together as if some of the oil had appeared on his fingertips. "Carbon-14 testing returned an age of two thousand years."

"Which puts it right at the time of the fall of Jerusalem."

"It's certainly in the ballpark. The Israel Museum verified that the composition of the oil is unlike any other oil they have evaluated. After intensive testing by the pharmaceutical department of Hebrew University, which verified the composition of the substance, the oil was turned over to the two chief rabbis of Israel. They have taken precautions to protect it."

"Okay," Beth said, "if I understand this correctly, the treasure is gold, silver, precious objects, and sacred artifacts that some believe are needed for a new temple. Am I close?"

"That's it. Of course, there is much more, but you get the idea." Chambers grinned. "And remember: you asked."

"It's all fascinating, but my head is spinning. I think I'll go forward for a bit and focus on easy stuff, like flying a jet at thirty thousand feet."

That made Chambers laugh. "Now that would make my head spin."

FIVE

The hands that would touch the object bore wrinkles, calluses, and age spots. The hands reflected the man, forged and shaped by a hard existence that ultimately led to wealth. These were hands that had worked cargo ships that plied the Mediterranean, hands that were slow to release a dollar. Those dollars became investments, and those investments became a comfortable living. Two decades later, the hands never had to work again.

Slowly, the hands opened a Plexiglas case. The act would have set off alarms throughout the mansion had he not entered the twelve-digit code known only to him. The alarms would have alerted the four security agents who patrolled the grounds, as well as the private security service a short distance away.

Above him, above the basement hideaway, were ten thousand square feet of opulence spread over three stories. Compared to the United Kingdom and the United States, Israel had few mansions like his. Property in Israel was too scarce and therefore too expensive for such wasteful self-indulgence. He had earned the right to be self-indulgent, and his wealth, when applied to the right bureaucrat, bought him special privileges, something he refused to let embarrass him.

With moves made easy by practice, he opened the case, removing the clear lid and then releasing the clips that held the sides in place. One by one, he lowered the sides until the object was exposed to the soft light that filled the room. The illumination poured from overhead bulbs designed to cast a neutral light, a light that would add no color to anything in the room. It was not enough just to look at an ancient artifact; the piece should be seen as it is. Harsh light could damage sensitive parchment or vellum; it could wash out centuries of patina on stone and prevent the observer from seeing the true essence of the centuries-old—in this case, millennia-old—object.

His breath caught in his lungs, despite having done this very act every day of the last fifteen years. For a moment, he understood how ancient people might be tempted to worship a bit of art made in stone. He, however, would not worship this object or any object like it. Still, his heart raced. He had never felt love for a woman, never dated, never married. He wondered if this emotion was what lesser men felt for a beautiful female. He would never know, and that fact never bothered him. His many mistresses bore names like Wealth, Power, and Influence. Artists had their muses; he had his. And they had been good to him.

The case lay open like a flower with its petals pulled back to reveal its sensitive heart. He bent over the slab of white marble and let his eyes pull in the color of the ancient artifact, the tint of a warm white stone with a light brown patina. He could smell the stone. Others would say he was crazy, a man who surrendered his mind a decade before, but he would swear that he could detect the stone slab's unique aroma. If someone were to chip away a corner—something worthy of a slow and painful execution—and mix it with other bits of marble, he would be able to find it by smell alone.

He also knew every branch, every vein of white marbling. He had never seen such intricacies in any other piece of stone.

The man stepped away from the open case and moved to a small sink in the corner of his personal museum. There he washed his hands using a powerful disinfecting soap. He washed again. Then again. He should wear white cotton museum gloves, but he could no longer bring himself to do so. He wanted to touch what had been touched twenty-five hundred years ago, to finger the surface upon which the body of the great man had been laid.

He moved from the sink to the display case with his hands held before him, like a freshly scrubbed surgeon walking into a surgical room. He paused, preparing himself for what had always been a sensuous experience.

Gently, as if his touch could shatter the slab, he touched one of the raised ancient Hebrew letters and moved his hand from right to left, following the text. Unlike most ancient writings committed to stone in which a scribe chiseled letters in the surface, the words on this slab were in bas-relief—the letters were raised above the surface. Twenty-five centuries before, a man, in what had to be arduous handwork, chipped away the surface, leaving just the letters. How long had that taken? How many people had worked on the tablet?

He had no answer to those questions, but he knew why such a difficult approach had been taken: by creating the message in bas-relief, they had made sure no one could alter the message. Stone could not be added where it had been taken away. Any attempt to alter the message would be obvious to everyone but a blind man.

The coolness of the stone, the smoothness of the surface, the edges of each letter thrilled him. So lost in the moment, he had to remind himself to breathe. His heart pounded, smashing into the back of his sternum, his hands shook, and tears rose in his eyes.

So beautiful.

So majestic.

So important.

Over sixty generations had passed since the hammer and chisel had removed the last fragment of marble.

The words.

The sentences.

The message.

His hands began to quiver just as they did every time he repeated this exercise.

He had very little formal education, but once he had gained his power, his influence, and his wealth, he undertook a self-education program, hiring professors from around the world to teach him what he needed to know, such as how to read ancient Hebrew, a language and writing very different from the modern version of the language.

Although he could recite the message forward and backward, he approached the material as if reading it for the first time, and in the custom of the ancient Jews, he read aloud.

"Blessed be *HaShem,* Lord of all, and his servant—"

A soft chiming filled the basement space. The man froze, his hand hovering over the next raised letter. He sighed, straightened, and looked at the ceiling-mounted, voice-activated intercom. "What."

"They're here." The male voice seemed unbothered by the man's curt response.

"Understood."

He returned to the tablet and began reading again. "Blessed be *HaShem,* Lord of all, and his priest Ezekiel son of Buzi…"

∽

The limo—long, white, new—was a nice touch, as if being flown in a private jet owned by the State of Israel hadn't been enough. Chambers had been in many limos. Anytime he appeared on a talk show, a limo would be sent. He soon realized he could judge a show's ratings by the size of the limo. A simple sixty-dollar-per-trip Lincoln Town Car meant the talk show was struggling; a stretch limo with a loaded bar meant cash was flowing into the coffers.

This limo said something else: Abram Ben-Judah had friends—powerful, wealthy friends. Field archaeologists were accustomed to less luxurious modes of transportation.

"I think he's trying to impress you, you know."

Chambers looked to his side and saw a smiling Nuri. "Yeah? How so?"

"Trust me, Ben-Judah would not send a limo like this for me. I'm just a lowly academician struggling to survive on a teacher's salary and what little I can squeeze from supporters."

"We're not far apart on that."

Nuri laughed so hard he came close to spilling his vodka tonic. Chambers sipped water from a plastic bottle but wished for strong, hot African coffee. His head hurt. Air travel never agreed with him, something he usually attributed to the stale, recycled air he was forced to breathe. In the rare moments he was honest with himself, he knew the head pain was somehow related to his mild claustrophobia.

"Oh, please, Dr. Chambers. You have two books on the *New York Times* bestseller list. You can't convince me you live in poverty."

Chambers shrugged. "I do all right, but I'm no Stephen King."

Nuri knocked back the last of his drink. "Oh, I don't know. I've read both books, and they struck me as horrors."

"You missed your calling, Nuri. You should have been a comedian. Then you could have brought some real value to the world."

"Let's not fight, David. We are here on a great mission."

Chambers bit his lip. "What is it with guys like you? You pick a fight, and as soon as someone tosses it back in your face, you act the innocent victim. You don't get to take free potshots at me, Nuri. You start a fight; I'll finish it. If you want to pretend to get along, then fine. Just keep your mouth shut around me."

"Fighting is second nature for Middle Easterners, or haven't you heard? We've been fighting for centuries. We are born with a bad attitude and barrels of mistrust."

"That doesn't mean you have to bathe in it, or worse, splash it around on everyone you meet."

Nuri poured another drink. "What can I say? I am a product of my upbringing and culture."

Chambers let the conversation wane in hopes of its death. Nuri sipped his freshened drink and stared out the window. "All the world comes here, David." His tone was civil, almost polite. "Just look at the people: white, black, Asian, Arab, Jews—"

"Who could have guessed Jews would be in Jerusalem."

Nuri didn't react to the jab. "They say Jerusalem is the center of the world. I once heard a radio preacher say that countries to the west of Jerusalem write from left to right; those east of Jerusalem pen their words right to left. Like Hebrew."

"And the Chinese write from top to bottom. Not everything a preacher says is true, Nuri."

"You've changed, David. You've become bitter like seawater. There is a reason people do not hug porcupines."

"I haven't traveled halfway around the world to earn hugs." He let his eyes take in the sights of Jerusalem and the irony it had become: ancient on one hand, a technological marvel on the other. Tourists crowded the bazaars and endured the cries of street vendors. Locals moved through them like trout swimming upstream, oblivious to anything but their destination. Armed soldiers dressed in green—men and women—stood on street corners eyeing everyone who passed. Jerusalem police officers, dressed in light-blue shirts and dark pants, patrolled the shops, letting their eyes linger on anyone who looked like a suicide bomber or gunman. The sight reminded Chambers that this land was as it has always been: a place of violence and hatred. The *"Jeru-Shalom,"* city of peace, had seldom known peace. Yet Nuri was right: people traveled to the city, despite possible danger, to walk the streets of the world's most famous city.

The city itself catered to three of the largest religions on the globe: Judaism, Islam, and Christianity. Three major faiths, none comfortable with the others.

When Chambers drew his eyes away from the street scene, he saw Nuri staring at him. "Are you now that cynical? Are you now such a misanthrope that only money and fame can motivate you?"

"I didn't say anything about money and fame."

"Not with words, this is true." Nuri frowned and looked away.

The limo driver lowered the privacy glass that separated the front seat from the large seating area in the back. "Five minutes more, Doctors."

"Thank you, driver," Nuri said.

Chambers said nothing.

Hebrew University was one university in several locations: Mount Scopus in northeastern Jerusalem, Giv'at Ram in western Jerusalem; Ein Kerem in the southwest part of the city; and the agricultural school in the city of Rehovot. What began as a humble effort in 1918 grew into one of the top universities in the world. Albert Einstein and Sigmund Freud served on the first board of governors. Four of Israel's prime ministers graduated from the facility; seven graduates had been awarded the Nobel Prize. Here 22,000 undergrads and postgrad students studied under the tutelage of 1,200 faculty. The school trained doctors, engineers, mathematicians, and scientists.

The driver parked the car and then opened the passenger door. Nuri slipped out first, leaving his glass tumbler on the surface of the tiny wet bar. Chambers followed. The air was heavy and surprisingly warm for the season and the 2,500-foot elevation. A wave of excitement rushed through Chambers as he looked at the three wings of the building that housed the Institute of Archaeology. Two of the wings had been constructed from dressed Jerusalem stone; the newest wing from sawn stone. The color and use of block stone gave the structure an ancient yet still very modern look, appropriate for its reputation, work, and location.

Chambers trotted up a short set of steps and marched toward a glass-and-anodized window wall and doors. He saw no need to wait for Nuri.

As he neared the entrance, the door swung open and a disheveled man in tan pants and a wrinkled white shirt exited, his arms held wide and a large grin beaming from his gray-bearded face. A yarmulke covered the crown of his head. Despite his sour mood, Chambers couldn't stop the growing insistent smile. He was slow to grant respect, but Abram Ben-Judah had earned a lifetime of esteem a long time ago.

"David, my boy. *Mah Shlomcah*?"

Ben-Judah looked frail, but Chambers knew him to be strong in body as well as mind. Still...

"Dr. Ben-Judah. *Mamash Tov.*" He let the older man embrace him and kiss him on both cheeks. The dark cloud that had followed him from his home dissipated. He patted the man's back.

"That's enough of formalities, David. You've served academic protocol; now let's speak as friends." He held Chambers at arm's length. "You do look well."

"As do you, Abram."

"Nonsense. I'm getting old and losing weight."

Chambers heart hesitated. "You're not ill, are you?"

"I am afflicted with age, that is all, David. No need to worry about me. I can still outwork my grad students."

There was no doubt in Chambers's mind about that. He had worked several digs with his mentor and often run out of energy long before the older man.

Ben-Judah stepped away and greeted Nuri. "*Shalom,* Nuri. It is good to see you again."

"*Shalom,* Professor. The joy is mine."

"Come, come." Ben-Judah motioned to the door. "I have refreshments waiting." He moved into the building.

"Is—"

"No, Nuri. Not yet."

Chambers shifted his gaze from one man to the other. "Is...what?"

"This way, gentlemen. The Institute has been good enough to let us use one of the executive conference rooms."

"I'm pretty sure the Institute does whatever you ask." Nuri moved alongside Chambers. "You are the executive director."

"Was, Nuri. Past tense. I no longer hold that position."

The news stunned Chambers. "What? Since when?"

"One month, two weeks, three days ago."

The two hustled forward until they were walking at Ben-Judah's side. "They fired you?" Chambers asked.

"Of course not, David. I quit. I have tea and *hamantashen*." He raised a hand as he walked, as if waving off unspoken objections. "I know it is not the festival of Purim, but an old man can have a cookie when he wants. No?"

The image of a three-cornered cookie filled with fruit preserve flashed in Chambers's mind. In Hebrew the pastry was called *Oznei Haman:* "Haman's ears" after the evil Haman in the book of Esther—the *Megillah*. Every year, Jews worldwide celebrate the salvation of the Hebrews from the pogrom promoted by the Persian leader working under King Xerxes.

Ben-Judah led the two down a hall. Students parted before him like water before the bow of a mighty ship. Chambers and Nuri followed in his wake.

Although it had been many months since Chambers last walked the corridors of the Institute, everything seemed familiar and comfortable.

Ben-Judah cut down another hall, his stride long and determined, belying his advanced years. How old was he? Chambers tried to recall. Seventy? Seventy-two? It didn't matter; his mind was faster and keener than any twenty-something undergrad. Living in the past seemed to fend off the future.

At the end of the hall, Ben-Judah opened a door and stepped into a large room dominated by a wide table. Unlike the contemporary furnishings found in other parts of the building, this table had a distinctive midcentury look. There was something familiar about it. Chambers laid a hand on its surface. "Is this *the* table?"

Ben-Judah was at the far wall lowering window shades, cutting off the view to a stone plaza and the faculty and students who walked there. "What's that, David? The table? Yes, of course. That is the table."

"Am I missing something?" Nuri said.

"Albert Einstein sat at this table. So did Sigmund Freud. They were two of the men on the first board of governors."

Nuri seemed impressed. "I would like to have been a mouse in the room when they were talking. What would the world's most famous physicist and the world's most renowned psychologist talk about?"

"Probably more than the weather." Chambers looked around the room. It was plain in every way. No art. No photos. No expensive wall treatment or thick-pile carpet. It was a room designed for the discussion of educational business, not a place to luxuriate. "Are we early?"

Ben-Judah closed the last of the shades. Sunlight filtered through the fabric, silhouetting the people moving outside. "Yes. Your driver made good time. Better than we anticipated. He is taking your luggage to the hotel."

"So he said." Chambers watched as Nuri snapped up a couple of the cookies and sat at what Chambers thought of as the foot of the table. For a moment he thought the man would prop his feet up on the historic piece of furniture. To his credit, he didn't.

"I see you found the *hamantashen,* Nuri. I was going to tell you to help yourself, but…"

"My apologies, Abram. I had a drink or two—"

"Or three," Chambers added.

Nuri sighed like a long-suffering father. "It was two drinks, David. Let's not exaggerate. Anyway, I thought a little food might be helpful."

The phone at the head of the table chimed, and Ben-Judah answered. A moment later he set the hand piece back in the cradle. He nodded at

Nuri, who set the cookies he had taken on a napkin and strode from the room.

"Where's he going?"

Ben-Judah moved to the table and pulled a tea service close. He poured hot brown liquid into five cups. *Five cups, five people.* Chambers expected more.

"Is it just me, Abram, or are you still being secretive?"

"Let an old man have his games, David. Soon the curtain will be drawn back, and all will be known."

Laughter oozed into the room from the hallway. It made Chambers tense. His mind began to sprint from thought to thought. He turned as the door opened. Nuri entered with a woman on his arm. Both were grinning; both looked like they had just won a lottery.

The woman had her eyes fixed on Nuri as they stepped into the room. He paused, then, "I believe everyone has met before."

The woman did the polite thing, turning her attention to the people in the room. Her jaw dropped.

"David!"

"Amber!"

SIX

They spoke in unison. "What are you doing here?"

Then a pause.

Chambers and Amber turned to Ben-Judah. Chambers spoke for both of them. "Abram?"

He clasped his hands behind his back and rocked up on his toes. A moment later he shrugged. "Would you have come had I told you?"

Again in unison. "No!"

"Well, there 'tis. I need you both; I need you here, and this is too important to let something as silly as love lost keep us from our goal."

"Silly?" Amber's face reddened. "There's nothing silly about this. You tricked me."

"Nonsense, young lady. I did no such thing. I may have withheld a minor detail or two so as not to distract you, but that's all I did."

Chambers crossed his arms. "I think you did more than that."

Again Abram shrugged. "Well, maybe I kept a few things from you, but I did so for good reason."

"Like tricking us into showing up in the same room when we don't want to be in the same country." Amber's gaze was pointed, and for a moment Chambers thought he could feel the barb.

This time, Abram looked pained. "Have you ever known me to play games with our discipline? What we do is too valuable. Archaeology in this land is unlike any other archaeology. I know I will sound like a foolish old man when I say biblical archaeology is the pinnacle of all scientific historical study. Perhaps that attitude is a little too superior for some, but what we do has more value than just uncovering ancient civilizations."

"Well," Nuri said, returning to his half-eaten cookie, "we can't overlook the life-changing work of those who study, oh say, the Olmecs."

"Can it, Nuri."

Nuri raised his hands. "To borrow an American phrase, 'Hey, I'm just sayin'.'"

Chambers drew a visual bead on him, like a sniper targeting his enemy. "Did you know about this?"

Nuri shrugged. "Maybe a little."

When a stout man with a thick neck entered the room, Chambers took notice but paid him no attention. His attention was on Nuri. "You weasel. You knew all along. You helped set me up."

"I just carried out the good professor's wishes. Such is my respect for him."

"Nuri, how could you do this to me?" Amber appeared to be getting angrier by the moment. She backed up a step, almost crashing into the room's newest occupant.

"You know I love you, my dear, but you have unresolved issues with David. Professor Ben-Judah feels you would make a great member of the team. He trusts you. I trust you. David—well, that remains to be seen."

"That's it." Chambers started for Nuri. "I've had my fill of you."

"Enough!"

The voice seemed to shake the windows and was delivered with such authority that Chambers seized midstep.

The corners of the stout man's mouth moved up a millimeter, and it chilled Chambers.

"David, my good friend, please stop. You are making a terrible mistake," Ben-Judah pleaded.

"I don't care. I will not tolerate being lied to."

Nuri raised a finger. "Professor Ben-Judah is right. Unless I miss my guess, our new guest is Shin Bet."

Chambers blinked several times. "Israel Security Agency?" He looked at the man in slacks and sports coat.

Nuri nodded. "Shin Bet, ISA, *Shabak,* choose your favorite name. My guess is he's internal security, but why don't you throw a punch his way and find out."

Ben-Judah rounded the table and put a hand on Chambers's shoulder. "Nuri is right, David. This is Hiram Landau. He works with ISA. The prime minister has been kind enough to send him our way." He paused. "I apologize, David, and to you too, Amber. My goal was not to deceive you, but I didn't want to give you a reason to say no until you've heard what I have to say. Then, if you feel you must still leave, I won't stand in your way."

Chambers looked at Amber. Man, she looked good, even with the red tinge of anger on her face. His heart did jumping jacks at the sight of her, and he hated it for doing so. "We're here. I guess we might as well go the next few steps." He waited for Amber to respond.

She lowered her head, bit her lip for a moment, then nodded. Chambers pulled back one of the chairs for Amber and she sat. He helped her scoot closer to the table, then walked to the point farthest away from her and took a seat. Her expression told him she got the message. The room iced over.

Ben-Judah conjured a smile, then set out the filled tea cups and, ever the dutiful host, made certain everyone had at least one of the filled cookies. When he finished, he filled one more cup. Someone else was expected.

Abram Ben-Judah set the cup at the head of the table, then sat in the chair immediately to the right. Chambers couldn't imagine who deserved the seat of honor more than Abram.

After the confrontation a few minutes ago, the room grew as silent as a sepulcher. Nuri chewed another cookie. Amber stared at the grain in the historic table; Landau leaned back in his seat, his beefy arms crossed over a beefier chest; and Ben-Judah stared into the distance as if seeing what no one else could.

∽

In the States, he rode in a modest limo. For him, a stretch limo was ostentatious. Truth was, he'd rather drive than be driven. He missed the days when he could, at will, leave his home and slip behind the wheel of one of his sports cars or, better yet, one of his collectables, his favorite being a copper-colored 1952 Allard J2X. It looked fast just sitting in his garage. It was too futuristic for midcentury America, and over six decades later, it still turned heads whenever it cruised the streets of Boston.

Those days were gone. He had made too many enemies, and the world had changed. Most likely he could take a long Sunday drive in full safety, but the security agency he paid an embarrassing amount of money to insisted that such frivolity was dangerous. After all, he had his family to think about—a half-dozen billion-dollar companies.

What good was being numbered with the top fifteen richest men in the world, and the top five in the United States, if he couldn't enjoy an occasional drive in a car he paid three-quarters of a million dollars to obtain? Well, he decided, there were still a few things he could do. Change the world was one of them.

The "limo" that carted him from Tel Aviv into Jerusalem and up the road to Hebrew University looked nothing like the kind of vehicle twenty-first-century robber barons plied busy streets in. From the outside, the vehicle looked like the American Humvee, but unlike those bought at dealerships, this car came equipped with bulletproof glass, a hardened undercarriage shield to fend off improvised explosive devices, state-of-the-art communication, on-board oxygen in case of a gas attack, and several types of handguns. He had been trained to use the guns, but he despised them. He hated violence.

The thin driver was a former Navy SEAL with a half-dozen long-term deployments in Afghanistan and Iraq. He had served in other countries as well, places he never talked about. Next to him sat a former Army Ranger, and sharing the backseat was a chunk of a man who had spent many years with Israel's Mossad.

The former SEAL touched his ear as he received a message from a tiny monitor. "Plaza looks clear." His voice was soft—like molten steel is soft.

The driver nodded. "Three minutes."

A car sped around them. Any other time, this would have been cause for alarm, but the passenger had been briefed. The American-made SUV sped ahead. A glance back told him another car had moved into the position of the previous vehicle. He sighed and wished for the days of his childhood.

"You can just drop me off at the curb."

"I'm sorry, sir, it doesn't work that way."

"It was a joke."

"Yes sir," the SEAL said. "Very funny."

"I don't see you laughing."

"Trust me, sir. I'm busting a gut on the inside."

"I bet you are."

Exactly three minutes later, the Humvee pulled to a stop in one of the university parking lots. He had no doubt that it was the parking lot closest to the Institute of Archaeology.

"Hold on," the driver said.

No one moved.

As the only one in the vehicle without someone chattering in his ear, the man could only wait until he was told to move. He couldn't open the door if he wanted to. The lock system that kept abductors out, kept him in. He waited in the armored womb.

"Go." The driver pressed a button and the doors unlocked.

And John Trent exited the air-conditioned backseat and felt the warmth of the sun on his face. He lingered for a moment, eyes closed, face turned to the sky. A strong hand took his elbow. "This way, sir."

Trent didn't hesitate.

SEVEN

Chambers could hear his heart beat, feel it struggling to do its work an inch or so behind his breastbone. His face felt warm, as if the heating vents were turned on his skin. Not to be outdone, his stomach roiled with adrenaline and rage-heated acid. Normally a calm, reflective man, David was not given to outbursts of anger. He prided himself on his intellect and his cool, detached manner of analysis. Unchecked emotion was a road traveled by lesser minds, not a disciplined scientist. Something in his brain screamed, "Liar." His unbidden self-evaluation was correct. He had known many objective scientists who became loudmouthed gasbags when others refused to take their work seriously or challenged some minutia of their logic. Many were driven by pride instead of curiosity. He saw himself as an intellectual cut from a different cloth. Today was proving him wrong, and he was beginning to hate himself for it. Lately his mouth seemed to have a mind of its own.

Maybe Nuri, the perpetual burr under his saddle, had irritated him beyond any human endurance. Maybe he was suffering from travel fatigue. Maybe he was feeling guilty about returning to biblical archaeology so soon after leaving it all behind. It could be one or all of those things. Or it could be that Amber walked in on the arm of Nuri, smiling and giggling like a high school girl.

He told himself that was the least likely reason. The thing in his head with the single-word vocabulary repeated its mantra: "Liar."

Ben-Judah sipped his tea. Amber continued to study the table as if trying to memorize the fingerprints. Nuri had given up on the cookies, and Hiram Landau had removed a small penknife from his pants pocket and was working at whatever rested beneath his fingernails.

The door to the conference room opened, and a man with blond hair cut close to the scalp entered. Chambers looked across the table and tensed. Something about the man said he was dangerous. Hiram had picked up the same vibe. He was on his feet and reaching beneath his sport coat. The visitor did the same, while raising his other hand.

A second man entered, and Hiram paused. "You lookin' to get your man shot, Jasper?" Hearing Hiram speak a full sentence for the first time, Chambers detected a slight Jersey accent. He had ceased being surprised by such things after his first visit to Jerusalem. No doubt, Hiram was a transplant from the States.

The man he called Jasper was a third the size of the man who entered before him but looked twice as mean. "Still jumpy I see, Hiram. They have medication for that, you know."

Chambers expected the conversation to turn angry, but instead Hiram laughed. "Everybody, this is Jasper... You're still using the name *Jasper,* right?"

"For now." The man shrugged and glanced around the room before opening the door wide. "It suits me."

Hiram flashed a snide grin. "He's with...another agency."

Chambers got the idea and tried to will his heart back to an even rhythm. A glance at Nuri showed a man trying to look nonchalant even though he was about to pass out. Pulling in a deep breath, Chambers pressed back in his seat and hoped he didn't look as shell-shocked as the others.

Jasper stepped aside, and a tall man in a white polo shirt, tan pants, and expensive-looking brown leather loafers walked in. He had seen the kind before. It was hard to forget a five-hundred-dollar pair of shoes. The man could have stepped from the glossy pages of a men's magazine. He was trim, with a square chin, intelligent-looking blue eyes, flat belly, and—best Chambers could tell—a gym-toned body. He most likely owned his own gym. Gray painted the hair at his temples, and his face bore enough wrinkles to show the man was on the north side of fifty.

Ben-Judah stood and beamed, then rounded the table to take the man's hand and shake it with enthusiasm. "So good to see you, Mr. Trent. Please come in. Come in. There's a seat for you at the head of the table." Ben-Judah swiveled to face the others. "Everyone, please meet our primary benefactor: Mr. John Trent of the United States."

"Just Trent if you don't mind." He let Ben-Judah lead him to the head of the conference table. "I'm one of the last-name-first kind of guys. It's the advantage of having two first names." He sat and leaned back in his chair. Chambers could imagine the man sitting this way at board-of-directors meetings. He wondered if Trent demanded the head of the table. Trent nodded at the security men, and they stepped into the hall, then gently closed the door behind them.

Ben-Judah slipped into his seat, the two-hundred-watt smile still plastered to his face. "Mr. Trent has long been a supporter of biblical archaeology. He's funded several digs for the Institute, as well as those from several universities. His generosity is legendary."

Ben-Judah was not prone to overstatement or effusion, and he hadn't surrendered to it now. Chambers had heard of the man and knew that some of his own research had been backed, silently and secretly, by Trent.

The group greeted the man with head nods and hellos.

"Allow me to make formal introductions," Ben-Judah said.

"No need. I'm not one for formality." Trent smiled in a way that Chambers found unsettling. "I already know this team." He turned to Ben-Judah. "I know I've said this in private, but let me say it before the group: you have assembled the best of the best for this project. I am humbled to be in their presence."

Chambers wasn't sure what to make of the situation or the man.

Archaeology was as dependent on donations from wealthy patrons as any science, maybe more so. Men like Trent made possible some of the greatest discoveries in the field. Some gave to gain fame and admiration, others in hope of financial return. Others gave from their coffers because they needed a tax write-off, and others wanted to see their names on the wing of some university building. What little Chambers knew of Trent—and it was precious little—suggested that the billionaire didn't fit the mold. Trent, from what Chambers had heard at symposiums and around the Harvard archaeology facility, was in it for the knowledge. That made him a true patron.

Trent looked each person in the eyes, like a man who had been invited to hang out with Academy Award winners. He seemed as enthralled with the gathering as the others were with him. Chambers wasn't easily impressed with a man, even if the man made more in an hour than he made in a year. The pesky voice in his head returned.

"How much do they know about me, Ben-Judah?"

The old man looked concerned. "I have told them nothing. Only that I had funding for the project."

"I'm not accusing you, old friend, just trying to find out where we stand." Trent addressed the others. "Let me give you a little background about me. Not much. I am a man who appreciates his privacy. It's the reason I don't grant interviews to the business magazines and newspapers, although I receive a dozen requests every week. Some of you know how the press can be." He looked at Chambers. "Isn't that right, Dr. Chambers?"

"I suppose so, although I've had very little trouble with them."

"I'm sure you haven't; I find them a distraction. That will lead to a statement I'll make in a moment."

He leaned forward and rested his hands on the table. They looked like soft hands to David. "We are about to undertake a grand adventure, so it is only right that you know a little about me, especially since I know a great deal about you."

He shifted in his seat. "I was born into a privileged family with the clichéd silver spoon in my mouth. I was rich the moment I entered this world. I went to the best of schools. That includes Harvard, Dr. Chambers."

"That explains your winning ways." Chambers cracked a crooked smile.

"It didn't hurt me, that's for sure." He returned his attention to the others. "For the bulk of my adult life, I built on my father's foundation. He made money in oil; I took it the next few steps, buying and revamping struggling companies in the same industry. Then I turned to pharmaceuticals—making them, that is. I also own several computer-related companies. Never mind which ones."

The group chuckled politely.

"Long story short, I made more money than a man can spend. I also became bored with business. It took several years, but I've separated myself from the day-to-day workings of corporate life. I've hired good people. I keep an eye on things of course, but I spend most of my time giving my money to worthwhile causes. I'm especially interested in biblical archaeology, so I've funded quite a few digs, but this one will be where I invest my soul."

An odd phrase. Chambers kept the opinion to himself.

Trent faced Ben-Judah again. "I assume you've stayed with our story?"

"I have, my friend."

"Wait a minute." Chambers leaned over the table. "Story? You mean we're not here because of the Scroll?"

"Easy, Dr. Chambers." Trent raised a hand. "You haven't been misled."

"Actually, I have." Chambers glared at Ben-Judah but couldn't maintain the scowl. His respect for the man quenched the heat of his anger.

"You say that because we didn't tell you about Dr. Rodgers?"

"Call me Amber." A smile parted her lips.

David rolled his eyes. "Yes. This isn't how I do business."

"Isn't it?" Trent raised a hand to his chin. "Then perhaps you better leave."

"No, Trent." Ben-Judah looked stunned. "We need him. He's the only one who can do what needs to be done."

"I doubt that," Nuri said.

Chambers stood. "Before you go, Dr. Chambers, you need to hear a few more things. I can have on this team only the best in their field and those I can trust. Most of all, you have to be able to trust me, or at very least, trust Dr. Ben-Judah."

Ben-Judah's face had gone white. "Please, David, sit."

The look in Ben-Judah's eyes forced Chambers back to his seat. He folded his hands on the table and determined to sit in silence until the ordeal was over.

Trent pushed back from the table and stood. "I am not ignorant of the interpersonal dynamics of this group. If this were any other field investigation, then Professor Ben-Judah and I would have chosen differently. But the magnitude of what we are about to do requires sacrifices on everyone's part."

"With all due respect, Mr. Trent," Chambers said, "what sacrifice are you making?"

Trent answered with a look that Chambers was certain could ignite wood across the room. "How about $200 million to start? How about my reputation? There's even a good chance I could lose my life. I don't travel with security because I'm lonely."

"Your life?" Chambers was disappointed that he hadn't hidden his sarcasm better.

"That's right, Dr. Chambers, and let everyone in this room understand this one thing: what you do may put you in danger." He stepped back to the chair at the head of the table but didn't sit. He placed both hands on the back of the chair and squeezed in a way that made Chambers glad the chair couldn't feel pain.

No one spoke, but the body language conveyed how ill at ease the group had become.

Finally, Nuri spoke. "Anything done in this land is dangerous. Archaeology is no different. I think you'll find that we don't intimidate that easily."

Chambers waited for the inevitable dig from his longtime adversary, but it never came. Was he being discreet? polite? Or had the man found one quality in Chambers's life to admire?

Trent straightened and held up several fingers. "Three things before we take the next step. One, I have to know that you will do your jobs to the best of your ability. Two, you must be able to trust me and Professor Ben-Judah fully, completely, and without question. I can assure you that you will be doing nothing untoward or illegal. You have my word on that. Three, you must be able to do your work without knowing all the details of the goal."

"Seriously?" The last comment seemed to catch Amber off guard. "Forgive me, but how can we promise our best work without knowing everything up-front?"

"Security," Chambers said. "He's playing spy. Need-to-know compartmentalization and all of that."

"Believe me," Trent said, "this has nothing to do with trust. If I did not trust you, you would not be in this room. Still, Dr. Chambers is right. For now, you just need to know that you are about to change the world. Forever."

He nodded to Ben-Judah, who picked up the handset of a phone at his end of the table. "We're ready."

A moment later, a young man with an uncut beard entered the room carrying a stack of what first appeared to be black leather folders. The man set the stack next to the professor, then opened the top folder and looked at a sticky note attached to the inside. That's when Chambers realized he was looking, not at a stack of notebooks, but at thin tablet computers. A few moments later, each person in the room had one of the touchscreen computers. Chambers pulled back the protective cover and saw a blank screen. Tempted as he was, he resisted the urge to press the power button at the top.

The bearded student left without a word.

Trent remained at his position behind the high-back chair as if it were a lectern. Once the door closed and the latch clicked, Trent spoke. "These are the latest in slate computers from one of my companies. They won't be released to the public for another year or so. The screen is touch sensitive. I've had my engineers and programmers make a few adjustments. They will work on the local cell system, but all e-mail, voice mail, anything for that matter, that is sent over open systems is encrypted. Each of your computers can decrypt the messages once you enter your password."

"What's the password?" Amber didn't look up from the thin device.

Trent shook his head. "You will set that the first time you turn the device on. First, power up the device."

Chambers and the others did. He was surprised how quickly it came to life. It was the closest to "instant on" he had seen in a computer. A small window appeared and a digital keyboard below it.

"Enter these numbers and letters," Trent said. "Seven, seven, one, one, zero, eight, *J, E, L*."

"Should the numbers mean anything to us?" Nuri asked.

"No," Trent said. "They were generated randomly by a computer. You don't need to memorize them since you'll be putting in your own, unique password. Make it something easy for you to remember but something no one would guess."

Chambers thought for a moment, then smiled. He entered the ISBN number of his first book. As instructed by the computer prompt, he entered it again. The computer came to life showing several small panes on the screen. He didn't have time to explore. Trent demanded their attention again.

"Each computer has information specific to your roles. I think you'll be surprised at what you find. As we progress, I will send more information your way." He stepped around the chair and sat. "Here is what you are to do next. First, review the material on your tablets. Remember, every bit of it is for your eyes only. We will meet again, and I would like to hear from our three archaeologists about the best way to proceed." He turned to Hiram. "Your device will give you some of the basics necessary to provide security."

"Understood."

Trent straightened and took a deep breath. "I am not a man given to exaggeration, so when I say we are about to undertake an adventure that will never be forgotten by the world, I mean it."

EIGHT

The thoughts in David Chambers's mind spun like debris in a tornado, scraping, gouging, smashing other thoughts to tiny pieces. His heart followed suit. He felt like a boulder rolling, bouncing down a long, steep hillside, moved by immutable laws of physics. He had no right to be angry, but he was; he had no reason to feel betrayed, but he did. He chose to remain behind longer than the others; not out of courtesy, but to avoid contact with Amber and Nuri. At the moment, he didn't trust his emotions. The prospects of a new dig would in the past have made him almost as giddy as a schoolgirl asked to the prom. In such predig meetings, he would normally be the one to ask the most questions, the one to plumb the depths of details. He wasn't that man today.

Ben-Judah and Trent were the first to leave, disappearing into some corner of the Institute, leaving the others to vacate the conference room. Seconds passed like epochs. Once he was certain that he had placed the reins on his emotions, Chambers picked up his tablet PC and exited the empty room.

Before the door behind him could close, he saw the one thing he didn't want to see: Amber standing at the end of the hall, leaning against a wall, her gaze directed at the floor. Alerted by the sound of the conference-room door closing, Amber looked up, gazed at Chambers for a moment, then looked away. Chambers's first impulse was to duck back into the room, like a child hiding from a bully. Pride prevented the maneuver. He started down the hall, doing his best to avoid eye contact with the one-time love of his life. *Keep your mouth shut, Chambers. Just walk on by. Nothing more needs to be said.*

Five steps later: "Where's your new boyfriend?"

Amber pressed her lips together as if trying to hold back a more pointed first response. "He's in the little archaeologist's room."

"The what... Oh. He's in the head." A pause. "I figured you'd be gone by now."

Her chuckle held no humor. "I thought you drifted off toward the end there. Hiram Landau said we'd be riding to the hotel together. Something about security. I was just about to go get you. I thought maybe you got lost trying to find the door."

"Cute. Still have the acid tongue, I see."

"Me? You're the one that came in with guns blazing."

"Yeah? Well, I have a right. Seeing you hanging on Nuri's arm and gazing at him like a high school freshman was more than irritating."

"I took his arm because he offered it—something you never did. The high school freshman crack is just plain stupid and mean. Besides, it's none of your business what I do with my life."

The truth stung, but Chambers didn't let it linger. "What do you see in a guy like Nuri? There are things about him you don't know." He thought of how Nuri flirted with the female pilot.

"I'm not going to stand here and listen to any more of this." She raised her tablet to her chest as if shielding her heart, turned on a heel, and marched from the hall into the lobby, taking long, purposeful strides to the entrance doors.

"Amber. Wait." Remorse percolated from the less callous part of his soul. He followed her, matching step for step, not wanting to draw the attention of students and faculty milling in the lobby. By the time Chambers had closed the distance between them to lay a hand on her shoulder, they were outside, standing on the stone plaza. She stopped at his touch, then stared at his hand as if it were leprous. "Okay, listen, I admit I'm a little off my emotional game, but you don't need to walk away. We are going to be working together after all."

"Had I known that, I might have refused Ben-Judah's offer." She shook off his hand.

Chambers smiled. "Not even you could do that. I'll admit that you're strong-willed and determined, but no one who knows Ben-Judah can turn him down. I know. I tried, yet here I am."

She turned her back on him and looked at the access road and nearby parking lot. He followed her gaze. Cars glistened in the afternoon sun.

"What has happened to you, David? I can't determine if the David I knew was a carefully orchestrated act and I'm seeing the real David now, or if you've changed."

"We are what life makes us."

She spun and faced him. Her face had grown a shade redder. "The David I knew would never have said that. He would have said, 'Life is what we make it.' You *have* changed even more since I last saw you, and you were horrible then."

"I was never horrible with you, Amber. I was *honest.* Do you know what honesty is? I don't think you do. You insist on living in your imaginary world of faith."

"You were a person of faith—once. Now you're a…a…I don't know what you are."

"I am a man who is honest with himself. I'm done pretending. I'm finished walking on eggshells to keep sensitive people like you from getting their little feelings hurt."

"Honest?" She pointed a finger at him. "Honest with yourself. Is that what you said? That's a lie."

Chamber saw several passersby staring at them. "Let's not fight, Amber. We used to be a couple. We used to have something. Once we spent time planning our wedding."

"That's before you lost your mind."

"I didn't lose my mind; I lost my faith."

"It's the same thing."

Chambers laughed. "Then why are you hanging out with Nuri? Last I looked, he was the antithesis of faith. He's not even a good Jew. You don't get to sleep with him and then play the faith card with me—"

The slap jarred him enough that he had to take a step to the side to keep from falling. He raised a hand to his stinging, hot cheek. Amber moved close. "I didn't sleep with you, and I haven't slept with Nuri—not that it's any business of yours."

Chambers reached into his bag of insults but found it empty.

"Did I miss something?"

Nuri's voice bored into Chambers's brain. He lowered his hand and clinched his fists. A large, strong hand landed on his shoulder. Chambers knocked it away as he turned, ready to unleash his adrenaline-laced anger on whoever invaded his private space, and found himself staring into the cold, unblinking eyes of Hiram Landau.

"You may want to reconsider your next action, Dr. Chambers." Landau's voice was soft, steady, and as cold as a glacier.

Chambers waited for Nuri to make a wisecrack, but a glance told him that the annoying archaeologist was just as intimidated. Slowly, Chambers's fists loosened.

Landau remained quiet to allow the heat of the moment to dissipate. "I have an SUV waiting for us." He narrowed his eyes. "Perhaps you'd like to ride in the front seat while I drive, Dr. Chambers."

It wasn't a suggestion.

Nuri took Amber by the hand and started for the parking lot. The sight of it infuriated Chambers. He started forward, but Landau clamped a viselike grip on his elbow. "A moment of your time, Dr. Chambers."

"I thought you were eager to get going."

Landau sighed. "I want to make sure you're clear on my role in this operation."

"I'm clear. Your job is to keep us safe."

"My job is to keep the dig safe. Please don't make me defend it against you."

"Are you threatening me?" Chambers struggled to appear unconcerned.

"I've never made a threat in my life." Landau slipped his arm over Chambers's shoulders and started toward the parking lot. "I have, however, implied a few." He squeezed Chambers's shoulder enough to cause mild pain. "I'm very good at what I do, but I have two shortcomings: one, I'm impatient; two, I have no sense of humor."

"This is one of those veiled threats, isn't it?"

Landau shrugged. "Come along, Dr. Chambers. You'll feel better after a hot meal and a little rest. International flights can wear on a man."

Chambers thought it wise to cooperate.

❧

John Trent stood just outside the lobby doors. Abram Ben-Judah stood next to him. "Is this going to be a problem, Professor?"

"David is a good man, with a good heart."

"I know his work very well, but I don't know him. Can he be trusted to do the job?"

Ben-Judah, nodded. "Once the work begins, you will see a focused man. I would not have recommended him if I had doubts."

"With all due respect, my friend, just seeing what we've seen, I have doubts."

Ben-Judah faced him. "No one knows the ancient tunnel systems like David; no one pursues the truth like him. He's our best choice. I have faith in him."

"I hope you're right, Professor."

The old man smiled. "He will be no problem."

"See to it, Professor—or I will."

∽

"So what's your story, Mr. Landau? Or should I be calling you by some military rank?"

Amber's voice wafted forward from the backseat of the black GMC Yukon Denali. Chambers sat in the front passenger seat, eyes forward, mouth turned down.

"No rank, ma'am. Just call me Landau. What do you want to know?"

"If I'm being nosy, just let me know, but you don't sound like you grew up around here. Is that a New York accent I hear?"

Chambers caught Landau glancing at him, perhaps waiting for a reaction to the "nosy" comment. Chambers started to say something just to prove that Landau hadn't intimidated him but couldn't find the courage.

"No ma'am, I'm from Jersey. Trenton to be exact."

"You're a long way from home," Nuri said.

"No sir. I am home. I was born in the States and lived there until I was nearly thirty. Went to college there and served in the military."

"What branch?" Amber said. She sounded cheerful. Chambers was still angry about the confrontation. "Or am I allowed to ask?"

"Marines, ma'am. Served a good number of years before moving here."

"And why move here?"

Chambers stared at the other cars on the road. He had been able to identify at least three vehicles as part of the security escort, although none bore any markings.

"Two things. My parents moved here after my father retired from medicine. He was a surgeon. I first came to Israel as part of a joint military-training detachment and fell in love with the place. My father was a frequent contributor to several Israeli causes, so he had made some friends. When he grew ill, I moved to Israel. He pulled a few strings, and soon I was working for the ISA. That was seven years ago."

"And your father?" Amber asked softly.

"He died a year after I arrived. Mom passed soon after that. By that time, Israel had become my home."

"I'm sorry about your parents."

"Life happens, Dr. Rodgers. So does death."

Chambers, against his will, thought of his mother. He could see her in her bed, dying inch by inch, while his father remained removed and in a distant land—this land.

He should have been there. He should have been there.

NINE

The upscale King Solomon hotel was the newest large hotel in Jerusalem and catered to wealthy tourists. When Chambers had last been in the city, the structure was still in the planning stage. He had heard rumors about the future hotel's opulence. The rumors were true. The building was beautiful inside and out. Like many hotels in the city and surrounding areas, this one was built according to plans by architects and interior designers who tried to reflect the ancient city's past without losing sight of the twenty-first century.

The interior floors and walls were made of cultured stone. Chambers had seen enough of the real thing to know the difference between real limestone, granite, and marble and "stone" manufactured in some factory. Still, light browns gave the lobby a warm and welcome feeling. Decorative lights shone up towering Romanesque columns with ornate capitals. Colorful drapes embroidered with gold pomegranates made Chambers think of biblical descriptions of the temple's interior.

The team walked through the expanse: Nuri and Amber first, Chambers following. Landau walked to the side, scanning the room, making eye contact with everyone looking their way. Chambers noticed several men and at least two women who looked too casual. He saw that Landau ignored them, focusing instead on the tourists and hotel employees. Chambers assumed the others were operatives. A bald man, in a suit one degree removed from a tuxedo, approached, smiling like a used-car salesman. Landau moved forward and took the lead in just a few strides. He greeted the man in Hebrew and held out his hand. The manager took it, then looked nonplussed when Landau didn't let go. They spoke in soft tones. Landau must have liked what he heard because he released the man and turned to the group.

The man led them to one end of a long marble counter away from the other guests waiting to check in. In a few moments, the three archaeologists had electronic room keys and the profuse welcome of the day manager. "Your luggage has been delivered to your individual rooms. If you have any questions or special needs, please let me know. The senior management will take care of all matters personally. We shall be at your service twenty-four hours a day."

As the manager recited their room numbers, Chambers felt a sense of shame over the relief he felt hearing that Nuri's room number was different from Amber's.

They rode an elevator to the twelfth floor. Chambers faced the matte-finish metal doors, thankful they were not reflective. He didn't want to face anyone, not even their reflection. The tension seemed heavy enough to slow the elevator cab.

They stepped from the elevator into a wide lobby. It smelled of new carpet and fresh paint.

"Before you go to your rooms, just a couple of things." Landau stood with his back near the far wall. "The locks on the doors of your rooms are tied to the hotel security system. Each time the door is opened, a record is made." He pointed above his head where the wall and ceiling met. Chambers saw a small security camera. "There are cameras spaced throughout the corridor. One is directed on each of your doors. They send a wireless signal to a monitoring station I've had set up in the hotel. We will know anytime anyone moves through the halls or uses the elevator to this floor. You may have noticed that I used a card key in the elevator. No other guests are on this floor, nor can anyone without the right key even access the floor. Of course, hotel services will be allowed into the area, but we will know who they are and when they come and go. If you order room service, the hotel will notify me or one of my team. We will make sure that only an approved employee makes it to this floor. Clear so far?"

The three nodded.

"Professor Ben-Judah tells me that he may send people your way, but he's promised to let me know first. Should someone show up at your door that you're not expecting, wait for the password."

"Which is?" Nuri asked.

"Shibboleth."

Chambers chuckled. "Clever." No one asked for an explanation. *Shibboleth* was a password used by the ancient Jews in the time of the judges to distinguish Ephraimites from the men of Gilead. The Ephraimites of the day could not utter the "sh" sound, just as some contemporary ethnic groups have trouble with English consonants. It became a way to distinguish the good guys from the bad.

"Yeah, well, I had to look the word up." Landau moved from the elevator lobby into a wide corridor. "All the rooms up here are suites, so you'll have a bedroom, a living room, and a small kitchen, although you won't need it. There is a desk in each room, and you have full Internet access for general e-mail. Please do not give away your location or what you're doing. Any message sent from the tablet PCs will be encrypted. You cannot transfer the material on the tablets to any other computer without the proper encryption codes."

"So we are not to be trusted." Nuri looked hurt.

"You we trust, Dr. Aumann. Others not so much. The limitation is meant to keep someone from wirelessly accessing your tablet PC and copying information or planting a virus. If you need outside consultation, say from some stateside university, you will need to talk to me. I will arrange for that to happen—assuming Professor Ben-Judah agrees."

"Of course," Amber said. She shifted from one foot to the other. Landau got the hint.

"Okay, I'm sure you all would like some time to rest and review the material on your tablets. You know your room numbers, so I won't keep you any longer. Oh, the management has set aside a special area of the dining room for dinner tonight, should you decide to eat together. Otherwise, call for room service. Everything is paid for, including gratuity. Well, until later."

Amber wasted no time, turning and fast-stepping to her room. Nuri looked at Chambers and shrugged. Chambers walked away. Maybe a nap would put everything into new perspective.

His room was spacious and offered a view overlooking the Old City. The bed was wide enough to sleep six. The bathroom sported bronze fixtures, a shower, and a deep soaking tub. The living room had a well-padded sofa, a contemporary-looking coffee table, and a working table. A flat-screen television rested on a cherry-wood dresser. Next to it, someone had installed a small security monitor. Chambers could see the hallway just beyond his door. He had worked digs requiring security before, but this was shaping up to be a spy operation. He felt silly.

He also felt weary. Away from the scrutiny of the others, he allowed the hard-nosed facade to fall. The trip, hours with Nuri, the unexpected arrival of Amber, meeting John Trent, and the skulduggery surrounding the work ahead had let the air out of him. He sat on the bed with the intention of removing his shoes but made the mistake of reclining on the mattress.

∽

"Are you sure you don't want something stronger to drink?"

Nuri reached across the table in the dining room and laid a hand on Amber's forearm. He smiled, but it came across as a sneer.

"No. Coffee is fine."

"How about some wine? It will help you relax. Maybe a nice dessert wine."

She pulled her arm away from Nuri and set her hands in her lap. "No thank you. I don't care for alcohol." He seemed disappointed. "I appreciate the offer."

"I understand. Dealing with David can destroy an appetite for food or drink." He looked at the vodka tonic sitting on the table. "If need be, I can drink for both of us. It will be a sacrifice, but I'm willing to offer myself for the mission."

"You know that doesn't impress me, don't you? Drinking, I mean."

Nuri shrugged. "To be honest, my dear, I'm drinking for me. Your David has gotten...what is the phrase? To burrow beneath the tissue?"

The question drew a smile. "Under the skin. David has gotten under your skin."

"Ah, that's it. My English is very good, but I have trouble with American expressions and colloquialisms."

"Most clichés aren't worth knowing anyway." She picked up her cup and held it in her hands, drawing the heat from the coffee inside. The chill she felt had nothing to do with the temperature in the air-conditioned space. She looked around. It was too early for the evening meal, and the only patrons were doing what she was doing, sipping strong coffee, tea, or soda. A few sucked down more potent beverages.

"I missed most of the, um, conversation." Nuri drummed his fingers on the tablecloth-clad table.

"It wasn't a conversation. A conversation is civil. This was anything but that."

"Did he attack you? Verbally, I mean?"

Amber looked around the room again, expecting the other patrons to be leaning her way, listening to every word. No one showed any indication of eavesdropping. "No. Not really. He doesn't do that. He's more subtle."

Nuri's eyebrow shot up. "He's not subtle with me."

"You do have a way of bringing out the best in a person." She softened the statement with a smile.

He turned his palms up. "I am but a simple archaeologist who is very attracted to the woman across the table from him."

Warmth ran up Amber's cheeks. "I suppose that was the most hurtful thing David said. He implied we're more than good friends."

Nuri blinked. "You mean we are not?"

"Nuri…" She stopped and set her cup down. "I don't know what we are. You have been kind, loving, supportive, and always interesting. I felt empty when you had to fly to the States a few months ago. Not knowing when you'd return made me uneasy."

"Here I am, thanks to the good Professor Ben-Judah. Maybe he would attend the wedding."

Amber furrowed her brow. "Wedding? Whose wedding?"

"Ours, of course. You don't know it yet, but you are falling madly in love with me. Who can blame you? My personality, my rugged good looks, my keen intelligence—"

"Your modesty." Amber laughed.

"My one fault."

The laughter felt good. For a moment, the heavy regret that clung to Amber lifted. "What am I to do with you, Nuri?"

This time both eyebrows rose. "I can make a few suggestions."

Again Amber blushed.

"I'm sorry. My humor is too often…what's the word?"

"Crude? Rude? Ribald?"

"You wound me." He put on a pout, but Amber wasn't buying it. "I will try to conform my teasing to your sensibilities. Tell me what troubles David so. What makes him so combative and hateful?"

She thought for a moment. Was this a conversation she wanted to have? Why not? Nuri was one of the few people who listened, who might understand. "He's hurting."

"Hurting? He is ill?"

"No. And your concern would appear more genuine if you didn't ask that question with a smile. I mean that he's hurting emotionally, spiritually." She turned the cup on its saucer and stared at the dark fluid. It reflected the ceiling lights and her face—a face that looked drawn and tired.

"What hurt him?"

"His father. The loss of his mother."

Nuri rubbed his chin as if hearing an interesting scientific problem. "Everyone experiences loss. I have lost a father, a mother, and two brothers. Why should David be any different?"

"It's not just the loss of his mother." She sighed. Talking about David this way made her uneasy, but she was betraying no secrets. Anyone who knew David well knew of his feelings about his father. "You should ask these questions of David."

"David would never confide in me. I only ask because his behavior has such a negative impact on you; that, and I will be working with him for many weeks to come. Maybe I can be less annoying if I know what troubles him."

Amber considered the statement. If revealing a little of David's past would ameliorate the tension already present in the team, then telling a little of what she knew could be good for the project.

"There's not much to tell, really. Do you know who David's father is?"

Nuri shook his head, then stopped as if his neck had stopped working. "There was a Charles Chambers who worked in the field. A good archaeologist. They're not related are they?"

Amber nodded. "He specialized in early Iron Age sea peoples, Philistines mostly. He was excellent with burial motifs. I only met him once. It was at the end of his career. He gave a lecture at UCLA, where I was doing some postdoc work. He wasn't well then. He's grown worse as time passed."

"He's ill?"

"Yes. I don't know what ails him, but he looked frail then. When David and I were engaged, he mentioned his father's illness but wouldn't say any more. He hasn't seen or spoken to his father in at least two or three years. I tried to convince him to mend the relationship, but he wouldn't hear of it. It was the only time he ever snapped at me. Told me to mind my own business. I know the basics and that's it."

"He doesn't seem to have a problem snapping at you now."

Amber felt an expanding emptiness. "He's changed. Once he was driven by faith, by love of the biblical narrative and the people who used to populate this land." She rubbed her eyes as images of the past played on her brain. "He was passionate back then. For the work, I mean. He was always the first at the dig site and always the last to leave. He has a near photographic memory, you know. He may be the smartest man I've ever met."

"Present company excluded, of course."

Amber didn't respond to the quip. "When David's mother died, his father was still in the field and—"

"And David resents him for not being there."

"Yes, but there are things that David doesn't—"

"I suppose he has a right to be angry at his father. That does seem unnecessarily cruel."

Amber tightened her jaw. She hated being interrupted. "If you say so."

Nuri seemed immune to Amber's pique; he sipped his drink. Silence filled the gap between them, interrupted by the laughter of an elderly couple across the room. Amber had noticed them earlier. They had the aura of two people who have been in love a very long time. Once she imagined that she and David would one day be like that couple, sitting in a coffee shop or restaurant reliving past adventures and talking about new ones.

That vision, however, was over. It had dissolved long ago.

"He turned his bitterness on you, didn't he?"

The question jarred Amber from her reflection. "What? Yes, I suppose so."

"You only suppose so?"

She shrugged. "Maybe I pushed too hard. I didn't have all the information. I was just the new fiancée, a woman in love with love."

"Pushed too hard? Nonsense. You were about to marry the man. You had a right to know the details of his life. He should not have shut you out."

She wrapped her hands around the cup of coffee again. It was growing cold, like so many other things in her life. "It was more than that. He…"

Nuri leaned over the table and cupped his hands around hers. "I'm not David, Amber. I am trustworthy to a fault. You know that. Say what's on your mind. It helps to talk about such things."

She had heard that before but harbored doubts about its accuracy. "He lost his faith. It's why he gave up biblical archaeology. His mother's death was lingering and painful. He told me he couldn't worship a God who let His followers suffer so. His father is a deeply spiritual man but not a demonstrative one. David saw his reluctance to leave a dig even though his wife was dying as a betrayal and proof that faith doesn't really change anyone." Her eyes began to burn. She had lost not only the only man she had loved but also a fellow believer. That was the deepest wound of all.

"I see my insistence has upset you." He patted her hands and sat back. "I apologize. I have added to your grief."

"No, no, you've been a gentleman, a friend. You have a right to know why David is, well, the way he is these days."

Nuri paused, then spoke softly. "You know I wish to be more than friends."

The comment warmed Amber, but it also made her uncomfortable. It was good to be wanted, but she and Nuri were so different. Perhaps if she gave him a chance, let him in a little closer…

"Thank you, Nuri, but I think I'd better go review the material Ben-Judah gave us. I hate being behind in anything." She stood.

"Don't go. We have all evening. Maybe we can study together. It will be like our college days. You had study groups in America, right?"

The smile she wore was genuine. "Yes, but I always preferred to study alone. Sorry." She turned, then stopped. Over her shoulder she said, "Thank you for listening."

"The pleasure was all mine."

Amber walked to the elevator.

～

Nuri watched as Amber walked away, his eyes first fixed on her bouncing, swaying hair, then on the sway of her hips, then her legs. He smiled.

TEN

There was a knock on the door. Then another.

Chambers opened his eyes and blinked several times. The bed was not his; the smell of the room was different from home. His sleep-fogged mind tried to sort through the information scattered around his brain. Clarity came a moment later. This wasn't his condo. He was in Jerusalem. The day's events seeped into his consciousness.

"Wow." He rubbed his eyes. "I must have really been out." He looked at his feet. He had slept with his shoes on.

More knocking, this time accompanied by a muffled voice. He couldn't make out much, but he did hear his name. "Just a minute," he shouted.

Pushing himself from the bed, he walked on uncertain legs from the bedroom into the adjoining living space, wagging his head from side to side to loosen the muscles in his neck. He started for the door, then stopped. Landau had sounded serious when he warned the team to exercise caution.

"Who is it?" He turned his eyes to the security monitor next to the television. A young man, clean shaven with short brown hair, stood outside the door looking at the video camera near the ceiling.

"Rubin. Joel Rubin. I'm one of Professor Ben-Judah's graduate students."

The voice came through the door, but a tinny version of it came over a small speaker on the monitor. Chambers found the volume knob and turned it up. "What do you want?"

"I'm your assistant." The voice had a slight Irish or British accent. Chambers couldn't tell which.

"I didn't ask for an assistant."

"I didn't ask to be left in the hall talking to a door."

Chambers chuckled. He had to admire the young man's wit. "If I told you to go away, would you?"

"I'd rather spend the night in the corridor than tell the professor I failed to do my job."

"Okay. You win, but I don't want or need an assistant." He moved to the door and opened it. The man stood in place, a tablet PC in his hand. He was also shaking his head. "What?"

"Mr. Landau said you'd do this."

"Do what?"

"Open the door before asking for the password." Rubin looked disappointed.

"I'm not very good at playing cops and robbers. Come in, but don't get comfortable. I plan to send you packing." Rubin didn't budge. "What now?"

Rubin just stared.

"Oh, all right. What's the password?"

"Shibboleth."

"You got it right. You even pronounced it correctly, which is pretty good for what? An Irishman?"

"You don't like the Irish?"

"I was referring to your accent."

"Odd, I thought you were the one with the accent." Rubin stepped in.

"Do you talk that way to Professor Ben-Judah?"

"No sir. I like what I do and want to keep doing it."

Ben-Judah had two reputations. If you were his peer, then he was respectful, gentle, and polite. If you were a grad student, he'd grind you to dust with work. One had to earn the old man's respect, but once you had it, you also had a friend for life. Chambers was glad to be on the peer side.

"Have a seat." Chambers motioned to the sofa.

"Thank you."

"How long have you been in this country?" Chambers looked for a clock. He had no idea how long he had been asleep.

"This is my third year. I finish my dissertation, then I'll be done." He paused. "Dinner is in two hours. It's four o'clock now."

"I'm that transparent?"

"Sleepy eyes, disheveled, no watch. I took a guess."

"I see why Ben-Judah likes you."

"Sometimes I think he hates me."

Chambers chortled. "He tortures the ones he loves. If he didn't like you, he'd ignore you."

"Good to know. I think."

Chambers sat in a plush, leather chair across from the sofa, then ran a hand through the hair Rubin called disheveled. "Okay, so tell me again why you're here."

"I'm your new assistant, as I said."

"And as *I said,* I don't need or want an assistant."

Rubin frowned. "Dr. Chambers, you heard me say Professor Ben-Judah sent me."

"I don't care."

"I care. The professor cares."

"He'll understand. We go way back."

Rubin set his tablet down and crossed his legs. "I was told to say John Trent cares."

Chambers rubbed his face, exasperated. "Okay, okay, but I don't want you in my way."

"My job is to help you do your job."

"And what qualifies you to do that, Joel—you said your name was Joel, right?"

He nodded once. "Joel Rubin. Dr. Joel Rubin."

"Wait. You said you were still working on your dissertation. You don't get to use the title until you earn it."

For the first time, Rubin smiled. "I have a doctorate in geography. I'm working on my second terminal degree."

"You didn't like geography?"

"I love it, but I have many interests. I became interested in archaeology while studying the changes in the Jordan River and the impact it had on the political history of the region. As you know, the Jordan has been changed a great deal over the last few decades. There's the Al Wahda Dam, Ziglab Dam, the King Abdullah Canal, all of which have changed the river."

Chambers was starting to like Rubin. He was sharp, conversant, intelligent, and apparently impossible to intimidate.

"Since I can't throw you out without offending an old friend and a billionaire, I suppose we should do a little work. What do you know of our work?"

"Not a great deal, Dr. Chambers. I know that the work permits have been expedited and that some people very high up in Israel's government are making the path straight, as it were. I also know that you have a presentation to give tomorrow, as does Dr. Aumann."

"What do you know of my work?"

"I've read everything you've published."

"That's nice." Chambers felt a moment of pride.

"Professor Ben-Judah made me read everything." Rubin waited a few moments before defusing his statement with a crooked grin. "I had already read your material."

"Is this how it's going to be, Joel? You cracking wise about important matters like, well, me?"

"Yes sir. I'm afraid I'm incorrigible. My own mother says so."

"And I'm annoying on many levels. Just ask the others."

Rubin picked up his tablet PC. "We should make a good team."

"If we don't spontaneously combust first." Chambers rose and retrieved his computer, then returned to his seat. "Do you know anything about the Copper Scroll?"

"I do."

"Let's hear it."

For the next half hour, Chambers quizzed Rubin, who had answers to every question. At least Ben-Judah didn't send an average student. Rubin just might turn out to be an asset. He hoped so. He'd hate to offend his friend by sending back his choice disciple.

∽

Time passed unnoticed by Chambers. Once his mind was fixed on a project he lost track of the clock. Many times he had said to himself and others, "Time is irrelevant."

First, Chambers reviewed the material he had been given. The tablet PC held maps, current and ancient, of Jerusalem and the surrounding region. It held numerous articles on first-century topography and articles by biblical archaeologists. The theme was easy to determine. All the journal clippings dealt with the Copper Scroll and other literature pertaining to the Essenes and the second temple period, primarily King Herod's time. Little of it was new to Chambers. His own articles and relevant chapters from his books were included.

He then tried to access a hidden set of files. They were listed by number, not title. Whenever he tried to access one, a photorealistic image of a clay seal appeared, a seal like those used in ancient times to show if a scroll had been opened. It bore the alleged pictogram of King Solomon: a star with six points set in a circle.

"An odd choice," Chambers said. "Do you know what this image is?"

Rubin nodded. "It's a stylized version of the supposed ring of Solomon. Two interlocking triangles in a circle with a raised dot in each space formed by the circle and star."

"Odd choice of iconography." Chambers tilted his head as he studied the image. "It's a mythical symbol. Everyone and their neighbor has adopted something like it. I've seen it as the basis for Christian, Muslim, and Jewish symbology. I've even seen it adopted by practitioners of the occult."

"That's to be expected, since the legend says it gave Solomon power over demons."

"Or genies, if you like Arabic literature."

"Somehow, I don't think Professor Ben-Judah has that in mind here."

Chambers had to agree. While there were many nonpracticing Jews in the land, Ben-Judah wasn't one of them. He was a man as comfortable with phylacteries and prayer as with dusty artifacts and detailed journal articles. It was one of the things Chambers admired about him. Science and faith were partners in his mind, never enemies.

"So why can't we get past the symbol." Chambers tapped the image again. It responded by growing larger for a moment, then returning to its original state. "Wait a second." He touched the screen, tapping the top of the star. It lit up. He touched another part of the star, and the first point dimmed. "It's a key. A type of password. I think we have to tap different points of the image in the correct order to get in."

"That could take awhile. I count eighteen points of connections—assuming those are the only touch sensitive areas."

Chambers watched Rubin activate the calculator on the computer.

Rubin talked as he worked. "If I do a little combinations and permutations math… Let's see, eighteen possible choices; assume we have to make eighteen right choices in the right order, then…"

"Then what?"

"Then we spend the rest of our lives punching the screen. There are 4×10^{22} possible permutations, assuming order matters." He looked at Chambers. "We don't have enough seconds in our lives to pull that off. I recommend we ask someone."

"I'm with you there—"

Another knock on the door. Chambers glanced at the monitor and saw Landau standing at the door, his hands clasped behind his back as if standing at ease in a military lineup.

"He looks serious," Rubin said.

"I think he was born with that look." Chambers went to the door and opened it. "Should I ask you for the password, even though I already know who you are?"

"Good evening, Dr. Chambers. Your presence is requested at dinner tonight."

"Well, thank you, Jeeves, but I was just going to order up some room service. Before you object, I remind you that you gave us that option."

"I did. Now I'm rescinding it."

"Nonetheless, I think I'll dine in today."

Landau looked down for a moment. When he raised his gaze, his eyes had turned to flint. "Dr. Chambers, there's been an incident, and I need the team in one place so I don't have to repeat the info."

"Send a memo. I'm busy." Chambers began to close the door when he heard a loud thud followed by the sound of the door hitting the wall. Landau was in the room, his face inches from Chambers. "What the—"

"I asked; now I'm telling you. You're coming downstairs, and we're leaving now." He looked at Rubin. "You too."

Rubin was on his feet in an instant, his face pale and his eyes wide.

Chambers had had enough. "Look, if you think you can just barge in here..." The anger on Landau's face kept Chambers from finishing the sentence.

"Would you like to arrive at dinner conscious or unconscious?"

"Man, you weren't kidding when you said you had no sense of humor." Chambers exited the room, trying to keep Landau from seeing how much he had frightened him. For a moment, Chambers thought of fleeing, but he had no idea where to go. Besides, he was pretty sure Landau would crack-back tackle him before he had taken five steps.

David Chambers walked quietly to the elevators.

ELEVEN

D ead? What do you mean by dead?"
      Chambers struggled to make sense of the announcement.

"Really, David?" Nuri said. "Must Mr. Landau explain the word *dead* to an archaeologist?"

"What I mean is, how did he die?" Chambers sat next to Ben-Judah, who had been waiting in the rented meeting room when Chambers and Rubin arrived. Amber and Nuri had already taken their places at the table. Plates, water glasses, and coffee cups decorated the cloth-covered table. Landau explained that it wouldn't do to announce the death of a college student in a crowded hotel restaurant, so he had arranged for private dining.

Landau didn't pause. "He was shot in the left temple, small caliber, no exit wound. It was a professional assassination."

"That's horrible."

Amber raised a hand to her mouth. Nuri laid a hand on her shoulder. The sight of it turned Chambers's stomach. He looked to Ben-Judah who stared into the distance, face pale, gazing at what only he could see.

"And you say he was a student?" Rubin looked shell-shocked. "May I ask his name?"

Landau remained standing, hunched forward just enough that he could rest his fingertips on the table. "Herman Rosenthal. He was a medical student, second year. Do you know him?"

Rubin shook his head. "No, but I didn't hang with the medical guys. Different worlds."

"Okay, this is sad," Chambers said. "I mean that, but murder is not new, certainly not in this country. What does this have to do with us?"

"Several things." Landau walked away from the table. A waiter stepped in, but Landau waved him off, holding up a hand with fingers extended. Chambers assumed he was asking for five minutes more of privacy. "One, the murder takes place on the same day that we meet. That may mean nothing, but it can't be overlooked. Next, his body is found in the parking lot near the Institute's building."

"Still, that is far from conclusive," Chambers said.

"Agreed, but we did some checking. Young Mr. Rosenthal was broke. The police, and some of my team, interviewed people who knew him. He was always looking for ways to make money for books and his tuition. He comes from a lower-middle-class family that has had some financial trouble. It appears Rosenthal was on his own for the rest of his education."

"Sounds like a dozen students I know," Rubin said.

"No doubt, but Rosenthal had thirty-five-hundred shekels on his person."

"That's about a thousand US dollars," Amber said.

"Correct. Somehow he found a way to line his wallet. It's not a lot of money, but to a starving student, it might prove to be tempting. Especially if he did what we think he did."

"Which is what?" Nuri moved his chair back from the table, as if putting distance between him and the horrible news being shared.

Landau lowered his head for a moment. "Before you arrived, before the meeting in the Institute, we did an electronic sweep of the conference room and nearby rooms. We found nothing. After Rosenthal's body was found, we did another sweep, inside and out. We're paranoid that way. Again, no devices, but we did find a small glue mark on the outside of the window between the plaza and the conference room."

"A glue mark?" Chambers didn't understand.

"It's a special glue. Think rubber glue that holds something in place but doesn't set."

Amber looked puzzled. "Someone glued something to the window?"

"And removed it later. The mark is about the size of a small coin. There's a very good chance that someone attached a remote listening device to the window."

"They can listen through the window?" Amber said.

"It reads the vibration of the window. For years, people in the intelligence business used a device that measured the minute vibrations in a window caused by voices inside. Certain government offices come equipped with speakers that play music at the window to mask any conversation going on inside. That system, however, requires a laser system. That would have been seen too easily.

"There's a different, more subtle device that vibrates with the window and sends the message to a nearby receiver. Its range is extremely limited, but someone within twenty meters or so should be able to receive the signal, then pass it along through a larger transmitter."

"I saw him." Ben-Judah whispered.

"You saw whom?" Chambers snapped his head around.

"The young man. The student. Rosenthal. I saw him when I was lowering the shades in the conference room so we could have some privacy. He was walking by. At least, I thought he was walking by. There were many students on the plaza this morning. I see them every day. I give it no thought." He set his elbows on the table and rested his head in his hand. To Chambers he looked like a man who had just lost everything.

"Excuse me, Professor." Amber spoke in a soft, motherly tone. "If you haven't met Rosenthal before, then how do you know it was him you saw?"

He didn't speak; he just shook his head.

Landau answered for the elderly man. "I showed him a picture taken at the scene. I'm afraid it wasn't a pleasant photo. It took the professor a moment, but he realized Rosenthal had been in the courtyard."

"I had no idea. How could I know?" Ben-Judah covered his face, and Chambers expected to hear sobbing any moment. It never came.

"You couldn't know, Professor." Chambers tried to sound firm yet comforting. "There are hundreds of students at the university and around the Institute's building. One student walking by wouldn't alert anyone. You did nothing wrong."

The others voiced their agreement.

"Best guess at this point," Landau said, "is that someone retained Rosenthal to walk to the window and stick the listening device on the glass. Somewhere nearby another person recorded the conversation on a laptop computer. Every student has a laptop these days. No one would notice someone sitting on a bench nearby gazing at a computer." He paused for a moment. "We checked the security cameras. Rosenthal did approach the window a few moments after the professor lowered the shades. He reached to the area where we found the glue mark. The device was too small for the security camera to pick up, but we're having the footage enhanced to see if we can identify it."

"Does that really matter now?" Nuri asked.

Landau frowned. "No, not really. If we can identify the device, we might be able to track down people who purchased it, but I doubt that will lead anywhere. Anyone who would go this far to listen in on your conversation probably took precautions to conceal the purchase. If it's a government, a terrorist group, or a foreign spy agency, we'll never be able to track the purchase. Still, we will follow every lead."

Amber inhaled deeply. "I'm afraid to ask, but why would someone kill Rosenthal if he did what he was hired to do?"

"I can't be certain at the moment, but Rosenthal must have had face-to-face contact with an operative. He had to be recruited, so he had a conversation with someone. That would make him a danger. There may be other reasons. What I can't figure out is why they left the money. Amateurish. The killer should have taken the wallet to make it look like a robbery. Perhaps he was interrupted. We just don't know."

"Okay," Chambers said, "where does this leave us? We know someone is willing to kill to get at what we're doing. Why? The Copper Scroll treasures? I suppose that would be high motivation."

"We have enemies," Ben-Judah said. "Many, many enemies."

"They couldn't have learned much." Amber wrapped her arms around herself as if cold. "We spoke in generalities. John Trent became poetic toward the end, talking about changing the world, but he never gave details."

"First rule in the intel business is this: always assume the enemy is a step ahead of you."

"So what do we do now?" Nuri asked.

"Our security here is already in place and every base is covered. You will not be returning to the Institute. Tomorrow's meeting will be held in the hotel. I've reserved five of the conference rooms. When the time comes, I'll lead each of you to the right one. They can't bug every conference room. Of course, we'll make a sweep of the room and surrounding areas. I'll also post a man outside the windows. I will make sure we have a jamming device operating as well. No one fools me twice."

Chambers wondered.

౼

Maybe it was the nap he had taken earlier; maybe it was "travel brain," which afflicted him every time he traveled more than three time zones; maybe it was hearing that some down-on-his-luck student took a bullet in the brain because of a project Chambers was involved with; or maybe it was seeing Nuri and Amber sitting together again. Whatever the reason,

Chambers couldn't sleep. The clock by his bed displayed 1:30 a.m. in blue letters. Just 7:30 in the evening back home.

His eyes were tired. He and Rubin had worked until nearly midnight, digesting the material they could access on Chambers's tablet. He kicked himself for not asking Ben-Judah for the passkey to use on the symbol, but the man looked too fragile to bother. The murder had unsettled him greatly. Ben-Judah was at heart a very gentle man. He didn't suffer fools easily or for long, but he'd help any honest person in any way he could.

Chambers rolled over, turning his back to the clock. He had tried all of his tricks to settle an overactive mind. He did math with the numbers on the clock, dividing the minutes by the hours, multiplying all the digits, adding, and subtracting in hopes of boring himself into slumber. He tried to recall the names of characters and the actors who played them in classic television. Having worked through *Bonanza, Star Trek* (all versions), and *The Bob Newhart Show,* he gave up.

He left the bed, washed his face, and slipped back into his clothes. A few minutes later, Chambers left his room behind and found the bar in the lobby.

Pop music filtered down from overhead speakers. To his surprise, it was a series of blues songs. *New Orleans and Chicago come to Jerusalem,* he thought. The bar had a contemporary feel: yellow lights shone from floor fixtures up the face of the long, marble-topped bar and around the two dozen booths spread across the floor. He was not alone. Couples and loners had taken positions at various places. Chambers found an unoccupied booth, sat, raised a hand to gain the barkeep's attention, and began an alcohol-fueled pity party. He felt fortunate that bars in Jerusalem didn't have official closing times, except before *Shabbat.*

He raised his glass as if offering a toast, then brought the glass to his lips. The bourbon burned his throat: consumption-based numbness came with a price. Everything came with a price. *Just ask the dead student.*

∽

Amber had always been an early riser. It was a family trait and one nur-
tured by many seasons spent digging in very hot climes. The best digging
was done before the sun had time to scorch the cool from the day. When
not at a dig site, she often jogged along the streets near her home. She had
trouble sleeping. Word of a murder linked to her work had unsettled her
soul. An hour of Bible reading and prayer had helped, but she still woke
before the sun arrived on scene.

What she really wanted to do was take to the streets of Jerusalem for
a long walk, but Landau's security probably wouldn't let her through the
tall lobby doors. It was to be the workout room this morning. A treadmill
was no match for her outdoor-loving spirit, but it beat sitting on the edge
of her bed waiting for time to pass.

She exited the elevator, iPod in hand, earbuds in place, and started
through the lobby. Last night's news had made her paranoid. She scanned
the open space, taking in the opulence and quiet ambiance. Two men sat
on thickly padded sofas. One read a newspaper; the other appeared to be
playing a video game on his cell phone. That impression lasted only a moment. Amber hadn't taken two steps before both men glanced her way.
They were dressed like tourists. One wore jeans, while the other wore
khaki shorts, revealing some of the hairiest legs she had seen. She wondered why he wasn't the one wearing the jeans.

One of the files on her tablet PC had been a series of photos of men
and women serving on the security detail. She recognized them. The man
in the jeans and San Diego Padres T-shirt made eye contact, then directed
his gaze to the bar. He stared that direction for several seconds, then returned his attention to the newspaper. She wondered how long he had
been pretending to read its pages.

Then the man in the shorts directed his gaze to the bar. Amber got
the idea and strolled that direction, intending to just walk by and glance

in. David Chambers sat in a booth, head down but body still upright. He swayed to the music filling the space from above.

"Oh David." She muttered the words, not knowing whether to be angry or disappointed. She marched into the bar and glared at the bartender, who replied with a halfhearted shrug. She moved to the edge of the booth and stood there. Chambers didn't seem to notice. She cleared her throat. He opened his eyes but appeared to have trouble focusing. "So this is the new David Chambers. A drunk."

"Well, well, well, look who's here. Ms. Heartthrob of Jerusalem herself." The words dribbled from his mouth. "Hey, you look good with earbuds. Nice touch. You should stick with it. Beats earrings."

"I don't believe what I'm seeing. I hardly recognize you."

He picked up his empty glass and raised it two feet above the table. "You know, Dr. Rodgers, this is a bar. I say that since I doubt you've ever been in one. You see, people come here to anestiz…anestethiasize…" He worked his lips as if warming up for another go at the word. "Numb themselves against life's foibles and pains."

"You know we have a meeting in a few hours, right?" The words had a serrated edge to them, just as planned.

"So?" He set the glass down and looked heartbroken that it was empty.

"So? You're drunk, David. Drunk as a skunk."

He chuckled. "Drunk as a skunk. Just what does that mean anyway? I've never seen a skunk drunk… I mean a drunk skunk. Have you?"

"Not until now."

"Wait. I see what you did there. You turned my comment around on me so that it would be an insult. You are one clever gal, Dr. Rodgers."

"I repeat: you're drunk."

"And you're ugly, but in the morning, I'll be sober and you'll still be ugly." He laughed at his version of the quote.

"I'm not Lady Astor, and you're not Winston Churchill. It was funny when he said it. It's just pathetic coming from you."

"Oh, I'm sorry. You know I think you're beautiful. Always have." He picked up his glass and held it out to her. "You don't mind getting me another drink do you? The bartender knows what I want."

"It's just a little after four in the morning."

"It's the beauty of being in Jerusalem: no last call."

Amber took the glass and stepped to the bar. She returned a moment later, the glass filled with fluid. Chambers narrowed his eyes. "I switched to Scotch. That's clear. What is it? Vodka?"

"No, but it is what you need." With a flick of the wrist, Amber flung the fluid in Chambers's face. "It's ice water, David."

He sputtered and wiped his eyes. "What are you doing!"

"Would you like another drink?"

"That was... was..."

"Uncalled for?"

"Yes. Uncalled for."

"Perhaps, but it was necessary. Let's go."

"I'm not going anywhere."

Amber placed her hands on the table. It wobbled slightly. "You walk out of here with me right now, or I'll drag you out."

"I doubt you can."

"Do you really want to find out?" She prayed he wouldn't.

"Fine. I was done anyway." He inched out of the booth, stood quickly, then teetered like a tree that's just been cut by a logger. "Whoa. The floor is moving."

"Here, let me help." She took him by the arm and squeezed. "Better?"

"Ow. Not so hard."

She directed him to the exit. "You should see what I really want to do to you."

"Is that a come-on?" His grin was lecherous. "Ow. You're doing it again."

"I've got lots more where that came from."

She marched him from the bar, into the lobby, and toward the bank of elevators. "Really, David. I should have left you there for Landau or Ben-Judah to find."

"So what if they did? I'm an adult."

"Are you? I'm having trouble seeing that lately."

"Yes, Mother."

"I can't believe I almost married you."

"You had your chance. Of course, I might consider a new offer."

She stopped in the middle of the lobby, not caring that the two security men were watching and listening. "That opportunity…" She hesitated, her voice growing softer. "That opportunity died when you walked away from the Truth. I'm using a capital T with that word, David. I don't just mean the truth about us, I mean the Truth about faith in Christ."

"Jesus did nothing for my mother; He certainly didn't change my father's heart…not in any way I could see." He pulled his arm free. "I don't need you to tell me what is true and not true."

Before she could reply, he staggered away.

"Please don't walk away from me, David—"

A hand touched her on the shoulder. The man in the jeans and Padres shirt was at her side. "I'll make sure he gets to his room, Dr. Rodgers. We don't need a scene here in the lobby."

Tears began to run. "I suppose you're right."

The security man was already on Chambers's heels.

TWELVE

David Chambers was alone again and sitting on the balcony outside his room. Next to him was a coffee cup with the dregs of his fifth cup. On his lap rested the tablet PC, but he was having trouble concentrating on the presentation he was to give. He nibbled on another piece of toast. The security man Amber had sicced on him had left an hour ago. Thirty minutes later a man from room service arrived with a cart upon which rested a plate of fried eggs, potatoes, and fruit. The hotel waiter started into the room, but Chambers, not ready to face a meal even after twenty minutes in a hot shower, stopped him.

"I didn't order this."

"Yes sir. I know, sir." He pushed into the room, the cart in front of him. "Your friend did. He said you might object but that I was to leave the food anyway." The man was short and dark-skinned and sported a thin beard.

"Well, I don't want it." He saw the carafe and assumed it held coffee. The caffeine might round the points of the spiked ball rolling inside his head.

"The man said I was to leave it no matter what."

"This is my room. I decide what you leave and what you don't."

"Yes sir. You're absolutely right, sir. Shall I put the cart on the balcony? It's early but the morning is warm."

"You're going to leave that no matter what I say, aren't you."

"Yes sir."

"And if I call the hotel manager?"

"He's expecting your call. He told me to tell you that you may call at any time."

"So *my friend* really frightened you, didn't he?"

"Yes sir. He also tips very well."

Chambers rubbed the back of his aching neck. "Well, don't expect a tip from me."

"I understand fully, sir." He wheeled the cart to the balcony and set the meal on the small table. He then poured a cup of coffee, which Chambers drank in three gulps.

"More."

"Yes sir." Three minutes later, the employee was gone.

The sight of food turned his stomach, but that changed after his first bite of fruit. Also on the table was a plate of sweet pastries. Before long, Chambers had finished the meal, having eaten more in that one sitting than he had the entire day before. It took another half hour and four tablets of pain reliever to halt the wrecking ball in his skull.

The sun had crawled over the distant hills and bathed Jerusalem in the golden light of a new day. Sunlight fell on ancient walls and modern buildings; it warmed Jews, Muslims, and Christians without discrimination. A dozen floors below, the timeless city came to life. Old blended seamlessly with the new. Where once donkey-drawn carts plied the streets, modern cars and buses moved through all but the narrowest streets. Dimming street and building lights cast golden rays on buildings and walkways. A small group of soldiers wearing green uniforms and darker green vests patrolled a short distance away. A bearded man dressed all in black walked through the street, perhaps on his way to pray.

David loved this city, despite the crowds, the occasional violence, and the hordes of tourists. His bitterness began to wane. Here King David once walked, as did his son Solomon. Good and bad kings followed in their wake. Two thousand years ago, Roman soldiers monitored the streets, pressing their will on others with short sword, knife, and javelin. Here Essenes shared space with the Pharisees, Sadducees, and Herodians. Roman women of means, dressed in their finery, crossed paths with simple Jewish women dressed in robes, headdresses, and scarves.

Archaeologists, Chambers realized early in his training, were time travelers without machines. They were transported to the past one layer of dust at a time, one potsherd at a time. The real time travel took place in the mind. With a brain that still ached, Chambers had no trouble seeing the city transform, back through the ages, to a time when the streets were choked with people wanting to be near Jesus. This was the city where His fans later called for His crucifixion. Here the newly formed church came to be. Not far from here, Jesus ascended into heaven.

Back and back, through occupations, wars, and times of peace, to the first temple and back further still to a time before the temple was made of stone and cedar, back to a day when the tabernacle was the place of worship.

Countless battles had been fought for this land, and the blood of tens of thousands stained the soil. Here the Romans destroyed the second temple, looting what riches had not been removed prior to the rebellion. Here and in Galilee, the Romans killed well over one million Jews, a pogrom hard to imagine even two millennia later. He could see the ancient city, hear the cries of men, women, and children being slain by the brutal Romans. He could hear the invaders' curses, see the smoke that darkened the sky. Brutality. Pain. Torture. The sound of Hebrews calling for deliverance from *HaShem*—even in the moments of death unwilling to call God by His name or title. To the contemporary mind, God was God, but to the Jews of ancient Jerusalem, He was *HaShem,* "the Name."

They died.

They died by the tens of thousands.

Yet, two thousand years later, they were back in their city. Living, procreating, rearing the next generation of Jews. He admired them. As a people, they faced the worst that humanity could inflict on others and survived to be a nation again.

All of it was history now, but a history that left its fingerprints in the strata. The most important events in the world happened in and around this city. That was what had captured his attention as a youth and what drove him for years.

He looked at the tablet PC. In a short time, he would discuss what he knew with the others. From there, a new adventure would begin. He thought of his behavior last night—well, just a few hours ago—and felt shame.

∽

Chambers emerged from the elevator to find Rubin waiting for him. The young man looked concerned. Word must have spread about Chambers's descent into intoxication. It didn't matter. Chambers understood that no matter how much someone studied the past, he couldn't change it. That went for his recent past as well.

"Good morning, Dr. Rubin."

The younger man looked surprised. "Um, good morning, Dr. Chambers. Are you—"

"Ready? Of course, I'm ready. Why wouldn't I be?"

"It's just that… Never mind." Rubin fell in step with Chambers, who marched like a man on a mission. "I don't suppose you asked Ben-Judah about the Ring of Solomon symbol in your tablet?"

Chambers shook his head. "I didn't have the heart. News of the murder seemed to undo him. Besides, I have a feeling he'll tell us when he's ready."

"The suspense is killing me."

"You'll live."

Chambers walked through the lobby to a wide corridor that ran through the west wing of the hotel. As he did, he caught sight of the security man who had helped him to his room. Chambers started to cut his eyes away but then decided to do something else instead. He smiled and saluted. The man frowned. For some reason, that made Chambers feel good.

The conference room was just large enough for a long table and a dozen chairs. As he entered, he saw the rest of the team waiting for him. He was three minutes early, so they had no room to complain. His eyes met those of Amber. He grinned and winked. The act seemed to stun her. *Expecting a drooling drunk, eh?* He mouthed the words, "Thank you." She gave a slight nod. He didn't notice if Nuri caught the silent communications, and he didn't care if he did.

Chambers and Rubin took two chairs near the head of the table. As before, Ben-Judah sat in a chair immediately to the right of the one at the head of the table. John Trent filled that space like a medieval king on a throne. Ben-Judah looked drawn, a half-empty balloon. Chambers was not the only one in the room who had slept poorly.

Ben-Judah rose and took the time to look at each person in the room. He forced a smile. "Thank you for coming and being so prompt." He glanced at Chambers but didn't linger. "I am aware that I have gathered some of the finest minds in archaeology to this project. As I mentioned yesterday, I am able to do so because of the great generosity of Mr. Trent."

Trent raised a dismissive hand as if he poured tens of millions into such projects on a daily basis.

Ben-Judah nodded in response. "This morning, I want us to spend a few moments making sure we are all on the same page, as they say. I also believe this will be beneficial to Mr. Landau and Dr. Rubin, who is aiding David. I will assign assistance to you, Nuri, and you, Amber, later in the day."

He paused for a few moments, as if his next words tasted bad in his mouth. "Mr. Landau, has there been progress on the murder of the student—Herman Rosenthal?"

"No sir. Nothing to speak of. Ballistics has analyzed the bullet, what's left of it. Impact with the skull and the brainpan left it in bad shape. Based on the size of the wound, the fact that it didn't exit, and the weight of the fragments, the police are pretty sure that the round was a .25 caliber, possibly a .22. Small weapon means small sound. Even if they could get a good image of the bullet's grooves and marks, we have no gun to compare it to. Not yet anyway. The coroner told us what we already knew: death by gunshot to the head."

"But the police are still looking?" Ben-Judah seemed worried.

"Of course, Professor. I have a man working with them. He will keep me informed."

Ben-Judah nodded slightly. "A great loss. So many are heartbroken over this." He ran a finger beneath his eye and an uncomfortable, dark silence filled the room. He took in a deep breath and raised his head. "David. Speak to us." Ben-Judah sat and leaned to one side, a position Chambers had seen before. It was what the man did when pondering something said in conversation. Ben-Judah was ready to listen.

Chambers rose. "Joel and I have prepared a slide presentation, but I don't see a projector."

"You don't need one," Nuri said. "Here." He rose and walked to Chambers, took his tablet PC, and tapped the touchscreen a few times. Everyone in the room had an identical tablet, and they all came to life at once. "The tablets are linked, David. Whatever is on your screen will now appear on ours." He grinned. "This is the twenty-first century, you know."

"Really? I hadn't heard." Then he forced another word from his throat. "Thanks."

Nuri bowed slightly and walked back to his seat, his self-satisfied grin adding to the light in the room.

Chambers regained his mental footing. "As the professor alluded to, most of what I have to say will be well known to the other archaeologists in the room, but I've been asked to give a quick review on the archaeological evidence for the historical truth of the Bible." He tapped his screen and a quote appeared in large letters. A quick look told him the same image appeared on the other tablets in the room:

> It may be stated categorically that no archaeological discovery has ever controverted a Biblical reference. Scores of archaeological findings have been made which confirm in clear outline or in exact detail historical statements in the Bible. And by the same token, proper evaluation of Biblical descriptions has often led to amazing discoveries. They form tesserae in the vast mosaic of the Bible's almost incredibly correct historical memory.

"Dr. Nelson Glueck made that comment in his book *Rivers in the Desert* in 1959. Over fifty years later, the statement is just as true. We can cite similar comments from Robert Dick Wilson, Dr. J. O. Kinnaman, and others. Those men and others like them inspired my own interest in the biblical authenticity as proven by archaeology."

"Until recently," Nuri said.

Chambers started to fire back but refrained. Talking to Nuri was like talking to a potsherd, except the broken bit of pottery was interesting. "Of course, not everyone shared their belief. With the rise of German higher criticism and the new archaeology, many scholars and textbook writers went out of their way to prove that the biblical narrative is fabrication, a collection of myths compiled long after the traditional dates of writing. For example, scholars have maintained for some time that the monarchies of David and Solomon are myths. This became the assumption of many Arabs, who previously accepted the historical David but now contend that there never was a Jewish kingdom or a first temple. Yasser Arafat and his followers denied the existence of David and the Jewish monarchy. Odd since the first Muslims referred to Jerusalem as the 'city of the temple.'

"Add to this," Chambers continued, "an inscription found by Dr. Avraham Biran at Tel Dan in northern Israel, near Mount Hermon. It appears that the stone inscription had been part of a stele which, for some reason, had been purposely destroyed. Other pieces have since been found. The stone includes the phrase, 'House of David.'"

He tapped the screen again and a new image appeared. The image was of a circular pad of clay with an impression pressed into its center. Three lines of paleo-Hebrew could be seen. "This is an image of the Baruch bulla. As was the custom of the day, papyrus scrolls were sealed with such bullae. Dr. R. Hecht acquired this clay seal sometime in the 1970s. Nahman Avigad published the bulla. Amber, you're our language expert. Care to translate?"

"I'm familiar with it," she said. "It reads, "Belonging to Berechiah son of Neriah the scribe." It is interesting to note the writing is preexilic, linear script, not the postexilic script."

"Which means what?" Landau asked.

Chambers answered. "It means that it was written before the Babylonian captivity, which makes it the right age to belong to Baruch ben Neriah, the prophet Jeremiah's scribe. His name is mentioned in Jeremiah 36:4." He advanced to the next screen. "I won't read all of these, but this is a list of other significant bullae, including that of Seraiah ben Neriah, the chamberlain to King Zedekiah. The biblical reference to that is Jeremiah 51:59. As you might have surmised from the names, they were brothers.

"The New Testament is supported by scores of archaeological finds." He advanced the presentation. "Two important discoveries come to mind." Another tap of the screen and the image of a faded yellow box with intricate carvings on one side flashed on the linked screens. "This is not new to most people here."

"The Caiaphas Ossuary," Nuri said. He didn't look up from the screen.

"Correct. Sometimes archaeology happens by accident. In November of 1990, a dump truck unwittingly broke through the roof of an unknown tomb. This happened on the southwest side of Old Jerusalem, across the Hinnom Valley. An ossuary is a bone box. After decomposition—and remember that Jews did not embalm—the bones of the deceased would be place in a box like this. The wealthier the family, the more ornate the box. As you can see from the rosettes and patterns carved into the stone, this belonged to a family of means."

He showed another photo of the ossuary. "On the undecorated side, the family carved a name. Actually, they carved the name twice: Yehosef bar Qafa—Joseph, son of Caiaphas."

"The high priest who led one of the trials of Jesus," Amber said.

"Exactly. This ossuary held the bones of several individuals. Six to be exact: Two infants, a toddler, a thirteen- to eighteen-year-old teenager, an adult female, and an adult male who was about sixty years old at the time of his death. As Amber said, this is the final resting area for the High Priest Caiaphas."

Another slide. A white-gray stone with Roman block letters. "For many years, some historians and archaeologists questioned the existence of Pontius Pilate, the fifth governor of Judea under Rome. This despite the fact that the man is mentioned in nonbiblical texts from Josephus, Philo, and Tacitus, and despite the existence of coins from his time as ruler. Italian excavator Antonio Frova found a dedication stone in Caesarea Maritima on the coast. The text reads: 'Tiberieum, Pontius Pilatus Praefectus Iudaeae—Tiberius was the Roman emperor at the time, so we have Tiberius, Pontius Pilate, Prefect of Judea."

Chambers felt something in his chest; something warm, inviting, convicting. As he spoke he began to feel the old enthusiasm that had put him on the course of his life. The bitterness that had grown weedlike over the months tried to reassert itself, but for the moment, Chambers relished the old enthusiasm. He had missed the sensation. What was it Ben-Judah told him a decade ago when Chambers served as one of the student archaeologists on an Institute dig? *"It is far easier to fall into a pit than to climb out of one."* The thought made him smile.

"Are you still with us, David?" Chambers looked at his mentor, who starred back quizzically. "Yes, of course. Just remembering something someone once told me."

"It is good to see you smile."

Chambers's face warmed, and he redirected his attention to his presentation. "We could spend the rest of the day listing all the finds that give the biblical record credibility. Instead, I've prepared a list of the key finds you can review later. I do want to add a few things.

"In recent years, I've had the opportunity to work with Jewish archaeologists on the tunnels that parallel the Western Wall of the Temple Mount. We discovered Zechariah's Tunnel, a secret passageway that leads north from the Temple Mount, beneath the city's Muslim Quarter, and connects with Zedekiah's Cave, also known as the Royal Cave. This tunnel runs below the northern wall of Jerusalem to Golgotha. Golgotha, of course, is the place where Jesus was crucified. It also leads to Jeremiah's cistern prison. As you know, King Zedekiah was the final king of Judah and escaped with his family through this ancient tunnel.

"There is another ancient tunnel-stairway beneath the City of David. It's a half kilometer long and runs from the ancient Pool of Siloam up to the southern entrance to the Temple Mount."

Ben-Judah raised a hand like a schoolboy. "David, what would you like to find?"

"Many things, Professor. Too many to list."

"Humor me."

"Well, we've already discussed the treasures of the Copper Scroll. I assume that's why we're here, but finding the Table of Shewbread from the temple days would be amazing. Or the jeweled breastpiece of the high priest." He hesitated. "But I suppose finding the long-lost subterranean tomb of King David and King Solomon. The wealth contained in those tombs boggles the mind."

"It is always about the money with you, isn't it, David?" Nuri said.

"That's unfair," Amber said.

"Oh, so now you defend him. I suppose it is only natural. What is one to do with such a lost puppy?"

Chambers fought the instinct to throw his tablet PC at the man, but there was a chance he would hit Amber. He started to speak but Trent beat him to it.

"Dr. Aumann, may I have your attention for a moment."

"Of course, Mr. Trent."

"Shut up."

"Excuse me?"

"You heard me, and your English is better than that of most of my countrymen. Shut your yap."

Nuri looked at Amber. "*Yap* means mouth, Nuri."

Nuri's face reddened, but he said nothing more.

Trent turned his face to Chambers. "Thank you, Dr. Chambers. Just for the record, you may get your wish."

"I don't understand."

"You will." Trent directed his gaze at Nuri. "Your turn, Dr. Aumann."

THIRTEEN

N uri gathered his composure and stood as Chambers seated himself. "Thank you, Mr. Trent." He tapped his screen several times, and the image on Chambers's tablet switched to an image of Jerusalem taken from a satellite. "I have had a wonderful time reviewing the documents provided. I thought I knew all the latest technology, but I must admit, I didn't know it had advanced this far."

The image changed to a tighter shot of the city. Chambers could see the old City of David, the new construction, the main roads, and even small dots he took to be people at the Wailing Wall. "Over the last few years, my focus has been on using technology to speed up the process of archaeology. Some of my peers love me for it; others, the traditionalists, think I'm a heretic for believing that what now takes years can be done in months. Unfortunately, most people in the field still work with a nineteenth-century mentality."

"Be that as it may, Professor Ben-Judah and Mr. Trent have provided me with some interesting material." The clear satellite photo of Jerusalem changed to a white-and-gray image with dark lines and blurry shapes, like an old, poorly developed photo from a century ago. Something about it, however, seemed familiar.

"What am I seeing here, Nuri?" Chambers leaned closer to the screen. "Is this an x-ray scan of the city?"

"Close, David. Not bad. I'm impressed. No, it's not an x-ray. It took me a moment to realize what I was seeing. Using satellites to search for lost cities is not new. Some Egyptian settlements have been found just by using Google Earth. A few years ago, a previously unknown meteor crater was found in the desert of Egypt, the result of an iron meteor strike. But satellite photos only reveal the surface of the earth. Some areas are covered with vegetation, so archaeologists searching for hidden cities of Mesoamerican peoples used infrared cameras to peer through the jungle canopy and had great success with it."

"But this isn't infrared, Nuri," Amber said.

"That's true, my dear, nor are they ultraviolet." He puffed out his chest as if he had taken the photos himself. "These are T-ray images."

"T-rays?" Landau inched closer to the table. "I've heard of those, but never in this context. They have a security application."

"Right, Mr. Landau. Absolutely right. The term *T-rays* is shorthand for *terahertz rays,* waves between infrared and microwaves on the electromagnetic spectrum. Their frequency is up to a thousand times lower than visible light. Scientists and engineers have been using T-ray devices to analyze the composition and density of objects. As Mr. Landau states, one of the early uses of these machines was in security, replacing x-ray machines that can be harmful to people. They can be used to see through a person's clothing, say at an airport. Hidden guns, knives, and explosives are easily seen. The T-rays pass through clothing, plastics, cardboard, and the like. Medical doctors are using them for everything from dental examinations to searching for cancer. Remarkable really."

"I thought you said that this was new to you," Chambers said.

"Not the basic technology. What I was unaware of was its use from space. You see, David, T-rays are another way—well, let us say a *better* way—of looking belowground without lifting a shovel. Oh, of course we've all used ground-penetrating radar to search for objects or voids below grade. Very useful tools, and they get better every year, but T-rays not only show what we cannot see with our eyes but may allow us to detect the material composition of an object. In other words, we will know a clay jar is clay before we touch it."

Chambers had used the technology in his work, but like Nuri, he had never seen it used to scan a whole city at one time. "Wow."

"Not scientific, David," Nuri said. For a change, Chambers didn't hear distain in his tone. He seemed genuinely impressed with the technology.

Chambers looked at Trent, who sat still and quiet. So did Ben-Judah. This was information they'd had for some time.

"David." Ben-Judah spoke softly. "Your face tells me you see something on the image. What has caught your attention?"

On a hunch, Chambers put two fingers on his tablet's screen and moved them apart. The image zoomed in. He saw the other tablets match what was on his computer. A dark line ran from the Fortress of Antonia to Jericho, about eleven miles outside the Old City. "Herod's tunnel."

Ben-Judah grinned for the first time since Chambers entered the room. "I thought you might notice that."

Chambers eyes scoured the image. He saw lines where he and others had uncovered ancient tunnels, including those he had just mentioned in his presentation. He also saw a few lines he couldn't recognize.

"Thank you, Dr. Aumann. Exceptional as expected." Ben-Judah pulled his tablet close.

"But Professor. I have more."

"There are things you haven't seen yet, Nuri. Please sit."

Nuri did, looking like a child just scolded by his teacher.

Ben-Judah looked to Trent, who nodded. The image on their screens changed to the mysterious Ring of Solomon. Chambers watched as Ben-Judah tapped in the password, touching each point of the star and three of the dots between the star and the circle enclosing it. "This is the Ring of Solomon. Is that news to anyone?" Ben-Judah looked up. Only Amber and Landau raised a hand. Ben-Judah grunted. "Over the centuries, it has been used by occultists for many distasteful things, and there is much silliness associated with it: magic, mysticism, control over demons, that sort of thing. I prefer not to surrender its use to those who have no respect for accurate history."

The screen changed to a list of files. Ben-Judah tapped one, and an image similar to the one before appeared, but this one sported more detail.

"In the interest of full disclosure," Trent said, "you should know that the material you are now seeing has not been seen by anyone other than myself, the professor, and a few trusted technicians employed to take these readings. I have access to this technology because I paid for its development. You don't need to know the details; just know that I come by it honestly." He pointed at the image in front of him. "What is the first thing you notice?"

Nuri answered. "The detail and the clarity."

"Exactly. What we gave you, Dr. Aumann, represents the best and newest in satellite surveys. To my knowledge, no other archaeologist has had access to this technology. Still, a satellite does its work far above the earth. As you have seen, what it does, it does remarkably, but for the real detail, the T-ray emitter must be closer. So Professor Ben-Judah was able to persuade the government to allow several flyovers. We had to promise that we would reveal to the military anything of…um…interest to them: a hidden weapons cache, biologicals, hidden areas."

"I'm surprised the Israelis didn't ask for the technology in return," Nuri said.

"They did." Trent didn't blink.

"And you gave it to them?" Amber asked.

"That is not pertinent to our discussion, and I advise against making assumptions. Your job is to use this and other technology to take our mission to the next level."

"Mission?" Chambers looked up. "Interesting choice of words."

"I'm a businessman, Dr. Chambers, not an English professor. You know what I mean."

Chambers did know, but wondered if the billionaire had other secrets. "No offense meant."

"None taken." He rubbed his face, showing his humanity for the first time. For a moment, he looked like a man with a great weight on his shoulders.

Amber tapped the table, something Chambers had seen her do when her mind was in high gear. "Okay, I'm just going to admit my ignorance and ask. Yesterday you said that we were going to change the world, and with all due respect, you just mentioned a mission. The Copper Scroll has come up several times, including when the professor recruited me, but I'm feeling more and more lost about our work. Why do I think you're after more than the Copper Scroll treasures? You don't strike me as a smuggler, and I know the professor well enough to know that he'd give up both arms and legs before participating in illegal archaeological exports."

She waited and no one spoke.

Chambers felt a sense of pride. The woman had courage. Not many people would speak to power and wealth that way. "She has a point," he said. "What exactly do you want us to do?"

Trent looked at Landau. "You're confident?"

"High confidence, sir," the security man said. "I swept the room myself, then had my best tech do it again. I have people in and all around the building. It's safe."

Trent inhaled deeply, then spoke: "We are going to find the temple artifacts."

Chambers said nothing. He knew this from the beginning. Now everyone knew it.

PART 2

FOURTEEN

The three weeks that had passed had changed several things, including Chambers's attitude. Work had always been his drug of choice. While he enjoyed teaching, nothing invigorated him like poring over documents, planning a dig, and moving dirt.

Ben-Judah headed the team but delegated most of the authority to others. He handled the administration and paperwork, communicated with local and national leaders, and smoothed feathers at the Institute of Archaeology and Israel Antiquities Authority. He also was the go-to guy with the media. Fortunately, there had been very little need for that last skill; at least not yet. That would change in the days ahead. This much activity could not go on in such a small country without someone noticing. David was impressed with his mentor's smooth handling of operations. He did so with humor, aplomb, finesse, and more circumlocution than an American politician.

David Chambers supervised and directed all fieldwork, making him the team leader, something that made Nuri even more unpleasant to be around. Still, to Chambers's amazement, the man went about his work with purpose and dedication to detail. As promised, Ben-Judah had appointed an aide for him. Nuri protested, saying he preferred to work alone, but Ben-Judah quietly insisted. Nuri's tune changed when he learned the aid had several hundred hours working ground-penetrating radar and other such equipment. Soon the two appeared to be old friends.

Amber coordinated documentation, making certain that all artifacts, no matter how small or seemingly unimportant, were logged, photographed, and stored for future study. She excelled at the task and enjoyed having access to the half-dozen digs going on simultaneously, which kept her in the forefront of all the activity. The conversation between Chambers and his former love had warmed to polite civility but nothing more. She kept him at arm's length, while best he could tell, allowing Nuri in a little closer. He still didn't understand their relationship and told himself he didn't care.

Landau, whom Chambers considered paranoid to begin with, had grown even more suspicious. He had asked for more people and technology and received both. No one got close to Ben-Judah or any of the team without first being cleared by Landau. The death of the student and the evidence indicating someone had been spying on the team ate at Landau's stomach, a fact he admitted in a rare personal moment while he and Chambers shared coffee late one night in the hotel bar. Once the dig had begun, Chambers confined his fluid consumption to tongue-curling strong coffee, vitamin water in the field, and soda in the evening. He decided he would not embarrass himself or the team again no matter how often temptation came, and it came often.

"So how long have you been working on this?" The question came from a young man with a shaved face and brown hair, bleached at the ends, giving his head a two-tone look. His eyes were blue, bright, and always on the move, an asset for a photographer.

Chambers turned from the papers, printouts, photos, and other information tacked to the wall of the Institute's conference room. This room, unlike the one where the team had first met, was big enough to hold only a dozen people. It was situated at the back of the building and had no windows. Landau's caution had struck again.

"Working on what? The dig?" Chambers looked back at the paper-covered walls. Some of the documents, drawings, and photos were covered with thick paper to keep unwanted eyes and cameras from seeing what should remain secret.

"The Copper Scroll thing." Edward Cove was the choice of *National Geographic,* which along with other magazines, had bid for the opportunity to be the onsite photojournalist. Such things weren't done in scientific endeavors, but John Trent didn't seem to care. He wasn't a scientist, but he had what every research needed: money. A great deal of scientific protocol could be overlooked if the money pile was high enough.

David grinned at the "Copper Scroll thing" remark. "I first translated the scroll as an undergrad student, then did it again as a grad student at Harvard. Back then it was a lark."

The photographer chuckled. "Only an archaeologist would think translating a two-thousand-year-old scroll was a lark. When I was in college, drinking beer was our lark."

"I know the type."

Cove cocked his head. "That sounded like resentment."

"I was one of those students who did nothing but study. If I felt like doing something wild, I'd sit at a different table in the library."

"Wow, you were a party animal."

"It served me well. Things change as we go through life."

Chambers liked Cove. He was a straight shooter with his opinions as well as his camera. The man's dossier arrived before he did, and it had a long list of awards and photo assignments that had taken him around the world several times. The sample photos were powerful and at times emotionally moving. The man knew how to put a face on the best and worst the world had to offer.

"Such as?"

"Let's stick to the business at hand, shall we?"

Cove shrugged. "Sure thing, chief. So you translated the scroll in school?"

"Technically, I translated from photos of the scroll. The original is in Amman, Jordan. I've seen it several times, but the museum is reluctant to release such a precious object into the hands of an American archaeologist."

"Why is it in Jordan? It's a Jewish document, right?"

"Jordan controlled the area in 1952 when the scroll was discovered. That gave them control of the object. You might have noticed that Jordanians and Israeli officials aren't prone to sharing with each other."

"Yeah, I picked up on that my first time in the country. That was ten years ago. Do you think it will be different ten years from now?"

"Not a chance. A decade is just a blink in tensions that go back centuries. It doesn't matter. At least not now. Over the decades, many photos have been taken, and artists have rendered the writing on paper. It's a tough thing to translate."

"Why is that?"

"Didn't they brief you before they gave you this assignment?"

Cove nodded. "Of course, and I did some research on my own, but to be honest, I flew here from Ethiopia where I was doing a video shoot, so my study time has been less than I prefer. Besides, I prefer to hear from the experts I deal with. It's more interesting that way. Mr. Trent said you'd school me."

"Those were his words?" Chambers leaned against the wall and stared at the seated man. He was thin and wore a khaki photographer's vest. That and the tan hat made Cove look like a poster boy for photojournalists.

"Well, not exactly. He was a little more formal. And remember, I've signed an NDA. Trent made it part of the deal."

"That would be our benefactor. We've all signed nondisclosure agreements. Okay, here are a few things you may not know about the scroll. First thing: it's still highly debated. Some think it's a fantasy, a list of treasures that don't exist."

"But you don't agree with that."

Chambers walked to the end of the wall where a computer-generated rendition of the scroll hung. "Not for a moment. Look, I can understand why other scholars think that. After all, the content is a long list of treasures written in twelve columns; treasures that would amount to a billion dollars or more. Actually, when you factor in the archaeological and historical value, it's worth much more."

A flash of light made Chambers turn. Cove was holding his digital SLR camera to his eye. He lowered it. "Sorry. Just a background photo. That's the beauty of digital photos: I can take as many shots as I want and delete what I don't like."

"You could warn me."

"No way, Dr. Chambers. Then you'd want to pose. I prefer natural shots." He set the camera down. "You were saying?"

"I was saying 3Q15—the official reference to the Copper Scroll—is a list of treasures scattered around the country, probably close to Jerusalem. Second thing to know: the language is not the literary Hebrew used in the parchment and papyrus Dead Sea Scrolls. No one is sure why, although I suspect that it was copied from an older document. The orthography, paleography—"

"It's what?"

"Sorry. Orthography is the study of spelling. Experts in orthography date a manuscript by its use of words and revealing spelling choices. Spelling changes as culture changes."

"Really? How?"

Chambers thought for a moment. "Okay, let's try this: what's a cupboard?"

"It's a place to store cups."

"Right. Spell it."

Cove did. "What's that prove?"

"It proves you can spell. It also proves that you, like everyone else, use words without thinking about their origins. *Cupboard* is a compound word, meaning it is a single word that started off as two or more words. A cupboard is a *cup-board,* a board for cups."

Cove raised an eyebrow. "I didn't realize that."

"It's called a closed spelling. What's a necklace?"

Cove didn't miss a beat. "Lace for the neck."

"Exactly. There are hundreds of compound words in English. Those who study such things can look at an old document, look at the spelling, and make a good guess as to the time it was written. Ever see the Declaration of Independence with its original spelling?"

"Yeah."

"Many of the words look strange to us because American English has changed over the last couple of centuries."

"So if I read a document that spells *colour* with a 'u,' then I know it's British English."

"That's similar to what an orthographic specialist does, but he or she does it in much greater detail. Add to that the work of paleographers, who study the forms, uses, and shapes of letters, and we get a good idea of when the scroll was written."

"Which is around the time of Christ?"

"Yes. The writing is similar to Mishnaic Hebrew—the kind of Hebrew used in recording the Jewish oral traditions, called the Mishnah." Chambers pointed at the long paper image of the Copper Scroll. "There are some intriguing anomalies."

"Other than the fact that it was written on a copper sheet."

"Now you bring up something interesting. You're right that the writing was chiseled into copper, making impressions into the soft metal. That must have taken a great deal of effort. Why go to that trouble?"

"You're asking me? I'm just a camera jockey."

"You're a logical man. Guess."

"Okay. Let's see, the other scrolls are parchment or papyrus. Papyrus is paper made from plant material; parchment is made from animal skin. Do I have that right?"

"Yes. Papyrus is made from a reed. We get our word *Bible* from the ancient city of Byblos, where papyrus was made. *Bible* refers to a book written on papyrus. Later it took on a greater meaning. Parchment is made from animal skin: lamb, calf, goat. Under the right conditions, it can last a very long time."

"But copper lasts longer."

"That's right. The copper itself is interesting. It's a very soft, almost pure copper. The ancients used to mix tin with copper to make bronze. That was a later development which makes some think the scroll is older than it is."

"Why would anyone use a softer metal?"

Chambers shrugged. "Impossible to say. Most likely it was so they could roll it like a scroll. Maybe that's what the Essenes had on hand."

"The authors and keepers of the scrolls?"

Chambers gave a nod. "They were a strict religious community that lived in and around Jerusalem. It's because of them that we have the Dead Sea Scrolls."

Cove rose and walked around the battered table to the long image of the scroll posted on the wall. "I'm no expert, but aren't those Greek letters?"

"You have a good eye. Seven of the location names are followed by two, sometimes three Greek letters. No one knows why. Why just seven listings out of sixty-four? There's something else. The scribe wasn't all that good."

Cove looked puzzled. "Isn't this an important document? I mean, they chose a difficult and probably costly way to make a shopping list of treasure. Why use a lousy scribe?" He paused, then, "And what do you mean by 'not all that good.'"

"I mean he was probably illiterate." Chambers let that sink into Cove's brain.

"Why would a group of literate men chose an illiterate man to record something so valuable… oh."

"Got it?" Chambers crossed his arms.

"I think so. Give me a sec. Let me see if I can get this." Cove began to pace the room. He picked up his camera but didn't aim it. Chambers guessed the camera was an extension of the man. He wouldn't be surprised if the guy slept with it on his pillow. The photographer moved around the room with his head down as if searching for the answer in the carpet.

When Cove stopped and pivoted to face him, Chambers could see the idea flash in the man's eyes. "What better way to keep a secret than have a man who can't read record your list of treasure?"

"Very good, Mr. Cove. You see, some of the words—about thirty such cases—are misspelled in a way no natural Hebrew reader would misspell them."

"I don't follow."

"Okay, you grew up speaking English. Your home is where?"

"Born in Detroit. I live in Austin now."

"Okay, so in Detroit you learned your English from your parents and from school. You know the difference between a Q and an O even though they're very similar, just a small pen stroke difference. Still no matter how similar they are in appearance, you'd never confuse them. You just can't substitute a Q for an O and have a valid word. There's no way you'd write *IRAO* when you mean *IRAQ*. One is a valid word; the other is not. But what happens if you don't know the English alphabet? A smudged O might look like a Q or vice versa, but the word would tell you everything you need to know. We could make the same argument about a P and an R."

"So they hired…what, an illiterate metal smith?"

"That's what I think. They might have given him the list written on parchment and, for security reasons, stayed and watched the work he did, never leaving the original scroll alone. The metal smith might be able to reproduce the letters, but he couldn't read them."

"Why would they leave mistakes?"

"You can't erase a copper sheet. Make a mistake halfway through the process, and it's too late to start over." Chambers leaned against the wall and crossed his arms. Before he could object, Cove took another photo. "You know I'm camera shy, right?"

"I'll cure you of that soon enough."

"We'll see." He waited for a response but didn't get one.

"So they use a man who can't read so he won't dig up the treasures himself?"

"Or tell anyone else. The most the copyist could do is try to remember what he had done. I doubt he could recall much. There's even a chance that Hebrew was a foreign language to him. Of course, there's no reason to believe that he had any idea what it was he was making."

"Sounds like a conspiracy theory."

"Some conspiracy theories have truth behind them. Those were turbulent, violent days. There's a reason the Essenes preserved and hid the Dead Sea Scrolls. They knew Rome would not tolerate a Jewish rebellion. Rebellion came, and Rome did what it did best: it killed people by the thousands."

"So they hid treasure as well as the scrolls?"

Chambers nodded. "Or at very least, knew where others hid them. Your comment about conspiracy theories fits nicely. In fact, it brings up one of the problems we face."

"Let me guess: the terrain has changed over the last two thousand years."

Pushing away from the wall, Chambers began to pace. "Yes, a great deal. The scroll contains lines like this." He moved to the scroll image, pointed to the oddly shaped, chiseled letters, and translated: "At the sepulchral monument in the third course of stones—one hundred gold bars." He turned back to Cove. "Of course, that's a paraphrase, but you get the idea. What sepulcher? Does this refer to the ruin of Horebbah in the Valley of Achor mentioned in the line above? When this was written, such places were common knowledge, at least to the Essenes. Now the best we can do is guess at many of these."

"How do you know that after the destruction of Jerusalem some of the surviving Essenes or priests didn't retrieve the treasure?"

"We don't know that, but it's unlikely. The Romans destroyed and desecrated the temple. Most of the treasures are associated with the temple one way or another. There was no reason to retrieve the treasures except for their monetary value."

"That sounds like high-octane motivation to me. I mean, I wouldn't mind finding a few tons of treasure." He paused. "Who wouldn't?"

"We Westerners think that way, but ancient religious Jews didn't. Selling off the gold and silver would be the same as stealing from God. The people who hid these treasures would never think of picking God's pocket. They'd rather die first." He paused. "Many did."

"Okay, if the topography has changed, old buildings long gone, then how can you hope to find anything?"

"Ah, that's the challenge for guys like me. Finding ancient treasures is my business, and by treasures, I don't mean just silver and gold. Archaeologists can get pretty excited about uncovering a bit of artwork on the wall of some house. The team and I believe that some, probably most, of the treasures are still out there. Will we find it all? Probably not. Maybe. I don't know. We might just end up spending John Trent into bankruptcy. Then again…"

"I still don't know how you hope to find anything."

"We're going to search where things are least likely to change: belowground. Maybe the cisterns mentioned in the scroll have long ago been filled in. Several sets of stairs are mentioned, and maybe they've been demolished and replaced by other structures; maybe rivers have changed course and new buildings have been placed on top of older ones, but the underground topology is not as likely to change. In this case, we're not looking *up* for guidance; we're looking *down*."

The door to the room opened, and Joel Rubin poked his head in. "We got something, Dr. Chambers. You may want to grab a hard hat."

FIFTEEN

The Agusta 109 business helicopter rose from a cordoned-off area of one of Hebrew University's parking lots, blasting bits of dirt and sand airborne with its thudding rotor thrust. Chambers's stomach dropped like a freight elevator, leaving him queasy and dizzy, but the sensation lasted only a moment. The chartered craft had room for six passengers. Four of the seats were taken by Chambers, Cove, Rubin, and Ben-Judah, whom Chambers had retrieved from his cluttered office. He glanced around the cabin. Everyone else seemed fine with the sudden liftoff and steep bank initiated by the pilot. Those who had seen Chambers on talk shows or read his books considered him the personification of the rugged, untroubled archaeologist. Only he knew how much things like flying in a wingless craft bothered him. That and his aversion to tight spaces. The small cabin didn't help with the last stressor.

Still, Chambers kept his jaw tight and his expression determined. Just because he felt like tossing his breakfast didn't mean the others needed to know.

Minutes later, Ben-Judah began rubbing his hands together and sighing every few minutes. "Why is the machine slowing?"

The comment conjured a smile from Chambers whose great-grandfather used to call cars and aircraft "machines." A true Luddite. Ben-Judah embraced technology, but he seemed uncomfortable with some things: like abrupt-moving, loud helicopters.

"No problem, Professor," Chambers said. "The site is on the other side of an Israeli military training range. We need permission to fly over. Wouldn't want to get shot down."

"That could break my camera gear," Cove said. He had been taking shots since taking off, aiming his lens out one of the side windows.

"I have all that taken care of." Ben-Judah crossed and then immediately uncrossed his legs.

"You know that. I know that. I'm not sure the pilot knows it."

"He's been told."

Before Chambers could respond, the Agusta picked up speed.

The ground below changed from city to farmland and then to open, desolate wilderness. *Familiar territory to the Essene religious community.* He could imagine a line of men in rough, well-worn robes making their way on foot from Jerusalem, through the Essene Gate, which today is a buried ruin, to their compound in Qumran near the Dead Sea. The distance from Jerusalem to Qumran was not far by car, shorter by air, but by foot over uneven terrain and hills, it was a different matter. Once again, Chambers was reminded how difficult life was in the days when an iron chisel was considered high-tech, when something as simple as aspirin was beyond the imagination.

He imagined a line of men walking two abreast, snaking their way along a path the wind could remove in minutes, chatting, praying, unsheltered from the elements, beaten by the sun, skin raw from blowing sand. Yet, they would consider such a trek a service to *HaShem,* to God.

Chambers had never lived in a repressed society, one ruled by an occupying force of foreigners who hated the sight of him and all like him. No Roman, whether politician or soldier, wanted to be condemned to work in Judea among the Jews. Jews would rather die than obey a Roman order.

The Copper Scroll and the moving of one hundred thirty tons of precious metal and religious objects worth more to them than the gold and silver were a stinging reminder that people will suffer greatly for their faith. What was pain in light of eternity? He once thought the same way.

Once.

He blinked several times and noticed Cove and Rubin staring at him.

"You okay, Doc?" Cove looked worried.

"Yeah. Sure. Great. Why?"

"You look...pained."

"It's genetic. You'll get used to it."

"Is it permissible to ask where we're going?" Cove rested his camera on his lap.

"To an area near the Dead Sea. Not far from Qumran. That's all I'm willing to say for now." Chambers hoped he didn't sound too conspiratorial.

"Okay." Cove shrugged. "Just so long as I don't have to walk back, I'm good with a little secrecy."

The copter banked sharply and headed south.

"What's he doing?" Ben-Judah's seat faced the back of the helicopter to the other row of three seats. He turned in an attempt to look at the pilot.

"What's wrong?" Cove seemed alarmed.

"He's going the wrong the direction." Ben-Judah reached for his safety belt, but Chambers, who sat opposite him, laid a hand on the old man's knee. Then he held up a finger indicating his mentor should wait a moment. Reaching to the side, Chambers pulled a handset from its cradle and tapped the call button. He waited for a voice, then asked, "Why have we changed course?" Chambers listened, then pulled the receiver from his ear. "We're being followed."

"What?" Ben-Judah's eyes widened. "How can that be?"

"Another helicopter has been on our tail since we took to the air."

"That was quick," Rubin said. "It's less than a thirty-kilometer flight. They'd have to be sitting in their helicopter waiting for us."

"They would have had time," Chambers said. "We had to call for our ride. That would give them time. But you're right: they'd have to plan this."

"What do we do?" Ben-Judah looked frightened.

"The pilot said he moved off course until the matter could be resolved."

"Resolved?" Cove grinned, apparently enjoying the excitement. "That's the word he used?"

"Yes."

Cove's grin broadened. "Think he'd turn us around a little so I can snap a few shots?"

Chambers snapped up the receiver and passed on the photographer's request. A second later the copter pivoted forty-five degrees on its axis. In the distance, Chambers saw a dark craft approaching. Cove aimed his camera at the other helo and snapped a series of shots. "It's slowing. I think it's a tourist flight. You know: see the Dead Sea from the air. That sort of thing. I can see lettering on the side. Gotta love a telephoto lens."

The phone next to Chambers sounded. He answered. Listened. Then said, "Thanks." He hung the receiver in its cradle. Ben-Judah stared at him. Chambers could see the worry in his eyes. Not for his safety, but for the security of the dig site. "The military's air-traffic control has warned them off."

"Then why are they still approaching?" Cove had his digital camera glued to his eye.

"I don't understand." Ben-Judah was growing more agitated. "All tourist flights have been restricted in this area. I received promises from the government." His agitation was morphing into anger. Chambers had only seen Ben-Judah angry a couple of times and didn't want to see a fresh expression of it in the confines of a charter helicopter hovering five hundred feet over the shore of the Dead Sea.

"Well," Cove said, "someone is about to deliver a reminder memo."

Chambers strained to see past Cove. "Let me borrow your camera."

"Sorry, I don't loan my equipment out."

"Listen pal, I've handled three-thousand-year-old artifacts and haven't broken anything yet. Hand it over."

Cove looked at the others.

"I'd hand it over," Rubin said. "He holds the keys to the dig sites."

Cove complied but said something under his breath that Chambers couldn't hear. Through the lens, Chambers saw a military helicopter bearing down on the tourist craft. Within moments, the craft caught up to the trespassing aircraft and shot past it. Once beyond the other chopper, the military helicopter spun to turn its nose toward the trespasser. Chambers knew nothing about military aircraft, but he knew a big machine gun when he saw one, and he saw one protruding from the front of the army chopper.

The other craft slowed to a hover. A second later, the craft turned and headed back in the direction of Jerusalem.

"I think there will be a few sightseers demanding a refund. Seeing a heavily armed war bird looking at you must have raised a few heart rates," Chambers said.

"I'd pay money for that experience," Cove said and reached for his camera.

"You're a bit of an adrenaline junkie, aren't you?" Chambers relinquished the camera.

"Yep, it's a requirement in my job."

The pilot turned the craft in a wide arc over the Dead Sea and then started north again.

SIXTEEN

In the Valley of Achor, in the ruin, under the steps
at the east entrance, forty long cubits: a chest of
money, seventeen talents.

— *The Copper Scroll*, 3Q15, COLUMN 1, lines 1–4

T he diploma on the wall gave a name and degree: "The Board of Directors and Regents of the University of Chicago do hereby grant on this day the degree of PhD in Archaeology to Hussein Al-Malik."

Al-Malik had earned that piece of paper three decades before. Once he took great joy in it. After all, he had spent four years earning his bachelor's degree, two years adding a master of science degree, then three more years finishing his dissertation and defending it before he was granted the privilege of calling himself Dr. Al-Malik. The educational journey had started off as one of joy. The opportunity to study in the United States seemed an honor. But he was a young man then, full of hopes and dreams of a world made better by science. "Through understanding the past," his major professor had told him one day, "is the means of changing the future. Only by knowing what we were can we hope to be what we want to be."

Like Al-Malik, the professor was an Arab living in the Jew-loving nation of the United States. How such a spiritually backward nation as America could have become so strong and so influential and built such a magnificent education system was beyond Al-Malik. At first, he could tolerate the Americans, although his fellow students were either geeky wallflowers who hid in their rooms or hard-drinking, drug-taking barbarians, intent on satisfying their insatiable hunger for sex and fun.

Not once had he associated with the infidels. He was in the country because of the knowledge he could gain and because he could study under Dr. Mazin Moufej, the famous Lebanese archaeologist. The highlight of Al-Malik's education was returning to his Lebanon homeland to do fieldwork in Gebal, where one of the earliest alphabets was formed. He also spent several seasons working with his mentor in the archaeologically rich towns of Tyre and Baalbek, areas with history that stretched back nearly seven thousand years.

Young men, however, grow old, sometimes faster than they should. Lebanon and Israel could never be called friends, and Al-Malik grew up in the midst of hatred and invasion. It was part of life in his land. The Palestine Liberation Organization had settled in southern Lebanon, making the region a target for Israel. That was one reason Al-Malik sought his terminal degree outside his country.

He, his mentor, and a team of students were in the country when Israel invaded in what they called Operation Peace in Galilee. Peace? When it was over, 17,825 Lebanese civilians had been killed and another 30,000 wounded. Professor Moufej was numbered in the first category; Al-Malik in the latter. The bomb that killed his mentor and fellow archaeologists had shredded one of his arms and half his face. Every mirror Al-Malik passed gave him more reason to hate Israel. Yes, he knew that PLO actions led to the conflict, but the lopsided number of deaths, especially of civilians, could not be forgotten. His scars wouldn't let him forget.

He let the sight of the diploma take him back to happier times. It was a luxury allowed for only a few moments.

He picked up the phone and dialed. At the sound of a male voice scarred by years of strong tobacco, Al-Malik spoke. "It was as I expected. They were turned back." He listened, then, "I just received the report. No casualties, but they made no gains. The other pilot must have been warned or saw our helicopter. Whatever the reason, he veered from course and took a position over the Dead Sea. He stayed there until the AH-64D Saraf came on scene. I am sorry to say, the effort was a failure."

He listened some more. "Yes, I understand. We shall prevail."

He hung up and stroked the scars on the right side of his face.

∽

A man stood in an open plain, waving his arms as the A-109 circled overhead. Chambers estimated he was a good two hundred meters from the dig site on the hill just to the southwest. As the pilot lowered the craft, Chambers recognized the young man as Simon Bartholomew, Nuri's assistant. No doubt guiding the chopper in was just one of the unpleasant duties Nuri made the twenty-five-year-old do. As they neared the dusty, bare ground, Simon scampered away, his arm raised to protect his face and eyes from the flying dust and gravel.

The pilot set the bird down as if landing on eggs. Chambers barely felt the skids touch down. He waited with the others as the large rotors slowed, then he popped the side hatch. First he helped Ben-Judah make the long step to the ground, then he led him from the craft. Both moved with heads down until clear of the rotors, which still pounded air downward. A dozen steps later, they turned and saw Rubin and Cove jogging their way. Chambers waved, and the Agusta took to the air again. A brightly painted executive helicopter sitting on the bare ground near Qumran would be noticeable. The area was supposed to be secured, but those who took chances often succumbed to them. Extra caution was the order of the day, now and for all coming days.

A pair of four-wheel-drive Toyota FJ Cruisers sped their direction and stopped a few feet away. One of the driver doors opened, and Nuri slipped from the vehicle. He wore a broad-brimmed hat stained with perspiration. "Someone call for a cab?"

"That would be me," Ben-Judah said.

Amber exited from the driver's position of the other vehicle. "Your chariot awaits. These are great cars but not very big inside, so we offer you a choice. Just so you know, Nuri is having trouble finding the steering wheel."

"Nonsense." He walked around his black SUV and opened the passenger door. "Let's not waste time. We have something you want to see."

Ben-Judah moved to Nuri's car, but Nuri stopped him. "Let the young guys crawl into the back." He motioned for Simon, who trotted to the car and climbed in. "How about you." He pointed at Cove. "You want to ride with a real archaeologist?"

"Sure," Cove said. "You know where one is?"

Nuri laughed. "I see you've been spending too much time with David."

Cove slipped into the back, and Chambers watched Nuri hold the door for Ben-Judah, then moved to Amber's car. Rubin followed in his shadow. He let Rubin take the backseat.

"You're smiling." Chambers shut the door.

"And with good reason." Amber started the car, turned the steering wheel, and hit the gas hard enough to make the wheels spin and fishtail the vehicle. "You'll be smiling in just a few minutes."

"I could use some good news. What did you find?"

Amber shook her head. "I'm not saying. You're going to have to draw your own conclusions."

"You like being coy, don't you?"

"Yep. Makes me feel powerful, and a girl does like to feel powerful."

"Hey, Joel, how should I respond to that?"

He huffed. "With silence. With cold, hard silence."

"Perhaps you're right. She can turn mean in a blink."

Rubin sighed. "I don't think you understand the concept of silence."

They laughed, and Chambers suddenly realized that this was the first time he had laughed in Amber's presence in a very long time.

Nuri's car pulled beside Amber's, then sped into the lead. "Boys and their toys!"

Several small shade canopies rested at the foot of a lone hill. Amber and Nuri parked beneath the largest one. The others had folding tables set up and folding chairs around them. Several workers sat at the tables talking and eating snacks.

Amber led them up a rocky path, which couldn't be more than two feet wide. "This is the original footpath." Amber walked slowly, pointing to places on the ground. "Of course, we had to do some clearing, but we found some broken pottery that we believe dates back to the first century. It's too early to be dogmatic about the age, but that is our first guess. We also found a few perimeter stones marking the old path. Our first best guess is that the path used to be wider but some of it was lost to erosion and small landslides. Twenty centuries changes things, but then you know that."

"Twenty minutes can change things," Chambers said.

She stopped midstep and glared at him. "What's that supposed to mean?"

"It doesn't mean anything. I'm talking about the site, not about you." She didn't move.

"Excuse me, Doctors," Rubin said, "but would you like me to wait in the desert while you two hash this out?"

"There's nothing to hash out, Joel. Let's just keep moving."

Amber spun and marched up the path.

"I like what I do, Dr. Chambers. I've already learned a great deal from you, so I hope I don't lose this job, but I gotta say that I wasn't kidding about keeping your silence."

"We're that obvious?"

"Oh yeah. You guys are as subtle as an earthquake."

"You think you can give me advice?" The phrase was sharper than Chambers intended.

"Me? No sir. At this point in my career, I don't give advice. I just do what I'm told."

Chambers followed Amber up the grade. He already knew everything she had said about the path. He kept track of all the digs in all their stages, but hearing her speak gave him a sense of joy.

The others waited for them at a small crevicelike opening. Chambers's practiced eye could see that the opening had once been larger but had long ago been covered over—intentionally. He moved closer and crouched to study the base of the gap. "Stacked."

"That's what we think," Nuri said.

"Can someone fill the new guy in?" Cove sounded lost.

"Stones don't stack themselves, Ed. The opening looks natural, but there are stones set one on top of another in a pattern. That means the place was sealed and then, over the centuries, covered with natural debris."

"So there's something important in the cave," Cove said.

"It's not a cave, it's a tunnel."

Nuri added more of an explanation. "Using satellite T-ray technology, we've been able to locate several tunnel systems." He took a moment to explain how T-rays can see what lies below grade. "We then used airplanes carrying the same kind of technology to get a more accurate picture. This area, we believe to be a previously unknown Essene compound."

Chambers continued to study the opening. "The Copper Scroll is not as useful as some believe. The laundry list of treasures is intriguing, but so much has changed, and the references are so vague, that no treasure associated with the scroll has ever been found. We've talked about this."

"I remember. The scroll isn't a map, it's an inventory." Cove looked in the opening.

"Right. The first lines read, 'In the Valley of Achor, in the ruin, under the steps at the east entrance, forty long cubits: a chest of money, seventeen talents.'" David moved Cove aside and peered into the tunnel. "The problem we had is that no one knows where the Valley of Achor is. Several have made educated guesses. We figured it would be a place the Essenes had traveled. We know that most of the sect lived in a compound near here; many lived in Jerusalem. Josephus wrote that the group didn't live in one city but in large numbers in every town. The historian Philo said there were more than four thousand in Palestine and Syria."

"They lived here?" Cove asked.

"Maybe," Chambers said. "We won't know until the site is properly excavated. At this point, I'd assume that this is what's left of a fortress monastery."

"But I don't see any buildings."

"That's not unusual," Amber said.

"You've been inside?" Chambers stuck his head into the opening.

"Yes, David, we have. We've done some GPR work. That's why we called you."

"Wait." Cove stepped back and took a few shots. "What's GPR?"

"Ground-penetrating radar," Chambers explained. "Radar signals are sent into the ground, and a computer program renders a color image based on the returns. Solid rock looks different from sand on the screen. Air pockets look very different. Someone hand me a flashlight?"

"Here." Simon gave him a thick flashlight. He also held out a hard hat.

Chambers took the objects and crawled through the opening, which he estimated to be just under a meter high and about a half meter wide at its broadest point. A tight fit. To enter, Chambers had to crawl over fallen stone, natural and cut. His first desire was to stop and analyze the marks on the tooled stone, but there would be time for that later. First things first. Reconnoiter the narrow passage, then return to the details.

As he swept the space with his flashlight, the beam revealed a corridor roughly carved from the natural rock. The ceiling cleared the top of his head by the length of his arm. If he stood on his toes, he could touch the cool stone. The passageway was a consistent meter in width. The floor sloped down at about ten degrees. The air was dry and smelled of dust.

Kneeling, Chambers pushed aside a few rocks, each the size of a grapefruit. They rested on packed dirt. With his bare hand, Chambers dug a small hole until he hit unyielding stone. A little more digging revealed the stone was the tread of a step. He replaced the dirt. It was common practice to leave such stairs covered to protect them for future study.

He rose and paused. Something was chewing at his enthusiasm. His heart began to pound harder, but not from the thrill of a new find. His old friend claustrophobia demanded to be noticed. He determined to ignore the phobia. He had done so many times before; he could do it again.

Focus on the task at hand.

A familiar soft glow six meters into the tunnel grabbed his attention: light from a laptop computer. Next to it rested a device with a long handle. At its end was a narrow metal plate: the GPR.

The sound of others entering the tunnel echoed off the stone walls.

"Not bad, eh?" Nuri sounded pleased with himself.

"Not bad at all," Chambers admitted.

"David?" It was Ben-Judah. He stood behind Nuri. Chambers had to admire the elderly man's ability to climb through tight openings, but then he had been climbing in and out of holes for decades. "Is it...I mean, could it be?"

"Too early to tell, Professor, but I've got a good feeling about this."

"I thought you'd be impressed." It was Amber.

Chambers turned and directed his light toward the voices. The tunnel was filling with people. "Amber, tell the others to wait outside. We've got too many boots in here as it is. Everyone will get a turn." To Nuri he said, "Fill me in."

"Yes sir." Nuri saluted.

"Can the attitude, Dr. Aumann. You made a stellar find here. Let's not ruin it with childishness." Chambers wanted to be the voice of reason, but he knew Nuri and the others were thinking the same thing: he had been the most childish of all.

"Don't forget, David, he found this with your planning." Ben-Judah sounded like a father trying to soothe a pair of angry children.

"Thanks, Professor. We might be a quarrelsome team, but we are still a team," Nuri said.

Amber stepped to a spot just behind Nuri and to the side of Ben-Judah. "We've got some unhappy campers out there. Especially the photographer. He said something about us preventing him from doing his job."

"Yeah, he's a tad pushy. He'll live and we'll make certain he has some time in here, but first I want to hear a rundown. How about it, Nuri?" A second later he added, "If you please."

Nuri moved past Chambers and picked up the laptop. "Based on an analysis of the T-ray surveys, we found this site. We surveyed it by eye for most of the day when Amber noticed the patch of loose rocks you saw at the base of the opening. It matched the airplane T-ray survey. We moved some of the stones and felt a slight breeze. You know how caves 'breathe,' drawing air from the outside and later expelling it."

"Right. It's caused by the difference in air temperature between the inside of the cave and the exterior."

"As the tunnel expert, you know that the same is true for underground structures. We felt air coming from the spaces around the debris field. Actually, Amber noticed it. Further investigation led to the opening. We noticed the same things you did about how the opening had been sealed. At some point, perhaps because of a tremor or just centuries of weather, a portion of the seal wall gave way. We widened the opening and made entrance."

"You've walked the tunnel?"

"Wouldn't you?" In the dim light, Chambers saw Nuri cock an eyebrow.

"You bet I would, especially one this clean. What's at the end?"

"A pile of stone. A portion of the ceiling caved in. We can't explore farther until the way is cleared. It might be a dead end, or it might be another seal wall." He shrugged, then turned the laptop to David. "I think you will find this interesting." He pointed at two white smears on an image of dark red and blue lines.

Chambers took the laptop and studied the GPR image. "Air pockets. Where is this?"

"You're standing on it. Well, almost on it." Nuri walked a few more strides into the tunnel. "Here."

Chambers looked at his feet for a moment, then looked at Ben-Judah. "East entrance, in the ruin, under the steps—"

"Forty long cubits, a chest of money—seventeen talents."

"Forty long cubits," Chambers mumbled. "A standard cubit is about half a meter, a long cubit might mean a royal cubit. That's about twenty-two inches. So something near to twenty to twenty-four meters." Chambers judged the distance to the opening. "We're about that far from the entrance."

Amber spoke up. "While we waited on you, we took a few measurements. It fits."

Chambers couldn't help smiling. This was what he lived for. "Outstanding." Then he reined in his joy. "We still don't know what we have, but if all we ever find is this tunnel, then we've made a significant discovery." He thought for a few moments. "Okay. You know the drill. Let's get some lights in here so the workers can see what they're doing. Professor, we need more people to work the surrounding area to verify that this is an Essene fortress or monastery—"

"No." Ben-Judah spoke softly, but the word struck Chambers like a shout.

"No? I don't understand." Chambers studied Ben-Judah's face. He seemed sad but firm.

"Open the chambers. Work stays in the tunnel for now."

"We can't open the chambers, Professor. We don't even know they are chambers. They could be natural voids in the rock strata." Chambers was uncomfortable with rush.

"The shape on the image looks man-made. They're chambers. I want them opened as soon as possible. And the wall at the end of the tunnel. I want to know what's behind that. I want to know right away."

The tunnel grew silent and cold. Everyone looked at Chambers. He couldn't believe what he was hearing. He had to object.

"Professor, I know you said we would be moving quickly, but there is scientific protocol to be observed. If we rush, we might destroy important evidence, not to mention what the archaeological community would say. The Israel Antiquities Authority alone would shut us down—"

Ben Judah shook his head. "That's been taken care of. We can conduct a more thorough investigation of the settlement later. Right now, we must verify the veracity of the Copper Scroll. That takes precedence."

"Even over established protocol?" David felt his muscles tense. "Even over science?"

Ben-Judah looked him in the eye.

"Yes."

SEVENTEEN

David Chambers marched up the tunnel and out the opening. He heard Amber call after him, but he refused to slow. He emerged into the open air and squinted against the bright sunlight.

"Hey, what'd ya see, Doc?" Cove looked ready to burst.

"Not now, Ed." He waved him off.

"When do I get to go in… Hey, you okay?"

Chambers didn't answer. He moved down the hillside so quickly he slipped twice. He didn't care. He pushed himself to his feet and continued to career down the slope until he reached the open-sided canopies. The workers, taking advantage of the long break, watched as he moved to the area where the Toyotas were parked. He reached for the handle on the driver's door of the vehicle closest to him. A strong hand landed on his shoulder. Chambers spun, knocking the hand down. A man, a good four inches taller than he, stood a foot away. He had the look of a man who could knock down a half-dozen men and feel only slightly inconvenienced by the process. Chambers expected to see anger but saw an emotionless face; something that frightened him even more.

"Excuse me, Dr. Chambers. May I ask where you're going?"

"You're Landau's man, aren't you?"

"One of them, Dr. Chambers. You know that."

"Brooks, right? Harry Brooks."

"Henry, sir. Henry Booker." His voice had an almost imperceptible growl.

"Close enough. To answer your question: I'm leaving."

"Yes sir. Wouldn't it be better to wait for the helicopter?"

Chambers was emphatic. "I don't have the patience to wait."

"Sir, please. It would be best if you just waited. The chopper can be here in a few minutes."

"I want to drive."

"I understand. There's so much to see in the wilderness."

"Ah, sarcasm, the last resort of the slow mind."

Booker showed no offense. "The helicopter is for your safety, sir. Mr. Landau made it clear that key members of the team shouldn't be driving without an escort."

"I don't care what Landau made clear. I'm leaving, and unless you knock me out, which you won't, you can't stop me."

Chambers opened the car door, found the keys still in the ignition, and cranked the motor. A moment later, he was speeding over the ancient ground, leaving a dust cloud to envelop Booker and the workers.

For the next two hours, the Toyota four-wheel drive was Chambers's decompression chamber. He had put up with more than he thought possible over the last few weeks but had finally come to accept the challenge of leading multiple digs and doing so without concerns about a budget. He was willing to work with Amber again, even though seeing her daily brought him pain; he finally reached the point where he could tolerate Nuri for several hours at a time; and working with his old mentor was joy—until now.

Chambers was a bit of a celebrity back in the States, but he had never let that go to his head. Appearing on talk shows to discuss the newest finds in archaeology was fine. He saw it as his duty to his science, a way of creating public interest, but he never let it interfere with his work. Scientists worked with a plan, with procedures proven over time. Gonzo research could ruin a career, destroy a reputation. What Ben-Judah was suggesting might seem a small thing to the uninitiated, but it was anathema to any field archaeologist. Projects were measured in years, not in days and weeks.

He drove for two hours, going nowhere, exchanging one crowded artery with another until he felt civil enough to return to the hotel. He wanted a shower. He wanted quiet. He wanted to be left alone.

After parking the car, Chambers made his way through the hotel lobby, to the elevator, and then to his room. The door had just closed when he heard someone insert a card key. He looked at the bed. It was made, and the room bore evidence of the maid's visit. Someone must have confused his room with their own—

The door opened. Chambers spun. "Don't you know how to knock?"

Landau took three steps, seized Chambers by the throat, pulled forward, then placed a foot behind Chambers's heel. Before he could speak, Chambers found himself on the bed looking into the angry eyes of Hiram Landau.

"What is my job?"

"What are you doing?" Chambers had to force the words out. He grabbed the man's wrist and tried to pull himself free.

"I asked you a question." The viselike grip tightened.

"Okay, okay. I'll play along. You're head of security."

The grip loosened a little. "My job is to keep you alive; to keep the rest of the team alive. It's a tough job, Dr. Chambers. Real tough, and you're making it harder."

"Let me go."

"Not yet. You may think you're calling all the shots here, but you're not. There's stuff you don't know. You do not get to override my security instructions. You do not get to ignore my men. You don't get to endanger the lives of my people or your team members."

"All I did was take a drive to cool off."

"Did my man tell you to wait for the helicopter?"

"Yes, but—"

"He had to blow his cover because of you. Now I'll have to reassign him." Landau released him.

"I can have you fired for this." Chambers sat up.

"Don't flatter yourself. You're stuck with me. But feel free to try."

"You think you can rough me up without consequences?" Chambers rubbed his throat.

"I don't just think it, pal. I know it." Landau pulled out the desk chair, turned it, and sat. "I'm sorry I had to do that, but you are one thickheaded man. Not to mentioned self-absorbed."

"Oh, you know me that well, do you?" He looked at the door.

"Feel free to try, Dr. Chambers. I have a man out there, one by the emergency stairs and another by the elevator." He motioned to the sliding-glass door and the balcony. "Of course, there's always that way out."

"So, what: you're holding me hostage? Just because I took a joyride?"

Landau's face hardened. "You didn't take a joyride, Chambers. That's your problem. You contextualize everything to be about you."

"'Contextualize.' That's a big word."

"Yeah? Well, I read a lot." Landau removed his pocket knife and began to clean his already immaculate nails. "You did more than take a joyride. As I said, you blew my man's cover."

"There was no one there but the team." Chambers moved to the other side of the bed so he could face Landau. Not that he wanted to.

"Really? Rethink that."

He did. "Okay, there were half a dozen workers, but you did background on all of them. So what's the problem?"

Landau sighed. "Just because a man appears to have a clean past doesn't mean he'll have a clean future. People can be persuaded to go against their history and nature. You just need the right motivation."

"Such as."

Landau closed and returned the knife to his pocket. "Money, power, fear. Love."

"Love?"

"You can't have spent that much time hidden away in a library, Doc. Okay, suppose there's something I want you to do for me, something unpleasant, untoward. I take someone you love, say, your lady friend—"

"Amber? I prefer you leave her out of this."

"That's the whole point: it doesn't matter what you want. If I want you to do something so contrary to your beliefs, then I have to find something you love more than those beliefs. So I kidnap Dr. Rodgers and send you a photo and maybe a finger or an eye. If you love her, then you'll do anything to save her. I've seen it repeatedly. Take suicide bombers. There are some who will kill themselves and others because they believe in the cause, but many do so to save their families."

"You're disgusting."

"No, I'm quite pleasant. However, there are many truly disgusting people out there. I've been dealing with them for years. Here's my point: the work is going to require a lot of workers. My team can run background checks on them, but someone could get them in the future. Yes, I'm paranoid. I have the scars to prove I earned the right to be paranoid. Wanna see them?"

"Not really."

"Good. Am I getting through to you? I cannot have a loose cannon like you on my deck, if you know what I mean. You do know what I mean, right?"

"I've got the picture."

Landau leaned forward, his expression softening. "I hate to barge in and bust your chops like this, but I saw no way around it. So I'll make a deal with you: you don't interfere with my work, and I won't interfere with yours. If all this talk about the Copper Scroll is true, then you're on the adventure of a lifetime. You're also walking through dark valleys. There's already been one murder related to this project; I refuse to let there be another one, and if that means I have to move into this room with you or handcuff you to the biggest, ugliest man on my team, then I'll do it."

"The stuff of nightmares."

"If you want nightmares, Dr. Chambers, then you can have a few of mine. I'd like to shed a few."

"No thanks. I imagine yours would turn my stomach."

Landau looked distant for a moment, and Chambers wondered what the man had been through. "I know they turn mine." He stood. "I apologize for my approach, but I felt it was necessary. We good?"

For a moment, Chambers thought Landau would offer his hand. He didn't. "I guess, but my throat still hurts."

"Don't worry. I didn't leave any marks. I never leave marks."

Landau nodded and walked from the room as if nothing had happened.

Chambers moved into the bathroom and looked at his neck. Landau hadn't been kidding, his neck was free of any marks and showed just a general redness. He thought about what had just happened, reliving the worst moments.

He stepped to the toilet and vomited.

༄

Amber was tired of the roller-coaster ride known as David Chambers. When they had first met as assistant dig directors working in the ruins of what had once been called Caesarea Maritima, she found David charming and winsome, quick with a joke, and long winded about the work. At times he would forget that she knew the history of the city and harbor as well as he and waxed on in almost poetic prose about Herod the Great and how he had built the city shortly before the first century. She let him ramble. There was something about his voice and his zeal that captivated her.

That was then. Now her stomach tightened at the sight of him. Over the weeks, things had settled, and she was once again beginning to relax in his presence. Then he marched out of a tunnel that may hold archaeology's greatest find.

The professional part of her agreed with him. Haste had no place in archaeology. She was used to moving through time one layer of dirt after another, and then only after everything had been mapped and a grid laid out. Professor Ben-Judah was suggesting that decades of field practice be chucked and with it his reputation as well as hers, Nuri's, and David's.

Had he just protested, she might have taken his side, but to storm from the tunnel like a disappointed teenage girl was too much. She decided there was nothing more she could do for him. She would do her work with excellence. It was all she could do.

That and pray.

She had been lax in that. Her prayer life had taken a backseat to research and preparation. When she wasn't involved in those things or sleeping, Nuri was pressing her to spend time with him.

Amber walked the tunnel again, videotaping every detail she could. She had some of the workers clear off a few of the stone treads so she could record their size and construction. Edward Cove had taken, by her estimate, close to one hundred photos and downloaded them to a small laptop he carried in his kit. In David's absence, Ben-Judah had taken charge, not that it was needed. He made no decision that she or Nuri couldn't have made, but they deferred to him and greeted each decision with enthusiasm.

She watched the elderly scholar oscillate between joy over discovery of the tunnel and disappointment in David. Why couldn't a man as intelligent as he see the pain he caused in others? *Myopic, plain and simple. He refuses to acknowledge that other people know what they're doing.*

She started down the tunnel again, this time taking footage with the benefit of a string of lights that had been set on metal stands every few feet. Details of the tunnel were much easier to see. She spent ninety minutes making the recording. It was all the time Ben-Judah would allow. He wanted to open the chamber below the stairs first thing in the morning. He also wanted the rubble at the end of the tunnel cleared. The workers would have an even longer night.

Before exiting the tunnel, she paused to wonder how many people it took to carve out such a straight tunnel and to do so with only iron hand tools. The number of man-hours must have been enormous. *It was faith that drove them to do this. Most people have no idea what a powerful motivator faith is.*

She moved up the low grade and for a moment imagined she could see a line of men in robes walking before her.

Outside, the sky had turned from blue to a dark cobalt. Soon the dome would be black, sequined with stars. "It's all yours, Professor."

"Thank you." Ben-Judah nodded at Nuri, who clapped his hands and ordered the workers to follow him into the tunnel.

"I will supervise the removal of the debris; Amber will supervise its placement for later study." Nuri pointed. "While you were recording, I had some of the men clear an area just a few meters to the side. How do you want us to proceed?"

"I suggest that we distinguish between tooled stone and natural. We'll be able to make some assessment on the tools and techniques they used." She stopped. "I mean, after we open the voids."

"You should do this for a living." Nuri smiled at his own joke, then headed into the tunnel, followed closely by his assistant, Simon. Amber's assistant had the day off for a wedding, which was fine with her. She liked working alone.

Cove stood near the entrance snapping photos of the men entering to work.

She looked at Ben-Judah. "You should go back to the hotel and eat, Professor. There is nothing more you can do here. It will take hours to remove the debris, and we won't be opening anything until tomorrow. We certainly won't open anything without you present."

"And you?"

"I'll stay here. We need to feed the men, though."

"I'll send someone back with food for everyone."

Amber smiled, then let the corners of her mouth dip. "I'm sorry about David."

"You have no reason to be sorry, my dear. David is a passionate man and a great archaeologist. I'm making him do what I myself would have never done, and wouldn't if things were not so...pressing."

"Pressing? I don't understand."

"Nothing, Dr. Rodgers. Just a tired old man talking out loud."

"Come on, I'll walk with you to the bottom of the hill. We can have the helicopter here soon. I suggest taking Joel with you. David may need him. You might take that photographer with you, too. He's starting to get underfoot."

Ben-Judah chuckled. "They warned me about him."

Amber led the professor down the slope to the tiny base camp.

EIGHTEEN

Amber looked exhausted, and Chambers knew why. She had worked at the Achor site until the wee hours, returned to the hotel for a shower and a few hours of sleep, eaten a quick breakfast, then met him and other members of the team in the lobby. The hotel, one of the top choices for wealthier tourists and businessmen, had a helipad on the roof. Chambers was sure it was the reason Landau had chosen this location.

Photographer Edward Cove and Nuri's assistant, Simon Bartholomew, had already made the short hop to the area outside Qumran. Chambers let Ben-Judah board the craft first, then Amber and her assistant, Elizabeth Harvick, a Hebrew University grad student working her first dig.

The helicopter pilot made a smooth rise into the cool morning air and started a circuitous path to their destination. After yesterday's event with the tourist helicopter, Landau had decided they should take a less direct course, forcing any other aircraft following them to reveal itself.

"I've heard from Nuri," Ben-Judah said. "He said the night work went well. We should be able to start the important work soon after we arrive."

Chambers wanted to remind his mentor that all archaeological work was important but found the discipline to keep quiet.

"Did he get any sleep?" Amber asked. She sounded motherly.

"He said he slept for a few hours before dawn. I think he slept in the tunnel."

"He's a dedicated man." Amber looked at Chambers, as if daring him to disagree. Chambers turned his attention out the window. They had crossed from the realm of buildings and paved streets to wide expanses of brown, bare ground.

"Has the crew been changed?" David didn't bother looking away from the window.

"Nuri sent them home this morning." Ben-Judah drummed his fingers on his leg.

"Eager, Professor?" Chambers grinned.

"Yes, David. I am. Aren't you?"

David admitted he was.

They set down in the same spot as yesterday. Chambers unloaded his backpack and helped Elizabeth with Amber's photo- and video-equipment bags. This time she brought several adjustable light stands. He toted the heavier bags to a Toyota that waited outside the rotor-blast area.

"Thanks, Dr. Chambers." Elizabeth was short and blond and could be the poster child for perky. She spoke like a teenager. "You must work out."

Chambers felt his face warm and caught Amber rolling her eyes. "Some men pump iron; I pump heavy books."

"Dr. Rodgers didn't say you were funny too."

"I'd hate to hear what Dr. Rodgers said about me. Let's go." He loaded the equipment in the back of the SUV and slipped into the backseat with Amber and Elizabeth. The car seemed much smaller than last time. Only Ben-Judah and the driver seemed comfortable.

"Landau, I didn't expect to see you here."

"I'm an outdoor man at heart." Landau directed the car across the short span of desert that separated the landing area from the dig site. "Dr. Aumann has things well in hand. The workers have been sent away, so it will just be the dig team present. That is what you wanted, Professor?"

"Yes. The fewer eyes the better. The equipment has arrived?"

"Yes. Everything is in place. Dr. Aumann and Simon are clearing the dirt from the stairs."

"And the debris at the rear of the tunnel?"

"All removed and set aside for Dr. Rodgers. If you ask me, it all looks like a bunch of rocks."

"That's because they are a bunch of rocks—important rocks," Amber said. "That's how you woo a female archaeologist: you bring her stones with tool marks."

"What, no roses?" Landau said.

"Doesn't hurt."

"Anyway, the tunnel is clear of debris. The only things that remain are some equipment bags. Cove's stuff."

"Cove is the *National Geographic* photographer," Amber told Elizabeth. "I mentioned him to you, didn't I?"

"Yes, but I don't know why we're taking photos if he's already doing that."

Amber blinked several times as if she couldn't believe the question. "Cove is recording the dig for the magazine. His job is to take photos that tell a story, that interests readers. My job—our job—is to taking scientific photos. We focus on the details. Our job isn't to take pretty photos, but meaningful ones. Same goes for the video work."

Landau directed the vehicle under one of the canopies. Yesterday, a dozen workers milled around, waiting to return to work. Now the area was empty of human life.

Chambers and Landau shouldered the bags and started up the hill. Ben-Judah moved as if the tunnel were his fountain of youth. There was a spring in his step that Chambers hadn't seen since arriving in Israel several weeks ago. Amber had positioned herself near Ben-Judah's side, but he was moving up easily without her help.

The area outside the tunnel had changed. The opening had been enlarged by removing more of the stacked stones. Chambers saw them arranged neatly to the side, each numbered with chalk marks that indicated the order in which they had been removed and an arrow that showed their orientation in the wall. A small generator hummed a short distance away.

A collapsible circular duct and an electric fan sent fresh air into the tunnel.

Setting his load near the opening, Chambers followed Ben-Judah into the tunnel. Nuri and Simon were on their hands and knees, filling small bags with the dirt that covered the stairs over the air void revealed by the ground penetrating radar. The rest of the stairs maintained their protective dirt.

At the sound of the others, Nuri looked up, then stood. He looked worn. He may have told Ben-Judah that he had slept, but Chambers doubted it. Weary or not, the man smiled broadly. "Welcome back. Anyone in the mood to make history?"

"You have done a remarkable job, Nuri." Ben-Judah sounded like a proud father.

Chambers couldn't decide what irritated him more: Ben-Judah's praise of Nuri or the fact that he was right. Had Chambers not let his temper get the best of him again, he would have been here working through the night.

He glanced around. Lights had been set on aluminum stanchions spaced about two meters apart. A thick orange cable ran from each light along the tunnel and out the opening to the gas-powered generator.

Then he saw something that made his professional soul shrivel: a pneumatic chipper, often called a jackhammer. Next to the unit were two large compressed-air cylinders.

Cove walked up from the lower end of the tunnel, snapping photos, his flash stabbing Chambers's eyes. David raised a hand, and Cove stopped. "Sorry."

Chambers moved to the area where Nuri had been working. The steps were indigenous stone, carved into the base of the tunnel. They had been used frequently and for a long time. Wear marks made by countless footfalls over decades. Maybe even a century. A harder stone like granite might not have shown such wear. "May I have your brush, Nuri?" He held out his hand.

Nuri handed over a well-used painter's brush that had seen many digs. Much of the basic equipment had come from Ben-Judah's department at the Institute. Most of the dirt in the target area had already been removed to expose three treads. Chambers focused on the juncture where the tread met the wall of the tunnel and where the treads overlapped. The joints were tight. So tight he assumed the stairs had been carved in place.

"Amber, direct your video light over here. Low angle."

She moved to his side, lowered herself to her knees, and aimed the bright light on the area Chambers indicated. "Helpful?"

"Yes. It looks like the stairs were carved in place out of base rock, not made elsewhere and brought in."

"Wouldn't that, like, be impossible?" Elizabeth said.

"No. It would be, like, so very possible." He stopped and looked at the young woman. "Sorry, Elizabeth. I tend to be a little cranky during waking hours. I apologize."

"For what?" Elizabeth looked puzzled.

Amber came to the rescue. "I'll explain later."

"Okay, I'm lost," Cove said. "If there's a man-made void beneath the stairs, then how did the ancients bury it beneath stone steps. I mean, the steps can't be moved, right?"

"Right, and I have no idea how they could do that." Chambers sat on his haunches and rubbed his chin. "First, we don't know that the voids shown in the GPR image are man-made."

"I don't agree," Nuri said. "The voids appear to have right angles. Nature doesn't use right angles."

Nuri had him there. While it was still possible they had found a pair of natural voids, Chambers wouldn't put any money on it. "What are we left with? If the Essenes had carved out a chamber beneath the stairs, then the GPR would have seen it. Either the voids are natural, or they found some way to make it look like the stairs are a continuous construction from beginning to end. Nuri, are you sure this is the right spot? Maybe we're too far up or too far down the staircase."

"Of course, I'm sure. I checked, double-checked, and even ran the GPR over it again."

"What about the portable T-ray?"

"Not here yet. I was a little busy last night while you were, what, sleeping?"

"Okay, I had that coming. Sorry. I was just hoping for a loose tread or something, but I guess that would be too easy." Chambers moved to the area where tread met wall. There he found a tiny line that looked more like a stress fracture than a seam. He ran the brush over it several times.

"I saw that earlier. It's a crack from the ground shifting."

Chambers knew Nuri was right. He was puzzled, then an idea struck him. "Amber, pick a direction: up or down?"

"What?"

"Just pick one or the other: up or down?"

"Okay, um, down."

"This may be a dumb idea, but it's an idea. Joel, Simon, give me a hand here. I want to move the dirt away from the tunnel walls. Start with what Nuri has cleared and work down two, no, make it three treads."

"I told you that I confirmed the void is right below you. Must you doubt everything I say?" Nuri's jaw tensed.

"I don't doubt you, Nuri. I believe the void is where you say it is. The question is, how could someone hide a treasure beneath a stone step that is carved out of the ground? I'll bet Joel's salary that we'll find the tread we want a little farther down."

"Hey, leave my salary out of this." Rubin began moving dirt with a small trowel.

"Why down and not farther up?" Ben-Judah inched closer.

"Because Amber told us that down was the right direction."

"What? No I didn't. You just said to choose—"

"I'm just kidding, Amber. If I'm right, then we have a fifty-fifty chance that the tread we're looking for will be down from where we are."

It took twenty minutes to delicately remove the dirt along the wall for a length of three treads. At the third tread, Chambers found what he was looking for: a slight gap, just two millimeters wide, where wall met tread. They found a matching space on the opposite side of the tunnel.

"Well, this is interesting. Amber, let's use your light again." She shone the bright beam from the video camera on the area. The blinking red light told him she was recording. "I need a pick."

In any other context, someone might have handed him a big tool with a point and blade on one end. Instead, Rubin placed a dental pick in Chambers's hand, which he used to scrape along the narrow gap. Dirt came out easily. He moved past Rubin and Simon and did the same to the other side. "Clever men, these Jewish monks."

He handed the small instrument back to Rubin and started pushing and pulling centuries of dirt away from the step; much of it landed in his lap and around his legs. Rubin joined him, and soon another three treads were cleared and brushed clean.

Cove snapped several shots. "I'm afraid I don't follow. You think this tread leads to the treasure several steps up? Is that it?"

Chambers nodded. "The scroll gave enough hints and even a distance —forty cubits—from the east-facing entrance. Of course that's vague, probably purposely so. Remember, these treasures are meant to be found— not by us—but by the people who hid them, or at least the next generation. It's unlikely anyone else would find the hiding place, but if they did, the monks didn't want to make it easy on them."

"So what do you propose now, David?" Nuri didn't seem pleased. "We still have the same basic problem. If we're going to hammer our way into the chamber, then why not just break through the stairstep directly over the cache?"

"Look, I know we're supposed to be working fast, but that doesn't mean we can't take a little time to learn how these men thought and worked. It may be important later."

"What do you propose, David?" Ben-Judah stroked his long beard.

"Let's see if we can't move this stone tread before we start chiseling things to pieces."

"But it fits into the walls," Elizabeth said. "Doesn't that, like, mean it's wider than the corridor?"

"Yes, it does, Elizabeth—"

"People call me Lizzy."

"Okay, Lizzy. You're right, but the tread had to be placed here in the first place. The tunnel is carved out of natural rock. Obviously they didn't build the tunnel after the stairs. My guess: the stone slides to the right or left." He looked at Amber. "Choose right or left."

"Not this time, bub. You make your own choices."

Chambers smiled. "This is what I love about archaeology." He rose, stepped to one end of the tunnel, placed his back against the stone wall, positioned his boot-clad feet on the tread, and pushed.

Nothing.

He tried again, straining. Rubin and Simon tried to help by pushing with their hands. The stone moved a quarter of an inch but no more. It felt to Chambers like the end hit something. "Let's try it from the other direction." This time the stone moved an inch, then three. The sound of sand grinding against stone filled the space.

Chambers and the two aides struggled. Despite the cool air in the tunnel, sweat dotted Chambers's brow, then drew together in streams.

He pushed back into the tunnel wall until he could feel the chiseled stone pressing through his brown work shirt and used his legs to apply as much pressure to the tread as possible. The tread alone had to weigh hundreds of pounds, and trying to move it along more stone was nearly impossible.

"Let me have a go at it." Landau didn't wait for permission. He elbowed Chambers aside. The day before, Chambers learned firsthand that Landau was strong. Recalling the event made his neck hurt.

Landau followed Chambers's technique, putting his back to the wall and using his legs to slide the stone slab to the side. It moved, but not far enough. Just as Chambers had convinced himself that they would have to destroy the tread with the handheld pneumatic hammer, Landau grunted, then groaned loudly. The stone moved another inch, this time pulling away from the hand-cut socket in the wall.

Landau stopped and sucked in a lungful of dusty air. Sweat dripped from his face. "That's a workout."

"See, and you probably thought I was just a wimp." Chambers looked into the small gap.

"What makes you think I've changed my mind?" Landau followed the quip with a weak grin. "Give me a sec, and I'll give it another try."

"Hang on. It's time for a little physics." Chambers moved up the tunnel, stepped outside, and found what he was looking for: a long-handled shovel and a crowbar. He returned to the others and set the blade of the shovel in the thin gap between the end of the tread and the wall. He pushed against the wood handle, using it as a lever. He repeated the action and each time the block moved a few millimeters. When he looked up from his work, he saw Landau holding the long metal bar.

"Say when."

"I think now would be good. We have enough room to swing the stone over the lower tread and from beneath, the one above."

"So turn the stone?"

"Exactly." Chambers hoped the set hole on the opposite side was wider than he could see. It had to be. There was no other way to explain how the stone had been placed two millennia ago.

The men repositioned themselves. Cove and Elizabeth took turns snapping shots. Amber kept the video camera going but was still able to direct her assistant.

It took fifteen minutes for Chambers and Landau to move the stone another four inches and pivot the one end away from the wall. With the help of Nuri, Rubin, and Simon, they finally dislodged the step, pushing it to the north side of the tunnel. Chambers was breathing hard and dripping with perspiration. Only his pride kept him from sitting down.

Behind the area where the stone had rested for two thousand years was packed dirt. Chambers lowered himself, studied the packed fill. "I need a trowel." One was handed to him. He began digging, slowly at first, then faster. It took close to half an hour for him to clear the space beneath the upper tread. He piled the dirt to either side of him. No one spoke. The drama before them might be missed by others, but not this collection of people. "The tread bridges the distance between the walls. The dirt doesn't seem to be structural—" He stopped suddenly. His trowel hit something other than dirt. "Found something. Feels like wood. Spongy wood."

Chambers lay on his stomach and pointed his flashlight into the cavity. He pushed to a kneeling position and drew a dirty hand across his brow. "I'm going to try to break through the wood with the crowbar." He looked at Nuri. "I don't suppose you thought to have a remote camera brought in with the other equipment."

"It just so happens, I did."

"That's good thinking. Let's get that ready to go."

Chambers returned his attention to the void and the wood barricade at the back of the fifteen-centimeter-high space. The wood put up no resistance. Several sharp thrusts with the crowbar produced a small, ragged opening. Chambers reached under the stone and gently fingered the hole. The wood was about as thick as a two-by-four but much softer. The fact that it had remained at all impressed Chambers. He pulled back a piece of the wood. It was dark and crumbled in his hand. He paused and wondered about the last hand to touch what he was holding.

Nuri reappeared with a handheld device connected to a coil of what looked like thick wire coated in black insulation. Chambers moved to the side to give Nuri room to work. Taking Chambers's place, Nuri went to work, uncoiling the fiber optic "snake" and activating the handheld control and display.

"What are you doing?" Cove asked.

Nuri looked at Chambers. "This is your baby. You tell him."

"This is a camera. Sometimes called a snake camera because"—he held up the black cable—"it looks like a snake. Clever, no?" He pointed at the end of the device. "There are tiny lights, which the camera needs to take good video. We can see the image on this handheld monitor, and we can control the light and direction of the camera here."

"Like what plumbers use to look inside pipes?"

"Yes." Nuri activated the device and pointed the end of the "snake" at Amber. "Say cheese."

She aimed the video camera at him. "You say cheese."

"Just making sure the camera is working." Nuri slipped the lens into the space cleared by Chambers.

Looking over Nuri's shoulder, Chambers watched the small video screen in the monitor. The monitor went from black to a dark image with a white glow made by the inline light. A second later, Chambers saw the hole he had created. "That ought to be big enough."

Nuri huffed. "By a factor of ten, David."

"I was using a crowbar, Nuri; hardly a delicate tool. It's still better than a pneumatic hammer."

Nuri didn't respond. He paused as the camera reached the uneven-shaped hole, then looked up at Ben-Judah. The others parted to give the professor room to move down the steps. Landau helped him take a stand that allowed a view of the small screen.

"Shall we?" Nuri asked.

"Proceed." Ben-Judah's words came with a tremor.

Nuri pushed the camera through the hole.

NINETEEN

Chambers sat in the dirt on the side of the hill a few meters from the tunnel opening. He watched as the delivery truck with the familiar brown paint job pulled away, headed along the same course he had used yesterday in his anger-fueled departure, something he now regretted. What he could not see was the armor behind the paint and gold lettering. The fact that such an armored truck had been created proved Ben-Judah and Trent's belief that the treasures not only existed but would be found. Chambers had shared their belief in the reality of the treasure but had serious doubts anyone could find them, if they still existed. After all, not a single treasure had ever been found. Until now.

There was a great deal of work to do before they could say much about the horde with any authority. The wood chest would be carbon dated, the tool marks in the tunnel would be analyzed, and the silver would be tested by a metallurgist. Those things had to be done. Science required it, but Chambers and the others already knew what they had found: silver from the temple treasury. A pomegranate emblem had been stamped into each bar. A pomegranate was one of the emblem motifs of the first and second temples.

A haze blurred Chambers's thinking. His mind, normally sharp, quick, and analytical, was awash in a boiling emotional stew. Thrilled as he was with the find, moved as he was with its importance, he also felt shame for the brutish techniques they used to retrieve the artifacts. He had been successful in minimizing damage by removing the keystone step, but once Nuri had slipped the snake camera through the pilot hole Chambers had created with his own brutish wielding of a crowbar, he knew there was no way they could remove the chest, which was too damaged by age and decay and too large to fit through the narrow opening. How the ancients managed to get the box into the void in the first place was a ship-in-the-bottle mystery. Given time, weeks—maybe months—he might have been able to figure it out, but Ben-Judah gave the command.

"Retrieve it."

Nuri took the handheld pneumatic hammer and placed the hardened-steel chisel in the center of the tread over the void. It was done with brute force instead of finesse, and Chambers couldn't help feeling a bit like the grave robbers who used to steal artifacts from Egyptian tombs and sell them to the highest bidder. He could still hear the sound of the pneumatic hammer, powered by compressed air, as it split the tread. To Nuri's credit, he hesitated before pulling the trigger. As much as he disdained the man, Chambers had to acknowledge he was a good archaeologist in his own right.

The silver ingots found in a decayed chest would not be sold. They had too much historical value for that, and the way Ben-Judah wept at the sight of them told Chambers that their significance to the Jews was more than he could imagine.

"You okay?" Amber stood by his side. He hadn't heard her approach. "You look a little lost."

"Not lost, just conflicted."

"What is there to be conflicted about? We just broke every dig rule in the book."

His eyes traced her dirt-powdered face. She was never more beautiful than when on a dig site. "Why the rush? This isn't like the professor. He's always been…been…"

"Cautious? Pedestrian? Rigid about rules?"

"I was going to say orthodox, but you're spot on. This isn't like him."

"He's hiding something." She pushed back a strand of hair.

"Like what?"

She lowered herself to the ground and sat next to him. "If I knew what it was, then it wouldn't be hidden." She smirked. "I do know this: it takes a lot to move a man like Ben-Judah off center. I'd hate to see our new technique appear on the *Discovery Channel*."

"Not much chance of that. Although Cove was snapping photos as if his life depended on it. I'm not sure *National Geographic* will consider keeping the pics to themselves. What are the others doing?"

"Ben-Judah told them to take a break. Nuri wants to do another GPR survey on the back wall."

"Why? The first one showed a dead end." Chambers stretched out his legs and leaned back on his arms.

"The idea of a stairway to nowhere bothers him. I'd think it'd bother you."

"Are we going to argue now?" Chambers looked away. "Because I'm a tad spent. Maybe we can reschedule the fight to another time."

Amber turned her gaze to the flatland that separated the Dead Sea from the hill. Two thousand years ago, the Dead Sea was larger, but since dams had slowed the flow of the Jordan River, evaporation had slowly reduced its volume. At one time, the water would have been much closer to the hill they sat upon.

"I'm not trying to pick a fight, David. Really, I'm not."

"What are you trying to do?"

"You know, some people go through life avoiding emotional land mines; you seem intent on jumping from one bomb to the next. I came over to compliment you."

"A compliment, eh. I suppose I could tolerate one of those." He grinned.

"I know the technique...the lack of technique in this dig has been a problem for you. That's true for all of us. You did a magnificent job in there."

Chambers appreciated the comment. "Thanks. I wish I could have figured out the rest."

"So does Nuri. That's why he wants to explore the back wall. He thinks it may hold the secret to how the Essenes did what they did. He thinks they may have built the stairs as a ruse or that they never completed the work—"

"That they had to rush to hide some of the treasures because the Roman army was bearing down on Jerusalem, so they made a small side tunnel." Chambers thought for a moment. "The GPR showed no voids beneath the stairs other than the one we found."

"Not under the stairs, David. Along the stairs on the other side of the tunnel."

"Not a bad idea, but then why create a tread that could be removed?"

She shrugged. "I don't know. Maybe to frustrate people like us. People searching for the treasure, I mean." She picked up a small stone and rubbed dirt off its surface. "Do you want to tell him he's wasting his time?"

Chambers looked at the late afternoon sky. "No. His idea makes more sense than mine."

"What's your idea?"

"You looking for a good laugh?"

"You know me, I love to laugh."

"Okay, just laugh at the idea not me. I am a delicate flower." He tried not to grin at his own comment.

"Sure you are. Just a daisy struggling for your share of sunlight."

"When I was thinking about this a few moments ago, I told myself it was a ship-in-a-bottle mystery. Have you ever seen anyone build a ship in a bottle?"

"No."

"I had an uncle who used to do it. When I was a kid he tried to show me how it was done. I didn't pay much attention. I didn't like my uncle much and only went to his home on holidays. I do remember seeing him insert small parts of the boat into the bottle. The parts were hinged. I don't mean with metal hinges, but somehow they were attached in such a way that once their binding was released, usually a small string or rubber band, they would open. You can't do that with the whole model but you get the idea."

"Wait a sec." Amber's forehead wrinkled. "Are you saying they built the chest in the cavity?"

"I told you it was a wacky idea, but it could be done. When we analyze the chest, we'll know more."

Amber dropped the pebble. "What kind of hinge would they use?"

"It doesn't have to be hinged. Okay, I'm doing this off the top of my head, but let's say they used a pin-and-hole system. Or maybe a mortise and tenon joint. First they put the base of the chest in the cavity, maybe with the back side already attached. I'd have to test this, but they might have been able to insert the base and attached side. Maybe not. Anyway, the base either has holes for pins or mortises for tenons. They would insert a side with glue on the tenon and set it in place and so on. It'd be a pain, but it could be done. If it was done that way, then I could imagine someone practicing the procedure over and over until he had it down. The last two things they would do would be to reach through the opening and drop in the silver ingots one at a time, then slide the lid over."

"That's ingenious. I mean that's brilliant. It could work."

"I wish I had thought of it earlier. I could have checked the chest before we packed it up and sent it off to the Institute."

"You should tell Nuri this."

"I'll let you tell him. He's your beau."

"Don't go there, David. You don't know what you're talking about."

"Sorry. I'm afraid being surly has become my default."

"You weren't always that way, you know. You used to be different."

"People change, Amber. Life changes them."

"Sorry, David, I don't buy it. I believe people change because they want to or because they allow it."

"Are you a psychologist now?"

"I don't need to be. You used to be like him." Amber pointed down the hill where Ben-Judah stood, facing west toward Jerusalem. He had slipped on a prayer robe with a hood that covered his head. David could see a small box with leather straps attached to his forehead and another phylactery tied to the back of his hand. He stood alone and with his hands raised. David had seen Ben-Judah pray many times. Like many religious Jews, he prayed three times a day, usually in private. Out here there was no privacy.

"I was never Jewish." Chambers couldn't pull his gaze away from his mentor.

Ben-Judah must have come to the end of his prayers. He removed the phylacteries and uncovered his head. He exhibited great care with the objects and the prayer shawl. Chambers watched as he walked to one of the Toyotas and placed the property in the backseat.

"You know what I mean. You used to be a man of prayer, a person of belief. That's the David I fell in love with—the one who prayed; the one who studied the Bible for more than archaeological and historical clues. You used to be so—"

"Please don't say I was on fire for the Lord. I hate that phrase. Always have."

"I was going to say committed."

"Now you think I need to be committed. Right?" He was the only one who laughed at his joke.

"What you need to do is find yourself, and there's only one way to do that: find your faith."

"Well, if that's all there is to it, then no problem."

"More sarcasm. Since when has that become your currency? Look at Ben-Judah. That man has been through more than the rest of the team combined. He is considered one of the best Holy Land archaeologists in the world. People travel from all around the world to sit in his classes and to shovel dirt at one of his digs. Look, he even pulled you from your academic cave. Yet every day, several times a day, he prays. For him, archaeology is an act of worship and service. It's that way for me too. It used to be that way for you."

Ben-Judah started up the side of the hill. He seemed lost in thought.

"Amber, I don't need a sermon."

She stood. "Oh yes you do. You need that and a lot more."

She started back to the tunnel. Chambers rose, brushed off his trousers and turned to follow, intent on apologizing yet again, when he saw Nuri approaching. He brushed by Amber and marched to Chambers.

"Did Amber tell you my plan?"

"She did. I think you'll come up empty, but you should go ahead with it."

"Then you need to move your stuff. Professor Ben-Judah wants to watch the test."

"What stuf?"

"I have Simon and Rubin moving the compressed-air tanks closer to the lower end of the stairs so we can use the pneumatic hammer if need be, but before I can run another GPR test, I need the whole area clear. That includes your duffel bag. It's in the way, and it is not my job to move it."

"It's not my bag, Nuri." Chambers started to the tunnel. He wanted to see the GPR results as they came in.

"It still needs to be moved."

Chambers left Nuri behind and caught up to Amber. They walked into the tunnel and down the stairs, careful to avoid the piles of dirt and broken stone. Near the base of the stairs they saw Simon and Rubin struggling with one of the compressed-air tanks. Cove was with them but not offering any help.

"Man, this is heavy." Rubin set his end down. "I became an academician to avoid physical labor."

"You picked the wrong discipline, Joel," Chambers said. "Archaeology isn't for softies." He looked at the base of the wall. "Edward, is this some of your photography equipment?"

Cove turned his hands palms up and shrugged. "Not mine, boss. I thought it belonged to one of you guys or one of the workers."

Chambers looked up searching for Nuri, but the man had yet to return to the tunnel. Then at the entry, he saw two shadowy forms. Nuri was talking to Ben-Judah. "Anyone know where Landau is?"

"Last I saw him, he was headed to one of the portable outhouses," Cove said. "I suppose even someone like him needs a bio break now and again."

"You think it might belong to him?" Amber stood at the back of the small group.

"Could be," Chambers said.

"Well, someone should check with him, and it might as well be me." Amber jogged up the stairs and out the entrance, stepping aside when she met Ben-Judah coming down the tunnel.

Chambers watched her go and wondered if he owed her yet another apology. He watched Amber stop as another figure entered the tunnel. It took a moment, but he soon recognized Amber's aide, Elizabeth. The perky grad student trotted down the steps, moving around the slower Ben-Judah. When she reached the bottom, she said, "Dr. Rodgers wants me to videotape the test. Can I set up?"

"Just leave things as they are. If they belong to Landau, then it could be filled with secret spy stuff and a rocket launcher."

"Pretty small rocket launcher," Simon said.

"I was making a funny. I'll be right back." Chambers started up the stairs to meet Ben-Judah.

"I don't know what the big deal is," Rubin said. "Let's just move it out of the way."

Chambers turned just as Rubin picked up the bag. "I said to leave things alone—"

He heard a loud click and the sound sent scorching terror through him before he could think why. "Run!" Chambers spun and sprinted toward his mentor.

There was light.

There was heat.

There was a roar.

Chambers was airborne, propelled by fire-laced air.

A heartbeat before the explosion, David Chambers had jumped toward Ben-Judah, his arms spread. He landed on the older man as the force and fury of the blast rolled over him. Bits of rock struck his back like bullets from an automatic rifle.

He felt no pain; just the slap of the concussion, which hit from behind like a giant fist.

He landed on Ben-Judah, shielding him with his body, but was on his feet a blink later, pulling the man to his feet, then lifting him over a shoulder.

Through the smoke, through the dust, Chambers ran as fast as his adrenaline-fueled legs would carry him. He had one thought: get Ben-Judah out of the tunnel.

A glance up revealed a ceiling spider-webbed with cracks. Bits of stone began to fall. Chambers pressed on harder.

"God no. Please God. Let me get him out."

His back began to complain from stress and injury. He didn't listen. Step followed step up the steep stairs.

A knee buckled. "No. God. No." He righted himself and kept plodding upward.

More rocks fell, but he couldn't hear them. The ringing in his ears drowned out all other sounds. Something warm and sticky dripped into his eyes.

A meter felt like a mile. Every step seemed five times taller than the last time he had ascended them.

The air was foul with a stench he fought not to identify. He knew but didn't want to know.

Again a knee buckled under the weight of the old man and the physical strain of running up stairs.

Ben-Judah hadn't spoken, hadn't moved. Tears ran from Chambers's eyes. If something happened to the old man, if...if... No. He wouldn't allow it.

The corridor had been plunged into darkness the moment the flash of the explosion dissipated. Chambers could barely make out the edge of each tread. Several times he caught a toe and nearly went face first to the stone. Each time he caught himself.

Something in his leg snapped and pain scorched up his spine. He forced one foot to follow another.

A few meters from the opening, the shape of a man appeared. Chambers could no longer see well, but the shape was familiar. The figure moved toward him.

Ben-Judah's weight on his shoulder disappeared. Chambers looked up and into Landau's face. His lips were moving but Chambers could only hear the chain-saw roar in his ears. He stumbled forward to the entry, trying to make his brain work, demanding his thoughts to line up into something cogent.

Fresh air poured over him as he stepped into the daylight.

Familiar hands grabbed his arm and steadied him. Amber stood next to him. She was speaking, but he heard nothing. She tried to lead him away from the tunnel, when his mind found a forward gear. "The others."

He turned, but Amber wouldn't let go. He started forward again, but she pulled him back.

"Let...let me go." He pulled free and started for the black maw of the tunnel, fearful of what he might find. With a glance to the side, he saw the large frame of Landau laying Ben-Judah on the ground. He also saw the security man motion for him to stay away from the tunnel. Chambers turned his gaze back to the opening.

Nuri appeared from his right and tried to step in his way. Chambers rewarded him by finding enough strength to shove the man to the ground.

Darkness hovered at the periphery of his vision.

With diminishing vision, waning strength, and ears that no longer worked, Chambers marched into the darkness.

Time ceased. He had no memory of the steps he had taken to the bottom of the tunnel or how long it took. Nor did he recall when he started weeping. One by one he removed a stone from the fallen ceiling. With each stone he pulled from the pile that kept him from his team, he called out a name.

"Joel...Simon...Cove...Lizzy...Joel..."

Amber stepped to his side. In the darkness, through the ringing in his ears, he could hear her sobs running counterpoint to his own.

Another stone landed on the ground, and Chambers waited for the rest of the ceiling to fall, then he realized Amber was digging next to him. A moment later, Nuri was at his other side.

Ten rocks later, maybe twenty, Chambers didn't know, the tunnel went completely black, and his face hit the pile of stones before him.

Everything disappeared.

TWENTY

Darkness gave way to bright light. Numbness gave way to pain. Chambers wished for the former. It took a few moments for the world to make sense to him again. The tunnel was gone; the hard stone upon which he had fallen had been replaced by a soft bed with the whitest sheets he had ever seen.

Then he saw the bed rail. A hospital bed rail.

He blinked several times, forcing his eyes to clear. Last he remembered, his eyes were full of dust and grit from…from what? Explosion. He tried to rise, but a hand pressed him back to the bed. "No you don't, Dr. Chambers. I'm not done yet."

A male voice. It came from behind him, calm, sure.

"Where am I?"

"Beth Israel Hospital in Jerusalem." Accent saturated the words.

"How did I get here?" He tried to turn to face the doctor.

"Stay still, please, I'm trying to do a little medical art back here."

"What kind of art?"

"Stitching. I'm an artist when it comes to stitching up wounds. I have a reputation to protect."

Memories were coming back like jigsaw pieces, leaving him to put things back together. "I don't feel anything."

"That's twenty-first-century drugs. This won't take long."

Chambers relaxed on his side and tried not to move. He decided he didn't want to see what the doctor was doing.

"I'm Dr. Karlin. You are a lucky man, Dr. Chambers. Fortunate indeed."

"I'm not feeling all that lucky. How bad…I mean…wounds…" It occurred to him that he could hear more clearly.

"You're going to live, but you'll have a few scars to frighten the grandkids with."

"I was hoping for something a little more medical."

"I can do that, but I'll keep it simple. I imagine you're still a little groggy. Your injuries are minor compared to what they could be. You presented with second-degree burns to the back of your neck and arms. Not serious, but your bed sheets will probably feel like sandpaper. There is some blistering but not much. We'll send you home with some ointment to help with the surface pain. You also received several impact wounds to the back. There's some bruising, and I had to dig out a few stone shards. All superficial, though it won't feel that way once the local wears off. While you were out, we did a few scans and x-rays. No broken bones, but you damaged a tendon in your right knee. I imagine you noticed that when you did it."

"I seem to recall a massive, stomach-turning pain."

"That would be the reason. We're going to treat that with an elastic brace since the tendon is still attached. There is a good chance, however, that you may be facing a leg surgery in your future. How's your hearing?"

"Some ringing still."

"That should pass with time. Hopefully. Sometimes tinnitus is permanent. Only time will tell. You'll be happy to know that your eardrums are intact. Which surprises me. From what I hear, I expected to see more damage than I do. Again, you are a lucky man."

"Dr. Ben-Judah—"

"I didn't work on him. I have no news for you."

"How do I find out?"

"I'll see what I can learn, but that may take a little time, especially if he's had to go in surgery."

Chambers tried to rise again. This time the hand pushed him down with more force. "I told you to stay still. I didn't say they took him to surgery. I don't know what they've done with him. I just know he's not in the ER, so maybe they're taking x-rays and a CAT scan. Really, it could be anything."

Glancing around, Chambers was struck by how similar hospitals could be. If he didn't know he was in Jerusalem, he could be in almost any hospital in the Western world. His bed was kept private by a curtain with pale-blue stripes. The polished floor reflected the overhead fluorescent lights. The smell was like every hospital he had visited. Until this moment, he had never been a patient.

"David?" A familiar, tentative voice pushed into the small ER treatment area.

"Over here, Amber."

The curtain moved. "May I come in?"

"Doctor?"

"Fine by me. Your wife?"

"No…colleague."

"Well, I'm done here."

Karlin rounded the bed. Chambers had pictured a squat doctor with a head of dark hair. Instead he saw a man in his thirties, tall, thin, and completely bald. He pulled the curtain back enough to let Amber in. She clasped her hands in front of her and made Chambers think of a shy schoolgirl.

She smiled and the room brightened. "They tell me you're going to be all right." She looked at Karlin. "Is that right, Doctor?"

"He should be fine. We're going to keep him overnight for observation. There are no signs of a concussion or internal injuries, but we need to be sure." Karlin watched them exchange glances. "I'll let you two talk." To Chambers he said, "I'm going to prescribe some antibiotics. Be sure to take them all. I'll also make sure you get some pain relievers. We'll have you in a room soon." He excused himself and left.

Amber looked hollow, cored out. Dust clung to her hair, and she smelled of something acrid, something he assumed had to do with the explosives used to bring down the tunnel. Red, angry-looking scratches covered her hands, evidence of her barehanded effort to save those who were beyond salvation.

She studied him as much as he examined her. For the next few moments, all communication was nonverbal. Words failed. No string of terms could be composed to relate the darkness they shared.

Amber moved closer and took Chambers's hand. Hers felt hot to the touch. She squeezed as if confirming that she wasn't looking at a ghost. Then "Oh David." A flood of tears carried the rest of the message. His vision blurred, and he turned away, hoping the breaking of eye contact would allow him to keep his composure. It didn't.

He pulled his hand away and covered his face. The flesh and bones of his hands were powerless to stop the outpouring of a soul ripped in half.

Time stopped. A minute may have passed, maybe an hour. Chambers couldn't tell and didn't care.

"It should have been me." It took herculean effort to push the words out.

"Don't talk that way." She drew a hand under her eyes. "I thought I lost you."

"I...I sensed something was wrong, but a bomb... It just never occurred to me. I was going to find Landau—"

"There's no way you could have known. No way. You can't blame yourself."

"I'm the team leader. Their safety is my responsibility." He returned his gaze to her. Her lower lip trembled. The sight of it ground to dust a heart already shattered.

"Not from bombs. Sure, you oversee dig site safety, but Landau and his people are responsible for our personal safety."

He repositioned himself on his side. "There's no hope, is there? For the others?"

"Landau is back at the scene. The army is there doing rescue work—"

"Answer my question."

This time Amber looked away. "No. They're dead. I don't see how they can't be. Gone." She paused. "You saved the professor. I don't know how you carried him up the tunnel and to safety."

"How is he? He was unconscious when I—"

Amber raised a hand to her mouth.

"What? Amber, what is it?"

Her lips moved, but the words were too soft to hear. He waited. She tried again. "I asked about his injuries, but they wouldn't tell me. They just said he was critical and not expected to live through the night."

Chambers's brain raced to process what he had just heard. "Help me up."

"No. You need to stay in bed. The doctor said—"

"Help me up, or leave. Lower the bed rail."

She hesitated, but then did as he ordered. Feeling less pain than he expected, Chambers swung his legs over the side. The room began to spin. He waited for the revolution to cease, then eased his bare feet to the cool sheet-vinyl floor. He noticed he was standing in his underwear. "See if you can't find a robe or hospital gown."

Amber slipped through the opening in the curtain and returned a moment later with an open-back hospital gown. "You shouldn't be doing this."

"I've been doing a lot of things I shouldn't lately. I want to see Ben-Judah. I owe him that."

"That may be more difficult that you think, Dr. Chambers." The voice was male and steady.

Chambers saw a pair of expensive-looking dress shoes just below the curtain.

The man spoke again. "May I come in?"

"I'm not in the mood for visitors."

A hand pulled aside the curtain anyway. The man who entered was stately, with an aquiline nose, gray hair that looked polished, and a suit that had a hand-tailored quality about it.

"Listen, pal, I said I wasn't in the mood for…visitors… Sir?"

"You know who I am?"

Chambers glanced at Amber, who looked dumbfounded. "Yes sir. I'm not much on foreign affairs, but I recognize Israel's prime minister when I meet him." He motioned to Amber. "Prime Minister Yakov, this is Dr. Amber Rodgers."

Yakov gave a small bow in her direction, then faced Chambers again. "Are you going somewhere?"

Chambers was suddenly aware of how silly he must look standing in a hospital gown, struggling to work the tie in the back. Amber came to his rescue. "Yes sir. I was going to check on one of my people."

"Dr. Ben-Judah?"

"Yes sir. He was injured—"

Yakov raised a hand. "I've been briefed. The professor and I go back many years. We did undergraduate work together. Obviously not in the same field." He smiled like a politician. "I wanted to personally thank you for your valiant efforts at the dig site. I understand you risked your own life to save the professor's and then returned to a tunnel which could collapse at any moment."

"No thanks necessary, sir. I just did what anyone would do in the same situation."

Yakov said an expletive in Hebrew. "I am a student of human nature, Dr. Chambers. I have to be in my position. Most men would have fled to save themselves. You did a heroic thing, and while you are in my country, I'll thank you not to dismiss my praise. There are hundreds of people who will tell you I don't do it often."

"Yes sir. I apologize."

"I have another question. The report I received said the cave-in was caused by a bomb. Do you agree?"

"Absolutely, sir."

"No chance that it was a buildup of flammable gas or a natural cave-in?"

"With all due respect, Mr. Prime Minister, I didn't get these burns from a natural cave-in." He turned to show the back of his neck and arms. "I can assure you that there was no gas buildup in the tunnel. We guard against such things."

Yakov nodded. "Thank you for being honest and straightforward with me. The nation of Israel owes you a debt of gratitude."

"Please, Mr. Prime Minister, do you have any word on the professor?"

Yakov's eyes narrowed. "What have you heard?"

"Amber...Dr. Rodgers said he's not expected to live through the night."

"An honest answer deserves one in return. Dr. Rodgers is correct. Ben-Judah is dying. We are about to suffer a great loss."

Chambers pinched the bridge of his nose in an effort to stop the emotional dam from breaking again.

Yakov's voice softened. "I am sorry to share that news with you. I know he counted you as a dear friend." The prime minister turned to leave.

"Mr. Prime Minister," Chambers said. "Were you serious when you said Israel owes me a debt of gratitude."

Yakov looked over his shoulder. "Of course."

"I'd like to call in that debt."

Yakov's eyebrows lifted. "Is that so, Dr. Chambers? What do you have in mind?"

TWENTY-ONE

Chambers and Amber followed Yakov as he and two security men moved through a back door of the ER and down a corridor. The painkillers he had received allowed David to walk without much of a limp, but the pain was making itself known. Doctors and nurses parted before them. They turned down another hall that led to a bank of elevators, which they rode to the top floor of the hospital. David saw a sign that read PRIVATE WING. He knew that hospitals in cities filled with dignitaries, ambassadors, stars, and high-ranking politicians had designated wings with private rooms where they could provide security and privacy from paparazzi. Rooms lined the corridor, each with its door closed. Two security officers stood at the start of the passageway. Their suit coats were unbuttoned, and Chambers could see handguns in shoulder holsters. They stepped aside as the prime minister led the way. They passed a nurses station where another guard sat watching video monitors.

Chambers felt conspicuous in his newly acquired robe. Apparently if the prime minister wanted a robe, he got a robe.

At the fifth door down on the north side of the wing stood one more suit-garbed security person: a woman who looked as if she hadn't smiled since grade school. At the sight of Yakov, she stepped to the center of the aisle and leaned to the side to see who followed the country's leader.

"Sir?"

"They're with me." Yakov answered the unspoken question.

"I was told it would just be you and the security detail."

"I know what you were told, and you are right to check, but as I said, they're with me."

Chambers could see her juggling the change in orders. She looked at the men with Yakov. "They're clear."

"Very good, sir." She moved to the door and opened it, then stepped aside. Yakov led them into the private room.

Chambers noticed several things: first, the room was large, more hotel than hospital; it had been professionally decorated; and Ben-Judah was sitting up in the hospital bed eating a sandwich and watching the news on television. He looked good. If he was on death's threshold, it was a very wide threshold. Ben-Judah switched off the television.

"David. I did not expect to see you." He pushed up in the bed and wiped at his beard. "You're not supposed to know I'm here."

Yakov moved to Ben-Judah's side and took his friend's hand. "He out-politicianed me, my friend. It's a shame he's wasting his time digging in the dirt and rescuing old men from cave-ins."

"I should have warned you about him, Nathan. He has his own way about him."

He calls the prime minister of Israel by his first name? Chambers was impressed.

"You can say that again," Amber said. "He's a snappy dresser too."

"David, my friend, I owe you my life. How are you? Your injuries?"

"I'm fine, Professor. Just a little dinged up, but you... I was told—"

"That I was dying. Yes, I know. In a way I am."

Chambers shook his head. "I don't understand."

"We would have told you eventually, David, but some things are out of our control." He seemed to have aged several years. "Five gone now. The student, and..." He couldn't finish the sentence. He addressed Yakov. "Nathan, is there any news from the investigation?"

"No, not yet. It is still too early. Dr. Chambers assures me it was an explosion. Our man Landau said he heard the blast. I've asked the army to investigate. I can keep a tighter lid on it with them than with local police."

"We have feared this from the beginning." He thought for a moment. "We must bring David, Amber, and Nuri into the circle. This is no longer just an academic dig or even a treasure hunt. They are risking their lives and the lives of others at the digs. They have a right to know."

"I am not so sure," Yakov said. "Secrecy has been our companion from the beginning."

"And it will continue to be so. David did save my life. I trust Amber as much as I trust you, Nathan."

"That's because she's prettier." The prime minster joked without changing his expression.

"Yes, this is true."

This time Yakov laughed, and it sounded genuine. He looked at the two men who had been at his side. "I need the room."

They left without a word. "Shall we?" Yakov pointed to a small seating area to the side of the room.

The space had a sofa, coffee table, and two leather chairs. Chambers lowered himself onto the sofa, careful about the stitches in his back, and stretched out his bum leg. It felt good to be off his feet. While he pretended to be untroubled about his injuries, the walk from the ER, the elevator to the top floor, and the few minutes standing in Ben-Judah's room had worn him out. He noticed Ben-Judah was a little wobbly, and the most powerful politician in the land had to help him to the chair.

Once seated, the politician and the professor exchanged glances. Ben-Judah took the lead. "First, I offer my apologies for not bringing you into my confidence earlier, but these decisions are not made by me alone."

Chambers began to feel uncomfortable.

Ben-Judah continued. "I have been up-front with you about the Copper Scroll and about John Trent's desire to find the treasures and artifacts. All of that is true, but there is more. We have a greater, more pressing desire. We believe we can change the world, not just with significant artifacts and the recovery of Jewish treasure, but in another way."

"You don't mean..." Chambers couldn't take his eyes of his mentor. "The temple? No, you can't be thinking that."

Ben-Judah fell silent.

"You are thinking that? Really? The temple. You think you can re-build the temple."

"Yes." Ben-Judah didn't waver. "We know we can."

"Oh Professor," Chambers said, "that's an illusion. It's been a long-held dream of the Jews since the first century. I know that. I get that. If I were Jewish, I'd want the same thing, but this isn't the first century. Things have changed."

"Not the important things, David."

Chambers rubbed his face. "I'd say the Dome of the Rock that sits on the temple location might be a problem. I'm just guessing here, but I don't think the Muslim Quarter is going to help you relocate their most holy site."

"Don't be snide, David," Amber said. "Give them a chance to explain."

"If this gets out, then we'll all be in more danger...than...before. Wait. It has gotten out, hasn't it? It must have."

"What are you getting at?" Amber looked frightened and embarrassed at the same time.

"Think about it, Amber. The explosion. Why blow up the tunnel if they were after the treasure? They weren't trying to get the treasure; they were trying to keep us from getting to it."

"Who?"

Yakov cleared his throat in the authoritative way a father quiets children without saying anything. All eyes turned his way.

"We don't have proof yet, but our intelligence forces believe Hussein Al-Malik is behind the troubles. He's a former Jordanian archaeologist turned terrorist leader working with an elite Hamas group. He has been very vocal in ridiculing the idea that we Jews have a connection to the Promised Land."

"You mentioned this back in one of our initial meetings, David." Ben-Judah rubbed the back of his neck.

"I did. In the 1980s, PLO head Yasser Arafat denied the historical kingdoms of David and Solomon. No one in the field took him seriously."

"But his followers did, and others have joined that chorus," Yakov said. "Al-Malik, a trained archaeologist, gives the lie credibility in the world, if not in the scientific community. We think he might be behind the murder of the Hebrew University student and the bombing of the tunnel. He has many followers, and it is very possible that he put one of his men on the team of workers who helped bring in equipment during the night. Such groups keep a large number of *clean* operatives on their payroll; people who have never been in trouble, have no police record, and have never been seen with known terrorists. They're sleepers, called upon only on special occasions. It will take some time to find out who carried in the explosives. I should tell you that investigators will want to talk to you both, especially you, Dr. Chambers, since you're the only living person to have seen the device." He stopped abruptly. "Forgive me. That was insensitive. I'm afraid that this job has made me more callous than is socially acceptable."

"You know for certain that Al-Malik is behind this?" Chambers hadn't had time to think about the *who* of the explosion, just the *fact* that it happened.

"We believe so, but don't ask how we know. I won't tell you." The prime minister sat stone faced.

"So how does Al-Malik know your intention? I lead the field teams, and I didn't know. Although I should have guessed."

Yakov answered. "My intelligence people tell me there is a mole in your group."

"Who?"

Yakov shook his head. "We don't know. If we did, we would know a great deal more."

The comment sounded ominous, and Chambers didn't want to know the threat behind the comment. He slipped to the edge of the sofa in preparation to stand, but the pain in his leg made him rethink the idea. He settled back. "I go back to my original comment. You can't rebuild the temple without destroying the Dome of the Rock, and you know what would happen then. Blood would flow in the gutters. Jewish blood. Muslim blood. Innocent blood."

"David," Ben-Judah began, "as you know, the exact location of the temple has been debated for centuries. We now have evidence that the true location is just north of the Dome of the Rock. We believe the ancient temples stood in a direct east-west line from the sealed Easter Gate to the Western Wall. It's a vast, open space with no significant Islamic shrines or mosques. There is no need to tear down their structure to build ours."

"This is madness. It's too dangerous, Professor. The Arab nations and their allies will stop at nothing to keep you from erecting a third temple in the middle of Jerusalem."

"Dr. Chambers, listen to me. My people are behind this. Two-thirds of the Israeli population want to see the temple rebuilt. That includes religious and secular Jews."

Amber spoke up. "Why would nonreligious Jews care?"

"Because the temple will make a statement to the world. Israel is here to stay. The Jewish state will be here forever."

"David, this is our land," Ben-Judah said. "God gave it to us through Father Abraham. The temple is the heart of our nation. Yes, there will be opposition. There was opposition against the world recognizing Israel as a valid country. The temple must be built."

"And you need the treasures mentioned in the Copper Scroll to fund its construction?" Amber asked.

"It's more than that, Amber." Chambers spoke before the others. "Think of the treasures mentioned. Our attention is drawn to the billion dollars of silver and gold, but there is mention of priestly garments, oil of anointing used for kings and high priests, gold vessels given as offerings, cups, sprinkling basins, libation pitchers, tithe vessels, sacred garments, and more. Now that I think about it, a billion dollars of gold and silver isn't that much in today's world. There are scores of billionaires, including John Trent. He could sell off a company and fund the rebuilding himself. The real treasure they want us to find has to do with temple artifacts. Isn't that right, Professor?"

"It is, David. As usual, you cut to the heart of the matter." Ben-Judah leaned forward. "Imagine it, David. A temple to rival the one of the first century, standing in the heart of the greatest city in the world. And you're making that happen."

Ben-Judah's word's ignited something in Chambers, but he kept his dour expression. "This can't end well."

"It can, David." Amber touched his arm. "If God wants this, then it will come to pass. You used to believe that. This is the kind of thing you lived for. Finding evidence proving the Bible's accuracy. Imagine the statement that would be made by finding artifacts associated with the temple."

"And it is not just the rebuilding of the temple, David. There's more." Ben-Judah spoke with renewed enthusiasm.

"Professor, please," Yakov said.

"He has the right to know everything. He nearly died for our mission."

Yakov frowned but waved the professor on. "You know, Abram is the only man on the planet who can speak to me that way."

"I have many childhood stories to tell on you, my friend. That's why you tolerate me." Ben-Judah sobered again. "You of course know of the Sanhedrin."

David cocked his head. "Yes. They were the ancient Jewish court. Twenty-three judges sat in every city in the land, and the Great Sanhedrin had seventy-one members. They met in the Hall of Hewn Stones at the

temple—well, in the first century they did. That body served as the su-
preme court. They dealt with religious and political life. Jesus was tried
before them."

"But it ended with the destruction of the temple by the Romans,"
Amber said.

"Not quite," David said. "Its power was greatly reduced, and it relo-
cated to various cities over time. Gamaliel VI was the last president. That
was in…" He struggled to recall the date. Ben-Judah rescued him.

"It was 425 of the Common Era. What else do you know, David?"

"There have been several attempts to revive it. Maimonides argued
that it should be reinstituted. That was during the twelfth century. If
memory serves, several rabbis have tried to re-create the Sanhedrin."

Ben-Judah nodded with each statement Chambers made. "Rabbi
Berab in 1538, Rabbi Shklover in 1830, Rabbi haCohen in 1901, Rabbi
Kovsker in 1940, and Rabbi Maimon in 1949."

"The most recent attempt," Yakov said, "was undertaken in Tishrei
5765—October 2004. They followed the suggestions outlined by Maimonides eight hundred years earlier and performed a ceremony in Tibe-
rias, the city that saw the end of the Sanhedrin. It was controversial and
did not receive full support."

Amber looked puzzled. "Are you telling us that you plan to reconsti-
tute the Sanhedrin?"

Ben-Judah grinned like a man with a deep, rich secret. "Not planning, my dear. We have done as you say."

Chambers blinked several times. "What?"

Yakov answered. "It remains a secret, but the assembly exists. Dr.
Abram Ben-Judah is the president. Our membership is select and includes
key Israeli cabinet ministers, as well as leaders from the Orthodox Jewish
religious party."

Painful leg or not, Chambers couldn't sit any longer. He paced the
space, head down, mind a tornado of whirling thoughts. "I should have

guessed this. I should've seen it coming." He ran a hand through his hair. "Madness. Insanity. Jerusalem isn't a unity; it's a composite of Jews, Christians, Islamics, and the secular. Each claim ownership. Now, I'm sympathetic to the Jewish plight. I have always sided with Israel—"

"You have been a friend to Israel," Ben-Judah said. "We need your friendship more than ever."

"What you're asking goes beyond dangerous. It's suicidal. Not just for us, but for everyone who lives in the city. You mean it for good, but it will be seen as an act of war."

"Let me worry about that, Dr. Chambers." Yakov had crossed his arms in front of his chest, a defensive bit of body language. Chambers didn't care.

"Forgive me, Mr. Prime Minister, but I am not known for subtlety—"

"I've heard."

"Okay, I have that coming. Maybe I am a little reactionary of late…" He looked at Amber. "But this goes beyond that. I just lost four members of my team. Blown to bits. Their burned and fractured bodies crushed by tons of stone. A student just trying to earn a little money was murdered because of this. Maybe that's made me a little paranoid, but all of that will seem insignificant compared to what will happen if this gets out. If we find what you're looking for, if you set up a third temple, then half the world will descend on you. On us. How many more are you willing to let die?"

Ben-Judah's face revealed how much the question pained him. "Such things rest in the hands of *HaShem,* David, not in ours. We are responsible to do only His will, not ours or our neighbors."

"Such is the problem of religion. People do what they want and shove the responsibility off on God."

"David!" Amber snapped her head around to see the still pacing Chambers.

"You didn't used to think so, my friend. Once your faith was as deep as the ocean." Ben-Judah's words were saturated with sadness.

The old man's tone sent an ice pick through Chambers's heart. He loved Ben-Judah more than he loved his own father. To see his mentor wounded by his words grieved him, but the heat of anger refused to be extinguished.

"I don't want any part in starting civil war." He rethought the phrase. "A world war. I'm done." He stared at Amber. "If you have a brain, you'll quit too."

"No. And you won't insult me into making a decision I don't want to make. You can bail if you want to. You're good at it. Just leave me out of your decisions."

"David," Ben-Judah pleaded. "Please. The work is so important. I believe *HaShem* has called you to help with this great effort. It's why I brought you into our confidence."

"If God has called me to this, then I didn't get the memo. You'll have to carry on without me. I'm not ready to die yet."

He started for the door, stopped, and turned. "I'm glad you are well, Professor. I'm sorry it all had to end this way."

Ben-Judah turned his face away and said nothing.

Yakov stood. "Dr. Chambers, what you have heard requires the utmost secrecy. I must insist you keep these things to yourself."

"No worries, Mr. Prime Minister. I plan to do my best to forget I was ever part of this conversation." One last glance at Amber. She looked like a delicate crystal he had just thrown to the concrete.

David Chambers walked from the room leaving behind the only friends he had.

∽

Amber was in a battle with her emotions. Profound sadness diluted the anger she felt over David's outburst. Pain from hearing his snide remarks about God mingled with impatience over his childishness. Most of all she felt a part of her die when he stormed from the room. A part of her, a very secret part of her she kept hidden from the rest of her mind, held onto the spider-web-thin strand of hope that he might once again become the man she loved.

A hand touched her shoulder. Ben-Judah had moved to the sofa and sat next to her. "There is still hope, my dear. There is always hope."

She couldn't speak. One word would unhinge what little composure remained.

Yakov rose and walked to the door. He whispered to one of his security men, then left the room.

TWENTY-TWO

The local anesthetics began to wear off before David arrived back at the hotel. The cab ride, piloted by a cabby who leaned on the horn as much as he did the brake, didn't help. Although his doctor and nurses warned him that leaving the hospital early was unwise, they were gracious enough to send him away with a bottle of Vicodin, and Chambers wasn't too proud to take it. Every muscle complained about the strain of having carried Ben-Judah up the steep, narrow tunnel. The scratches and puncture wounds from flying bits of stone were not deep, but they stung as if the doctor had used salt to cleanse the wounds.

By the time he exited the cab, made his way to his room, and removed his dirt-caked clothing, he was feeling enough pain to slow his movement. He had planned to throw his belongings into his suitcase and travel bag and be out the door in fifteen minutes. An hour later, he was still emptying his closet and gathering his toiletries.

Jumbled thoughts tumbled in his brain, all of them bathed in a wash of anger and incredulity. He should never have accepted Ben-Judah's invitation. He had been right to leave biblical archaeology. Another year wouldn't matter, he had told himself, then he could turn his back on it all, but the lure of hidden treasure and the history-changing artifacts got the best of him. Now he regretted his decision. It all started south when he learned Nuri would be one of the lead archaeologists. Then learning that Ben-Judah had recruited Amber—well, he told himself, that's when he should have walked away and never looked back.

He was laying another pair of well-worn jeans in the suitcase when he heard a knock on the door. He followed his first impulse and ignored the intrusion. More knocking, this time more insistent. Chambers moved to the door and peered at the security monitor.

Amber.

He sighed, leaned forward and rested his head on the door. He was tired. So tired. Tired of his past, tired of this day, tired of the pain—physical and emotional.

"I'm not going away, David." The door muffled her voice.

"I'm not here."

"Very funny. You're a real comedian. Now let me in."

"I'm not decent."

"Yeah? Well, everyone in the world knows that. Open up."

"Go away, Amber."

There was a pause. He could see on the monitor that she stood, arms crossed. "Here's the deal, David. I'm going to stay here and get louder and louder until you let me in."

He unlatched the door and pulled it open an inch, then walked away. He'd let her open the door for herself. Which she did. He returned to his packing.

"I see you're packing."

"It's insights like that, that make you such a fine scientist."

"This is so you, David. Things change, things refuse to go the way you like, and you pack up and leave."

He faced her. She still wore the dusting of the catastrophe a few hours earlier. "You know me that well, do you?"

"I know your history. I'm part of it."

He moved to the closet, removed the last of his hanging clothes, and returned to the bed where he had set his bag and suitcase. "You don't know me as well as you think you do."

"I know you better than you know yourself. You love the limelight. You like being the center of academic attention. But when things get rough, you love to leave."

"That's nonsense."

"I don't think so, David. You are a self-centered egotist who enjoys feeling lousy about life."

"No one enjoys feeling lousy about life—"

"You do. I've never met anyone who was so dissatisfied with happiness. You sabotaged your relationship with your father and with me. Now you've blown up the bridge that linked you to the kindest, most loving man in this hemisphere."

"I did no such thing."

"You turned your back on the professor. It crushed him."

"I doubt that—"

"I was there after you left. When will you learn your words have consequences? Your mother would be ashamed of the way you've been acting."

"Well, she's not, and do you know why, Amber? Because she's dead. She died with just me by her side. My father couldn't be bothered with her terminal illness. He was too busy digging in this forsaken land, trying to prove his faith was real. He would have done better by me if he showed the love his faith promotes."

"Like you're doing?"

"I gave that up. When I was a child, I thought like a child—"

"Don't you dare misquote Scripture to suit your purposes! You don't do that in my presence, ever."

"I'll be out of your presence soon enough. Besides, you don't get to dictate to me what I can and can't say, not when you use my dead mother to manipulate me."

Amber moved to the other side of the bed and turned down the heat in her tone. "You know, she lied to your father."

"Be careful, Amber; be very careful what you say. My mother was a saint."

"I know she was. I love her for her patience and strength. Most of all, I love her for her faith."

"You only met her a few times."

"It was enough. And we talked on the phone several more times. My heart broke when she died. At first, I thought I was feeling bad for you, but I was grieving too."

"Yet you stand there and tell me my mother was a liar." He tossed his shirts into the suitcase unfolded.

"I said she lied to your father. He was here in the Holy Land in the middle of an important dig. He told her he was coming home, but she objected. In fact, she forbade it. Your mother told him she was doing better when she wasn't. He continued to work thinking she was on the mend."

"She was not in the habit of lying to him or to me."

"That's the point, David. Your father trusted her without question. If she said she was getting well, that the doctors were very positive, then he would believe her. And she did. And he did."

The words came like a sledgehammer to the sternum. "How do you know this?"

"Unlike some people I know, I've talked to your father. Your father and mother loved each other. They loved the Lord. They shared a passion for truth and archaeology. Too bad their son didn't inherit any of their more noble qualities."

Chambers didn't speak, couldn't speak.

Amber raised a hand to her forehead, a hand that trembled. "You know what? I'm done. I've got nothing more. Do what you want. Leave. Run away. We'll take care of the dead. You fly home. You go back to your condo and feel sad about how life has been unfair to you while we bury four people who died doing their job."

She stomped to the door, then stopped just short of it. "I just realized something: I'm glad you're leaving." She opened the door and turned. "One last thing: call your father!"

Chambers heard a sob, then the sound of a closing door.

෪

The cab ride to Tel Aviv lasted a millennium. The cabbie was a talkative Russian Jew who had an opinion about everything and didn't seem to care that Chambers had stopped listening by the time they exited the hotel parking lot. Chambers spent the hour-long, traffic-hindered drive to Ben-Gurion International Airport fighting off the gut-twisting memories of the tunnel explosion, Ben-Judah's heartbreaking countenance, the bizarre plan to rebuild the temple and reestablish the Sanhedrin, and Amber's words that burned him like hot coals dropped into his stomach.

"Don't you agree?" The cabbie said. To Chambers it sounded like the man gargled with battery acid.

"About what?"

"The Iranians. Haven't you been listening?"

"I'm afraid I'm preoccupied."

"You do look like you have had a rough day."

Chambers pursed his lips. "I tell you what: you stop talking and drive, and I'll toss an extra ten shekels on the tip."

"Done."

The stinging, angry bees of regret swarmed his mind again. What he wouldn't give for a few hours in oblivion. Amber had no right to speak to him like that. Especially on a day so full of turmoil. He nearly died in that tunnel, but she seemed to have already forgotten that. Then he recalled her digging at the fallen mass of ceiling that had crushed their team. She had raced into the tunnel after him. How could he overlook that? He couldn't. It was a memory branded on the soft tissue of his brain.

The cab pulled to the passenger unloading area, and the driver unloaded Chambers's luggage. As promised, Chambers bumped up the tip. The Russian said thank you with a gap-toothed smile. Lugging the bags out of the room had reminded Chambers of his injuries. The thought of schlepping the luggage through the airport was too painful to consider. He motioned for a baggage man and slipped him a few shekels to carry his things to the ticket counter.

As they started forward, Chambers noticed a man wearing a beige polo-style shirt, a pair of slacks, and blue blazer. He was Chambers's size, a little round in the torso, and wore wire-rimmed glasses. He looked like an accountant or midlevel executive. Except for his eyes. The man's eyes lingered on David a tad too long. Something set off alarms in his mind.

Chambers returned the gaze, then followed the porter through the glass entrance and into the lobby. They moved through crowds and over highly polished floors. He was directing the porter to the El Al counter when a movement caught his attention. The man with the wire-rimmed glasses had followed them in. Why one man in the midst of scores of other people moving in the busy airport gave him a sense of dread, he didn't know. It had to be nerves. He had, after all, barely escaped death.

It seemed like a year ago. He had expended more energy in one day than he had in the previous several months. A woman moved in front of him; a woman who looked remarkably like Amber. The resemblance brought Amber's words, anger, sadness, and dedication to mind in a tsunami of emotion.

Why? Why should he care? She was the one who broke off the engagement.

Because you changed, moron. His inner voice never minced words. He was as brutal with himself as he was with others.

Chambers stopped at the long line of people waiting to buy tickets or check luggage. He wondered how long he'd be on standby before an empty seat became available.

"You go back to your condo and feel sad about how life has been unfair to you while we bury four people who died doing their job." Amber's words would not go away. He tried to focus on other things, tried to imagine how good it would feel to sleep in his own bed.

It was useless. He couldn't exorcize Amber's words or the way she appeared at his doorstep. How could he leave? Departing in such a hurry would look bad to the investigators. Ben-Judah would cover for him, but what right did he have to expect that? He had no right. He had made a commitment to this project and now he was walking away. Worse, he was leaving Amber behind to face any danger alone. Nuri would be no help. She might like him, but Chambers didn't trust the man.

"The line has moved."

Chambers came back to the present. "Excuse me?"

A man who looked twenty and wore his hair in dreadlocks pointed at the line. "It's moving, man. You going to close up the gap, or what?" He sounded British. London accent.

Chambers looked at the ticket line that had moved several feet in the cue. "No. No, I'm not. Go ahead."

Ignoring the pain, Chambers grabbed his bag and rolling suitcase and hobbled to the lobby doors. Two realizations came to him at once. First, he was not the kind of man who quit; two, he loved Amber Rodgers and he was going to prove it.

⤳

The ride back to Jerusalem took less time than going. Night had settled on the city that some considered the heart of the world. The day's events and the trip to and back from the Tel Aviv–located airport had drained Chambers of what little strength he had left. He felt like a shipwreck. As he limped through the lobby, he saw Amber, Landau, and Nuri walking into the restaurant. He set his luggage by the front desk and asked that a bellhop take it to his room. Since the floor was secured and had no other guests, he had no doubts that his room would still be available. He then walked into the restaurant and headed to what had become "their" table. Landau was the first to notice him.

"Dr. Rodgers just told me you had left for good."

"I did. I'm back." He made eye contact with Amber. "Word from the site?"

Landau gazed at the table and looked like a man who wished he was anything but what he was.

"The army recovered the bodies. No word on the type of explosive device."

It was the answer Chambers expected but didn't want to hear.

A moment later, Amber asked, "Care to join us?"

Chambers saw Nuri roll his eyes, which was almost enough reason to say yes. Instead, he said, "No thank you. I'm going to order room service, then go to bed. Tomorrow we start working to make sure our team didn't die in vain."

TWENTY-THREE

Four weeks later

O fficially, David Chambers was the leader of the multiple dig sites; unofficially, Chambers still reported to the sequestered Abram Ben-Judah and to John Trent. Landau and his superiors believed it best to let the world think Ben-Judah had died with the others. Although Chambers never asked, he assumed the other secret members of the new Sanhedrin had been informed of the ruse, but he had no way of knowing if such was the case.

What he did know was that he spent more time traveling between sixteen search sites. Most came up empty, although several interesting artifacts had been found. And some very valuable ones. Using new satellite sweeps and airborne T-ray scans, Chambers, Nuri, and Amber had been able to find the tomb mentioned in lines five and six of the Copper Scroll. Since the land was littered with ancient tombs, finding the right one seemed impossible. The description, like all descriptions in the Scroll, was vague: "The third course of stones in the tomb, one hundred wrought gold articles." The question was, which tomb?

"It has to be a tomb well known to the Essene community at the site of our first find. Simply saying in 'the tomb' with no more details indicates a sepulcher of someone significant, maybe one of the sect's leaders. Let's focus on tombs near site one. There must be a cemetery in the area."

"It would probably be off the site," Amber said. "They wouldn't bury their dead in their compound."

Chambers assigned the search to Nuri, who surveyed the region using helicopter-mounted ground-penetrating radar followed by detailed electronic surveys over any promising site. It took two weeks, but Nuri found a likely candidate: a tomb buried two meters beneath a hillside slide. A one-meter-high stone marker lay on its side covered with the landslide debris. The team estimated that two acres of cliff-side material gave way, perhaps during an ancient storm.

As before, Chambers wanted to take as much time as possible to excavate, but digging began almost immediately. The site looked like a military camp. Even then, Landau remained nervous. Surveillance aircraft buzzed overhead; every worker was searched before being allowed on the camp site; armed guards in military vehicles and on foot kept a ready perimeter around the area. No cameras other than those used by Amber were permitted.

There were other changes. There would be no more aides. Chambers and Landau agreed that having people that close to the primary archaeologists was a danger to all involved. In a private moment, Chambers admitted to Amber that he could not stand the thought of losing someone like Joel Rubin again. His nights were often disrupted with nightmares; nightmares that included the image of Joel's broken body being excavated from the rubble.

Chambers and Nuri uncovered the tomb in short order. As a matter of professional protocol, David let Nuri oversee every aspect of the excavation, leaving David free to observe and occasionally help Amber with photo work and other recording of data.

The Essenes had built the sepulcher from indigenous cut stone and laid it in an ingenious manner. It had endured centuries buried beneath the fallen side of the hill, yet its walls remained unbowed and with no signs of cracking, which was especially remarkable since friction, not grout, held the blocks in place.

A thick stone covered the entrance, reminding Chambers of the wheel-like stone said to have been rolled in front of Jesus' tomb.

"A square sealing stone," Amber had said. "We know what that means."

Nuri nodded. "It wasn't a family tomb. No need to open it again."

"The Essenes were celibate, which means no families, therefore no need for a family tomb." Chambers touched the thick stone door. "Of course, they might have used burial caves for the regular members. This is for someone special."

"Or something special," Amber said. "Like a treasure."

"Only one way to find out."

The workers were sent home except for a crane operator, one of Landau's men. It took several hours to prepare for the removal of the stone. When the nylon straps were in place, the crane operator gently removed it. Air that had been sealed in the tomb for twenty centuries rushed out the moment the door had been pulled away.

With flashlights blazing, the three entered where no one had been since it was first closed.

"I estimate the interior to be five meters by five meters." Chambers scanned the room.

"About the size of a bedroom," Amber said.

"Except the ceiling is also five meters up." Nuri aimed the beam of his light up. "A perfect cube."

"Gotta love their symmetry." Amber's voice echoed in the space.

"Mind if I join you?"

Chambers didn't have to turn to know it was Landau speaking. "There's plenty of room."

"It's empty." Landau joined the three huddled in the middle. "I was expecting a corpse."

"Or a mummy, maybe."

"I'm not that ignorant, Dr. Aumann. I know the ancients didn't mummify the dead. I mean there's no bone box. There's nothing here."

"So where do we start?" Amber said. "The Copper Scroll says 'in the third section or course of stones.' Does that mean the third up from the floor, or the third down from the top?"

Chambers counted the courses. "I count fifteen courses of block, all the same size. Placing it low would make it easier to hide, but placing it high would make it more difficult to retrieve." He considered the situation. "What little we know of the Essenes tells me they would choose the difficult over the easy."

"Makes sense," Amber said. She directed the beam of the light to the ceiling, then moved it down three courses of stone. "That's a tad out of our reach. It's what? Twelve feet above the floor?" She looked at Landau, who got the hint.

"Sure, all my training and experience makes me the ideal man to retrieve a ladder."

"You're very gracious," she said. "A little sarcastic, but gracious."

"You thinking what I'm thinking, Nuri?" Chambers moved to the back wall and touched it. The stone felt cool.

"I am if you are thinking the tomb was partly built into the side of the hill—which would make it easier to create a space with a false wall."

"Exactly. But it's still just a guess."

"As much as it pains me to agree with you," Nuri said, "I think your guess is a good one. I'll get the portable T-ray scanner and the GPR. If there is a space somewhere in the wall, we'll find it."

They found it ninety minutes later. Three courses down from the ceiling and three meters from the east wall, the GPR revealed a cluttered space. Nuri set up the T-ray device, and Chambers operated the business end while Nuri analyzed the readings.

A few moments later Nuri began to laugh. "Gold, my friends. We have strong readings of gold."

Chambers pushed against one of the stones, but it refused to budge. "There's no way to get a hold of an edge."

"Leave that to me." Nuri set down the monitor and exited the sepulcher, returning a few moments later with a cordless power drill and an extra battery. He also carried a large framing hammer. Chambers's stomach turned, but he didn't object. Silently he descended the ladder and surrendered to Nuri.

Nuri had thought to bring a masonry bit. The hand drill filled the space with its high-pitched whine as the bit bored into the stone. Amber recorded every step of the process. Several minutes after he began, Nuri stepped down the ladder a few rungs and handed the power tool to Landau, then asked Chambers for the hammer. Chambers frowned as he handed it over.

Back up the ladder, Nuri removed from his jeans pocket a cylindrical metal sleeve that he inserted into the borehole. He tapped it in with his hammer, then retrieved an eyebolt from his pocket. He threaded it into the expansion sleeve, which widened with every turn.

"Mr. Landau, if you please."

Landau jogged from the tomb and returned with a coil of nylon rope, which Nuri threaded through the eyebolt and tied off. He descended the ladder and moved it out of the way. He paused and looked at the others for a moment, as if seeking their permission to proceed.

"Do it." Thrill dulled the regret David felt about moving so fast with such an ancient find.

Nuri tugged. Nothing. He tugged again, and Chambers thought he saw a tiny bit of grit fall from one of the joints.

"Do you want me to give it a try?" Landau seemed eager to have something to do.

Nuri didn't hesitate to hand over the rope.

"You can catch the stone when I pull it free." Landau smiled. Chambers was stunned.

"Hilarious."

Nuri didn't return the grin. It was an odd change of behavior. As the days passed, Nuri became more sullen as Landau became a little more approachable, almost human. Chambers barely understood himself, so he had given up trying to understand others.

"Stand by." Landau tugged, then yanked. On his third try, he put his weight behind it. The stone came free, plunged to the floor, and broke into three pieces.

Chambers stepped to the fragments. "It's thinner than I expected. More of a veneer stone."

"Makes sense." Amber stood by his side. "The wall isn't structural. At least not this part of it."

"Make room." With Landau's help, Nuri muscled the ladder back in place. "Time to demonstrate my genius again."

Chambers and Amber stepped back and gave the man the room he needed. He wasted no time climbing to the opening left behind by the stone. He directed the beam of his flashlight into the void.

"What do you see?" Amber asked.

"Nothing, my dear." He reached into the space. "Nothing but gold." He removed an ingot of dust-covered gold. "And this little one has many friends."

True to the description in the Copper Scroll, there were one hundred bars.

~

There were other finds: the remains of a small, simple wood chest filled with nearly two hundred ancient shekels; a clay jar holding a vellum scroll with guidelines for life in an Essene compound. Opening the scroll was delicate work, and Chambers assigned the work to specialists at the Institute, but he was able to see enough of the writing on the fragments broken away over the years to recognize it as a copy of a document found in the fifties. Presumably, every conclave of Essenes had one or more of the documents.

Chambers met with Ben-Judah weekly in the hospital room that had been converted to a small apartment. Often the meeting included a teleconference with Trent. In each of those cases, the background behind the billionaire was different. Chambers got the idea that Trent was in a different location every time.

This time the meeting was just between the professor and Chambers. Landau drove Chambers to these meetings. He explained it was for security reasons. The explanation was unnecessary since Chambers had become a member of the society of paranoids. Having nearly been killed and buried at the same time had made him suspicious of nearly everyone. He didn't question Landau's circuitous path from the hotel to the hospital. It was never the same. Chambers guessed that several of Landau's men followed in other cars.

This night, they entered the hospital through the emergency room. Seeing the place where he had been a patient made David uneasy, but this night, at least, he wasn't in need of stitches or a leg brace. For that he was thankful.

Landau escorted Chambers past the ever-present guards and into Ben-Judah's room. As was Ben-Judah's custom, he rose the minute Chambers entered the room and embraced him.

"David, my son. Seeing you always does my heart good." Ben-Judah led him to the seating area.

"Always a pleasure to spend time with you, Professor."

They sat, and Ben-Judah settled into the leather side chair. Chambers had always known his mentor to be a frugal man with simple tastes and doubted that he had such a nice chair in his own home.

"Do they ever let you out of here?" Chambers sat on the end of the sofa closest to Ben-Judah's chair.

"They do, David, but I can't say more than that. It is for my own security, and I find it quite comfortable here. I am able to do my work and follow your progress. I do the same here I would do from my office. It is important to keep things as they are."

"I'm glad you're comfortable."

Ben-Judah stroked his beard. "Your latest find is more than amazing, David. So much gold in one place, and the way you discerned its location. You are amazing."

"It was Nuri who made the find. He is a technical whiz. It pains me to admit it."

"You still do not like him? After all these weeks? After the success you and he have had?"

"And Amber. I have no problem with Nuri's research and field skills. He just rubs me the wrong way. Always has."

"Of course. I did not mean to exclude her. You harbor ill will because you think he is taking Amber away from you."

Chambers cut his gaze away. "Amber doesn't belong to me. We're not a couple anymore."

"Not yet." A moment later, Ben-Judah added, "But this is none of my business. You are adults, and I am not your father."

"I don't always act like an adult."

Ben-Judah gave an exaggerated nod. "Yes, this is very true."

"You were supposed to contradict me."

"Yes, I know."

They shared a laugh, then Ben-Judah turned serious. "David, great progress has been made in finding the treasures of the Copper Scroll. Two significant treasures amounting to tens of millions of dollars..."

"But..."

"But I need you to focus on the nonprecious metals. Continue your search of course, but we are most eager to find the other artifacts."

"By other artifacts, you mean things listed in the scroll that have to do with the ancient priestly work?"

"Am I that obvious?"

"No, just logical. You want to rebuild the temple, and a temple is useless without a priesthood."

"Gold and silver hordes we've found prove the validity of the scroll, so we can trust that these items are there, too. For us to reach our goal—our larger goal—then we must focus on the greater treasure: the holy artifacts of the temple."

The change in emphasis did not surprise Chambers. He had been expecting it. During the first phase of the search, they had focused on things that high-tech space, air, and ground surveys could show them: underground cavities, tunnels, and tombs. Since so many of the locations described in the Copper Scroll were intentionally vague and the terrain so different after two thousand years, Chambers focused on "hard sites," with well-defined structure that could be detected at a distance.

"You know those will be the most difficult things to find."

"Of course I know that." Ben-Judah paused. "I am sorry, David. For the first time in my professional career, I have been afflicted with impatience."

"Impatience is an archaeologist's greatest obstacle."

Ben-Judah lowered his gaze. "The student quotes the teacher's lesson back to him."

"I meant it as a compliment."

Ben-Judah rose and paced the room, his hands clasped behind his back, head down, eyes fixed on the carpet. Chambers let the man have his silence. Finally:

"There's more I have to tell you, David. It has to do with a tunnel. Your tunnel."

"My tunnel. Which one... You mean Herod's tunnel?"

"Yes. We've found something."

Chambers sat in silence pondering the sudden revelation. Ben-Judah took the silence to mean Chambers was upset.

"I am sorry to give you this news so suddenly. I should have been more up-front with you, but you have been… I'm not sure how to say this."

"Reactive?"

"Yes, yes. Reactive. That is a good word. On several occasions you've been emotional."

"Don't I get some credit for coming back?" He hoped his grin softened his words.

The professor stopped his pacing. "Of course, David. Of course, it's just that I needed you to focus on proving the reality of the Scroll's treasures. You have done that." He pursed his lips before speaking again. "After your discovery of Herod the Great's escape tunnel and the initial survey and investigation, you handed the research over to the Institute and the Israel Antiquities Authority."

"I remember." Chambers remembered wanting to finish his portion of the work so he could leave the world of biblical archaeology behind.

"I'm sure you do. What you do not know is that I took an initiative and called in some favors. I oversaw the ongoing research."

"That's wonderful, Professor. I can't think of anyone else I'd rather have finish the work."

"I only provided oversight and direction. Others did the hard work."

"Why are you telling this to me now?"

Ben-Judah took his seat again, leaned forward and stared into Chambers's eyes. "We found something." He took a breath. "Another tunnel."

"Another tunnel. You mean an adjoining tunnel?"

"Yes. Cleverly hidden. It was in a debris area. We think it was built at the same time as the original tunnel."

Chambers leaned back and tried to take in what he was hearing. "Another tunnel—branching off the one I discovered? How could I have missed that?"

"You were in a hurry to leave. You had made up your mind to never return to God's land."

The words stung. He had missed a great find, probably one of significance. "What did you find when you opened it?"

"It hasn't been opened, David. That's for you to do. I continued the work while you and the others were searching for the treasures. The area has been cleared, and we have done GPR and echo work to identify the size and shape of the opening. The builders went to great trouble to conceal the location."

"Wait. No one has been in the tunnel? Why?"

"Because, David, it may hold what we're looking for. It may hold priestly treasures."

Chambers rose and began his own pacing. "This is remarkable."

"You are not angry with your old professor?"

"Angry with you? Of course not. I knew work would continue after I left, although I admit that an adjoining tunnel hadn't occurred to me. No, I'm not angry with you. I am, however, angry with myself."

"You are making amends, David. I want you to open the tunnel as soon as possible. Will you do that?"

"Gladly."

The phone on the side table rang. Ben-Judah answered, *"Shalom."* He listened, then said to Chambers, "It's John Trent. He says we should turn on the television."

TWENTY-FOUR

B ecause history belongs to all people, not just the Jews." Al-Malik spoke softly, almost contemplatively. He had been rehearsing for this interview. Anticipating questions. Planting prompts in his answers to trigger desirable questions in the mind of the questioner. He was planting something else. Key words would telegraph unspoken orders to his followers.

"Do you object to the advancement of science, Dr Al-Malik?"

Michael Mitchell, you are an idiot as well as an infidel. Al-Malik looked at the artificially blond, tanned, slim American reporter sitting in a chair on the other side of the small coffee shop table. The shop was empty. He had seen to that. Still, the smell of cigarette smoke hung in the air and clung to the walls. As the star overseas reporter for the world's largest cable news station, Mitchell had followers around the world. He had covered breaking news in Pakistan, India, Sudan, and throughout his own country. Al-Malik seldom missed a broadcast, more for entertainment than hard facts.

"Of course not, Mr. Mitchell. Your questions show your Western-world bias. We Arabs do not object to science. In fact, our ancestors created what has become contemporary math and made early advancements in medicine. I object to science that is conducted in secret, on or near land rightfully owned by Arabs. We are the father to many branches of contemporary science. Arabs are not a backward people. I, myself, have earned a PhD in archaeology. I object to the Israelis digging up land as they search for artifacts they do not share with the world."

"What kind of artifacts?"

Al-Malik couldn't believe the question or the questioner. "I am sorry, Mr. Mitchell. I know to your ears my accent is thick. Perhaps I was unclear when I said the Israelis were keeping the artifacts secret." He managed to sound sincere despite the fact he knew everything that had been found.

"Some might say that this is sour grapes, Dr. Al-Malik, that you're jealous of their finds."

"People are free to think as they wish, but they would be wrong. I, and many Arab leaders like me, believe that there is much to learn from our past. By that, I mean the past of the Arabs and the Jews and even ancient civilizations like the Canaanites, Hittites, Jebusites, and others who occupied this land before the Israelis."

"So you believe they are being unfair to Arabs?"

"To the whole world, Mr. Mitchell." Al-Malik swung his arms wide to emphasize his point, careful not to spill the untouched cup of coffee in front of him. "As they have done in the past, the Jews are showing that they believe they are more important than their neighbors, privileged above all others. This is offensive arrogance."

"What do you want them to do, Dr. Al-Malik?"

"They should stop working in secret. They should reveal what they have found. They should make important artifacts available for study."

"But isn't it true that the work began just two months or so ago?" Mitchell glanced at the camera and for a moment Al-Malik thought the man was going to wink at his audience.

"No, plans and early work began long ago. Now they have a dozen teams digging in the wilderness and in the towns and cities all over this land, disturbing commerce and the lives of people who wish only to be allowed to go about their business."

"Why do I think you believe there is more to their story?"

"Only you can answer that, Mr. Mitchell, but I would not be surprised if you are right. They are up to something, something that should cause not only Arabs to rise up in protest, but also the rest of the thinking world."

"Thank you for your time and insights, Dr. Al-Malik." Mitchell turned to the camera. "We have made repeated attempts to get a spokesman from the Israel Antiquities Authority and the Institute of Archaeology at Hebrew University here in Jerusalem to speak to us, but they have refused to return our calls. Perhaps Dr. Al-Malik is right; maybe something is being hidden. This is Michael Mitchell reporting from Jerusalem."

It took great restraint for Al-Malik not to smile.

∽

The report aired at 9:00 p.m. on the east coast of the United States. President Baker D. Meyers reached for the remote on the Queen Anne side table by the beige leather smoking chair in his office just off the bedroom he shared with his wife, Leah. He pushed the mute button. On his lap rested the first draft of a speech he was to give at UCLA in two days. A cold had sidelined his head of communications, and his staff had prepared the draft. It was good, but it still lacked something.

Alone in his private office, he found time to unwind and be creative. He seldom made it to the second floor residence wing before ten in the evening. Tonight he arrived a little over an hour early. His aides had told him that Michael Mitchell would be interviewing Dr. Al-Malik, and that was something that Meyers didn't want to miss, so he brought his work to the residence. It wasn't the first time. It wouldn't be the last.

With his own television silenced, he could hear the distant sounds of Leah's set playing in the bedroom. It sounded like a cop show. He wondered when he last watched a television show that didn't have to do with history or world events.

Meyers lifted the receiver of his phone and tapped a button connecting him to the office of his chief of staff, the only man who worked harder and longer than the president. He seldom left for home before eleven.

"Tony, did you catch the Al-Malik interview?"

At five foot seven, Anthony Cleese was shorter than the president by four inches, and vegetarian thin, but he had a mind that retained everything and could predict the political landscape months in advance.

"Yes sir. Let me guess. You want to know if Al-Malik was giving more than an interview."

"Right as always. Let's get info from CIA and NSA. I want to know if there's chatter out there we should be concerned about."

"Yes sir. I'll push your security briefing back a few hours to give them time to get their ducks in a row."

"Good idea. Let's make it a lunch. Casual. Tuna sandwiches or something. That'll give them the whole morning to shake the trees and see what falls out."

"Yes sir. Will do."

"Good. Then go home and hug your wife."

"Yes sir."

∽

"Did you see the news last night?" Amber was seated in the private dining room in the hotel restaurant. They ate all their meals there since Landau kept it locked when not in use and frequently swept it for listening devices. Nuri sat next to her.

"Yeah, we saw it." Chambers's stomach cringed as soon as the words left his mouth.

"We?" Nuri cocked an eyebrow. "Who is 'we'?"

"What? I can't have a friend?" Amber's eyes widened by a fraction.

Nuri smirked. "What kind of friend? Someone of the female persuasion?"

"Let it go, Nuri. Not everyone has an out-of-control libido."

Taking a seat opposite the two, he set down a notebook with loose pages. Amber spoke. "You look horrible. Didn't you sleep last night?"

"Some, and thank you for the compliment." In truth, he had slept—at his desk. Ben-Judah's new direction wasn't a surprise, but the timing threw him; that and the Al-Malik interview. He couldn't pin it down, but he had a bad feeling about what he heard. "We're going to make a change in our search emphasis."

"Oh, is that a fact." Nuri seemed put out. "And why are we doing that?"

"Because it is what the professor would want if he were still calling the shots. We owe him this and much more."

Nuri took a slow sip of coffee, then set his cup down. "I do not wish to sound unsympathetic, but the professor is gone." He shot up a hand before Chambers could speak. "I loved the old man as much as anyone, but unless you have become a medium channeling Ben-Judah's departed spirit, then you cannot know what he would want."

"He told me." The three words landed like bombs. Amber tensed.

"And how did he do that?" Nuri pushed his cup away. "In a dream?"

"It was part of his recruitment speech to me. Besides, I'm worried about people getting the wrong idea about what we're doing. Guys like Al-Malik are more than willing to paint us as treasure hunters. We need to find something more than gold and silver."

"The temple items?" Amber said. She played innocent well.

"Yes. I've spent most of the night going over the translations again." He removed several pieces of paper from his folder and gave a small packet to Amber and Nuri. "I've isolated those passages that refer to items used in temple worship. The first one is in column one, lines nine through twelve." He glanced at the paper before him. He had compiled three columns, each with a different translation made by an expert in ancient language. The fourth column was his own rendition. Chambers chose to read his translation:

"Priestly garments and vessels of vows are buried in the hill of Kohlit. This is the full votive offerings of the seventh treasure. The second tenth is impure. The opening is located at the edge of the canal on its northern side, six cubits in the direction of the immersion bath." He tapped the paper. "Then the line is followed by three Greek letters: *chi, alpha, gamma.* My guess is that these items are at the Essene site where the explosion took place. Remember the stairs ended at a wall. After the blast brought down the ceiling, we were unable to continue our work. I'm ordering the area cleared and shoring to be put in place. That will take a little time. They did some clearing to recover"—he looked away—"to recover the bodies of our team."

Nuri shook his head. "It mentions an immersion bath. I take that to be a ritual cleansing reservoir. It also mentions an entry point at the northern side of a canal. We didn't find a canal."

"That doesn't mean there wasn't one there two thousand years ago." Chambers rubbed his eyes. They stung with weariness. "A small canal could easily be covered over. Since the entrance to that site was buried, we can assume the ritual baths might also be covered over. Nuri, I want you to lead that team."

"What about the other teams?" Amber asked.

"We let them continue. Finding the gold and silver from the treasury is still important. I want the three of us to focus on the priestly and temple artifacts. I don't want the other teams to know what we're doing. Keep things vague."

"The team leaders have certainly read the Copper Scroll," Nuri said. "They won't have to do a lot of thinking to figure out that finding temple artifacts is part of the goal."

Chambers nodded. "They already know that. They just don't need the details of our work until we're ready to bring them in. Security requires that we be discreet."

"Now you sound like Landau." Nuri picked up the paper.

Chambers ignored the dig. "Seven times 3Q15 mentions items related to the temple, but we can't spread ourselves that thin. Besides, as with all things in the Copper Scroll, there is great mystery about what is meant by the place names and descriptions."

"What about me?" Amber asked.

"I need your help on my search."

"Oh, I see how it is." Nuri seemed offended. "You're just trying to get alone time with the love of my life."

"I'm not the love of your life, Nuri."

"Ouch. You injure me, dear lady." He grabbed at his heart. "You know how I long for you to be my love."

The words sat in Chambers's stomach like marbles.

"You're a sweetheart, Nuri. A lady likes to hear such things, but you're not the love of my life, either."

Chambers groaned. "As entertaining as it is to watch you make goo-goo eyes at each other, we have work to do."

"What kind of work are you going to be doing?" Nuri patted Amber's hand. It galled Chambers that she would allow it.

"I'm returning to an old friend."

"Meaning?" Nuri said.

"Meaning, it's time to get to work." Chambers rose. "Amber, I would like to leave in an hour."

"Aren't you going to eat breakfast?"

I had something sent to the room earlier—"

"Which one of you is Dr. David Chambers?"

The voice came from the door to the private room. A man with a dark complexion and a gray-black beard and wearing a suit walked in. Instinctively, Chambers moved toward the man to interpose his body between the interloper and Amber. From the corner of his eye, he saw Nuri still in his seat.

"Who are you?" Chambers noticed a second man enter with a small digital video camera that bore a small directional microphone. A flashing red light told Chambers the man was recording.

"Are you Dr. David Chambers?"

"This room is private. You need to leave."

"Dr. Chambers, I'm with the media, and I have a few questions for you. What is it you and your team are looking for?"

"A way to get rid of you." He started forward when a blur of a man appeared behind them. Before Chambers could fully understand what was happening, the man with the camera was back-pedaling.

"Take your hands off me," the cameraman shouted.

Landau gave no indication of obeying the command. The cameraman exited the room faster than he entered. A second later, Landau was back in the dining room, face to face with the reporter. "I will say this once. Leave of your own accord, or I will make you leave."

"Is that a threat?"

"It's more of a promise."

"You can't treat the press this way."

Landau put a hand on the man's chest and began to push him back.

"You dare assault a member of the Jordanian media?"

Landau cocked his head. "I haven't assaulted you. Yet."

The reporter grabbed Landau's hand and Chambers winced. He had had his own run-in with the man. For a moment, he pitied the reporter, but only for a moment.

"Dr. Chambers, what are you looking for? Why are you and your people tearing up the land? Is it treasure? Is it a scheme to bolster the Jewish position in Jerusalem and elsewhere?"

Another man appeared behind the reporter, a tall, ruggedly built member of Landau's team. The reporter disappeared through the opening. Chambers could hear scuffling, loud complaining, and curses in Arabic.

Landau shut the door. For a moment as he looked at the others, fury filled his eyes, then it slowly waned. "I apologize. That should not have happened."

"You're right," Nuri said. "How did it happen?"

"Three other men entered the hotel and went to the far end of the lobby. They started a ruckus. A fight really. While we were breaking them up, those two morons got by us."

"The three men were decoys?" Amber stood. Chambers could see her hands shake.

"It appears so."

Chambers shrugged. "At least they didn't get anything to broadcast. I assume you've confiscated the camera."

He shook his head. "The camera has a transmitter on it. I saw it when I yanked the cameraman out of his shoes. It broadcast what just happened to a van outside. I noticed the van when I arrived. I've got a feeling that the confrontation went out live to the van and was relayed to Jordanian television."

"It doesn't matter," Chambers said. "I didn't say anything they can use."

Landau looked at Chambers as if studying someone too naive to know what is going on around him. "They got a shot of your faces."

TWENTY-FIVE

Security exited the SUVs first and scanned the tourists walking near where the Antonia Fortress had been in Jesus' day, now just north of the Muslim shrine, the Dome of the Rock. From the car window, Chambers could see the golden dome sitting atop the eight-sided structure. Blue, white, and green tile decorated the upper half of each wall. Several men wearing Windbreakers and light coats strolled the tree-studded area just to the north. Tourists and locals moved along the concrete path that led through the peaceful-looking terrain.

"I wonder what it looked like back then," Amber said.

"Back when? Jerusalem has a lot of 'back thens.'"

"Back in the first century." She gazed out the window.

"There was much less traffic and few tourists." Chambers tried to keep the conversation light.

"My understanding is that old Jerusalem was crowded, especially during the holy days. It's an awfully small city to be inundated by hundreds of thousands of pilgrims from around the land."

"That's why so many set up camp outside the Old City, spending days, even weeks in the Kidron Valley. The smaller villages would have been full too. Especially on the Day of Atonement."

"That's where you found the tunnel?" She nodded to the north end of the raised plaza.

"Yes, a few meters from the north retaining wall. It's the location of the old Antonia Fortress, built to honor Mark Antony."

"That's the ground where Jesus first spilled His blood." Amber spoke in a whisper.

"Are you forgetting Gethsemane. He sweat blood there."

"Okay, technically you're right. I meant, that was the place He was flogged by the Romans."

"Except the four-tower building the Jewish historian Josephus describes is gone. So much has changed since then, but then why wouldn't it? Everything changes over time."

"Not everything, David. God remains the same, as does His love."

Chambers glanced at the driver to see if he was listening. He gave no indication that he was, but how could he not? There were just the three of them in the vehicle. "I suppose. Look, Landau is coming back. It looks like we're good to go."

"When does the rest of the team get here?"

"Any minute. I want us to be the first in the tunnel. The others know the tunnel well. They're the workers the professor's been using since I turned the project over to him and the Institute."

Landau opened the back door for Chambers, and the driver slipped from his place and did the same for Amber. Both archaeologists retrieved backpacks and donned them. It took all of Chambers's restraint not to jog to the concrete block building that covered the opening to the eleven-mile tunnel running beneath the streets of Jerusalem to Jericho. The building was about the size of a two-car garage and had no windows. A pair of steel doors blocked its only entrance. Landau worked the heavy lock that kept out the curious. Chambers and Amber stood to the side as Landau swung the doors open. Just inside the doors was another set of doors, except these looked as if someone had stolen them from a prison. Chambers looked at the space just beyond the bars. The building was not here when he last left Jerusalem, but such precautions were not out of the ordinary. The curious, and sometimes thieves, felt entitled to help themselves to whatever they could find and slip into a pocket or a sack. Iron bars kept pillaging down. In this case, they also kept people from hurting themselves. Chambers remembered the size of the hole in what was now the floor of the building. It would be bad for man or beast to fall down such a pit.

The barred doors swung on noisy hinges, filling the space with a fingernail-on-blackboard screech. Chambers entered first, careful with each step. His eyes had not adjusted to the dark, and the only light came from the open door. Until Landau flipped a switch.

"Better?"

"Much. Thanks." Chambers stepped to the door. Another barricade made of rebar welded together covered the one-meter-wide entrance to the tunnel below and was held in place by a lock on one end and hinge on the other. It took both Landau and his man to lift the grate up and out of the way.

"Is this the way you left it, Dr. Chambers?" Landau stood at the edge of the hole looking down.

"No. We had a small metal shed over the hole and that was it. The concrete floor and the metal sleeve in the hole came later." He looked around. "The forced-air system is my design."

"Not enough air down there?" Landau leaned over the hole.

"Not fresh air. Subterranean archaeology has dangers all its own: cave-ins and tick-borne fever to name a few."

"Ticks? You're kidding me, right?" Landau took a step back. "I hate bugs."

Chambers laughed. "Then tunnel work isn't for you. You'd be surprised to see what kind of creepy-crawlies live below. The ticks carry a disease called cave fever. It's a relapsing fever. The infection is caused by *Borrelia persica,* an organism that can change its surface antigens, causing recurring episodes of fever. *Ornithodoros tholozani* ticks transmit the infection through their bites leading to TBRF—tick-borne relapsing fever. It affects about ten percent of Israeli caves and tunnels."

"Now I am creeped out."

"Not to worry, Mr. Landau. Remember, it's a recurring fever, which, to an optimist like you, means that you only have the fever part of the time."

"Thanks, I feel much better now."

Amber stepped next to Chambers at the edge of the hole. "Now David, you know it's not nice to tease the security people."

"Are you going to need me down there?" Landau asked.

"No. The fewer the better. The workers will be here soon enough." He moved to the back wall and removed two caver helmets, each with an attached light. He handed one to Amber and donned the other. "We'll have light down there once I start the generator." He motioned to a yellow-painted machine in the corner, then spoke to Landau. "It's gas. If it dies, put some more gas in. There are a few five-gallon gas cans over there." Several backpacks and a portable GPS unit sat in one corner. Chambers had tried to anticipate what he might need. He'd even included two types of electric hammers, similar to the handheld pneumatic hammer used by Nuri at the Dead Sea compound.

"I hope it exhausts to the outside," Landau said.

"It does. You might want to keep the door open just in case. The generator provides power for our ventilation system." Chambers turned on the generator, tightened the strap of his helmet, and stepped to the opening. An aluminum ladder bridged the distance from the floor of the shed to the floor of the tunnel. He started down.

"What, no ladies first?" Amber said.

"Doors yes, ancient tunnels no. I'm just going down to scare off the scorpions."

"Now you're just being cruel."

"It's a gift." Chambers started down, taking care that each step was secure before making the next and that his backpack cleared the edge of the opening. The moment his head dropped below the floor line, his chest began to tighten and his breathing increased. He paused, took a breath, and fought to ignore the boiling emotion. For years he had told himself, *"It doesn't matter how you feel; what matters is what you do."* It was pop psychology, but it worked—some of the time.

Lights had been strung down this area of the tunnel, each connected to a thick orange wire. He doubted the string of lights ran the full eleven miles. Most likely there was a similar generator in Jericho and an identical set of lights coming up the tunnel. Even so, there was bound to be skin-crawling darkness along the way.

Amber descended the stairs. "Scorpions all gone?"

"Most of them."

"Most?" She sighed and stepped to the solid surface of the tunnel floor. "I don't see any bugs."

"Just goes to show how effective I am." He removed his tablet PC from the backpack and read the notes he had made on it. He had been careful not to provide any context with the cryptic comments and numbers. Should someone come into possession of the document, he or she would see only a series of numbers. Chambers, however, knew which numbers were accurate and what they stood for; the others were just a ruse, a magician's misdirection.

"I read about this place in your book and the journal articles you wrote. It's more impressive in person."

"She's a beauty all right. I often wonder if ol' King Herod walked this tunnel during his last years."

Amber shrugged. "Every historian knows the man's front-porch light was a little dim, if you know what I mean."

"I know what you mean, but paranoid as he was—and he probably had reason to be paranoid—he did some remarkable building. Just look at this place." He motioned around him. "Tunnel building is an exact and demanding science today. Imagine how difficult it was two thousand years ago to dig beneath the city of Jerusalem and the surrounding region for eleven miles without getting off course—and using hand tools at that."

His enthusiasm had squelched his claustrophobia for the moment. "They had to do this by torchlight. I imagine that made the air foul. I'd be lying if I said I knew exactly how they did this."

She smiled. "It's good to see you excited again. And to think you wanted to leave all this behind."

"Yeah? Well, maybe next year."

Amber saddened for a moment, and David's mind raced for something witty to say but came up empty. Instead, he stepped to the ladder. "Hey, Landau, how about you send one of your guys down with the portable GPS."

"Gotcha."

In a few moments, the long wood handle with the emitter head was lowered through the opening. Chambers took it. Then a pair of boots appeared, followed by their owner—Landau.

"I thought you were afraid of bugs and ticks."

"I didn't say I was afraid; I said I didn't like them. Besides, I haven't heard you screaming like a Girl Scout, so I figured it was safe."

"You have such an encouraging way with words."

"I am a man of many levels, Chambers. Do you need anything else from topside?"

"There's a distance-measuring wheel in one of the corners up there. I could use that. It's a little more scientific than pacing off the distance. When the crew arrives, have them bring the electric hammers and shovels."

Landau ascended the ladder just enough that his head poked above the floor. Chambers heard him pass on his request and the information about the crew.

The device Landau's men handed down was a bright-yellow contraption with a wheel on one end of an aluminum pole and a handle with a digital readout on the other, an improvement over the older analog devices with a mechanical counter.

Glancing at the PC's display, Chambers mumbled, "Three hundred meters. About four hundred cubits by the standard of the day." He looked down the long tunnel and remembered the first time he had walked its length. It was more cluttered then but still in remarkable shape. The floor was now clear of debris. Spaced unevenly along the path were heavy wood supports used to shore up areas that workers thought might be subject to cave in. The posts and beams gave the tunnel the feel of a mine.

Chambers moved slowly, letting the three-hundred-millimeter wheel move along the sloping base of the tunnel, clicking off the distance as it did. They walked the length of a football field, and Chambers stopped. "This should be it." He turned to his right, studied the wall, and saw four chalk marks left by the team that discovered the anomaly behind the wall.

"I see the marks," Amber said, "but I'm having trouble believing there's an opening behind the surface. The material looks the same all along. I've not seen any breaks, cracks, or anything else to indicate that a surface material was used to cover the opening."

Landau placed a hand on the wall. "How could they do that? Especially back then?"

"I don't know." Chambers set the measuring wheel aside.

Landau scoffed. "I was led to believe that you know everything, that you have all the answers."

"Nonsense," Chambers said. "I do, however, know all the questions. I'll tell you one. In one of the remaining walls of the second temple, there is a stone that weighs over six hundred tons, the equivalent of three hundred or more cars compressed into a twelve-meter by three-meter by four-meter space—bigger than the stones used in the pyramids. Tell me how they excavated that and moved it to its present location, and I'll tell you how they did this." Chambers studied the wall. "One of the greatest mistakes archaeologists can make is assuming ancient people were stupid. They might not have had cell phones, but they knew how to build structures that have lasted centuries. I doubt anything we're building these days can last as long."

Chambers removed his pack and set it to the side. "I want to verify the location." He set up the handheld ground-penetrating radar unit. "Amber, you run the computer. Give your video camera to Landau. You can work a camera, can't you, Mr. Landau?"

"I think so. I can even chew gum and walk at the same time. I'm just full of surprises."

"Sorry, I wasn't trying to demean you, I was just…never mind. The more I talk, the deeper I dig my hole. So to speak."

In a few minutes, Chambers was running the sensor head along the wall. It took only moments to confirm that the material behind the wall's surface was less dense and of a less compact material than that to either side of the tunnel.

"It's amazing they found this. There has to be close to a million square feet of surface area on the two walls and spread along eleven miles of tunnel."

"And that's not counting the surface area of the floor. You can add another third to that number." Amber kept her eyes fixed on the computer readout.

Landau lowered the camera, and the deep, ghostly shadows cast by the tunnel lighting returned, exaggerating the height of the three. "Do you think they scanned everything?"

Chambers shrugged. "I don't know. I have some of Ben-Judah's notes, but I doubt I have everything. Maybe the crew can tell us when they get here. Although the lead archaeologist is out of the country for a few weeks. Inconvenient if you ask me. I guess we'll have to ask you-know-who."

Even though the people who were standing alone in the tunnel with him all knew Ben-Judah was alive, Chambers had grown paranoid enough to assume that somehow, some way, someone was eavesdropping. A moment later he added, "That doesn't matter now. We have our mystery before us. That's what we need to focus on." He stepped back and looked at the chalk marks. The hidden opening was less than a meter wide and one-and-a-half meters high.

"A tight fit," Amber said.

Chambers nodded. "A king escaping through a tunnel would need it to be wide and tall to accommodate guards, aides, and family, although Herod cared little for his own family."

"What's that mean?" Landau looked puzzled.

Chambers faced the man. "Herod the Great was extremely paranoid. He believed that some in his family were trying to kill him. Maybe they were. Anyway, he had several of his family killed. He also saw to the execution of many rabbis. He was worried that when he died no one would mourn, so he ordered many respected dignitaries to come to Jericho. He planned to have them killed so that there would be tears in the land. Not a nice guy."

"I guess not," Landau said. "So why build this side tunnel?"

"I don't think he did. Herod died about 4 BCE—some think as late as 1 BCE. The temple was still safe at that time."

"So someone else created a side tunnel to hide temple artifacts?" Landau sounded genuinely interested.

"Most likely. We won't know until the investigation is complete, and that might take some time, but it's a reasonable hypothesis. The Antonia Fortress is very close to the temple. Although it was a place where many Roman soldiers spent their time, so most Jews stayed away. Do you know much about the trials of Christ, Landau?"

"Not really. Being a good Jewish boy in the States, I didn't attend many churches."

"Jesus went through three trials. Some say six, but it depends on what you classify as a trial. The Pharisees and others stacked the trials against Him. They wanted nothing more than to see Jesus dead, yet when asked to bring their charges against Him, they did so from the doorway of Pontius Pilate's building. They didn't want to defile themselves by stepping on Gentile floors. Herod, however, was a different animal. Just to be clear, this Herod is a descendent of Herod the Great I mentioned a moment ago. Rome appointed Herod Antipas to power after his father's death. He was one of three leaders who ruled various parts of the land. Herod Antipas ruled over Galilee but was in Jerusalem for Passover and during Jesus' trial and execution. Antipas didn't mind associating with Gentiles, since they provided his wealth and power. He would have no problem escaping from the temple or his palace to the Antonia Fortress and out a tunnel."

Landau's radio crackled. "Go."

"The workers are here," said the voice on the radio.

"I'll be right there." Landau handed the camera to Chambers. "I need to go. I want to check each worker myself."

"You have radio reception down here?" Amber said.

"My man probably descended the ladder. Our radios are good, but not that good." He jogged up the tunnel.

"Do you think we'll find temple artifacts?"

Chambers rubbed the back of his neck. "We'll know soon."

TWENTY SIX

P resident Baker Meyers slipped into the Oval Office three hours later than he had intended. His guests were seated around an art deco–style coffee table. The room was a mixture of disparate furnishings, something Meyers preferred to call eclectic but his wife called a mishmash. One year into his term, he agreed to let her hire an interior decorator to convert the place into something more suitable to the head of the world's most powerful country. If he had his way, the building would be midcentury modern, but his wife convinced him that a head of state should have something more refined than furniture that looked like it had been culled from the set of an old *Perry Mason* television show. The only thing he insisted on keeping was the contrasting cross-pattern floor of quarter-sawn oak and walnut laid down during George W. Bush's presidency. His wife objected, but the floor stayed. After all, he was the president of the United States and that gave him veto power.

He removed his jacket and hung it on an oak coatrack near his nineteenth-century walnut desk. "I'm sorry to keep you gentlemen waiting. I know we planned this as a lunch, but I got hung up with the secretary of the interior. There's been another blowout on an offshore oil rig. Just what I need—another oil-soaked coastline."

By the time he stepped to the seating area in the center of the room, two men and one woman were standing. "We understand, Mr. President." Tony Cleese was an old friend who insisted on formality when in the Oval Office. They had come a long way from his days as a California congressman. Back then it was just "Baker," at least when they were alone, but once Meyers took the oath, Tony ceased calling him by his first name.

Meyers shook hands with Vivian Roller, secretary of state; Hobert Allen, NSA; and Lewis Conah, CIA. Then he took his seat. The others followed his example.

"I'm sure Tony has brought everyone up to speed on my concerns." The president leaned back in the chair and steepled his fingers before him. "I caught Al-Malik's interview last night. I got a chill, and when I get a chill, it means something is going on but I can't identify it. Am I off base here?" They looked at one another. "You lead off, Lew. What does CIA know about Al-Malik?"

Although the man held a folder on his lap, he spoke from memory. "Dr. Hussein Al-Malik, PhD. His doctorate is in archaeology. He did his graduate and postgrad work at the U. of Chicago and graduated with honors. He's a Palestinian with connections to the PLO, and we believe he's behind several bombings and assassination attempts. There is reason to believe that he is the functional head of the PLO, although not the public leader. He is brilliant. His IQ runs north of one-forty-five. As a young man, he worked as a field archaeologist and taught a few years in Chicago, then he moved to Jordan, where he is officially retired from teaching and research. He maintains several layers of protection around him at all times, often working through subordinates."

"Which is your way of saying that if he were brought to trial, there would be no evidence linking him to the crime," the president said.

"Exactly."

"So why do the interview?" Tony poured a cup of the president's favorite African coffee for the commander in chief and one for each person present.

"I'll take that one," Hobert Allen said. "It's our job to keep track of various communications from suspected terrorists and others. Al-Malik has been on our radar for some time but to little avail. As Lew has stated, the man keeps his distance from problems. That doesn't mean his hands aren't dirty. I'll bet next month's paycheck that they are."

"What do you think he's up to, Hobert?"

"Nothing good, Mr. President. He has made no secret of his hatred for Israel. If a wind blew every Jew into the ocean, he'd do the dance of joy. But since that's not going to happen, he has to learn to live with them and undermine every effort toward peace."

"And the interview?" Meyers retrieved his coffee and sipped it. Strong, smooth, no bitter aftertaste. Just the way he liked it.

"My analysts agree on this, Mr. President. We think Al-Malik is sending a message through the interview."

The president set the cup down again. "I didn't hear anything but the typical blasts of hot air and sour grapes."

"That's the way it's supposed to work, Mr. President." Hobert shifted forward in his seat. A tall man, he found every chair and sofa to be at least three inches too short. "He's not sending the message to military troops but to followers, citizens who have been schooled to listen for key words and phrases. We've analyzed his message, voice patterns, and vocal inflections. We are seventy-six percent sure that he was sending a coded message to his civilian followers."

"Seventy-six percent? You couldn't be more specific?" The president smiled, but the joke shot past his NSA director.

"No sir. Seventy-six percent is high probability."

"Okay, what message do you think he was sending?"

Lewis took the lead. "Mr. President, a few months ago, a team of biblical archaeologists began digging in and around Israel. There are small teams working in conjunction with one another. Dr. Abram Ben-Judah out of Hebrew University and the Institute of Archaeology heads the dig." He paused just a second. "I should say, he headed the dig. There was an accident at one of the sites, and several workers were killed. Ben-Judah died in the hospital later. We have reason to believe that the accident might not have been so accidental. Sources tell us that the cave-in was caused by an explosion."

"How many died?" the president said.

"We believe four were killed at the site; Ben-Judah died a few hours later."

The president cleared his throat and thought for a moment. "Someone connect the dots for me."

Secretary of State Vivian Roller took the lead. "We discussed some of this while we waited for this meeting. It gave us a little more time to make calls and chase a couple of leads. We think the archaeology teams are after something important." She ran a hand through her light brown hair, hair that used to bounce and shine before she took what had to be the second most difficult job on the planet.

"Important how?" The president leaned forward to rest his elbows on his knees.

"We don't know specifically, but we have a guess, Mr. President. We have to ask ourselves what could a group of archaeologists be digging up that would upset the PLO specifically."

"Wait. The US has not considered the PLO a terrorist organization since 1991, and back in 1993 the PLO recognized Israel's right to exist. They denounced terrorism."

"Perhaps," Lewis said, "but no one knows how long that will last. The group is still composed of several radical, nonconforming factions. Dangerous ones, I might add. The region is still plagued with conflict. Anti-Jewish sentiment has grown over the last few years, especially in Iran. Mr. President, the place remains a powder keg. Something stupid could set off the whole thing. As you know, the world is like a table with dominoes set on end. Bump the table, and the dominoes fall. A chain reaction begins."

"They used to say that about the Communists, and it never quite worked out that way." Meyers kept his voice casual.

"It almost did, and several countries did fall to communism. I believe the analogy is still valid, Mr. President."

"I'm sorry, Vivian. You were about to say something else. You have an idea about what the archaeologists are doing?"

She drummed her fingers on the arm of the sofa as if wishing she hadn't brought it up. "This is a guess, sir."

"I'm not opposed to a little speculation, Madam Secretary. Let it fly."

She took a deep breath. "I come from an evangelical background. Something you already know. I've spent a lifetime in church. Everyone here knows my father was a minister." She looked away. "There is a great interest among evangelicals in the Second Coming of Christ and prophecy. There are lots of viewpoints, of course, but I remember my father talking about biblical prophecy. He said that one day the Temple of Solomon would be rebuilt and the Jews would begin to worship there again."

Hobert Allen laughed.

She turned on him. "Laugh if you want, Hobert, but I think that's what's going on down there."

"That's a quite a leap, Madam Secretary," Tony said.

"I know, but it's a reasonable leap. Listen, we're not talking about a single team digging along the Dead Sea or in some ancient Roman bathhouse. You read Lew's report. There are a dozen teams, maybe more, all working under Ben-Judah, until he was killed. And they're still doing the work. That takes big money. Tell the president who is funding this, Tony."

The chief of staff pinched the bridge of his nose before speaking. He looked tired. He always looked tired. The president didn't wonder. The COS's schedule was worse than his. "At Vivian's suggestion, I had the FBI do a little snooping. We believe John Trent is funding the whole thing."

"John Trent." Meyers leaned back as if the revelation were a punch to his nose. "He's one of my best contributors."

"Yes, Mr. President, he is."

"The law prohibits the CIA from investigating its own citizens, but our people in Israel have been able to verify his presence in the country several times over the last few months."

"Why would he spend hundreds of thousands of dollars to fund biblical archaeology?" the president asked.

"Not hundreds of thousands of dollars, Mr. President," Tony said. "Millions. Tens of millions."

"Wow. Have they found anything?" Meyers was beginning to feel unsettled.

"Yes, but we don't know what." The CIA director shifted in his seat. "There have been no announcements. The teams avoid the media. In fact, a Jordanian reporter was shown the door by special security at the hotel where the primary archaeologists are housed. We were able to identify a couple of the security people. They're Shin Bet."

That took the president by surprise. "Israeli internal security?"

"Yes sir."

"But that would mean…"

"Yes sir," Vivian said. "Israel is part and parcel of this. Not only do they know about it, they're involved."

"Unbelievable. Okay, Vivian, throw your cards down. What are they planning?"

The secretary of state took a deep breath and then spat out the words. "Best guess, sir: Israel is going to rebuild its temple."

President Baker D. Meyers was thankful that he was already seated.

TWENTY-SEVEN

Five men led by Landau trudged down the sloping tunnel. Chambers made eye contact with the security man, who answered the unspoken question with a nod. Landau had told him he would check each man personally. No one could blame him for the deaths at the ancient Dead Sea compound, but Chambers could tell Landau was blaming himself. He didn't speak of the event, hadn't changed his behavior or attitude, but something in the man's eyes said that he still felt the pain of his failure. Chambers knew that if he could excavate the man the way he did archaeological sites, he wouldn't have to dig very far to find a trove of guilt and remorse.

It took only moments to set up the power hammer with a wide, chisel-like blade.

"I want everyone on the up-slope side and back a ways. That's the closest exit should things go south." Chambers moved to the chalk marks on the tunnel wall.

"I'm staying close so I can record the work." Amber raised the video camera.

"No you're not. You and the others are going to go ten or fifteen meters up the tunnel."

Amber frowned. "You don't need to prove your bravery to me or anyone else—"

"Amber, I'm not trying to prove anything. I'm just being cautious and logical. It doesn't make sense to endanger anyone else. Besides, nothing else is going to happen."

"Then why send us back—"

"Landau. Would you please escort Dr. Rodgers away from the area? Toss her over your shoulder if you need to."

"Why don't you let me work the power tool, Doc." Landau moved closer. "Or maybe one of the workers."

Chambers lowered his head and his voice. "It's my call. This is going to be the way it is. Understood? Now beat it."

"Come on, Dr. Rodgers. Your man seems intent on doing this alone. It seems he has a stubborn streak."

Amber started up the low grade. "You have no idea."

"I heard that," Chambers said.

For the next three minutes, Chambers studied the marks, then decided to start at the top and work his way down each side. If he had read the GPR returns correctly, he would have a meter-wide opening that stood a little over a meter-and-a-half high. Not big, but big enough. His primary concern was the limestone facing giving way before he was done cutting, especially since the GPR revealed a loose material sealing the auxiliary tunnel.

He slipped on a pair of noise-suppressing ear protectors, hoisted the twenty-five-pound demolition hammer a little above his head, placed the three-inch-wide hardened-steel chisel to the rock face, and took a deep breath. He squeezed the trigger.

The noise, compounded by echo, ran the length of the tunnel. Even with a protective headset on, Chambers cringed at the sound. If it was possible to raise the dead, this noise would do it.

Bits of rock flew up and out; dust swirled, then hung in the air and clung to his goggles. He could taste the dirt. The blade cut the soft stone easily, and soon chunks were falling at Chambers's feet. It took ten minutes to cut across the top of the narrow rectangle he had inscribed. He started down the sides, chiseling down a short distance and then cutting another horizontal line to keep the stone from dropping on him as a single slab. Something he assumed might hurt.

Once he had created cut lines that marked off a meter wide by a half meter high, he stopped the power. "Sledgehammer, please."

A worker started forward, but Landau stopped him. He took the long-handled tool to Chambers but refused release it. "Stand back."

"I'll do it."

"I got more meat on my bones than you archaeology types. Whatcha think? Hit it right in the middle?"

"No, really, I can—"

"I'm sure you can, but what you can't do is take the sledge away from me. Now move back."

David backed up, grumbling with each step.

Landau set his feet, swung the sledgehammer, and hit the wall dead center in the rectangle Chambers marked off with power hammer. It moved but held its place. Again, Landau put his back into the swing, and the stone facing cracked. One more swing knocked a hole in the material. The next swing shattered the rock and it crumbled. A stream of sand poured from the opening and onto the ground. It took several minutes for the flow to stop.

"Well, now we know what the loose material sealing the auxiliary tunnel is," Amber said. She moved to the mound at the base of the opening and fingered the granules. "Nothing out of the ordinary. At least to the eye."

Chambers moved to the opening and peered in. He pulled back, activated his helmet light, and looked in again. "Folks, we have a tunnel, but it's not big." Claustrophobia began to roil in his stomach again. "Okay, let's finish this."

He picked up the power hammer, then felt a hand on his shoulder. "Let one of the workers do it, David." Amber looked worried. "You've made your point."

"I didn't have a point."

"Look, the tunnel seems sound. These men were hired to do this kind of work. You're embarrassing them."

Chambers looked at the group of men in dirty work clothes, then held up the power tool. A man stepped forward, and Chambers retreated up the tunnel. The man had been watching carefully. He followed Chambers's example, cutting the remaining portion of covering into two rectangles. Then he used the sledgehammer on each piece. The rectangles gave easily, crumbling at his feet and releasing sand into the tunnel.

Using shovels and a broom, the workers cleared the entrance of sand and rubble, piling the debris along the base of the tunnel's other wall.

Crouching, Chambers studied the opening. It was ragged, lacking the refined technique of the workers who had created Herod's tunnel.

"It looks like a natural fissure," Amber said.

"Perhaps. It would make sense that they would use a natural geological formation, or maybe they just want us to think it's natural."

"Why would they do that?" Landau asked.

"Who knows? To make treasure hunters think there was nothing in there to find. We have no way to know. The Essenes used natural caves to hide the Dead Sea Scrolls." He paused. "Well, let's see what's been kept under wraps for all these centuries."

Chambers heart began to pump like a piston in an Indy car, and sweat dotted his brow. For a moment, he thought he saw the ragged opening close like the mouth of a giant cave creature. He took a deep breath, then another.

"You okay, Doc?" Landau sounded concerned.

"Yep. Why?" He knew why.

"Because you look like you're about to toss breakfast, and I want to make sure I'm out of the way when you do."

"I'm fine."

Amber squatted beside him. "He's right. You look ill." They exchanged glances.

"Gee, thanks." He looked back into the opening. "I'm going to have to take my helmet off. It narrows…quite a bit in there." He took hold of a flashlight.

"Let me go, David," Amber said. "I'm smaller than you. It only makes sense."

"No, I'm going in first. I'll keep you posted as I go along." Chambers didn't wait for another objection, nor did he want to give his claustrophobia time to intensify. He crawled through the narrow opening. He was just an inch under six feet tall, which meant he was close to a foot too tall to walk in standing up.

He moved forward, his helmet in one hand, a flashlight in the other. "The passage narrows and lowers the deeper I go."

"How do you feel?" Amber asked.

"I feel like I'm in a vise." He pushed on but not before cracking his head on the inclined ceiling. He turned sideways and inched deeper and deeper in the crevice, pressing his back against one side of the rugged passageway. "I can't imagine trying to do this with just a torch. Those guys had some guts."

Every muscle tensed as Chambers lowered himself to his side and tried to push forward along the ground like an oversized snake. Every few feet the opening narrowed more, and his fear level hit maximum.

He stopped.

He couldn't breathe, couldn't draw air into his lungs.

The front and back walls touched his body. Sweat streamed from his face and into his eyes. His hands shook. His legs trembled. The walls were closing, pressing in, squeezing him, crushing him, pressing him flat.

Nonsense. Walls don't move. They're in the same place they were five minutes ago; the same place they were two thousand years ago. It's in your mind. When he was in college, he heard his psychology professor say, *"The mind cannot distinguish between fiction and reality. It's why we jump while watching a scary movie. We know the image is nothing more than a two-dimensional representation of actors playing a part, but when the killer jumps at the girl, we jump anyway."* He now understood what the old prof was saying.

Keep going. Don't think. Don't imagine. Just squiggle and squirm forward. It has to get bigger. It has to. And if it doesn't? Don't think that. Just move. Move. Inch forward. Move. Move. Move.

Sand filled his pockets and pushed beneath his belt. The grit dug at his skin.

A Bible verse flew to the top of his mind. Something from Paul. From the second book of Corinthians: "We are hard pressed on every side, but not crushed; perplexed, but not in despair; persecuted, but not abandoned; struck down, but not destroyed." *Hard pressed.* The phrase had new meaning for Chambers.

He clenched his teeth, tired of inhaling dust and dirt, and used his legs to push on. It took several efforts to move a meter, but he was moving. He had planned to estimate the length of the ragged passageway. His first guess was ten meters, but it was starting to feel like ten kilometers.

Still he pressed. Still the opening narrowed until he had just enough room for his chest to expand when he inhaled. If it narrowed any more, he'd have to turn back—except there was no way to turn. Slithering backward would be twice as hard, and not being able to see where he was going twice as claustrophobic.

"Having fun yet, Doc?"

"Every inch is a party." Chambers heard the concern in Landau's voice.

In the temple days, the priests used to tie a rope around the high priest's ankle before he entered the Holy of Holies to offer a sacrifice for the sins of the nation. They believed that if the high priest was unclean, God would kill him on the spot. If that happened, who would be brave enough to go in and retrieve the body? The rope around the high priest's ankle was a low-tech way of retrieving the corpse. Chambers wished someone had tied a rope around his ankle in case he became wedged between the rock face or lost consciousness. A good idea. Late, but good.

Chambers stretched one arm forward, looking for something he could grab and use to pull himself a little farther along, but found only emptiness.

He tried again. Then again. This time he pulled his arm back and felt the base of the tunnel drop off. He crawled forward another half meter until he reached the ledge. The passageway widened slightly, enough for him to roll on his belly. He picked up the flashlight he had been pushing along and let the beam scan the area.

Chambers stopped breathing.

"David?" Amber's voice sounded miles away.

Chambers blinked several times, then scanned the area again. He lowered his head and tears fell, swallowed by dust that had seen no moisture in centuries.

"David. Answer me. Are you all right?"

"Yeah. Better than all right."

"You sound…funny."

He chuckled, then laughed. A moment later, he filled the tunnel with the sound of laughter. His laughter filled the cavern before him.

"He's lost his mind?" Landau said.

"You might be right, Landau," Chambers shouted. "Amber, get in here. Landau, get the men out of the tunnel and secure the area. And I mean SECURE it. Got it?"

He heard something.

Shouting.

A gunshot.

Then a scream.

"Amber!"

Then he heard someone scrambling through the access tunnel.

TWENTY-EIGHT

Chambers wiggled forward, thankful that a short set of stairs was before him. The staircase had maybe six or seven steps. He hadn't had time to determine if they were safe to use. All he knew was there was more room in the cavern than in the narrow tunnel.

The stairs held, and he took his flashlight in hand like a club. He heard huffing, puffing, and groaning. A woman's voice. "David."

Amber.

Another gunshot, then three in rapid succession.

He shone the light down the opening and saw her safety helmet, its small bulb shining light on surfaces just a few inches away.

Another shot.

"David!"

A hand. Chambers grabbed it and pulled. Amber let out a small cry of pain as he pulled her from the cramped confines into the dark cavern. She landed hard on the stone steps. Chambers kept a tight grip so Amber wouldn't roll off the edge of the stairway or down the steps.

"What's going on?"

"Hush," she said. "Men. Gunmen. Came up the tunnel. Landau. He started shooting back. Before I knew it, he had shoved me into the crevice. The workers ran back to the entrance. I think...I think some of them may have been wounded."

"Why would they run toward... Wait, you said the men came 'up' the tunnel?"

"Yes, from the other direction."

"The tunnel ends near Jericho. It would take hours to make their way up this direction. They'd have to cover ten miles up grade."

"I can't explain it, David. I just know I was shot at."

The *pop, pop, pop* of a handgun rolled through the access tunnel and into the cavern. "What about the other security? Surely Landau called for them."

"I don't know. He pushed me into the tunnel before I could figure out what was happening. I didn't wait to ask questions."

"Wise. Come with me."

"Where?"

"Down the steps."

"What is this place?"

"We'll figure that out later. Right now, I want us away from this opening."

He let her descend first, placing himself between her and whatever might come through the narrow tunnel.

"Where do I go?"

He took her arm and guided her around the stairs. "This way."

"What's over here?"

"I have no idea."

More shots sounded. Chambers could hear not only the report of the weapons but the *ping* of bullets ricocheting off stone walls. He knew nothing about weapons, but he could distinguish the rapid fire of an automatic weapon and that of a handgun. There was more of the former and less of the latter, and that didn't bode well. Landau had a handgun.

Chambers extinguished his helmet light and flashlight. Amber did the same. The darkness became profound, almost tangible. It felt as if the darkness was crawling on his skin, looking for a point of entrance.

More shots. Yelling. Cries of pain. It seemed a world away; it seemed inches away. Chambers took Amber in his arms and felt her quiver. He wanted to protect her, to shield her from all harm, but if armed men came in, he would be able to do neither.

The sounds died. The gunfire ended. The shouting ceased. Minutes passed like epochs. Then a scrapping, scuffling, scurrying sound.

"What's that?" Amber pressed deeper into David's arms.

"I don't know." He let go and felt his way to the stairs. "Stay here."

"Where are you going?"

"Stay here, I said. Keep your light off."

"But—"

"For once, just do as I say." He scrambled up the steps, feeling for each riser with one hand, holding his flashlight with the other, and being careful to land each foot squarely on the stone treads. Dim light seeped from the opening, and Chambers headed straight for it.

He saw movement.

He saw a shadow.

Stopping where the top step met narrow ledge, Chambers paused and slowly raised his dark flashlight.

Scrapping, scrabbling, grunting.

A hand appeared. It held a pistol. Chambers raised the metal flashlight, readying it like a weapon.

A man oozed from the tunnel like toothpaste from a tube. Chambers started his swing.

"Hey Doc?"

Landau.

The flashlight missed Landau's head by inches.

"Yeow!" A string of curses followed the exclamation. "What are you doing?"

"Sorry, I didn't know it was you." Chambers helped him up. "Watch your step. There's about a two-meter drop-off.

"I'm surprised you didn't push me off the edge."

"I said I was sorry. What happened out there?"

"Sneak attack. They weren't wearing uniforms, but they acted like military, at least military trained."

"And?"

"Dead. There were five of them. Automatic weapons. T-89s."

"I don't know what that means."

"It's an assault rifle. Good thing I heard them coming."

"What about the workers? Are they okay?"

"No. They were cut down. There's no way to outrun a bullet, not in a tunnel. I ducked into the side tunnel and fired from there."

Chambers turned his helmet light on and directed it at Landau. "Your shoulder. You're wounded."

"I hadn't noticed."

"The blood gives it away. Let me see."

"Forget that for now. It's not much, probably just a rock fragment." He pressed on the wound enough to make Chambers wince just watching. "I don't feel anything in it. Blood is minimal. I'm fine for now. Where's Dr. Rodgers?"

"Down here."

Landau held out his hand. "Let me have your flashlight."

"It's kinda busted."

"Great. Then lead me down the stairs."

A few moments later the three were standing in the light of Chambers's and Amber's helmet lights.

"What is this place?"

"I don't know yet, but you can bet your paycheck there are some amazing things to be found here."

Landau nodded. "Okay, there will be time for that later. As soon as I know there aren't more bad guys headed our way, I need to get you out of here. When I hear from my men, we're going to exit as quickly as possible."

"What about the dead?" Chambers asked.

"That's my problem. I just want to get you far away from here."

"I don't understand," Amber said. "How did they know about the tunnel and that we were here?"

Chambers answered. "I wrote about the tunnel. Two scholarly articles and a chapter in my last book. I also did a few talk shows. As to how they knew we were in here, I don't know."

"Someone is feeding them information. Whoever *someone* is."

"But who?" Amber moved close to Chambers and took his arm.

"It's impossible to tell at the moment," Landau said, "but I'm working on it. These are serious people. They've taken ten lives. Ten." His voice turned ominous. "There will be payback."

Amber trembled. "Those poor workers. Their families. I'm not sure it's worth all this death."

Chambers had no words to offer. He wanted to comfort her, to tell her everything was going to be fine, but it wasn't all right. People were dying. People who had done nothing to deserve death.

"Are we safe here?" Amber asked.

"For now. I have backup coming. I sent several men down the tunnel to make sure we don't get ambushed again. I don't suppose I could use your flashlight, Dr. Rodgers?"

She handed it to him. With two helmet lights and one handheld flashlight, they scanned the floor and walls of the cavern. It appeared to be a natural formation. Most of the area was empty, but a series of twelve one-meter-tall clay pots stood in a line next to the wall opposite the short staircase. Most of the clay pots were intact and covered with a thick layer of dust. One lay on its side, fractured. Most likely a victim of one of the many earthquakes that shook the area over the centuries. Chambers was amazed that the others still stood.

What remained of four wood chests sat in front of the clay pots.

"Do you have your camera, Amber?" Chambers asked.

"Yes, but… I mean, is it appropriate, considering…" She pointed to the opening above the stairs.

Landau spoke before Chambers could. "You can't do anything for them, and I'm not letting you out of here until I have the tunnel secured. You might as well take a look around. Hopefully you'll find something that makes all this worthwhile."

Chambers moved carefully to the pots and stood a few feet away. "What do you think?" he asked Amber. The light beam from her helmet moved from pot to pot, tracing their forms from base to top. "They match the jars found with the Dead Sea Scrolls. Same pinkish-red color—best I can tell with this artificial light. The bell-like top is the same. Based on appearance, they seem to be of the same age, but that's just a guess. We'll have to do some testing."

"I agree. At least there's nothing indicating the pots are recent." He moved to the fractured pot and crouched for a better look. Amber moved to the wood boxes, which had lost the ability to hold their shape and their contents.

The light from the video camera threw its light against the Stygian darkness. Chambers watched as Amber did a full circle, recording the chamber and its contents. He let her continue her methodical survey while he studied the broken pot. At first he thought it was empty, or its contents rotted to dust, but then he saw a glint, a tiny flash. He redirected his light to the spot where he first noticed the flash.

He saw it again.

"Amber. Bring your camera."

"What'd you find?" She started toward him.

"I don't know, yet, but I want this recorded." A moment later, the camera's light blazed over the fallen pot. Gently, slowly, Chambers pulled away a broken piece of pottery, then another and another, until he fit his hand into the vessel. His fingers felt dust, dirt, and something hard. He drew the object from its resting place. It was a rectangle about eight centimeters by four centimeters. Not large.

Chambers wiped the dust from its surface.

"Is that what I think it is?" Amber whispered the words. "That is a diamond, isn't it?"

"I think so." Chambers put it in the palm of his hand. "I've never held a diamond this big, but it feels right."

"Do you think there are more in there?"

Chambers thought for a moment, then said. "Not if I'm right. This will be the only diamond, but not the only stone." Again he reached into the fractured jar and felt around until he felt several other stones. He removed two of them, wiping each clean and studying them in the harsh light of the camera and his helmet beam. One was red, the other green. "*Odem* and *tarshish:* ruby and emerald. The stones are engraved in Hebrew." He strained to make out the letters on the ruby. "Reuven—Ruben."

"So they had a collection of stones. A treasury of gems… What?"

"Amber, think."

"I am thinking. We've found a diamond, a ruby, and…oh my." She lowered herself to the dust. "That… I mean…the only thing this could be is—"

"The ephod, the breastpiece of the high priest. Twelve stones set in four rows of three: ruby, topaz, beryl, turquoise, sapphire, diamond, jacinth, agate, jasper, tarshish, onyx, and jade. One stone for each of the tribes of Israel."

"If that's true, then there should be other items in there."

"The linen apron is long gone."

"Exodus 28, David."

He knew the passage, a lengthy description of the high priest's garments: the apron, turban tunic, sash, robe, and sash. He thought some more. "There should be two more stones mounted in gold, six names on each stone."

"Right. They sat upon the shoulders of the high priest."

Chambers searched in the vase again and removed a handful of powder and small gold chains. Another search brought out a stone still in a gold setting and larger than those of the breastpiece. The stone had six names engraved on it. "Onyx."

"Just like the Bible says." Amber giggled.

It was contagious. Chambers chortled.

Footsteps sounded behind them, then Landau's voice. "What's so funny? I take it you found something?"

Chambers looked at Amber. "Yeah, you could say that."

"Well, what is it? What'd you find?"

The laughter stopped. A moment later, Chambers replied. "The voice of God. We found the voice of God."

TWENTY NINE

They spent the next few hours photographing the chamber and every-thing in it. Once Landau's men had secured the tunnel with addi-tional men at the Jerusalem entry point and spaced out along the corridor several miles, he allowed Chambers and Amber to set up lights that ran from the same power source that fed the tunnel lights. In bright light, the cave looked smaller than Chambers had thought. In a Hollywood movie, there would be torches spread around the perimeter, each easily lit despite centuries of inactivity. In real life, there were no convenient torches or other sources of light. There was just what they lugged to the site and pushed through the narrow opening. Instead of a breathtaking array, there were twelve clay jars and a couple of decayed boxes.

Nonetheless there was treasure. The boxes held gold and silver in ingot form, more money from the temple treasury. That should have been enough to thrill anyone, especially Chambers, but the real treasure lay in the artifacts: the stones of the high priest's breastpiece and linen apron. The linen had turned to dust centuries before, but the stones were unaf-fected by the passing of time.

Things might have gone faster had Chambers allowed other workers into the site, but he refused. A find of this magnitude had to be protected, which meant allowing only the minimum number of people to lay eyes on it. The value lay not in the gems but in the spiritual and biblical significance.

Nuri arrived an hour after being called. He had taken the helicopter to the hotel where one of Landau's men picked him up and took him on a long, winding drive through and around Jerusalem to make sure they weren't being followed. Landau said Nuri complained the whole way.

The complaining stopped after he inched through the access tunnel into the cavern. He was impressed by what he saw; he was speechless when Chambers put the inscribed shoulder stones in the archaeologist's hands.

"No." Nuri stared at the two multicolored onyx stones.

"Yes," David said.

"No." Nuri shook his head. "It can't be."

"It is." Amber's grin widened.

"No."

"Yes." Amber and Chambers spoke in unison.

Nuri sat on the dusty floor. "I'm holding the engraved stones of the high priest's ephod."

"Hold out your other hand, Nuri." Chambers was enjoying this.

Nuri did, and Chambers put a different pair of stones in his left hand. "Wanna guess?"

Nuri looked at the objects, then at the twelve stones near the broken jar. "If those are the stones on the high priest's breastpiece, then these"— he closed his hand over the engraved shoulder stones—"then these two stones must be…must be… No."

"We think so," Chambers said.

"I'm holding the Urim and Thummim. The Decision Stones."

"That's right," Chambers said.

"Could these be… I mean, they're not the originals. Right? I mean, how could they be?"

"We don't know," Amber said. "There are four centuries between Moses's day and when the first temple was built, another five centuries to the building of the second temple, and that stood from 516 BCE to 70 CE. Were the original stones there through all those centuries? Who knows? These could have been made much later. Or they could be the same ones Moses saw."

"Take these." Nuri lifted his arms. Chambers took the stones and watched as Nuri rolled and lay back in the dirt.

"Is he okay?" Landau asked.

Chambers nodded. "Yes. He's just overjoyed."

Landau shook his head. "You archaeologists are a weird bunch."

"That's a fact," Amber said.

Landau looked at the artifacts. "Okay, I admit it. I'm a secular Jew, and I've forgotten most of what I learned as a child. So forgive me for being ignorant, but what are these things?"

"This may sound strange."

"Everything sounds strange lately."

"The ancient Jews believed God spoke to Aaron and the high priests that followed him by means of the stones." Landau looked puzzled. "In Exodus 28, there is a long passage describing what the high priest was to wear. It's quite elaborate. Details extend to the color of the cloth to be used. That's not unusual in world religions, but what is, is the idea that God would directly communicate with His people. There have been several devices associated with communication with God. The high priest—the *Kohen Gadol*—wore vestments that were symbolic. For example, he wore a turban of fine white linen to show atonement; the turban had a gold plate showing holiness. He also wore an under tunic of fine linen and over that a blue robe that had a fringe of gold bells and pomegranates of blue, purple, and scarlet. Over that he would don a sleeveless garment called an ephod. It was embroidered with blue, scarlet, and gold. There was also a girdle, well, *sash* might be a better word, which wrapped around the priest's waist. You with me?"

"I think so."

"Okay, so far it just sounds like symbolic religious clothing, but he wore something else. Something some scholars believe served as a communication device, a way for God to answer questions."

"You mean God needs a device to be heard?"

Chambers grinned. "No. It's not about what God needs. The Bible shows God speaking directly with Adam and Eve, Elijah, Jonah, and even twice in the New Testament: once at Jesus' baptism and once at the Transfiguration. Those events are rare, and He seldom spoke to groups. He appeared in various manifestations to groups. Think of the children of Israel being led through the wilderness by a pillar of fire by night and a column of smoke by day. But when God had a message for the people, He spoke to Moses, who would then deliver it."

"It's God's way," Amber said. "The biblical record shows that He chooses leaders, speaks to them, and expects others to follow that message. In the Old Testament days, during the time of kings, God appointed prophets to deliver His message to the people or directly to the king. Seventeen of the Old Testament books are named after prophets. They are called writing prophets, because their messages were recorded. There were many other prophets."

"You're talking about guys like Isaiah, Ezekiel, and the like," Landau said.

"Yes, and many more." Chambers couldn't stop grinning. "The point is, God usually spoke through one person who then proclaimed that message. It's not a limitation on His part; it's a choice."

"Okay, but what does that have to do with these rocks?"

Chambers shifted his weight and studied the stones. They bore engraved Hebrew letters. "It's a bit of a mystery. Here's what we know. The high priest was to keep the Urim and Thummim *in* the breastpiece. Many scholars think the jeweled breastpiece had a pocket to hold the stones and the high priest would remove them when he or other leaders needed a word from God."

"How did that work?"

Chambers exchanged glances with Amber and Nuri, who was now sitting up. "No one knows. It's not clear. Some think *Urim* and *Thummim* mean "light" and "dark"; others think the words mean "revelation" and "decision." There are many ideas about the etymology, but no certainty. Some think the stones moved. Some think individual Hebrew letters would light up. There is no end to the speculation. The truth is no one knows. They haven't been seen in… what? Twenty-five hundred years?"

Amber spoke in a low voice. "Tradition says there were five things missing in the second temple that were in the first temple: the ark of the covenant, the sacred fire, the *Shekinah* glory of God, the Holy Spirit, and the Urim and Thummim."

"And there is the question," Nuri said. "If the Urim and Thummim disappeared fifteen hundred years before the Essenes, then what are they doing here?"

"I don't know," Chambers said. "I just don't know."

"We have another problem," Landau said. "I assume these things are extremely valuable."

"They're beyond value. They're priceless." Chambers returned the stones to the fractured jar.

"Then we need to move them to a safe place. We already know people are willing to kill to stop you. I don't think they're done."

"It's a shame the professor can't see this." Nuri stood, still shaken by the find.

Chambers said nothing.

∽

It was close to midnight when Chambers and Amber arrived at the hospital. As before, they came in through a side door to a hallway that had been cordoned off. Security men dressed as hospital personnel patrolled the area. Once the area in front of the elevators had been cleared, Landau led the two to the upper floor and to the private room, where Ben-Judah waited. Security on the wing had been doubled, as had the escort around Chambers and Amber. Chambers carried a computer bag.

"I'll let you two go in alone." Landau waited at the door. "You're sure the old man won't have a heart attack?"

"I nearly did," Chambers said. "I'll call if he keels over."

Chambers and Amber slipped into the room and received the always gracious greeting. "They told me about the attack in the tunnel. Sad. Horrible. Those poor workers. But what of you? You are well?"

"We weren't harmed." Chambers moved to the seating area. "Landau's men saved our lives. I heard that two were injured but will recover."

"Yes, I was told the same. I praise *HaShem* for your safety. I have also been told you found something important. Landau said so when he set up this meeting. Please, I must know what it is. He wouldn't say."

"I asked him not to say anything on the phone." Chambers waited for Amber to sit on the sofa, then joined her. Ben-Judah took his usual seat to the side and near the coffee table.

"I am sure that is wise, but please, don't keep an old man in suspense. Did you find votive vessels? priest vestments?"

Amber beamed. "Yes, in a way. Show him, David."

"First, you should know that Landau has arranged to use a secured vault on one of Israel's military bases. He had to ask for the prime minister's help, which he received. We'll keep these and some of the other things there we've found. He won't tell me where."

"You must trust him, David." Ben-Judah fidgeted and glanced at the computer bag like a child waiting permission to open a birthday present.

Chambers opened the bag and withdrew a metal case about the size of a large candy box. He set it on the coffee table. The box had a roller-style combination, similar to those on a briefcase. Chambers dialed a number. He slid from the sofa to one knee, moved the case in front of Ben-Judah, and without a word, opened it.

∽

For Landau, the day had been long. It began early and included helping find a secret tunnel that apparently contained religious objects beyond value and a gunfight that left two of his men injured, five workers dead, and an equal number of dead attackers. The investigation into the attack would be secret and run by the government. The prime minister would make certain of that.

The weariness he felt robbed him of some of his strength. He leaned against the wall next to Ben-Judah's door and allowed his eyes to close for a moment.

The he heard a howl.

He was in the room a half second later, his Jericho 941 handgun drawn and ready to be used.

Ben-Judah was in the middle of the room—dancing.

THIRTY

E ven from the twelfth floor of the hotel, Chambers could hear the disturbance. It began early. He had just stepped from the shower, towel around his waist, water dripping from his hair, when he noticed a sound he couldn't recognize. Distant sounds from the busy street often filtered through the thick glass window, and he had grown accustomed to their muted presence. This sound, however, was new and unsettling.

Chambers stepped to the window and gazed down the one hundred fifty feet to the street below. Cars and delivery trucks that had, day after day, flowed easily in front of the hotel were bunched nose to tail, moving only inches at a time. In the street and on the sidewalks were crowds, shoulder to shoulder, holding signs and chanting. He was too far removed to hear their words, but their combined voices hummed through the window.

He saw something else: vans with markings of local television stations. Picking up the remote from the night table next to his bed, Chambers turned on the television, something he had only done a few times during the last few weeks. A little searching found an English-language news station.

He sat on the bed and watched. Through the camera lens, the crowd looked twice the size as what he saw from his hotel window. Men, women, and children marched and carried signs, some in Hebrew, some in Arabic, and a few in English. One sign read, BLASPHEMERS, INFIDELS. That was disturbing enough; more unsettling was a large placard of his photo with a blood-red X painted over it. He recognized the photo. It was the publicity shot used for his last book.

A reporter pulled a man from the crowd. His dress revealed him to be an Arab. "Why are you here?" the reporter asked in English. Chambers was pretty sure the reporter already knew.

"Our holy site has been defiled by the infidel archaeologists from the United States and their Hebrew puppets." Spit flew from the man's lips as he shouted into the microphone.

"How have they defiled your holy site? Which holy site?"

"*Masjid Qubbat As-Sakhrah*. It is a holy site. The followers of Allah will not allow this to go unpunished."

"*Kipat Hasela*—the Dome of the Rock. Tell me, sir, how did they defile the site?"

"A tunnel. They have dug a tunnel beneath the blessed site."

"Oh brother," Chambers said to the television. He turned off the television. He didn't have the stomach for any more nonsense.

His phone rang. It was Amber. "Have you looked outside?"

"Yes."

"What about the news?"

"Yeah. A little. I just turned it off. It's ridiculous. Someone is feeding lies to these people."

"The problem with lies is that some people believe them to be truth."

"Well, there's nothing I can do about it. It'll settle down soon."

Amber disagreed. "I don't think so. Neither does Landau. I just spoke to him. He wants to meet with us in the conference room. He's setting up a video conference."

"With whom?"

"Guess."

"Okay. I'll be there. When?"

"Thirty minutes."

"That's quick. You know, this project is hard enough without this."

"You can't say you're surprised, David. Those who do God's work always face opposition."

Chambers didn't know how to respond. At one time, he would have quickly agreed; when he started this project, he would have wasted no time ridiculing the idea. Now he was content to ignore the comment. "I'll be there."

∾

A thirty-inch television monitor hung from the conference-room wall. Chambers, Amber, Nuri, and Landau looked at it, seeing the drawn face of Nathan Ben Yakov. To Chambers it looked like the man hadn't slept for several days.

Yakov wasted no time with pleasantries. He launched into the matter. "There are protests in Amman, Jerusalem, Tel Aviv, and several other cities. In one case, violence has broken out. Three Russian Orthodox priests were beaten. One may not live through the night. In Tel Aviv, twenty or thirty Jews began throwing rocks into the crowd of protestors. Of course, we've made arrests on both sides. Protests are nothing new for our country, but I have intel linking these back to Al-Malik, who is feeding the fury."

"He's the one who's fabricating the lies?" Nuri asked.

"I'm sure he's behind it, although there are probably many layers between him and the protestors." Yakov pinched the bridge of his nose. "Al-Malik gave an interview on Jordanian television. His bottom line: the people have a right to voice an opinion, considering the insult they've endured against the holy site."

"Doesn't it bother anyone that none of this is true?" Amber said. She was dressed in clean work clothes: jeans, brown long-sleeve shirt, and boots.

"The first thing you learn in politics, Dr. Rodgers, is that truth is not essential in persuasion. People will believe lies; they will believe the truth. Most days I don't think they know the difference."

"So what do we do, Mr. Prime Minister?" Chambers said. "I can have all the teams stand down for a while, at least until things settle. We have plenty of lab work and cataloging to do."

Yakov waited before replying. "It may not go away. My gut tells me they know more than they're letting on. They knew when you'd be in the tunnel; they knew when we were working by the Dead Sea and planted a bomb. Things may get worse before they get better."

"What do you want us to do?" Landau asked.

"I want Dr. Chambers to hold a press conference."

"Me?" Chambers snapped his head around. "With due respect, sir, I may not be your best choice. I'm American, and I'm the lead archaeologist. To the protesters, I represent the problem." He thought of the placard with his picture on it.

"That, my friend, makes you the best choice. Confronting this head on will show that we are being up-front about everything. Besides you have great experience with the media. Are you not the Carl Sagan of archaeology?"

Chambers tapped the table with his finger. "That might be an exaggeration. Sir, I don't wish to be argumentative. You have shown me nothing but the greatest kindness—"

"Now you sound like a diplomat, Dr. Chambers. Get to it."

"We're not being up-front with everyone. They know we're working in secret. They know we're removing artifacts, which we're keeping under wraps—"

"I've arranged for the conference to begin in one hour—"

"One hour?"

"I'm sorry about the short notice, but this is a delicate matter. My press secretary will release a statement saying that I've called for an investigation into the matter. For now, that's all I plan to say on the matter. Mr. Landau will make sure you are safely delivered to the Israel Antiquities Authority, where a room will be set up for the conference. The head of the

IAA will introduce you. He is…aware of all things. Please, Dr. Chambers, be diplomatic. I have seen video of your television interviews on American talk shows. That is the Dr. Chambers the people need to see."

Not the one who's been a pain in the rear, you mean. "Yes sir. I understand."

"Forgive me," Yakov said. "As always, there are other matters that demand my attention."

The screen went blank.

"Well, well." Nuri grinned. "Archaeologist, professor, author, and now worldly diplomat. And yet, for some reason, I don't envy you."

"Yeah? Well, I don't envy me either."

∽

"How did they know which hotel we were staying in?" Chambers sat in the back of a bread delivery truck. Across from him, on a small metal seat, sat Landau. Three other Shin Bet men filled the remaining space. The truck smelled of fresh baked bread, and the aroma was making Chambers, who had skipped breakfast, hungry. A glance at the deck showed holes where brackets had held metal shelves until the vehicle was pressed into duty.

"I can think of a dozen ways. They could have seen you coming and going; they could have been alerted by an employee; they may know more about me than I like to think. These are not stupid people. They have their ways, just as we have ours. That, and it's a small country."

"Do you think this is wise? I mean, having me speak to the press?"

"First, it doesn't matter what I think; it matters what Prime Minister Yakov thinks. Second, yes, it is a good idea. Al-Malik and his people are trying to demonize you. You saw the placards with your photo, right?"

"Yes, not very flattering."

Landau shrugged. "You've looked better."

"Hey!"

"Just trying to get you to relax. Look, just tell them the truth about everything you can, but not about the things you can't."

"Really? That's your suggestion? That's impossible."

"How many impossible things have you seen over the last few months?"

Landau had him there. If someone told him that yesterday he would help uncover the breastpiece of the high priest and possibly the Urim and Thummim, he would have laughed them to scorn.

"I'm going on record saying this is a bad idea. A real bad idea."

Hiram Landau leaned forward and looked Chambers deep in the eyes. Chambers expected to feel the man's hand around his throat again, but he made no threatening actions. "Listen, I know you and I have locked horns a few times." He chuckled. "No doubt we'll do it again, but you should know this: you are one of the most driven and capable men I've met, and I believe in what you're doing. I have a job to do and I won't let anyone stand in the way of my doing it, not even you. Still, you have my admiration."

"Thank you. I think."

"Don't let it go to your head."

"Man, you are a buzzkill."

One of the other Shin Bet men snickered, then stopped abruptly. Landau wasn't smiling.

"Two minutes," the driver said.

"Understood." Landau raised a cell phone to his ear, did a speed dial, then waited. "Status?" He listened. "Good. In two."

Chambers's stomach began to do flips. He suddenly missed the dull part of the year when he was teaching. "We still have time to turn around."

"Funny man." Landau checked the position of his shoulder holster. "Okay, here's what's going to happen..."

The bread truck pulled off the street and into the parking lot of the IAA's administrative building. Chambers had worked with the group several times before. In addition to education, the organization provided oversight of digs in Israel and even had a police force that kept an eye on looters. The bread truck pulled to the back of the building and backed up to a small loading area. Chambers could see a wide metal roll-up door. It opened the moment the driver stopped.

Landau held a hand in front of Chambers's face. "Wait."

A voice came over the radio. *"Clear."*

"Go." Landau said.

Without hesitation the agents opened the back door and stepped onto the loading platform just inside the door. Before Chambers could speak, Landau had him by the arm and was moving him out the back of the vehicle. Five steps later, they were inside the small supply room, and one of the agents was closing the rolling door.

"I'm starting to feel paranoid." Chambers pulled his arm away.

"Good. It's about time. This way."

They walked past wood crates and cardboard boxes. One area looked set aside for office supplies. They moved through a door into the office area, then walked by a copy room, a break room, and a kitchenette. Landau asked Chambers, "Are you ready?"

"I guess."

"They've set up in one of the lecture rooms. As a college professor, you should feel right at home."

"Except my students don't think I'm an agent of evil. Well, most don't."

"Humor. That's good. It means you're on your game."

"We'll see."

They started down a corridor. Chambers could hear the low rumble of people talking.

"Stay on my heels," Landau said. "We're going straight to the front."

They crossed the wide threshold between the corridor and the lecture room. The place was filled with men and women. The room looked like it could hold ninety to one hundred people, but it felt like twice that number was present. Those standing turned; those who had been seated stood. A chorus of "Dr. Chambers" filled the air. Chambers did as he was told; he kept his head down and followed Landau to the front. That's when he noticed the other agents had remained at the back of the room. He supposed there was some security reason for that.

A man Chambers's age sat in a fiberglass classroom seat just to the right of a highly polished wood lectern. He had coal-black hair, dark eyes, and a face that looked used to smiling, although the smile he offered was forced. He extended his hand. Judging by the man's damp palm, he was nervous.

"Dr. Asher Doron," Chambers said with a nod. "Thank you for hosting this."

"Dr. Chambers. I'm not sure I had a choice." His accent was profound, and his English exceptional. "I will introduce you. I'm afraid it will be short."

"Would it be more comfortable for you if I just started."

"Well—"

"I'll take care of it, Dr. Doron. You've done your part."

Chambers walked to the lectern. Before he managed to plant his feet, several people were standing, hands raised, shouting his name. "If everyone will have a seat, we'll get started."

More shouting, more camera flashes, more questions.

"Please, if you'll be seated I'll do my best to get to everyone—"

More bedlam. Chambers resorted to an old teacher's trick. He clasped his hands behind his back, took one step away from the lectern and waited. It took five minutes for everyone to get the point. Once everyone was seated and order had been restored, he returned to the lectern.

"Thank you. My name is Dr. David Chambers. I am a biblical archaeologist and the head of a team of archaeologists working in the Palestine area. It has been made clear to me that there is some confusion going on about our work. As is often the case in science, progress is sometimes kept secret until sufficient work is done to make certain that false information does not leak and thereby misinform the citizens, who have a right not only to the archaeology of their nations but to the *correct* information. This is the reason I am here with you this morning."

He paused to take in the crowd. It was a mix of Muslims, Jews, and secular media. "The first thing to understand is that we are working with the approval of the local authorities. Second, there is a misguided rumor that we have somehow committed an inappropriate act against the Muslim holy shrine. Know this: We have committed no such act nor would we. We are a team of scientists studying the past. That is all."

He let his gaze fall on a young woman with a dark *hijab* covering her hair. "Would you honor us with the first question?" He was careful not to smile. Americans had a bad enough reputation without him looking like he was hitting on an Islamic woman.

She seemed embarrassed by the sudden attention. Others shot their hands up, but he ignored them. The woman rose. "What exactly are you looking for in your excavations?" She sat quickly.

"As I mentioned, I and the leaders of my team are biblical archaeologists. That means we focus our attention on biblical history. For me, that means I focus on peoples and events in biblical times. While I've worked on digs dealing with pre-Abrahamic peoples, I have spent most of my time dealing with what Christians call New Testament times: events after about 30 CE. The primary focus of our research has to do with one of the early Jewish sects called the Essenes. We are focusing on some of their work."

A man in the back row popped up. His face was stern and his eyes narrow. "So you're out to prove the Christian Bible is true?"

"Archaeology doesn't work that way, sir. There are many historical events recorded in the Bible, and people like me often use that information as a starting point. However, every archaeologist sets out to find facts, not to prove a point."

The man started to speak again, but Chambers quickly pointed to a Jewish woman in the front row, hoping for a friendly question. "Can you tell us about the deaths at the Dead Sea?"

His heart stuttered.

The woman elaborated on the question. "I have received reports that at one of your digs, not far from the Dead Sea, a number of people died. Is that true?"

Chambers blinked and wished Yakov was here to see how bad an idea all this was. "Yes. It is true. Four people died in a cave-in: three aides to our team and a photographer."

"Dr. Chambers, what caused the cave-in?" The woman showed no emotion; she was a machine making notes on a small pad.

"That is being investigated. I have not heard final word—"

"But it was caused by an explosion, was it not?"

"Since I have not received a final report on the tragedy, I can't give a definitive answer, but yes, you are probably right."

"You weren't in the tunnel were you?"

Who was this woman? "No."

"That seems convenient."

Asher Doron stood and started to speak. Chambers waved him off. "Convenient? What's your name, please?"

"Amit Ferber, *Tel Aviv Post.*"

"There was nothing convenient about it. Lives were lost. I will never forget them or how they died. Would you have been happier if the body count was higher?"

She didn't reply.

"Does anyone have a thoughtful question?" It was a fight. His first inclination was to walk out. The question infuriated him.

A man in the middle of the room rose. Chambers had troubled placing his ethnicity. The man had a short beard and short dark hair with ample gray and wore a suit but no tie. He had an accent, but it was thin and indistinct, like a child born in one culture but reared in another. "If I may, Dr. Chambers. Your skill, intellect, research, and passion have gone before you. You are to be respected for your *past* work, but I must wonder about your present activities."

"Where I come from, that's called a backhanded compliment." A few people chuckled. Most, it appeared, did not understand the colloquialism.

"Do you deny being at the Dome of the Rock yesterday?"

"I, like thousands, was somewhere near the site."

"Is that where Herod's tunnel is?"

Chambers felt like he was being interrogated in court. "It is one of two entry points. The other is in Jericho."

"How far does the tunnel extend under the Dome?" The man flashed an insincere grin.

"Not a single foot. As I said it runs to old Jericho."

"You expect us to believe that?"

Chambers shook his head. "I have no expectations. I've told you the truth. You are free to fabricate whatever story you wish."

He nodded. "When will the construction begin, Dr. Chambers?"

Chambers stomach twisted. "We're archaeologists. We dig; we don't build. Perhaps you're thinking of an architect."

"Please, Dr. Chambers. There is no need to be rude. I am asking you when construction of the third Jewish temple begins."

Several gasps punctured the air.

His spine felt awash in ice water. "Mr.... Mr.... You never gave your name."

"Behzad Raad. I write for a small but influential paper in Iran."

"Mr. Raad, your people have a rich history and have shared many great scholars with the world. None of them would make the mistake you are making. I have said nothing about a third temple. Yes, I know there have been several movements among the Jews to build another temple, but none has ever succeeded. You will have to save that question for one of them."

"Isn't it true that a gun battle occurred in the tunnel yesterday? Isn't it true that several men died, including a number of your workers? Isn't it true, that the Shin Bet is providing security for you and your team?"

Chambers had always been an unsuccessful liar. The only thing he could think of was to refocus the truth. "I'm not sure who your source is, but I suggest you consult some other people. Let me make this clear. I am a biblical archaeologist. All my team leaders are biblical archaeologists. We are not in the business of building temples. As far as the temple goes, most think it's an impossible task."

"Would it be more possible if Israel had, say, the treasures of the Copper Scroll?"

He was in verbal quicksand. Every comment, every question drew him deeper and deeper into his doom. He cleared his throat. "A very interesting proposition, Mr. Raad. Perhaps you should give up reporting for fiction writing."

Two people were kind enough to laugh.

Raising a hand, Chambers said. "I appreciate your time and attention. This has been an honor, and thanks to Mr. Raad, entertaining. I'm afraid I must return to my work, but I want to say this one more time. We have not tunneled beneath the Dome of the Rock, nor do we plan to. Please don't let rumors keep you from being the professionals I know you all are. Thank you."

Questions flew like arrows, but Chambers ignored them all. He refused to look at the faces. Landau and the others rushed him from the room and into a side room to wait until the others had left.

"Did that go as badly as I think it did?" he asked Landau.

"I've seen worse."

"Really?"

"No."

THIRTY-ONE

H ow did the press conference go?" Amber sounded cheerful over the cell phone.

"That's like asking Abraham Lincoln if he enjoyed his Booth." It was good to hear her voice. For a moment it made him forget his embarrassment, but just for a moment.

"What? Oh, I get it. It's a pun." She paused, but Chambers could hear her breathing over the military-grade, encrypted cell phone. "That bad?"

"I suppose it could have been worse. No, wait. It couldn't."

"I'm sorry, David. I know you didn't want to do it. It was a lose-lose situation."

He looked at Landau, who rode in the back of the SUV with him. "I think it was a setup. A couple of the press members had information they couldn't possibly know without help."

"But who could be sharing information?"

"I can think of a dozen people. It's always the one you least expect. For all I know, ol' Hiram here could be on the take."

Landau glared at him. "You know I can hear you, right? I can also reach you, if you know what I mean."

Chambers tried to grin but his mouth refused.

"Where are you now?" Amber asked.

"Driving back to the hotel, where I plan to hide under the bed."

She chuckled, but he had the impression it had nothing to do with his weak humor. "Sounds uncomfortable. I have a better idea. Come to the... first site. We have something to show you."

That was Amber, cautious even over an encrypted phone. "Maybe later. I have a noose to make—"

"Stop it, David. Get your rear end over here, and bring your biggest smile."

"Just tell me what you've found—" The line went dead. "Amber? Amber?"

"Does that happen often?" Landau did a poor job of concealing his grin.

"What?"

"Women hanging up on you. I'm guessing you've grown used to it."

"Nice guy. Kick a man when he is down." A second later. "We need the helicopter."

"For what?"

"Amber says she and Nuri have found something."

Landau made a call.

∽

Within the hour, Chambers was walking up the slope to the staircase in what little remained of the previously unknown Essene compound. Landau walked behind. They paused long enough to watch the helo take to the air again.

Ascending the slope required Chambers's careful attention. One misstep and he could twist an ankle. For an instant, that seemed like a welcome idea. Physical pain was preferable to the emotional and intellectual beating he was taking.

"Glad you could make it."

Chambers looked up and saw Amber leaning next to the opening, arms crossed in front of her. Her wide smile gave Chambers a lift. "I'd rather be here than where I was a little while ago."

"Let me help you forget that." She disappeared into the maw of the tunnel.

"I think she's teasing you, pal." Landau passed him as they continued up the grade.

"More like tormenting me."

Moments later they exchanged the warm, bright sun for the dim tunnel. Chambers hesitated at the opening. He had not been back to the spot since the tragedy. Images of blood-soaked stone strobed in his mind.

"Sometimes it's best not to think, Doc. Just do." Landau started down the tunnel.

"Got that from a fortune cookie, did ya?"

"Personal experience."

What has this man seen in his career? What has he done? Chambers took Landau's advice and kept moving forward.

Workers, most likely the ones sitting in the shade of the canopies at the foot of the hill, had cleared the tunnel of debris and had even used thick hardwood to replace the steps they had destroyed to access the hidden treasure. The last portion of the tunnel showed damage from the explosion and cave-in. Posts, beams, and narrow metal slabs shored up the ceiling and weak areas of the wall. The dead-end wall was still in place but deeply chipped and cracked. There was something else: a ragged hole about a meter in diameter.

The smiling face of Amber appeared from the other side. "Come on in. We've been expecting you."

Chambers crawled through the hole, glad he had taken time to change into his work clothes. They suspected a space was behind the wall when they first examined the tunnel. The explosion and the deaths it brought kept them from pursuing the investigation. Now Chambers stood in a stone room with a low ceiling. He could stand straight, but Landau had to keep his head low. The whole space was the size of a bedroom. Lights filled the area with yellow illumination.

Nuri stood shoulder to shoulder with Amber, his hands in his pockets. He looked smug. Amber looked ready to explode with glee.

"Okay. I'm here."

Without a word, Amber and Nuri parted, allowing Chambers to see the wall behind them. Both retreated to side walls. At the back wall rested several objects covered in dust. The first thing to catch Chambers's eye was a table, a meter long and half that in width. Around the table top was a handcrafted ornamental edge. The table stood on four tapered legs. Nuri or Amber had removed some of the grime revealing gleaming gold.

Chambers let his eyes shift to another object, a large menorah, also made of gold. There were also smaller objects, flasks of gold.

"What do you think?" Amber asked.

Chambers leaned forward and placed his hands on his knees, his body swaying. The room spun. Sweat dotted his face. His stomach clenched.

"Yeah," Amber said, "we had the same reaction."

"Is this what I think it is?" Landau asked.

Nuri spoke for the first time since they arrived. "If you think that's the holy Table of Shewbread and the menorah that was in the Holy of Holies of the temple, then yes."

Chambers straightened, then walked to the table. With obvious respect, he extended a hand and touched it. The hand trembled. Tears formed in his eyes.

"Shewbread? I really should have paid attention in Shabbat school." Landau sounded puzzled.

"It's from Exodus 25." Amber moved to Chambers's side and placed a hand on his shoulder. "Twelve loaves of bread were to be kept on the table of gold. Once a week, priests would replace the twelve unleavened loaves with fresh bread. Tradition teaches that the old bread remained fresh and warm. It was a type of offering to God. Only the priests were allowed to eat of the bread, although King David and his men ate some during a difficult time."

"So this was in the second temple?" Landau asked.

"Yes." Chambers found his voice. "It's...beautiful."

A thudding, pounding sound poured into the small space.

"Sounds like a helicopter." Landau was out the opening a moment later. The others followed.

Chambers arrived at the tunnel entrance a few moments after Landau. He took a step back when he saw Landau unholster his weapon.

"Trouble?"

"I don't know yet. Are you expecting someone?" Landau scanned the sky.

"Are you kidding? I didn't know I was going to be here."

"There." Landau pointed to the north. "It's making a wide sweep. Indirect approach. Not something an unfriendly would do. I wish I had binoculars."

"It's not our helicopter?"

"No." Landau kept his eyes skyward. "Sounds like a military bird."

"Whose military bird?"

Nuri and Amber arrived and stood behind them. "Who is it?" Amber asked.

"We don't know yet," Chambers said.

The copter approached slowly and lowered to the landing area. "It's Israeli military. Sikorsky S-70, probably out of Hatzerim air base." Landau relaxed, and Chambers took his cue from him. Life was surreal to Chambers. His mind seemed to float in a sea of emotion from the press conference to the recent finds. More than anything, he wanted a couple of days to sort things out. He was sure he wasn't going to get one.

The moment the helicopter set down on the pad, Chambers started forward, but Landau stopped him. "Call me paranoid, but let's just wait to see who our guests are."

"Paranoid is fine with me," Chambers backed up a step.

The blades of the transport chopper slowed, and the side door opened. A man in uniform emerged first, then a man in casual clothes. The third man caught Chambers's attention. He wore a black hooded robe, and moved with less agility than the others. The distance kept Chambers from making an identification. The three walked toward the footpath leading up the side of the hill. The man in the hood seemed to know where he was going. At the foot of the path, the hooded person said something to the man in uniform. The soldier walked back to the aircraft.

"There's something familiar about them," David said. "The man in the hood...that couldn't be..."

"That's John Trent," Amber said. "What's he doing here?"

Chambers strained his eyes, and as the men started up the path, he realized she was correct. "The hooded man moves kinda like... No, it couldn't be."

"Who?" Nuri asked.

Chambers didn't answer. He knew just by the man's mannerisms who it was working his way up the slope. "If I told you, Nuri, you wouldn't believe me."

"Try me."

"I don't think so. Some things have to be seen to be believed."

They waited as the two men made the climb. Ten minutes later, the hooded man stepped into the tunnel and pushed back the hood.

"You're alive!" Nuri took two steps back as if he had just met a ghost. "But...but... I don't understand. I was told..."

"I am so sorry to have left you out of the loop, Dr. Aumann, but it had to be so." Ben-Judah embraced the man. "I have no right to expect your forgiveness. Circumstances sometimes dictate our actions."

"Professor. What if someone sees you?" Chambers was as puzzled as Nuri was stunned.

"I had to see what you have found. I cannot stay in my room forever. Not with so much going on."

"I advised against it," Trent said. "But he doesn't listen to me."

"Wait," Amber said. "How did you know about our find? David is the only person I called."

"Mr. Landau can explain as we walk. I must see what you have found. From the sound of it, it must be significant."

"What about it, Landau?" Chambers said.

"No big deal. Your phones are monitored."

"What? Our cell phones?"

"Hotel phones too. So is your Internet usage, e-mail. Pretty much everything. We can fix your position by your phones. Nothing new there. It's been done for years. Cell phones have GPS built in for a reason."

"Not to track people. This is outrageous," Amber said. "You don't trust us?"

"It has nothing to do with trust. Everyone's phone is monitored," Ben-Judah said. "It is the way it must be for many reasons, including your security. Now show me; show me what you've found."

Chambers and Nuri helped the two men through the tight opening, then stood to the side. This, Chambers decided, was one of those moments that words could not improve.

The professor stood in the middle of the space, his eyes fixed on the gold table, the menorah, and the gold flasks. Ben-Judah shivered, then trembled.

"Professor?" Chambers moved to his side. Amber was a step behind. "Are you all right?"

Ben-Judah crumbled to his knees and sobbed.

"Professor, it's okay, we're here with you." Amber knelt beside him. "What can we do?"

Ben-Judah leaned back on his heels, lifted his arms, turned his palms up, tilted his head back so much the tears ran down his face. His lips trembled but no words came. Then, in a clear voice, Abram Ben-Judah began to pray aloud in Hebrew.

Chambers moved away, to let a holy man do a holy work, and something inside of him warmed.

THIRTY-TWO

The day had been more than Chambers thought he could endure. He had awakened to the sight of hundreds of protesters outside the hotel; he'd done—at the prime minister's request—a press conference he wasn't and couldn't be prepared for; he'd been called to one of the original dig sites where he saw things he had only read about, objects some had suggested were only myths; and all that had come on the heels of the previous day's discovery of the Urim and Thummim. Were they the original stones? That would be debated for many years to come.

Odd that the scene that most moved him was his mentor on his knees, in the dirt of a concealed room that hadn't seen the light of day in two hundred decades. The objects were the rarest of the rare, and evidence of the Bible's historical accuracy, something he had long defended until he turned his back on his pending marriage, his love of biblical archaeology, his father, and God.

As he walked through the hotel lobby, glad that the police had peacefully put an end to the protests outside, Chambers wondered if a man like Ben-Judah could ever become so disappointed in life as to abandon all faith. He chastised himself for the thought. It would be easier to imagine the sea no longer sending waves to the shore or the stars ceasing to shine. Men like Ben-Judah did not *have* faith; faith *had* them. It was in the fiber of their being and grew with every beat of their hearts.

When Chambers had seen the legendary temple articles, they astounded him. His knees felt weak, his heart seized, and he knew he was viewing something any biblical archaeologist would give his life to see.

Ben-Judah saw more. He saw the hand of God; he saw objects built at the specific behest of the Almighty. Chambers saw a career made; Ben-Judah saw a need to worship.

He crossed the ornate lobby, eyed two of Landau's security men, who—in the absence of hotel tenants—looked conspicuous. Landau had trained him and the others to not acknowledge the security. It seemed silly to Chambers. The people who opposed them would not be fooled by such things.

Chambers, carrying the Bible from his hotel room, walked into the hotel bar. As it was most nights, the bar was empty. The dark space was punctuated with neon lights meant to lure patrons, but there were too few to make it profitable. He wondered if John Trent was footing the bill to keep the place open. He found his usual seat, the one in which he had drunk himself nearly under the table weeks before. These days, he consumed decaf coffee.

"*Shalom*, Dr. Chambers." The bartender was one of three he had met in here. Tall and lanky, he had the look of a graduate student. His accent was German.

"*Shalom*, Michael. Staying busy?"

"No, but I have a book to keep me busy."

"Ah, a scholar. What are you reading?"

He held up several comic books and waved them. "Food for the mind."

Chambers laughed and scooted into "his" booth. "The usual, Michael." He looked up as he spoke and saw the young man already pouring coffee into a mug.

A few moments later, Michael set down the cup and a plate with fruit pastry. "I saw you on the news today, Dr. Chambers."

"I'm sorry. You'll get over it." *I might not.*

"I'm no expert, but that looked like a setup to me."

"I could have handled it better. What's the pastry for?"

"I told you. I saw you on television today. I thought you might like something sweet to end the day."

"Thanks, Michael."

The young man retreated behind the bar and opened one of his comics. Chambers sipped the coffee and opened the Bible. The simple act sent a chill through him. He had intended to read Exodus 25's descriptions of the furnishings in the tabernacle, the predecessor to the first temple. Unlike Solomon's temple, the tabernacle was portable, a collection of curtains and objects that could be erected by the wandering Hebrews. It would be centuries before those objects found a home in the temple King Solomon built for the Lord.

That had been his intention, but he could not focus on the passage. He didn't need to read the verses. He knew the Bible better than most preachers. It had been a spiritual guide, then an archaeological one. He knew the words; once he had known the Truth behind them.

The last thought made him pause. He used the past tense. Was that true? Was his spiritual life now to be thought of in the past tense? Had God abandoned him in his time of need, turned His back on the godly woman he called Mother? Had God so consumed his father that the man found his work more important than his family?

Or had he been a fool? Amber was no intellectual lightweight. She was brilliant but never sought the spotlight. Theirs was a competitive field. All of science was a competitive sport. There were several things every young scientist learned once the idealism wore off: no matter how great your discovery, many of your peers will dismiss it or challenge it, and if they can't remove it, then they'll try to make sure it's swept under the carpet so as not to detract from their work. There were exceptions. Ben-Judah was the best of these, a man who cared only about the knowledge gained, not about the fame it brought.

A hot ache ate at the back of Chambers's sternum. He was one of the former in that list. Make a significant find and ride it for all it was worth.

Sure, add to the body of knowledge, but be sure to grab all the fame you can along the way.

When had that happened? His father hadn't set that kind of example. Was that it? A response to the idea that his father loved his work more than he loved his wife, his son?

Chambers ran a hand over his eyes. He was used to analyzing data, facts, and historical clues, not himself. The former could be frustrating; the latter was pure pain. What had Amber said? *"Your mother lied to your father?"* It sounded like blasphemy when he heard it. No woman was brighter, more dedicated, more loving—except Amber. She was a natural beauty. He had never seen her look more gorgeous than earlier today as she stood in the stairway entry, dressed in dirty work clothes, hair mussed, and flashing her million-watt smile.

The sight made him smile, and he covered his mouth in case Michael saw it and thought he'd lost his mind.

He tasted the pastry, enjoying the burst of sweet as it contrasted the bitter of his coffee.

The Copper Scroll had been proven to be true. He and his team had recovered gold and silver as ingots, coins, and vessels. They unearthed some of the holiest items known in the Bible. Time and time again, the Bible showed itself to be true. He had known that his entire life. Why had he allowed himself to drift? It cost him his relationship with his father, with Amber, with his friends, and with his science.

"You are a world-class idiot, David." He spoke softly.

"Did you say something, Dr. Chambers?"

Chambers looked up. "Just thinking out loud, Michael. Sorry."

"No problem." He went back to his comic book.

There—in Jerusalem, in a high-class hotel, in an empty bar—David Chambers made his apologies to God.

∽

The staff of Prime Minister Nathan Ben Yakov often called him The Man Who Never Sleeps. It was an exaggeration, but not by much. He maintained two sets of aides, one for business hours, one for late nights. Key staff, however, could not be duplicated, especially those privy to state secrets. They just had to learn how to go without sleep.

As the clock passed into the wee hours, Yakov sat in the office of his private residence, Beit Aghion on Smolenskin Street—named after a Russian novelist who wrote in Hebrew—and studied the video and photos delivered by armed couriers earlier that day. He alternated between pure joy and abject terror. The Table of Shewbread, or as he preferred, The Table of Presence, was stunning even covered in dust, its gold dimmed. He lingered over the photos of the gems of the high priest's breastpiece. If only the vestments, the ephod, the robes had been preserved, but that was too much of a miracle to ask. As it was, *HaShem* had blessed his nation with more than could be imagined.

Now he needed another miracle: protection for his nation. The protests in three cities were just the beginning. There would be more. Every security branch Israel had, as well as those of his country's allies, were feeding him information, all of it bad news. Several Arab nations, the Russians, and the Iranians were planning to file complaints with the United Nations stating that a third temple would create unbearable stress in the region. Their assumption was the one made so many times through history, that the temple must be built where the Dome of the Rock now stands. If they extended themselves with a little research, then they'd know that other sites have been suggested by scholars. All of that was secondary, of course. One either loved Israel or hated it. There seemed to be no middle ground, no ambivalence, and the numbers on the "hate" side seemed to be growing.

He pushed aside the photos, pulled an intelligence brief to the center of the desk, and then read it for the tenth time. Iran, which had been ratcheting up its anti-Semitic rhetoric, had also been testing a new medium-range missile "for defensive purposes." It was a missile that could easily reach Israel.

There had been a loud outcry from the United States, the United Kingdom, and many other countries, but such complaints never brought change. Iran had been spoiling for a fight for decades. All it needed was an excuse, and the sky would be full of death.

Yakov looked at his desk. The temple artifacts represented the best possible future: Israel, a holy nation. The intelligence reports represented the worst possible future: another war.

He closed his eyes and leaned his head against the high-back office chair. The cool leather felt good against his scalp, and he longed for the dark peace of sleep. Instead, he wondered if he should stop the search until things settled down. Perhaps they should move more slowly, deliberately. That would never work. John Trent was an impatient man, and the stone had already begun rolling down the hill. Somehow, the truth had become known.

Yakov had done everything he could to keep the State of Israel out of the search for temple treasures. The time would come when all would be revealed—his role in coordinating the effort, funneling money through John Trent, even his sending the hapless David Chambers to conduct a press conference he was ill equipped to handle. Anything to keep the appearance of separation.

The question he kept asking himself was whether it was prudent to bring this part of the world to the brink of war for the sake of rebuilding a temple torn down twice by invading armies.

He decided it was.

∽

Chambers left a healthy tip on the table for Michael and returned to his room. Although he was a man of letters, his prayer had been simple, almost childlike. No voices came, no apparitions, no dreams, no visions. Just a sweet sense of peace. He was home.

The elevator took him to the twelfth floor. His only regret was that it was so late and Amber would be in bed. She and Nuri had returned to the hotel late, having supervised the crating and moving of the recently found artifacts.

"You look like fifty miles of bad road," he had said.

"Sweet, just what every girl wants to hear."

Chambers tried to backtrack, but Amber put an end to it with a smile, then excused herself.

"Aren't you going to eat?"

"I'm going to bed, assuming I don't fall asleep in the elevator."

That was hours ago. Now, as he exited the elevator cab, he wished that Amber were available. He had apologized to God; now he needed to apologize to her. He walked the empty corridor to his room and had started to insert his card key when a light several doors down caught his attention.

Amber's room. The door was ajar.

That wasn't like her. Maybe she and Nuri—he forced the thought from his mind. That was the old David. Amber deserved better. Again, he started to insert his card key, but curiosity stopped his hand. He placed the key in his pocket and walked down the hall to Amber's room. Maybe she was up for a chat after all.

The door was barely open, just enough to let light escape into the hallway. He rapped a knuckle on the door. "Amber?"

Nothing.

"Amber, it's David. Did you know your door is open?"

Still nothing. Maybe she had fallen asleep. He wasn't certain what to do. He reached for the handle, intending to pull the door closed and return to his own room, but he stopped. He had no idea why. He just did.

He placed a finger on the door and pushed it open, calling her name again. He heard nothing. Not a radio, not the shower, nothing.

He walked in. The light was on in the small living room. So was the light in the bedroom. He felt like a Peeping Tom, but he wanted to make sure she was safe. The thought of seeing her peacefully sleeping brought warmth to his face.

Quietly, he stepped to the bedroom door and looked in.

What he saw sent a spear through his heart.

THIRTY-THREE

How could this happen, Landau? How?" Chambers paced his room. Landau had told him to wait for him there, but waiting only turned his fear into anger. "You're supposed to be the security guru. You're supposed to make sure we're safe."

"We've done everything we can—"

Chambers spun on his heel. "It wasn't enough. She's gone. Taken from a room you assured us was safe."

"Dr. Chambers, I have a team investigating her room, the grounds, everything. We'll find her."

"Really? That's a fact, is it? I'm just a lowly archaeologist, so I could be wrong about this, but wouldn't it have made more sense to prevent the abduction in the first place?" Chambers clenched his teeth, then his fists, digging his knuckles into his eyes and fighting for control.

"You need to calm down, Dr. Chambers. This isn't helping."

"Calm down? Calm *down*?" Chambers sank to the sofa. "I just don't know how this could happen. What about the video surveillance? What about your men? How did they get into her room? She would have checked the video monitor. None of this makes sense."

"My team is investigating that. The police have been notified, as have internal security agencies. I can tell you that the man monitoring the video system was nullified."

"Fell asleep?"

There was a heated pause, and Chambers realized he had let his mouth get him in trouble again.

"He's dead."

Chambers thought it best not to speak.

"The man has three children. I tell you that so you'll understand. I'm going to find who did this and make him suffer—suffer hard."

Chambers covered his face with his hands. This had to be a nightmare. It had to be. Amber's room empty; her blouse on the bed with a curved knife stuck through it and deep into the mattress; the note: "Tell anyone, and she is dead. You will be contacted."

Then there was the Polaroid photo next to the blouse: the image of Amber, tape over her mouth, knife to her throat. Her expression...the fear...the pleading in her eyes... "Oh, God, dear God."

He felt someone sit next to him. He couldn't bring himself to look up. A muscular hand landed on his shoulder and rested there. Chambers dissolved into tears.

"Dr. Chambers... David, listen to me. I need you to do a few things."

"What? I'll do anything."

"First, I need you to pull yourself together as soon as possible. I know this is tough, but when the bad guys contact you, I need you to be on your game."

"I'll try."

"No, David. This isn't one of those situations where you try. You *will* pull yourself together. There is no other choice. Use that high-octane brain of yours. Am I clear?"

"Yes. I'll try—I'll do it."

"Good. Next, I need you to stop all work on the dig sites. I mean all of them. I want the kidnappers to think they're winning. Now listen to me. I've already spoken to the prime minister, and he is activating every intelligence agency in Israel. That includes all the military intelligence branches of the Israeli Defense Forces. Shin Bet is pouring everything it has into this. Even Mossad is working with their overseas operatives. Yakov has also told me he's calling in favors from friendly intelligence groups like the CIA, MI6, and others."

"I appreciate that."

"Just to be clear, David, he's not doing it for you or even for Amber, although he is very concerned about her. He's doing this because we're sitting on a powder keg. Here's the good news: Israel is always in danger from within and without. That has made us paranoid and extremely good at monitoring our citizens and enemies. We are the best in video surveillance. Right now, a team of video-surveillance analysts are using the best computer software to analyze data. We've tracked terrorists this way before."

Chambers lowered his hands and took several deep breaths. "I understand. How do you think they will contact me?"

"Unknown. They might contact the hotel by phone, but I doubt it. They know we can trace that. My guess is they'll send an emissary, a third party who doesn't know what's going on—maybe a kid paid to deliver an envelope or an encrypted cell phone. We'll just have to wait and see."

"My mother used to say the hardest work a person will ever do is wait for someone they love."

"Smart woman."

"Yes, she was." He rose and walked to his window. Outside the new sun cast golden rays on the predominately brown Jerusalem. Buses of tourists passed along the road belching black clouds of diesel smoke as the vehicles pressed through traffic. Birds flew through a crystalline sky, oblivious to the pain raging in his soul. That was the way with the world, tragedies happened every few minutes—people died of starvation, criminals assaulted the innocent, wars took the lives of young men and women who had barely begun to live, cancer ate away the rich and the poor, and terrorists schemed to force their twisted sense of justice on society. Amber was one of seven billion people on the planet. To Chambers, she was the most important person.

"You'll keep me posted, won't you?"

Landau rose. "Yes sir. I will."

~

The hotel room proved too small for Chambers. He found Landau and told him he was going to the first floor for some coffee. He could have made coffee in his room, but it wasn't the drink he was after, it was space, something less restrictive, less claustrophobic. Hours had passed, and the stress of sleeplessness and shock drained him. He took a seat in the restaurant, refused a menu, and consumed cup after cup of strong black coffee.

Two hours later, Chambers could sit no longer. His mind was blurry, and his nerves on edge from the caffeine. He paced the lobby, but his restless energy didn't dissipate. Fresh air. That's what he needed. He passed the bar and looked in. One of the televisions mounted near the ceiling showed a local news program. The image of hundreds of protesters massing in the streets of the Old City reminded Chambers of the horde of angry people in the street yesterday.

Odd. The street in front of the hotel was calm, uncluttered. Maybe Yakov, the police, and Shin Bet had found a way to keep them away. What more could go wrong? He stepped into the street. The morning had grown warm. The sound of traffic and chatty pedestrians formed a cacophony of confusion. A helicopter circled overhead.

Inhaling deeply, he took in the aroma of the city, contemporary and ancient. What was Amber smelling? The thought of her bound, held in some room, enduring torment his mind refused to imagine eroded what little strength he had left. Never had he felt so helpless, so hopeless, so mentally and emotionally weak.

A cab pulled from the street and up to the covered porch. The driver, a dark-skinned man with East African features exited. "Will there be any luggage, Dr. Chambers?"

The sound of his name pulled him from the fog. "I'm sorry. What?"

"Luggage, sir." The accent was definitely African. Ethiopian, maybe Somali. "Baggage, sir?"

"I'm sorry, you must have the wrong man. I didn't call for a cab."

"I am so sorry. I thought you were Dr. Chambers. You look very much like his picture."

"I am Dr. Chambers, but I didn't..." He recalled the note stating he would be contacted. He also remembered Landau's comment about the kidnappers using an innocent third party. He should ask the man to wait and retrieve Landau, or at very least, one of the security men. Most of them, however, were still searching the grounds and empty rooms of the hotel. He made a command decision and prayed he wasn't making a mistake. "No, no luggage. Just me."

Shutting down his screaming subconscious, David Chambers entered the cab.

∽

"May I ask how you knew to pick me up?" Chambers sat in the back of the well-used cab.

"You called for a cab, sir." The driver, whom Chambers guessed was in his midthirties but was probably younger, looked confused.

"I didn't call for you."

"My dispatcher sent me." He pointed a finger at the radio. "Maybe one of your associates made the arrangements. It's all been paid for, sir, if that is what concerns you."

"No concerns." A moment later: "How did you know I would be in front of the hotel?"

"I didn't, sir. I was to call the front desk when I arrived, but you were already there."

Chambers started to ask where they were going, but the cabbie already looked too puzzled. He would wait. Ten minutes later, the driver stopped in front of a bank. Chambers tipped the man, feeling silly that he might be giving money to someone leading him to his demise. He exited the car and waited on the sidewalk. A moment later another cab appeared; this one from a different company.

The driver slipped from the seat. "You are Dr. Chambers, yes?" Arabic accent.

This time Chambers didn't hesitate. "Yes. I am."

The driver opened the rear door, and Chambers was on another ride, which ended in front a museum. Then another cab. Each time, he was told that a dispatcher sent the cab. It was in the third cab that he had a frightening realization: he had not brought his encrypted cell phone. What if Landau needed to reach him? What if he needed to reach Landau?

There was nothing to do about it now. He considered asking the driver to take him back to his hotel, but couldn't bring himself to do it. He knew nothing about spy procedures and intrigue. He just knew that a series of cab rides like this could not be coincidence.

The surroundings became familiar again. He had been driven through much of the city, but the sight of the Dome of the Rock and signs to the Wailing Wall told him his destination. The cab pulled to the open, tree-dotted area just outside the Muslim compound. "Here we are, sir. May Allah bless your day."

Chambers conjured a smile and reached for his wallet. The driver waved him off. "All is paid for, sir. Even the gratuity. Your people are very kind."

"Yes, they are." Chambers couldn't think of anything else to say.

He needed no directions. There could be only one place in mind. Chambers walked from the street, along the path into the trees, beneath the shadow of the Dome, to the concrete structure that protected the Jerusalem access to Herod's tunnel. He dialed the combination used the last time he was there just days ago. He had a hunch to leave the door unlocked. He did the same with the welded-rebar grate over the opening in the floor.

Every step Chambers took was laden with fear. Not for his own safety but for Amber's. His greatest terror was tripping over her body. He evicted the thought. If they wanted her dead, they would have killed her in the room. If they wanted him dead, he would have found them waiting when he retired for the night. If they wanted everyone dead, they would have set a bomb on the wing. If they could get past the video surveillance, if they could kill the guard at the monitors and steal his master key, they could have done any of that and more.

At the back of the wall, he retrieved a helmet with the attached miner's light and a flashlight. He shouldn't need either since the work lights in the tunnel would come on the moment he activated the generator, but old safety habits died hard.

He moved slowly, as if his concern and fear had weight. He slipped down the hole into Herod's tunnel. Was he supposed to do that? Is that what they wanted? He didn't know. It made sense. Why else arrange an elaborate ruse to get him here?

Rung by rung, he had descended into what had been his greatest archaeological find before returning to Jerusalem, down into the tunnel that led to a secret compartment that held items no one ever expected to see again.

Every other time he descended into the gut of the tunnel, Chambers felt the crushing, clawed hand of some invisible giant squeezing his heart and lungs, but not this time. Before, he had to remind himself to breathe and force his heart to slow; he had to remind himself that walls of solid rock don't close in on unsuspecting archaeologists. He expected the same fear, but it didn't come. He could no longer be bothered with fear for himself, not when the only woman he loved was in danger.

He walked a short distance down the tunnel, found one of the few level areas of floor, and sat. There was nothing else to do but wait.

Then he heard a sound.

THIRTY-FOUR

Footsteps echoed off the rock walls. In the distance, thirty or forty meters down the tunnel, was a man. He walked slowly toward Chambers like a man out for an afternoon stroll.

Chambers stood. The man wore a helmet light, which he kept directed at Chambers, leaving the visitor in silhouette against the work lights that trailed down the tunnel. He also carried a bright flashlight, the beam of which he kept in Chambers's face. Chambers raised a hand and squinted into the glow.

"Who are you?" Chambers's words rolled down the corridor.

No answer.

"I asked you a question."

"Yes, you did, David."

The voice stunned him. "Nuri?"

The man lowered the beam spotlight and switched off the light on his helmet. "Yes, David, it is me."

Chambers gave a smile, which quickly evaporated. "Wait. I didn't see you at the hotel. Amber. She's been taken."

"I know all about it, David." He grinned and motioned to the tunnel. "A fitting place, no? Your great discovery. Your legacy. Until, that is, our recent finds. Nothing compares to such marvelous religious artifacts."

"You know about Amber? I didn't see you at the hotel. I-I didn't even think about you."

"I have been working all night. With Amber."

Chambers tensed. "You know where she is?"

"Yes. I know how she got there, and I know exactly what you're going to do."

Fury boiled in Chambers, and he drew his hands into fists.

Nuri chuckled. "David, David. You have been so angry, so quick to attack those around you. It is your weakness, my friend. Do you want to attack me? Of course you do. Why shouldn't you? You should know that it would be bad for you and for Amber."

"You don't frighten me, Nuri."

Nuri's face hardened. "David, I can kill you in forty different ways. I practice daily. I have dreamed of it ever since we've arrived. Trust me. I'd love to do that right now, but that's not my mission. There is only one way to save your darling Amber."

"Say it."

"We want it all. Every ingot and vessel of gold, every ounce of silver, every religious artifact. You will turn it all over to us."

"Do you really think the professor will turn those things over to you? He won't. You know that. Your greed has made you stupid."

"Greed? Yes, I am greedy, but there's more to it than that. The Jews will not rebuild their temple. Not now, not ever. They might raise the money, but they will not have the instruments they need. I'll make sure those are destroyed. As for our dear Ben-Judah, well, you'll have to convince him. He loves you; he loves Amber. You might as well be his own flesh and blood. He'll listen to you. He'll do anything to save Amber's life."

"You're wrong. You're an archaeologist. How can you destroy such ancient artifacts?"

"Some things are more important. Who knows, there may be more political value in them than monetary. That will suit my superiors fine."

"You're crazy, Nuri. You've lost what little mind you had. You know I don't control those things. Ben-Judah and Yakov have them locked away. There's no way I can release them to you."

Nuri shrugged. "I admit, it seems impossible, but you can work miracles. Ben-Judah—and it wasn't nice of you to let me think he was dead all this time—will do it. As I said, he loves you and Amber."

"Then you don't understand the man. This is his life. He'd die first."

"That is his choice, but you must help him understand that Amber will die first. Maybe I could arrange a little proof for you and for him. Which of her body parts would you like sent to you?"

Chambers took a step forward.

"Please, David. Try. I'll be punished for killing you, but it will be worth it."

Chambers stopped, caught between fury that demanded blood and fear for Amber's life. Heroics here would do nothing for Amber, wherever she was.

"We trusted you."

Nuri raised an eyebrow. "Really? *You* trusted *me*." He laughed.

"I didn't say I liked you, Nuri, but I never doubted your skill, just your personality. Ben-Judah trusted you. So did Amber."

"I imagine that will change now." He motioned up the tunnel. "It is time you delivered my message. Go. Deliver the message."

"You know what the answer will be."

"Then you have a problem. Oh, and be sure to lock the grate over the entry. We wouldn't want anyone to fall in and get hurt." Nuri turned and started a casual stroll toward Jericho.

⌒

It took only one cab ride to return from the hotel, and when he arrived, he wished he had asked the driver to keep going.

"Where have you been?" Landau's face was red around the edges, and Chambers was sure he could see the man's carotid artery pulse. "And why don't you have your phone?"

"I didn't know I was going out." He started across the lobby. "Nuri's part of it."

"I know." Landau's voice had an edge to it.

"You do? Then why didn't you tell me?"

"Because we just found out. If you hadn't been out sightseeing—"

Chambers stopped and spun, taking a step closer to the man. "I wasn't sightseeing. Nuri or whoever he works for had it arranged." He paused and lowered his voice. "Look, it was stupid, I know. The note on Amber's bed said someone would contact me. When the cabbie called my name, I thought the time had come. I want Amber back, and if that means getting into a cab I didn't hire, then so be it. We have to know what they want. I'm helpless to do anything else."

Landau seized his elbow in a way Chambers knew would leave marks and directed him through the lobby, past the front desk, and into one of the empty conference rooms. For a moment, Chambers thought the Shin Bet man would push him through the door without opening it.

The moment the door latched behind them, Landau pointed at one of the seats that surrounded a small conference table. "Sit down."

"I don't feel like sitting."

"I can arrange that."

Chambers rolled his eyes but sat. "Fine. Tell me you have found Amber."

"Okay, we know where she is."

He was on his feet again. "Really? Is she okay?"

"I told you to sit."

Chambers did. "Is she okay?"

"I'll tell you this much, then you're going to spill your guts about Nuri and where you were. Then and only then will I give you more information about Amber. Clear?"

"Clear."

"We know where she is but not her condition. We assume she's still alive since they need her to manipulate you...us."

"Where?"

"About a year ago, in the east part of the city, the Muslims built a school to train clerics. She's being kept there."

"How did—"

"Despite what you might think at the moment, we're good at what we do. Jerusalem is a surveilled city. It has to be. I told you that the man assigned to watch the security monitors had been killed. We think Nuri was the murderer." He held up a hand. "You're going to ask why. This will go quicker if you sit and listen. We can't prove he's the killer, but we will. He was known to our man, so he could approach him without raising suspicion. Then he fired a small caliber round into the man's heart. Of course, the gun would have had a silencer. He then disabled the monitors and headed to your floor."

"So you didn't see him enter or leave her room?"

"Not on our cameras, but the hotel maintains a set of security cameras on the outside of the building to monitor the parking lot, entry way, and the like. We have him leaving the building with Amber walking by his side."

"She just walked out with him? She wouldn't do that."

Landau pulled out a chair and sat. "Yes she would. So would you." Again he stopped Chambers from interrupting with a raised hand. "I use a passkey to get into your room, I'm armed, and I tell you that one of my friends has Amber and is ready to put a bullet in her head the moment you speak, cry out, or resist. You have no way of knowing if that's true, but the gun is pretty convincing. You following me?"

"Yeah. But the tape on her mouth."

"Drama for you. If she thought you'd die if she resisted, then she'd cooperate. I've seen people do mind-boggling things to save someone they love." He paused. "Of course, Nuri might have claimed to have the professor at gunpoint. We don't know the line he used, and it doesn't matter. He got her cooperation. It doesn't take a genius to know she loves you."

Chambers stammered, then gave up trying to speak.

"We have video of a van pulling up to the rear exit of the pool patio. That gave us the make and model of the car. It also gave us a time stamp. My team was able to use traffic video cameras to track their movement. Jerusalem, like London and other cities, has cameras on most major streets. We lost them when they pulled onto the street where the facility is. We did an aerial surveillance and found the van inside the walls. The school has high walls for privacy—and apparently for other reasons."

"Men are on their way there now, right? Tell me you have a team on the move."

Landau shook his head. "There's a problem. Not only is the facility a college for clerics, it has a mosque. To make matters worse, several of the students are related to high-ranking Islamic religious leaders. Can you imagine the problems that would arise if a bunch of Israeli Defense Forces storm the place? The world is already on edge about the whole third-temple thing."

"I don't care."

"You had better learn to care. There's no way the prime minister would allow what the world would see as an invasion of holy ground."

"Oh come on. Israel has a history of making raids—"

Landau slapped the table with his palm. "It's not going to happen, at least not soon. Intelligence thinks the school isn't involved."

"Tell me where it is. I'll go."

"And do what? You going to kick down the gate, climb the walls, put up your fists, and duke it out with whatever the terrorists have set up there. Trust me on this. You'd end up dead in minutes, and Amber would still be in danger. What part of that makes sense?"

Landau was right and the knowledge made Chambers's bones feel like warm wax. "We can't leave her. Who knows what they've done to her."

"Stay with me, Dr. Chambers. I need you functional. You're no good to Amber if you're a puddle of emotions. Got it?" When Chambers didn't respond, Landau seized his jaw and turned his face toward his own. "Got it?"

"Yes."

"I told you what I know, at least all I'm going to tell you for now. Your turn. Tell me where've you been and don't leave out any details."

"Okay." Chambers took a deep breath and let it out. It took five minutes for him to relate the story, then he stopped and waited for a reaction.

"You know they'll never turn over the artifacts. I'm sorry, David, but I can't see Yakov, Ben-Judah, and Trent agreeing to such a thing."

"They would sacrifice her?"

"Yes, they would. Just as they're willing to sacrifice themselves." Landau leaned back, and for the first time, Chambers saw despair on the man's face. "I can't believe Nuri would drag you all the way back to Herod's tunnel to deliver that message."

"It's a way of rubbing his victory in my face."

"And he just walked down the tunnel toward Jericho? That's a long walk."

"Maybe he had a bicycle. I don't know..." Chambers straightened. "Where did you say they had Amber?"

"Northeast part of the city. Just outside the Old City, on the Kidron side—"

"Show me."

"Why?"

"Come on."

"Where are we going?"

"My room. I want to know exactly where this school-mosque is."

Chambers bounced on the balls of his feet as he and Landau waited for the elevator. For a moment, he considered sprinting up twelve floors. The doors had barely parted before Chambers leapt into the cab. Seconds crawled by as they rode to David's floor. He shot out of the cab and jogged to his door, card key in hand. He opened the door so hard it shook the adjoining wall.

He glanced around the room. "Where did I put it?"

Landau entered and closed the door quietly behind him. "Where is what?"

"My tablet PC. I know I had it here."

"The desk." Landau pointed.

"Of course." Chambers seized it and turned it on. A few moments later, he had a satellite image of Jerusalem on the screen. He examined it, then handed it to Landau. "Show me."

"Doc, if you're thinking of going there—"

"For once, Landau, just for once, can't you go along with me?"

Landau frowned, his face a mixture of concern and irritation. He indicated a populated area along the far side of the Kidron Valley. Chambers snatched the tablet PC from Landau and tapped the screen.

"Come on, be there…be there."

"What are you looking for?"

"Wait." Chambers paced and mumbled to himself. Then he stopped, looked up, and smiled.

"You're scaring me, Doc."

"What would you do if I told you I may be able to get you into the facility?"

"I've told you. They won't let us in, and we can't storm the gates without bringing the whole Arab world down around our ears—and a few non-Arab states too."

"What if no one could see you?"

"How is that possible?"

Chambers set the flat computer on the desk and pointed. "Remember all those surveys we did looking for tunnels? NASA did orbital surveys; we did aerial ground-penetrating radar and Trent's T-ray surveys. When we found something, we did ground surveys. Well, when we found something that looked like a tunnel. Some things we ignored, at least in the beginning. We gave them low priority."

"Okay. I'm following you."

Chambers touched the screen. "This is the facility you identified. You see this line?"

Landau said he did. "It doesn't look very straight. What kind of tunnel is it?"

"It's not a tunnel, and you're right—it's a very crooked space."

"If it's not a tunnel, then what is it?"

"That, Mr. Landau, is a karstic fissure."

"A what?"

Chambers tapped the screen and the computer zoomed in on the image. "A karstic fissure. A karst is a region of limestone that has been altered by water, like underground streams. Sometimes they form sinkholes. The ancients used some of these naturally occurring cisterns as catch basins for rain. Underground streams can carve fissures—natural tunnels. We're the first to find this one, and we only found it because Trent is paying for the best high-end equipment."

"So what are you saying?"

"I'm saying you might not be able to get your men over the walls, but I might be able to get you under them."

"You look like a man with a plan."

Chambers shook his head. "I'm a man with an idea. You need to come up with the plan."

One hour later they were walking into Prime Minister Yakov's office.

THIRTY-FIVE

D avid Chambers was well into his second night without sleep. The best he had been able to manage was the occasional ten-minute fade-out. He had reached the point where coffee no longer helped. He and Landau had come up with a plan that Yakov called the most "outlandish thing I've heard" and then approved.

He spent the evening in the lobby staring out the window, occasionally drinking coffee. Most of the time he spent in prayer. Within minutes of submitting to restoration with God, he had learned that Amber had been abducted. He waited for his anger against God to return. It never did. Every time he thought of Jesus, he reminded himself that hardship and unfair treatment happens to everyone. Jesus of all people understood that. He was abducted by a mob, tried repeatedly by people who had either made up their minds about His guilt or couldn't be bothered. He endured beating and scourging, then was nailed to a cross, an innocent man in the hands of evil people. All but one of the disciples died a martyr's death, and John had suffered plenty in his day. It was a modern church contrivance that only good things happened to Christians. Chambers had never bought that feel-good philosophy. Still, he wished it were true.

When he dozed, he dreamed of Amber; when he prayed, he prayed for Amber; when he thought, he thought of Amber. He regretted the grief he had caused her. He hated his quick temper and fast mouth. He regret-ted so much. If God would return her to him, he would be a different man. He'd be a different man, regardless.

Things were underway, and they needed to be flawless.

Chambers's eyes were closed when he recognized the familiar voice of Landau. "It's time. You ready?"

"Is it a bad thing if I'm scared?"

Landau smiled. "It would be a bad thing if you weren't."

Chambers rose, looked down at his work boots and work clothes. He felt empty, a hollow man moving by a force he didn't understand. It was show time.

They walked from the seating area to the back of the hotel and through the kitchen, which was empty—something Landau insisted upon. A utility van waited for them. Once inside the back of the midsize panel truck, the men began to change clothes. A driver pulled away. They rode in silence.

"Sunup is in two hours," Landau said. "You were right. There was an opening on the west-facing slope of the valley. We've had a couple of track-hoes from the utility company working the spot you indicated. You were pretty close. Just three feet off the mark."

"That's not close, Landau, that's spot on."

"If you say so."

In a few moments, both men had changed into uniforms and donned yellow safety helmets. Before Landau slipped his coveralls on, he changed into a black special-forces-type uniform common to military and police spec ops worldwide.

"I saw the news report," Chambers said. "The media seem to be buying the gas-leak story."

"That's good, especially since there are no gas lines in the area. We'll be done before anyone figures that out."

The short drive seemed hours long. Chambers's palms were slick with moisture. Out the windscreen, he could see splashes of yellow from the van's warning lights. They started down a road that branched from the Shmuel Ben Adaya. From there, the driver turned onto a dirt path that jarred the men and equipment in the back.

Landau grinned. "Sometimes the most dangerous part of a mission is the drive there."

"You're kidding, right?"

"Mostly. You up for this?"

"I'm up for it. Just get us in; I'll get you there."

Landau narrowed his eyes. "And as a reminder, you stay behind at that point."

"Of course."

"I'm serious. I don't want you to be the first one I shoot."

Chambers stared at the man. "You know threats aren't all that endearing."

"That explains the failure of my social life."

The van slowed, then stopped. Landau opened the door, and the sound of diesel engines and the glare of bright work lights mounted to towers assaulted his senses. Two trackhoes took turns dipping their buckets into the earth, scooping dirt, and piling it to the side. The roar of a generator competed with the noise of heavy equipment.

"Kind of obvious, isn't it?" Chambers asked.

"It's the principle of hiding in plain sight. If we were out here working in the dark, we would look suspicious. We have men stationed around the perimeter to keep sightseers away."

A short distance away, a panel truck waited, identical to the one they had arrived in. Chambers was pretty sure a half-dozen armed men were waiting inside.

"When do we go?" Chamber studied the void where the equipment had been digging. At the bottom, he saw a dark shape, a hole.

"Anytime. The operators were just pushing dirt around until we got here. We had the opening half an hour ago." Landau made a hand gesture to the heavy equipment operators, and they shut down, exited the tractors and walked to the side.

"What do they do while we're in there?"

"They're our men, from the army. Let's go."

Chambers followed Landau to the hole. It was three or four meters deep and five meters across. The sides of the hole were tapered to prevent a cave-in. A worker stepped forward and handed Chambers a backpack. He took it without question, slipped it over his shoulder, and started down the slope.

The dirt was loose but held their footing. Chambers had climbed enough slopes to know to walk sideways to give his boot greater surface area to grip the ground.

Bits of dirt flowed down the slope, looking like tiny rivers of sand. The artificial lights cast the men's shadows long and thin. The biblical phrase *valley of death* came to Chambers mind. His heart beat as if in the last mile of a marathon.

They paused at the bottom, standing in front of a meter-wide, two-meter-tall ragged opening. Darkness waited for them. Chambers turned his helmet light on and saw what he feared. Chunks of limestone varying in size from pebbles to the width of a basketball littered the uneven floor. Moving through the tunnel was going to be slow and possibly painful.

"Turn your light off, Doc."

"What? Why?"

"Just do it and don't move."

Chambers didn't like the sound of that, but he complied. He switched off the helmet light, then looked at Landau, who raised a radio to his mouth and spoke one word in Hebrew.

Landau disappeared.

Everything disappeared.

It took one second for Chambers to realize the generator that powered the tower work lights had gone silent. Then he heard the sound of pounding. Something brushed passed him, then several somethings. Fighting the urge to turn and run, Chambers obeyed Landau's command to stay put.

Ten seconds passed, then the lights came back on. Chambers stared at Landau, who shrugged and said, "Oops, power outage."

Chambers turned, then jumped. A half-dozen armed men dressed in black from helmets to boots stood just inside the opening. "How... Never mind. I don't want to know."

Landau stepped into the jaws of the natural fissure, and the armed men parted before him. Chambers followed, thinking the soldiers looked more mechanical than human. Each wore night-vision goggles and carried a small automatic rifle and a side arm. He had no doubt they carried other things harmful to the human body.

"Give Dr. Chambers your attention, men. He's going to tell us what to expect while underground." Landau began to strip off the oversized utility jumpsuit he wore over his military assault uniform.

All eyes shifted to him, and Chambers could swear that each pair was boring a hole in him. He cleared his throat. "Um, okay...you are in a natural limestone formation created centuries ago by flowing water—"

"Faster and funnier, Doc," Landau said.

"Okay. The ground is uneven. As you can see, there are loose stones and larger rocks. These are ankle breakers. Watch your step. I suggest giving yourself some space so you can see what's in front of you. This is not a tunnel. That means the width of the fissure varies. It is unexplored, so we don't know how narrow it gets, but you may have to strip off your gear to get through the tight spots. Anyone claustrophobic?" They shook their heads but didn't speak. *Figures.* "Okay, if you get a little panicky, just take deep breaths and keep your eyes forward." He paused. "I'll lead the way since I've spent a fair amount of time underground. I've calculated how far we need to travel. The fissure runs beneath the school, but there's no opening. Mr. Landau tells me one of you is an explosives expert."

Three of the men raised a hand.

"Redundancy is an asset," Landau said.

Chambers didn't know how to respond. Landau spoke up. "We go in silent. Once we blow out the floor, everyone in the compound will know it. We move fast, find the woman, and exit with haste. You've seen the photo of Dr. Amber Rodgers. We don't leave till we find her. Clear?"

"Clear." They spoke in unison.

Chambers noticed that none of the men wore an insignia of rank or army, nothing to identify them as individuals or the army they served.

"It's time, Doc. Take point."

He worked his way slowly along the cluttered path. The fissure was two meters wide, but he had no doubt it would narrow. His heart tumbled like a stone down a slope. He tried to distract himself by thinking about the rest of the plan. To buy time, Landau had made sure Chambers entered the prime minister's offices in full daylight, easily observed by any interested watcher. He had made several trips to Hebrew University and watched as crates were loaded into the Institute of Archaeology. Similar crates and packing material were sent to the other locations where treasures and artifacts had been stored. Nuri knew those places well, and he, or whoever was calling the shots, would be watching.

A loose stone shifted under Chambers's boot and a slight pain ran up his leg. He tested the foot by putting more weight on it. Still usable. He pushed on, his helmet light moving from side to side and up and down. The ceiling dropped lower with each step.

Chambers's biggest fear was choosing the wrong part of the tunnel below the school. GPS was useless belowground. Distance was impossible to measure over uneven ground. His only advantage was the T-ray and GPR readings and the fact that the fissure made a sharp turn north about twenty meters from the center of the school's plaza. Aerial photos showed a wide open space of grass with picnic tables spaced a few feet apart. The rest of the space was open and perhaps used for assemblies, a casual game of soccer, or even outdoor prayers made toward Mecca. Chambers didn't know, and at the moment, he didn't care.

The ceiling dropped another half meter, and Chambers had to hunch to continue. A dozen steps later, he had to remove his backpack and carry it so it wouldn't hang on the rough rock above. He wondered how Landau and the soldiers were doing but decided they were better equipped for this than he.

The fissure banked south for a dozen steps, then east again. Chambers had memorized the survey and knew every turn coming his way. What he hadn't expected was how small the space would become. It seemed that with every step the walls grew closer and the ceiling lower. Finally, Chambers stopped and looked at the area in front of him.

"Looks like a tight fit," Landau said. Chambers was sucking air, and even Landau's breathing was heavy.

"I think the fissure is bigger a little farther along."

"You think?"

"Only one way to find out." He handed Landau his backpack. "If I don't come back, you can keep my computer."

"Gee, thanks."

"Stay close. You should be able to hear me from the other side."

"We're still talking about the cave, right?"

"Funny. If I get stuck, send the skinniest soldier after me."

"Doc, none of them are skinny."

Chambers took a deep breath and let it out. He repeated the action several times. "Remember when I asked about anyone being claustro-phobic?"

"Yes. You're kidding. Tell me you're kidding."

"You're the first one I've told. Keep it a secret, okay."

"Look, let me go first—"

"No. If this doesn't work out, you need to find another way to save Amber."

Landau patted him on the shoulder. "Will do, but this will work out. I trust your scientific intuition."

One more deep breath, then, after a short prayer, he removed his helmet, shoved it in the hole and followed after. The light from the helmet pressed back the blackness. Sharp edges and rocky points dug at his skin, tearing his jumpsuit uniform. He pushed with his feet, pulled with his hands. Dust filled his nose and mouth.

He grunted and clawed another meter, then another. He felt as if he were crawling through a straw. Then his outstretched hand took hold of—nothing. Tilting his head up, Chambers saw the beam of his light shining on a distant wall, a wall with a large space in front of it.

Sweat poured into his eyes as he inched forward. Another meter, and Chambers's head emerged from the sharp confines into a wide corridor-like passageway. He wasted no time extracting himself. The distance to the floor was twice that of the entry point. The ceiling was three meters above his head. Chambers felt as if he had entered a ballroom.

He donned his helmet and looked around. What he saw gave him relief. The fissure continued just as the surveys indicated. Then a dark realization settled on him: the hard part was still to come. He returned to the space he had just escaped and directed his light down the dark gullet and wiggled it. The he spoke one word. "Clear."

A few moments later, Landau emerged, pushing Chambers's backpack in front of him. "That was fun."

"I should punch you."

"What's stopping you?"

"Fear of painful death."

"You know, Doc. I'm starting to like you."

Chambers started down the passageway while the other soldiers crawled through, pushing their weapons before them. He removed the tablet PC he had been carrying and activated it. The light pushed back some of the darkness. He studied the surveys and his calculations. They

320 Grant R. Jeffrey and Alton L. Gansky

were close. He waited for the others to join him, then he removed a long
cloth tape measure and handed one end to Landau. "Have someone take
this end back to the place where we turned north."

Landau did and the men parted for the soldier. Chambers then moved
up the grade until he had walked fifty meters. Setting down the tape, he
looked to the ceiling.

"We're here." He looked at Landau. "It's your show now."

                              ∽

Two men formed stirrups with their hands and lifted a soldier high enough
to place shaped charges of plastic explosive. One thing working in their
favor was the wider size of the fissure in this area. If it were too narrow, the
best they could hope for was a hole in the ceiling and a fissure so cluttered
with debris that the mission would have to be called off.

Chambers had made his way back to the small opening, ordered there
by Landau. This was as far as the security man would let him go. "You're
untrained and unarmed, and you present a danger to the mission, to us,
and to Amber." The words stung, but Chambers recognized the wisdom.
This was no movie. If he attempted to do what the trained soldiers were
about to do, he could get in their way and get someone killed. Or if he
were wounded, then the team would have two people to rescue.

Two concerns swirled to the top of his mind. One, he couldn't be sure
how thick the overhead material was. He had asked for and received a
handheld altimeter, which he carried in the backpack. He had been able to
establish the target area's height above sea level. By comparing that to the
top-of-the-line altimeter and guessing the distance to the top of the fissure,
Chambers estimated the rock material to be only two meters thick. The
other concern was that any hole that allowed soldiers to ascend into the
school would also allow terrorists to descend.

The sound of fast-moving boots drew him from his morbid thoughts. Six soldiers filled the space, crouching against the walls. One held a remote control. Landau was the last to appear. He remained erect and studied two soldiers as each removed a folding, telescoping aluminum assault ladder from their packs. With practiced moves, they unfolded each segment and locked it in place, creating a ladder two meters in length. Each tactical ladder had a pair of long, clawlike hooks on the end. When they finished, each man gave Landau a nod.

"Masks." Landau pulled a balaclava from a pocket and pulled the ski-mask-like hood over his head. Again, the soldiers followed suit without a word. For Chambers it was a reminder to don the construction mask he had been provided. It was going to get dusty.

Landau took a breath, then said, "Ears." He pulled a pair of earplugs from his pocket. The soldiers did the same. Chambers scrambled to find his pair in his backpack. Landau gave him a moment. Once Chambers had stuffed the red plugs in his ear canals, he looked at Landau, who took a moment to eye each man.

He held out a hand, three fingers extended, and drew them in one by one, then tapped the soldier with the remote on the shoulder.

Chambers saw a flash, felt the limestone in the wall behind him shudder, then heard the sharp report of the plastic explosive. A tsunami of dust shot down the fissure like smoke. Chambers closed his eyes against the flying grit. When he opened them again, he was alone.

THIRTY-SIX

A mber felt a rumble through the floor. She was seated on the concrete, and the vibration made her jump to her feet. She had no place to go. For two days she had been confined to a shed with nothing more than a cot to sleep on and a bucket for her bathroom needs. She didn't know where she was. Nuri had seen to that. Once in the van, he had blindfolded her. He uttered only one line. "David's life depends on your cooperation."

She wanted to ask why he would do this. She wanted an explanation but held no hope of receiving one. One thought came to mind: he was after the artifacts or the treasure. If that was the case, she was doomed. Yakov and Ben-Judah might offer money to save her life, but they wouldn't trade what they considered the revival of spiritual Israel for her. She wouldn't want them to. If she had to die, then so be it. Her prayers were more for David's safety than for hers.

Pacing like a caged tiger, Amber wished for a window. She tried to peek through the narrow opening between the shed doors but could see nothing. What little light crept in from the exterior lights blinked out. Power outage? Was that what had caused the vibration and noise? A transformer explosion?

The sound of a gunshot answered her question.

᠆᠆

Landau was the third man over the fallen debris but the first up the tactical ladder. Driven by his fury at the injustice of the deaths he had been forced to see over the course of this mission, especially the agent Nuri had killed,

Landau pressed himself through the ragged opening in the ceiling of the limestone fissure. It was a tight fit. The moment he emerged, he raised the Uzi submachine gun and scanned the courtyard and buildings. A slight moon hung above, enabling his night-vision goggles to reveal every movement in the dark.

Where were they keeping her? In the hours before the mission, Landau had studied everything he could find about the structure. He had been able to retrieve architectural plans, photos of the grounds, and publicity snapshots from the school's Web site meant to draw future clerics and Islamic theologians. He also learned that students were still on campus. Of course, that had been the plan of Nuri and his people. He couldn't prove it, but he had no doubt Hussein Al-Malik was behind this. Another problem for another time. His task was to find and rescue Amber without killing innocent students or faculty in the process.

But where?

Would Nuri hide Amber where some student or cleric could find her? No. He wouldn't put a woman in a male dormitory. Since classes were still being held during the day, he couldn't sequester her away there or anyplace where people traveled or congregated. That left outbuildings: storage structures, equipment buildings, groundskeeper's sheds.

Six other men poured from the rabbit hole and spread out. Landau, on a hunch, headed for the back of the compound. As he moved across the open plaza, he saw a door to his right open. It was one of the dormitories. Several young men spilled from the opening and found themselves staring into the automatic rifles of two of his men. It took less than five seconds to press the group back into the building. The soldiers followed according to plan. The best way to keep the innocent safe was to keep them out of the way. The rest of the team spread out along the plaza.

Landau knew of four structures that seemed too small to be used for anything but storage. He made for those. Reaching the edge of one of the longer, two-story classroom structures, he paused and did a quick check. Nothing moved. He rounded the corner and ran down an alley formed by the perimeter wall and the building. In a corner, nestled near the northeast corner of the lot, was a string of sheds, each about three meters square. Landau approached slowly, weapon at the ready. Two men stood at the doors of one of the sheds, each dressed in long robes. They looked nervous. That they hadn't raced to the site of an explosive noise told him the men were guards, ordered not to leave their post.

Landau had no place for cover. The men had seen him and each raised an AK-47 assault rifle his way. Human nature told him to duck, to run, to seek protection; training taught him to tap the trigger of his weapon to send three rounds from the automatic Uzi into the guards' chests. Training won out. Landau had made two perfect body-mass shots. The men folded before they could pull a trigger.

Advance. Step by step. Weapon up. Eyes scanning.

He rounded the corner of the building just in time to see a third armed man approaching. Another tap of the trigger, but this time, Landau's aim was off. He hit the man in the head.

Now he faced several sheds and hoped Amber was in one of them. "Amber?" He hoped she would recognize his voice.

"Here."

One shed down. "Amber? It's Landau."

"Yes, it's me. Help."

"That's what I'm here for." Landau studied the lock. It was an expensive combination lock set in a cheap latch. If he had time, he would have laughed at the irony. One side of the latch was held in place by five wood screws. The screws were strong; the wood door was another matter. "Stand back from the door." A recurring mantra in his years of training had been to attack the weakest link. He did. Landau kicked the door just to the inside of the latch. It took two strong strikes, but the wood splintered where the screws had been attached. The door slammed open, and Amber sprinted from the dark space. She threw her arms around Landau.

"You look beautiful in black."

He pulled her away. They were far from safe. "Beautiful? We have to work on your choice of adjectives." He studied her. "Are you injured?"

"Just a little roughed up."

"Okay, let's get you out of here. Stay close and stay behind me at all times. Do everything I say without question. Got it?"

"Got it. David's in danger—"

"No he's not. If God is good, you will see him in a few minutes."

"God is good. Lead the way."

Landau keyed his radio. "Package is in hand." He retraced his steps, stopping at the plaza-side corner of the building. He saw one team of two at the entrance point, each man on one knee, weapons raised. Another team of two joined them assuming the same posture.

"Wait," he told Amber.

The team that stopped the flow of students from the dormitory appeared and jogged to Landau's position. No words were needed. This part had been discussed and practiced. The two men with Landau formed a triangle of protection around Amber and ran toward the opening they had created in the ground five minutes before. When they reached the hole, Landau said, "Go."

Two soldiers slipped down the ladder.

"You're next," he said to Amber. She didn't question the direction. A minute later she was below grade. One by one the spec ops team disappeared down the rabbit hole leaving Landau to descend last. He was team leader: first in, last out.

He shouldered his weapon, glanced at the tactical ladder and the tomblike blackness. He took a step toward the ladder, then staggered sideways. Something had hit him in the arm. His arm grew warm, then exploded in pain.

"Off with the mask."

Landau looked at his arm and saw a hole in his sleeve oozing blood. The world seemed to spin. He reached for his weapon, but his arm wouldn't move.

A man approached. Nuri.

Landau tried to reach across his body for his sidearm, but the man was on him before he negotiated the move. A boot caught Landau's belt, doubling him over. Nuri yanked Landau's sidearm from the holster and tossed it to the side. Then he stepped back. "I said remove the mask."

Landau straightened, pulled his helmet from his head, and slipped off the mask.

"Hiram Landau. I might have guessed."

Landau didn't speak. He was saving his strength to remain conscious.

"You shouldn't have done this. If your people had been cooperative, no real harm would have come to Amber. I'm quite fond of her."

"You locked her in a shed."

Nuri shrugged. "She is just a woman."

The anger Landau felt stemmed some of the pain.

A helmeted, masked head appeared in the hole. The soldier swore. Nuri turned the handgun at the soldier. The man could do nothing but drop from the ladder, something that had to hurt. Nuri started for the opening but didn't finish the first step. Landau used his one working arm to knock Nuri's arm to the side. The gun went off but the round sank into the grassy surface. Before Nuri recovered, Landau drove a knee into the man's hip joint, an area filled with sensitive nerves.

Nuri grunted, then screamed in anger. The scream was short, cut off by Landau's fist striking the side of Nuri's neck and sending a pulse of blood to the brain. Stunned, Nuri wobbled to the side, toward the opening in the ground. Landau pushed him to the ground, then directed him headfirst down the hole. A cracking sound wafted up the opening.

Landau sat, hung his legs into the gaping maw, and took hold of the first rung of the tactical ladder. He felt his strength fading. He struggled down a meter, then dropped into the fissure. His boots landed on something soft. The moment his feet landed on Nuri's body, two of his team were there to grab him. "Retrieve my weapons, then secure the ladders."

"Yes sir." One of the soldiers started up the ladder. There was a new type of darkness swirling in Landau's eyes that had nothing to do with being underground.

"This way, sir."

"Report."

"One other injury besides you, sir. Twisted ankle. The woman and Dr. Chambers are following one of our men through the Straw."

"The Straw?"

"That's what Chambers called it."

"He was first through; he gets to…uh…name it."

The soldier keyed his microphone. "Have the medic ready. Gunshot wound."

Another soldier appeared and helped move Landau to the opening Chambers had dubbed the Straw. They sat him down. He was glad to see that Chambers and Amber were gone. So were two of the spec ops team. The medic, a required member of every team, had remained behind.

"First, I'm going to stop the bleeding, then I'm going to give you something for the pain. Can you move your arm at all?"

"No. Get the other men out of here. I'll make it."

"Sorry, sir. When it comes to injuries, I outrank you."

∽

Chambers watched as two soldiers emerged into the first segment of the fissure—one strung a nylon climber's rope behind him. Together, they pulled Landau through the opening. The medic was the last one through.

Amber was in tears. "Are you… I mean…"

"I don't know what the medic gave me, but I'm feeling pretty good. I can walk. Sort of."

With two injured, the egress was longer and more arduous than the ingress. Still they made it to the opening, where a stretcher and an ambulance crew waited. Chambers watched as they loaded Landau, the injured team member, and Amber into the ambulance.

He looked into the night sky, saw the stars and the thin moon, and said, "Thank You, God. Thank You."

THIRTY SEVEN

Spring 2015

Chambers and Amber rode in the back of a bulletproof SUV. They had been summoned at three in the morning and told to be ready in ten minutes. Ten minutes! The hour and the rush meant something was wrong.

The streets of Jerusalem seemed normal. Chambers knew they weren't.

∽

In just two years, the world came unhinged. Good things came to pass: David asked Amber to marry him—for the second time—and for the second time, she agreed. The wedding took place on the shore of the Sea of Galilee, and David's best man was his father, now frail but strong enough for one more trip to Israel.

The work on Copper Scroll discoveries continued with several remarkable finds, but none as amazing as the stones of the high priest's breastpiece and temple articles, including the Table of Shewbread.

Protector and now friend, Hiram Landau had regained the use of his arm but was spending most of his energy as a deputy director of Shin Bet, a job that recent world events had made almost impossible.

Most remarkable was something Chambers never guessed he would see: the groundwork on the third temple began twelve months after Amber's rescue. Tension between Israel and its neighbors grew geometrically, but property north of the Dome of the Rock, in an area not far from the entry to Herod's tunnel, was chosen as the proper site. Millions were spent for the property and millions more for added security. Yakov, working with Israel's chief rabbis, Ben-Judah, and other consultants, began operation under the principle that forgiveness was easier to get than permission. Forgiveness never came. The media kept the world apprised of the progress and the conflict, to the joy of some and the anger of others.

Although Chambers knew the importance of the temple, and although he understood the controversy surrounding it, he had not expected such a polarizing effect. In retrospect, he realized he should have. One in five people in the world called themselves Muslims. They were the *ummah,* the collective believers of Islam. The world was host to fifty-seven recognized Islamic states that made up the Organization of the Islamic Conference, most of which banded together to denounce Israel's "blatant assault on the peace of Palestine and the world."

Chambers hated politics and world affairs. His life was tied up in understanding the biblical past. His preferred world was the field and books, but his part in finding the treasures and artifacts of the temple made his name one of the best-known names in the world. He received bags of mail praising his accomplishments and an equal number of threats on his life. He tried to send Amber back to the States, to the condo he still paid for, but she refused to leave his side. This was her project too, and he was her husband. She would not be sent away.

As the world grew more tense, Chambers and Amber continued to search for artifacts with some success, but the search had been slowed by security needs. There simply wasn't enough security to maintain multiple dig sites. That didn't bother Chambers. While he loved the dirt, he was happy to be in the safety of a secured facility, cataloging and studying everything found so far.

That too had become a bone of contention in the world of archae-ologists. No one but Chambers, Amber, and Ben-Judah were allowed access to the finds. In the early years following the discovery of the Dead Sea Scrolls, scholars complained that information was being kept from the scientific community. But Ben-Judah and Yakov forbade sharing in-formation. These were not just artifacts. They belonged to Israel and the temple.

Over the months, Ben-Judah, often in disguise, took the two to the stone quarry where stones like those of the second temple were cut and shaped. A new set of masons had to be trained to build like the ancients. Jewish artisans learned to apply gold to walls and furnishings. The truth of the new temple hit home when a search was done to find those geneti-cally qualified to be priests. The amount of respondents, which numbered in the thousands, astonished Chambers.

Ben-Judah had changed as well. He showed a new life, additional spring in his step, and absolute conviction that God was behind every find. When Chambers first arrived in the country, he would have argued the point, but no longer. His own faith had grown beyond what it had been years before. Prayer was a daily part of his life, and he read his Bible, not looking for archaeological clues but looking for a deeper relationship with God and with his Savior.

స

The car pulled to the front of the multistory, square earth-brown building and stopped by the large bronze doors called the Gate of the Tribes. Four uniformed soldiers stood at the front. With them was Hiram Landau. He embraced the two as they exited the SUV.

"You're looking well, Landau." Seeing the man who had saved Am-ber's life filled Chambers with joy.

"You don't look so bad yourself." He turned and kissed Amber on the cheek. "Is your husband treating you with proper respect? If not, I can send a few guys over."

"He's learning."

They walked into the building, past the reception desk and to the elevators. Landau removed a card key and slid it through a slot, then punched a number into the keypad. The elevator started down.

Landau asked, "Do you know where we're going?"

Chambers answered. "I've been told there's a situation room below the building. I assume we're going there."

"Correct."

"What I don't know is why?"

Landau looked grim. "For your safety. It's all gone bad, David."

"How bad?"

"The worst. I'm not clear to read you in, but the prime minister is, of course."

Amber wrapped her arms around herself. "Should I be afraid?"

Landau looked at her. "You'll be safe in the sit room."

"Then what?" she asked.

"I don't know, Amber. I don't know."

She looked at him. "What about your family?"

Landau looked away. "We'll be there in a second. You'll need to stand out of the way."

"Why us?" Chambers asked.

"Ben-Judah insisted on your presence, and when the head of the new Sanhedrin makes a request like that, it happens."

"Will you be staying with us?" Amber asked.

"No. I have work to do."

"Will we see you again?" Amber looked on the verge of tears.

"Only *HaShem* knows."

The elevator opened and Chambers led Amber into a room that looked as if it had been plucked from the set of a science-fiction movie. A long table ran through the room. A dozen men faced the monitors. Chambers recognized Prime Minister Yakov. He was on the phone. Some of the other men wore uniforms representing the different departments of the Israeli military.

Ben-Judah approached. "Good of you to come."

Chambers looked at his old mentor. "We weren't given a choice, but we're glad to be here."

Ben-Judah put a hand on Chambers's shoulder. "Do not lose heart my friends. *HaShem* still sits upon His throne. He is not moved. He is not shaken, and He has not led us this far to abandon us now."

Chambers studied the myriad of monitors. Some were clearly images from satellites. On one, he could see ships moving in the Persian Gulf; on another, he could see tanks and troops moving along the ground. Others were direct feeds from combat control centers. "This doesn't look good."

Amber drew a hand beneath her eyes. "How did we get here? How could things get this bad?"

David knew and wished he didn't.

∾

Formal complaints about the "invasion" of the Islamic school for clerics led to more protest marches and more saber-rattling from Iran, Jordan, and several other Middle Eastern countries. Every member of the Organization of the Islamic Conference complained bitterly. Even Pakistan made its displeasure known. But nothing would be done. Not yet.

Iran took a more aggressive posture. Its president, Omeed Memar, had secured greater control of the country than any previous leader. Iran found a friend in a cash-strapped Russia. Between them, they controlled much of the world's oil. With Iran's new and powerful leader, oil-dependent countries, including the United Kingdom and the United States, were slow to criticize. In Memar they saw a man wielding enough influence in OPEC countries and others to limit the oil supplies to "infidel nations."

But President Memar was not satisfied with oil. He saw the future of his own country's energy needs resting in nuclear power and its defense in the by-product of the technology.

Yakov had a plan for the future. Memar was the kind of man who was not happy unless he was the center of attention and making Israel nervous. More than once he had called for Israel to be "wiped from the face of the earth." It was his mantra, and more and more people were chanting it with him.

Yakov had tough decisions to make. Israel had a history of being pre-emptive, as well as quick to react to any insult to its sovereignty. His advisors agreed, "Act first or you won't be able to act at all."

The first action was carried out by several elite Arabic-speaking Israeli commando teams, each targeting key nuclear sites. Explosives destroyed the centers, and the teams exited without a single casualty. They did, however, leave Iranian casualties in their wake.

The Iranian president was beside himself. Threats flowed like water. This was expected, but Memar wanted reparations. Israel denied any involvement. Israel's allies backed them—in word. Mossad brought a disturbing report. Iran was preparing missiles for an assault against the country. Yakov made another difficult decision: it was time to "take the head off the chicken." He ordered a Dolphin-class submarine in the Persian Gulf to take out suspected missile sites that could target Israel.

Two direct, unilateral attacks by Israel on its enemy stunned the world. The attacks successfully took the teeth out of the Iranian lion for a few months. The democratic nations of the European Union and those of North America were shocked. Not one supported the decision. Each chastised Israel for not using diplomatic methods and the United Nations.

But diplomatic avenues had not worked with Iran for years, and no one in Israel believed the approach would have worked then.

Protests were universal. Russia continued to align with Iran. Even China complained about the unwarranted act of war. David followed the news closely but preferred not to think about what might come in the months ahead.

As unstable as Memar demonstrated himself to be, there was another man who rivaled him: Chief of the General Staff for the Russian Federation, Army General Nicholai Agog. "It is time to deal with Israel before they can attack peace-loving people everywhere." That was how the Mossad, Israel's foreign spy service, quoted him.

First rhetoric flew, and while accusations were exchanged in a dozen different languages, alliances against Israel were being made, armies were being prepared, and missiles were being moved from the Russian Federation to Iran. Something noticed by US intelligence and warnings were given.

∽

"Operation Samson, they call it," Ben-Judah said.

"Operation Samson?" Amber stepped closer to Chambers, and he put an arm around her. She shivered. "Do I want to know what that is?"

"I don't imagine you do." Ben-Judah looked calm. "Our nation has nuclear-capable Jericho 3 missiles aimed at every Arab country that is moving against us."

"Oh, this is horrible." Tears washed her eyes. Chambers felt numb, barely able to think. Nuclear war was every sane man's nightmare.

"There is evidence that Iran and her friends are planning a biological attack. You might recall Iraq sent forty-two Scud missiles at Israel in the early 1990s. Our fear then was that the missiles carried chemical or biological agents. Fortunately, thanks to the American Patriot missile defense system, only one landed within our borders. The military has learned a few things since then."

"How can you be so calm, Professor?" Amber asked.

"I have told you, *HaShem* still sits upon His throne."

"Mr. Prime Minister?" Chambers watched Yakov turn to a man in an Israeli army uniform.

"What is it, General?"

"I...I'm getting odd reports. I don't know how to interpret this."

"Say it, General."

"Intel is saying that the Arab troops at the Lebanon border are firing on approaching Russian forces."

Yakov stood. "Why would they do that?"

"I don't know, sir. Intel says the enemy seems confused. I'm getting the same report from Jordan."

A rumble ran through the underground situation room, and Amber released a short scream. The floor vibrated, the walls rattled.

"Earthquake," Ben-Judah said.

Yakov raised his voice. "What was that? Have we been hit?"

Someone made a call and a few moments later announced, "Earthquake. Early location is somewhere in northern Syria. No damage estimates, but the first measurement put the quake at over eight on the Richter scale. There has to be damage. We can expect aftershocks."

"What is going on?" Yakov demanded. He turned to where Ben-Judah, Chambers, and Amber stood.

"Wait, Mr. Prime Minister. It has begun."

"What has begun?"

Ben-Judah smiled. "I think you know, old friend."

"Can it be?"

"It can."

Chambers touched Ben-Judah's arm. "Professor?"

He smiled. "And you call yourself a biblical archaeologist." He pointed to the monitors. "Wait and see, my son. Wait and see the hand of *HaShem*."

༄

Hours passed. Chambers found chairs for Amber and Ben-Judah. They watched events that could only be described as miraculous. A volcano in southern Syria, southeast of Damascus, erupted for the first time since 1850, ejecting sulfurous smoke and burning ejecta into a military encampment.

In desperation, the Iranian- and Russian-led armies launched truck-mounted rockets, all of which fell short of Israel's borders, dumping their load of genetically enhanced Ebola virus and concentrated Machupo virus, a hemorrhagic organism. Disease spread quickly.

The day wore on, and the attack against Israel failed.

Only Abram Ben-Judah seemed unsurprised.

"Professor, what are you thinking?"

Ben-Judah grinned, then spoke loud enough for all to hear: "In my zeal and fiery wrath I declare that at that time there shall be a great earthquake in the land of Israel. The fish in the sea, the birds in the sky, the beasts of the field, every creature that moves along the ground, and all the people on the face of the earth will tremble at my presence. The mountains will be overturned, the cliffs will crumble and every wall will fall to the ground. I will summon a sword against Gog on all my mountains, declares the Sovereign LORD. Every man's sword will be against his brother. I will execute judgment on him with plague and bloodshed; I will pour down torrents of rain, hailstones and burning sulfur on him and on his troops and on the many nations with him. And so I will show my greatness and my holiness, and I will make myself known in the sight of many nations. Then they will know that I am the LORD.'"

He looked at Chambers and Amber. "Ezekiel 38." He looked at the monitors. "*HaShem* has made His will known. We found the treasures and temple furnishings by His will. We are His servants. We are blessed and soon all the world will see His temple."

Chambers and Amber sat in the last row of a theater-style classroom at Hebrew University. Before them were the seventy-one members of the new Sanhedrin, as well as key government officials.

Ben-Judah stepped to the lectern. Next to him was a table covered with a white cloth.

"He who sits above the heavens has blessed our nation and our work on His temple. Much work remains. I am told that it will be two more years before construction ends. Still, our enemies are now powerless."

A gentle round of applause rose from the small gathering. Ben-Judah raised a hand. "We continue to search for the remaining treasures. How much we will find only *HaShem* knows. In short, all goes well, but something has been delivered to me. Dr. Chambers, Dr. Rodgers, and other trusted archaeologists have examined it and believe it to be authentic."

He stepped to the table and removed the cloth. Beneath the cover lay a small square of stones.

"Some of you know the Ezekiel tablets, stones with the words of Ezekiel chiseled on the surface in bas-relief. We have long thought that other such stones might exist. I do not know who our benefactor is, but he has sent us a great gift." Ben-Judah ran a hand across the raised letters on the slab's smooth surface. He read:

"Ezekiel son of Buzi, priest of the Most Holy. Here lies the furnishings of God: the ark of Moses, the tablets writ by the very finger of God, the rod of Aaron that budded…"

An elderly man in the back row caught Chambers's attention. The man rose, gazed at Chambers for a moment, then walked from the room.

DR. GRANT R. JEFFREY BIOGRAPHY

Grant Jeffrey is internationally recognized as a teacher on Bible prophecy and an intelligent defense of our Christian faith. Jeffrey's books have been translated into twenty-four languages and sold more than seven million copies during the last twenty-three years. He has been the main speaker at hundreds of prophecy conferences around the world, and with his wife, Kaye, has worked in full-time ministry since 1988.

Jeffrey's decades of dedicated research on military history, intelligence, and prophecy are reflected in his recent books: *The Next World War, Countdown to the Apocalypse, Shadow Government,* and his latest, *The Global Warming Deception.* His prophetic novel *By Dawn's Early Light,* written with co-author Angela Hunt, received the respected Christy Award for the Best Prophetic Fiction novel of 1999.

His popular TV program *Bible Prophecy Revealed* is broadcast twice weekly by Trinity Broadcasting Network in over eighty nations. He also appears frequently as a guest on numerous TV programs and radio stations internationally.

Jeffrey's passion for research led him to acquire a personal library of over seven thousand books on prophecy, theology, and biblical archaeology. He earned a master's degree and PhD in biblical studies from Louisiana Baptist University. He is the chairman of Frontier Research Publications Inc., a leading publisher of books, tapes, and videos, and created the Jeffrey Prophecy Study Bible. This two-and-a-half-year research and writing project was his doctoral dissertation for his PhD. Many prophecy teachers, including Hal Lindsey, Ed Hindson, and Chuck Missler, have declared that this is the most comprehensive Prophecy Study Bible ever published.

His dozens of research trips to the Middle East and extensive interviews with experts in the military and intelligence field, including political leaders Benjamin Netanyahu and Shimon Peres, provide the unique insights and background to his books *The New Temple and the Second Coming* and *Countdown to the Apocalypse.*

OTHER BOOKS BY GRANT R. JEFFREY

Apocalypse: The Coming Judgment of the Nations
Armageddon: Appointment with Destiny
Countdown to the Apocalypse
Creation: Remarkable Evidence of God's Design
Final Warning
Finding Financial Freedom: A Biblical Guide to Your Independence
The Global Warming Deception
The Handwriting of God: Sacred Mysteries of the Bible
Heaven: The Mystery of Angels
Jesus: The Great Debate
Journey into Eternity
Messiah: War in the Middle East
The New Temple and the Second Coming
The Next World War
Prince of Darkness: Antichrist and the New World Order
The Signature of God
Shadow Government
Surveillance Society: The Rise of Antichrist
Triumphant Return: The Coming Kingdom of God
Unveiling Mysteries of the Bible
War on Terror: Unfolding Bible Prophecy

Also from Alton L. Gansky

Ethical questions flavor this suspense novel about one man who fights world hunger by any means…and another who must decide if wrong can ever be right.

The book that brings
end-times prophecy to life.
Because it's happening right now.

The Prophecy That Points to
Christ's Return in Your Generation

THE
NEW TEMPLE
AND THE
SECOND COMING

GRANT R. JEFFREY
BEST-SELLING AUTHOR OF THE NEXT WORLD WAR

Grant Jeffrey investigates the Bible, obscure archaeological finds,
the ancient city beneath Jerusalem, and developments among rabbinic
authorities to reveal a prophetic, Temple-related timeline that points to
Jesus' return in the current generation.

Wondering about the end times?
Let Daniel answer your questions.

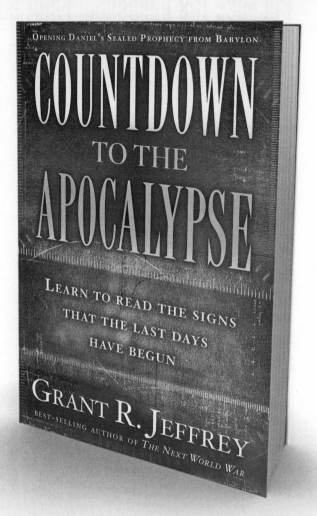

By analyzing Daniel's prophecies through the lens of the Hebrew calendar and the cycle of major Jewish festivals, Grant R. Jeffrey discovers the dates of many future end-times events—and identifies a number of already-visible signs of the impending arrival of the Antichrist.

Read a chapter of this book at www.WaterBrookMultnomah.com!

You are being watched.
And that's not the worst of it.

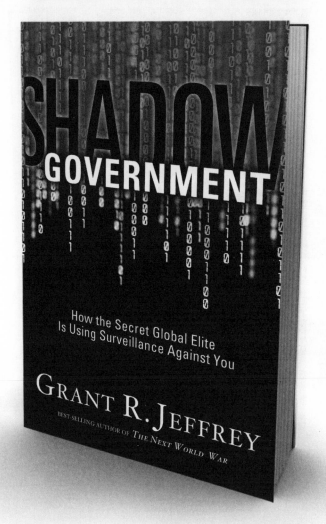

Grant Jeffrey reveals biblical prophecies that describe Satan's work at the end of the age, as the evil one installs the Antichrist as the world's unrivaled leader.

Read a chapter of this book at www.WaterBrookMultnomah.com!

More titles from Grant R. Jeffrey

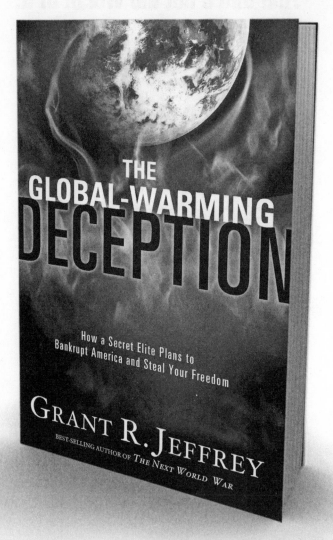

Bible prophecy expert Grant Jeffrey reveals evidence that proves the diabolical forces seeking to establish a centralized global government are using the lie of manmade global warming to destroy national economies, to steal your freedom, and to prepare the way for the Antichrist.

Read a chapter of this book at www.WaterBrookMultnomah.com!